What others are saying about

The Elimination Ga...

So good, you'll be sad when you finish it.

~Isaac Forsyth

This book is filled with thrilling action sequences, espionage, and deception that will keep you on your toes. The Zanadu brothers continue to capture my attention with their high-speed chases and sleuthing skills in this stunning winter adventure.

~Ray MacIntosh

I really enjoyed this book! It took me on an amazing adventure with the Zanadu boys and an old friend. At the end of each page, I couldn't wait to read the next one! The book is full of action, adventure, and mystery. I can't wait for the next one in the series.

~Christy Martin

The *Elimination Games Enigma* is an action-packed adventure guaranteed to keep you on the edge of your seat! Teen detectives Alex and Gabe Zanadu, with the help of their trusty canine companions Thunder and Lightning, take on corruption at every turn and prove that the most dangerous of situations can be conquered with a good plan and God on your side.

~Kelly Snyder, PhD

THE ELIMINATION GAMES

ENIGMA

AARON M. ZOOK JR.

Enjoy this French adventure!

Aaron M. Zook, Jr.

Matt 22:34-40

The Elimination Games Enigma

Aaron M. Zook, Jr.

Bold Vision Books

PO Box 2011

Friendswood, TX 777549

Table of Contents

Chapter 1 – A Chilly Clue

IEG Coliseum, Albertville, France

Saturday, 11 January 1992, 5:10 p.m.

I donned my ski jacket, tugged on my mittens and wool cap, and shoved the restroom door open to the International Elimination Games Stadium second-level concourse.

My older brother, Alex, trailed behind, grumbling. "Hurry up, Gabe. You've made me miss at least ten minutes of the Procession of Nations."

I faced him, a night breeze chilling my cheeks. "No big deal. The Elims are only the prep games for next month's world-wide competitions. And at least we got to warm up a little."

My brother gritted his teeth. "You're kidding, right? The Winter IEGs are nothing?" He pointed upward at the stadium seats over our heads. "Every event, including the opening ceremony, is a critical practice run for the world games. I'm taking great pictures from my seat to remember each moment—"

A metal clattering sound came from my right.

Alex and I swiveled our heads. The loud disturbance cut through the crowd noise.

A man swung a fist at someone on the ground. The person on the concrete rolled to avoid the punch and collided with a fallen trash can, knocking the contents onto the walkway. The few people present on the concourse looked the other way and hurried past.

I sprinted toward the men as fast as my thick clothing and winter hiking boots would let me. Alex surged ahead. He didn't need as much snivel gear as I did.

"Hey." Alex's deep voice boomed at the struggling men. "Stop."

The man on top leapt to his feet, pulled a square leather object that might have been a wallet from the other man, and raced away. Rolling to his side, the victim got to his knees and lurched to his feet. He stumbled and ran away, hand over his gut. Before turning onto an exit ramp, a rolled piece of paper dropped from his pocket to the ground.

Alex raced around the garbage can and arrived by the down ramp first. He scooped the paper off the concrete.

I rushed past him to reach the exit on the ground level. A couple of pedestrians ambled near the food kiosks. No trace of the mysterious men.

"What do you have?" I trudged back to my brother, unzipping my jacket and taking off my cap.

Alex unrolled the paper, turned it sideways for better lighting, and handed it to me. "Test results?" He retraced his steps to the fallen metal trash container.

I scanned the paper as I followed. The sheet looked like several lab tests, but I couldn't figure out what kind of test. When I reached Alex, I tugged my hoodie back and took off my mittens. "I'm sweating."

"You wear too many clothes."

"Easy for you to say." I stuffed the mittens in my coat. Alex always liked colder weather, like a polar bear enjoyed the ice. "I'm skinnier than you."

"You need to work out more." My brother checked out the barrel and the spilled trash.

Walking behind the can, I found a white paper sack crushed into a tight ball. I opened it. "Uh-oh."

"What'd you find?" Alex collected a few items and navigated around the other trash to stand next to me.

I opened the bag to let him see the contents.

He whistled. "We're going to have to report this." He held out his palm, showing me a few objects he'd found.

"Guess we need to tell Dad now." I closed the bag.

"Not yet." Alex pulled out his camera. "We need to take photo evidence in case someone disturbs this before the police get here." He snapped several pics, the Instamatic camera shooting out the developing pictures. Alex stuffed them in his pocket, but the breeze whipped one across the concrete. A woman, hurrying through the concourse, ground the image under a snow boot.

Alex chased the fluttering photo, slapping his hand on the concrete to keep the wind from snatching it away. He captured the picture, lifted and examined it, then threw it in the trash can next to me. "Ruined. One less piece of evidence for security."

I nodded. Sighed. "Yep. And there goes our vacation." Mom would explode, even though we weren't looking for trouble. But somehow, trouble found us.

Again.

Chapter 2 – Security Station Surprise

IEG Coliseum, Albertville, France

Saturday, 11 January 1992, 5:30 p.m.

The French emcee announced the United States team when we reached our parents' location. A massive swell of shouts and applause swept around the stadium.

Mom grabbed my arm and pulled me into my seat. "Gabe, sit. The people behind you need to see."

"Sorry." I took a deep breath. "I needed to show this to Dad."

Her forehead creased when she saw the crumpled white bag. "What is that?"

"Evidence."

She closed her eyes. Mumbled a few things to herself. Straightening her posture, she turned and whispered in Dad's ear. A few seconds later, they swapped seats. While the Procession of Nations finished, which took another half hour, Alex and I told Dad about the scuffle below.

For the next ten minutes, while the announcer introduced several speakers, including French Vice-President Phillipe Francios, the President of the International Elimination Games Organizing Committee, and world-famous skier Alexandre De La Fontaine, Dad sat back, watching the events.

When runners carrying a large IEG flag strode into the stadium while Alphorn players filled the air with music, Dad leaned close enough for both of us to hear. "Boys, is this all the evidence you found?"

Alex nodded.

"We took pictures of the trash can, the rest of the spilled trash, and searched the immediate area for anything else." I rubbed at an itchy spot next to my cap. "Since the men escaped, there isn't anything else."

"Here's the plan." Dad kept his voice low. "I'll talk to your mother, but we need to report this after the festivities for the Games are over." He tugged on his coat sleeve to find his watch. "That's about forty-five minutes from now."

"But the trail's getting cold," I whispered close to his ear.

"You're not listening, Gabe. From what you've told me, there is no trail." Dad held up one gloved finger. "I am not going to destroy our once-in-a-lifetime family vacation. Now sit back and watch the show." He scooted closer to Mom, wrapped an arm around her shoulder, and ignored Alex and me.

The rest of the show included torchbearers lighting the eternal flame, followed by drummers, accordion players, and various instrumentalists providing music, and dance groups and actors in wild costumes performing acrobatic activities while they paraded around the arena, dancing and singing. Performers wearing athletic outfits showed the different sports of the Winter Games—skiing, ice-skating, and bobsledding. One individual on a wire portrayed a glider which turned into a bird. A rushing parade of flag holders raced down the aisles of the stands, collecting in the center, and flew into the air on wires to conclude the show.

"What a beautiful opening." Mom beamed at Dad and us. "Two hours of gorgeous costumes, music, and entertainment. I loved seeing it in person."

I nodded, waiting for Dad to tell her about stopping at the police headquarters to deliver the evidence. When he didn't say anything when we reached the ground level, I lifted the white bag high and wiggled it. "Dad, remember?"

He caught sight of it and put a finger to his lips to silence me.

I tapped Alex. "Didn't Dad say we'd report this after the ceremony?"

He shrugged. "I'm not sure what he meant, but he'll take us in when it's time. Be patient."

"He promised."

My brother blended in with the masses, leaving us behind. He practiced this whenever we went to crowded events to improve his covert operations capabilities and hide from the bad guys. Dad let him work on his skills as long as he rejoined us at the end of the journey.

Dad, Mom, and I walked through the town's streets until we reached our hotel. I loved that our accommodations in Albertville weren't far from the Opening Ceremonies. All because Dad's chain of command wanted him, a Lieutenant Colonel in the Intelligence field, present for a super-secret meeting with other country representatives during the Games.

Alex joined us the instant we crossed the doorway into the hotel lobby. We rode the elevator to the tenth floor. Dad led us to their room, opened the door, walked inside with Mom, and turned. "Boys, I'll meet you in the lobby in fifteen minutes."

Thirty minutes later, Dad found us in the lobby. I sipped on a hot chocolate offered to me by a staff member. Alex played with his camera, taking a few pictures of the lobby and revelers out in the street.

"That took a little longer than I thought it would." Our father's timetable worked like a well-oiled machine, except when it came to matters that involved our mother. He preferred joint decisions that they both liked. "I've discussed what we're going to do and plan to be back here in an hour. Let's go."

We hustled out the door. Dad led us back to the coliseum and located a security man. He spoke passable English. The man directed us to the main IEG Committee Security Headquarters.

We arrived at a quiet location not far from the stadium. Like many European downtown areas, the buildings on this block seemed connected together. The front of the headquarters stood out with its stucco painted a light brown and the rounded steps leading to a wide landing. A classic European church, the Greater Evangelical Protestant Church of Albertville, stood alone lit by small floodlights at the end of the street. Black metal streetlamps gave off a soft golden glow, making the scene appear like something from an 1850s magazine. Upper apartments over businesses made the road a residential section of town. We climbed the stairs to the landing, facing a set of dark brown wooden doors.

"Charming." I turned to Dad. "Did we get the right address?"

Alex rolled his eyes. "You don't believe the security man?"

A uniformed security officer strode out the door, almost knocking us over. We scattered to the side without an apology from the man.

I tugged the heavy door open and stepped inside. Dad and Alex followed. An office complex filled the main room, all behind a hip-high handrail that you might see in a courtroom. We stood in front of a raised desk. A woman, hair pinned behind her head, scratched out something with a pen on the desktop. I couldn't find a rank insignia on her uniform.

The woman glanced at us. She tilted her head. "Americans?"

"That obvious?" Dad smiled.

The woman frowned. "The younger boy's overdressed, the older boy has cowboy boots, and you look like a military man."

"Bingo." I gave her a thumbs up.

Her frown-lines deepened. "May I help you with something? We're busy with security issues after the Games opening ceremony."

Dad's smile faded. "We don't want to bother you, but my sons saw someone being robbed today and found evidence that is drug-related."

"Where?" The woman scribbled something else on her desk.

"In the coliseum." I lifted my white paper bag. "Here's some of the evidence."

Alex held out his items.

The woman tapped her lips with the top of her pen. She spun in her chair. "Jil-bear. Come now."

A young man appeared from a doorway in the back of the room, dashing between desks to the woman. "Yes, Sergeant."

She spouted a torrent of French, pointing to her work on the desk, waving a hand at us, tapping one of her palms with a finger, and raising both hands in the air. She frowned at me and shook her head. The whole episode took about three minutes.

The young man nodded so many times I thought he might strain his neck. Any time he tried to interject into the avalanche of French, the Sergeant glared at him. When she stopped, he gazed at us and rubbed the side of his face. "Americans?"

The Sergeant went into another tirade of French until someone interrupted from the back of the room.

"Stop you're spewin', Sarge." The man's familiar voice and Australian accent took command of the situation. "Did you say we have some Yanks here?" He stepped into the reception room. His brownish-blond hair needed combing. His height appeared similar to my five-foot, eleven inches, but his body-builder physique set him apart. "I'm always pleased to take care of—"

"Willie." Alex and I shouted at the same time.

The Sergeant straightened in her seat, eyebrows arched in surprise. Her head swiveled from Willie to us and back again. Someone entered the building, and she focused on the new arrival instead of us.

"Mates." A huge grin spread across Willie's face. "What brings you to these headquarters?"

Dad walked to the railing and held out a hand. "Willie Gretzke. Haven't run into you since Salzburg, Austria, about a year ago. Good to see you."

When Willie grabbed our father's hand, he pumped it with great enthusiasm. "And you too, Mr. Zanadu." He opened a wooden gate in the railing and ushered us back to his office, where he hugged Alex and me. "You've grown a bit. How old are you now?"

Alex grinned. "Seventeen in three months."

"Fourteen-and-a-half." I checked out the room. "Do you have anything to drink?"

"You haven't changed a bit, Gabe." After sending a runner to get us a beverage, Willie motioned for us to sit and glanced at our father.

"What can I do for you?"

"I can't stay." Dad ran a hand through his short hair. "I promised their mother this wouldn't be long and we'd to get right back to the hotel. The boys' dogs, Thunder and Lightning, need some attention. We've been gone for a while."

"I'll bring them back to the hotel if that's what you need." Willie's green eyes stared at the ceiling for a second and refocused on our father. "In about an hour?"

"That'll work." Dad rose. "I know the boys are in good hands. Since I didn't witness anything, I can't give a statement, but criminal activity is never a good sign. And what they found is probably the tip of the iceberg. They'll have to fill you in on the details."

"No worries." Willie got to his feet, shook Dad's hand, and watched him depart.

The coffee arrived after our father departed.

"Cheers." Willie lifted his cup in the air, which we copied. Then we sipped the hot beverages, reminiscing for a few minutes about the adventures we'd shared in the German salt mines and Salzburg's medieval fortress.

"Now, give me a quick run-down as to why you're here and what you've found."

We talked over each other, explaining we were on a family vacation, that Dad's boss sent him on a special mission, and we brought Thunder and Lightning with us. Then Alex described the incident from his perspective, including documenting the scene by taking pictures. When he finished, I told the story from my point of view. I set the crumpled white bag on our friend's desk.

"You'll have to pass over the camera." Willie held out a hand. "I'll get you another roll of film and you'll be set for tomorrow."

Alex handed over a stack of pictures. "I have a Polaroid SX-70. An Instamatic. It develops the film in ten seconds after you take the pictures. The big problem is the ten-picture limit with one cartridge."

"I can take care of that." Willie put the pictures in an envelope and glanced at the clock on the wall to our right. "Guess I should get you boys back to the hotel."

"You didn't tell us why you're here." I swallowed a warm gulp of hot, sweetened coffee.

"Glad you asked." He shifted in his chair. "Here's the short version, since your parents are waiting."

"Don't leave out too much." Alex sat forward. "Details are important."

Willie chuckled. "No worries. I'm here because my department in Australia attached me to the Secret Intelligence Service, a.k.a. MI6, in London, England, to cover the drug surveillance program during the Elims. Australia bid on hosting the 2000 summer games. I'm supposed to learn the procedures to ensure there's no cheating or falsification of records. If someone's going to sneak into the Games system, the IEGs are the place to do it. Since the fall of communism, the International Elimination Games Committee ordered a special watch on the Cooperative Team composed of several former communist nations, the former Soviet satellite nations, and the combined Germany team resulting from their countries reunification in 1990." He tapped the Polaroid pictures. "The Elim Games are one day old and this is the first evidence I have of a problem."

Alex whipped out the piece of paper and the ripped pill containers he found earlier. "Here's a few more bits to add to your collection." He set them next to the white bag. "Dad's taught us how to recognize and gather information to stop the illegal drug trade and drug abuse."

"Check out what's in the bag." I pointed. "Dirty needles, I think."

Willie raised his eyebrows. "Your Dad's decided to expand your detective training?"

I puffed out my chest. "We do a lot on our own."

Our friend snatched the bag off his desktop, opened it, and nodded. He followed the same procedure with the pill containers and the paper. "Looks like a false set of documents for drug testing, some empty containers for illegal drugs, and possible blood-doping needles. I'm amazed you found them all in the same place."

"Was it a plant?" Alex set his coffee on a side table.

"Not sure." Willie made a few notes. "But that shouldn't concern you. You're here for a vacation, right?"

Alex and I glanced at each other.

My shoulders sagged. "I guess so. I hoped we could be involved in the investigation."

"Did you get a special message from someone, like a government official?" Willie winked. "Or maybe a sign from God?"

Alex sighed. "No. We haven't even received our typical box from G, our mysterious poet and forecaster who gives us clues for our mysteries."

I searched my pockets, caught hold of a chain, and pulled it out. "I still brought the key for our next adventure. The fifth of seven keys." I held it out to my friend.

"Good on ya, mate." Willie took the key, examined it, and tossed it back to me. "It might be helpful sometime."

I slid the chain around my neck. "G will get in touch with us. He's never missed an adventure, and this feels like we're about to get involved. Can't we do something?"

Willie stood. "We'll see." He put on his parka. We got our coats back on and he led us out of the station. "Time to get you back. Can you pop in tomorrow morning about nine-thirty? I'll have the analysis report on these items by that deadline." He smiled. "You'll have to let me know if God taps you on the shoulder for action by then."

Chapter 3 – G Strikes Again

Wild Boar Hotel, Albertville
Saturday, 11 January 1992, 10:15 p.m.

I scratched Lightning's head while I cradled him in my arms. He tried to lick my face and squirmed with excitement. Thunder rubbed his head against Alex's jeans to say hello.

"I don't think Mom wants us to see Willie tomorrow." I set Lightning on the floor and took off my coat and other extra clothing.

"Yep. The usual." Alex hung his coat in the closet, took off his boots, and flopped on his bed. Thunder joined him.

I pulled out my suitcase from under my bed to unpack and stopped. "Was our door locked when we got here?"

"Are you blind? You saw me open the door with our key."

"Someone else came into our room while we were gone."

Alex rolled over to look at me. "What?"

"I said—"

"I heard you. But our room isn't messy. The dogs would have made a racket and tore into the intruder's clothing." He pulled on Thunder's ear. "Did anyone come into our room while we were gone?"

His dog whined.

"See." I smirked at him. "I knew someone visited us." I bent to see under my bed. Pulled out a box wrapped in silver foil with American flags covering the top. A large G occupied the center. I set it on my bed. "We've got a mystery to solve."

"Don't open it yet." Alex sprang from his bed.

Two minutes later, we'd both examined the outside of the box. No wires, no oil, no external or internal sounds, and no rattling.

"Looks safe to me." I grabbed my Swiss Army knife from my pocket.

"Wait." Alex whipped the box away from me. "Dad needs to see this first."

I closed my knife, dropped it on my pillow, leapt after him, and tackled him on top of his bed. The package flew from his hands, tumbled, and dropped onto the floor.

Someone knocked. The dogs raced to the door.

"Now what?" I straightened my clothes and went to the door's peephole. Mom waited outside. I opened the heavy wooden door, which banged against the security chain.

"Amazing." Mom tilted her head. "You're more cautious in a hotel now?"

I unhooked the chain and opened the door wide. "You taught us well." I beamed, let her in, closed the door, and rehooked the chain. The dogs swirled around her feet.

She walked inside, noticed Alex's rumpled covers and his boots thrown in a corner, and fixed me with a stare. "Have you boys been roughhousing?" Walking to my bed, she collected my knife, waved it in the air, and spoke in a sharp tone. "Were you threatening your brother?"

"No." Alex came around his bed to stand next to me. "We disagreed about who would open the box and Gabe tackled me."

Her lips tightened. "When will you grow up? You're almost fifteen, Gabriel, yet you still act like a six-year-old." She thrust the folded knife at me. "Is this yours?"

I nodded and accepted it.

The dogs slunk in our direction and stood next to us.

"Why is it out?" She folded her arms.

This wasn't going to be pretty, no matter what I said to explain the situation. She didn't like our adventures and the directions we got from G. His package lay beside Alex's bed in plain view.

I pointed at the box. "G sent us another package."

Her voice cracked. "G?" Eyes widened.

Another knock broke off the interrogation. "Anyone home?" Dad opened the door until it stopped because of the chain. The dogs darted forward.

Alex undid the chain and let him in. Thunder and Lightning leapt to greet him.

Dad noticed the tension in one glance. "Honey, what's wrong?" Mom didn't answer. He walked to her, rubbed her back, and faced Alex and me. "Out with it, boys."

I cleared my throat. "At last we got a package from G."

"At last?" Mom waved a hand in the air. "Do you think this is a game? Every time G sends something, you're both thrown into danger."

"His packages and poems kept us safe." I tugged out key number five. "He sent us keys to—"

"I don't want to hear it." Her expression hardened. "Answer my first question. "Why the knife?"

"Gabe wanted to open the box first," Alex said. "When I took the package away, he tackled me and kind-of made a mess."

I glared at him.

Alex made his way to the bed, grabbed the package off the floor, and handed it to Dad. "We inspected it for tampering and any signs of a bomb. Nothing."

Mom went to a chair and sat. Her posture rigid, she turned to Dad. "We are in France." Her frosty voice chilled the warm air. "On a family vacation. Now this man wants to ruin our lives again."

Thunder and Lightning both sank to the floor and lay on their bellies. Lightning put his head on the floor and glanced at me with sad puppy-dog eyes.

Dad's eyes roved over the package. He flipped it over. "Let's see what's inside." He held out his hand for my knife.

I handed it over and stood beside him with Alex opposite me.

Seconds later, the contents of the box lay on my bed covers.

I snatched up several items to examine them. "Toys again. Skis, a snowmobile, and a picture of an ice-skating rink."

"I've got the note." Alex tugged it off the blanket and flipped it open.

"Read it to us." Mom sighed.

> *Choose your path with great care in the land of France*
> *Where drug lords would woo those seeking a chance*
> *For medals of bronze, silver, or gold.*
> *To keep the Games fair, you must act and be bold.*
> *The IEG Committee will do its part,*
> *But behind the scenes a villain will start*
> *A campaign of treachery, evil, and lies.*
> *Yet you and your dogs will ensure his demise.*
>
> *As light dispels darkness and brightens the skies*
> *You will find hidden a couple of spies.*
> *Though chased, harassed, even captured you may be,*
> *Hold true to your faith to achieve victory.*

Mom stood, strode to the door, and opened it. "I've prayed that these messages would stop." She swallowed hard. "That our household could live peaceful lives. Uneventful. Pleasant. But God seems to have different plans. I'm going to bed." She stepped into the hall and pulled the door shut with a click.

Both dogs raised their heads while Mom walked out. When the door shut, they slumped back to the floor, eyes flicking at us.

Dad tossed the box onto my bed. "We have a lot to talk about at breakfast tomorrow. Be there at seven sharp." He trudged to the exit.

"Dad?" I said.

He pressed on the handle and paused. His eyes bored into me.

"Willie wants to see us at the station at nine-thirty."

He swung the door wide. "See you at breakfast." With a firm thunk, the wooden door shut.

I locked the door and put the security chain on.

"That went well." Alex motioned Thunder onto his bed and patted his dog's side.

I sat on the floor and gathered Lightning in my arms. "Yep. Splendid, ole chap. Just splendid."

Chapter 4 – Scheduling Drama

Wild Boar Hotel, Albertville
Sunday, 12 January 1992, 7:00 a.m.

Breakfast on the second day of the Elim Games was an unhappy affair. We brought the dogs with us. Other than saying good morning, Mom and Dad weren't talking to us. I forced myself to be positive and eat, wolfing down the American breakfast buffet of French Toast, scrambled eggs, bacon, sausage, and some hot croissants with butter and jelly. The endless hot chocolate warmed my insides.

"Hungry?" Alex lifted an eyebrow. He seemed to be taking his time and ate half the food I did. He focused on his meat and eggs.

I stuffed the rest of the French Toast in my mouth. "Not really, but we need to be ready for the nine-thirty meeting. Who knows what will happen?" I dropped a piece for Lightning to eat.

"Before you do anything, you'll come to our room and discuss the day's schedule." Dad tapped my plate with his knife. Seven thirty-five. No deviations. And be ready to go to church."

"Church?" I scanned the bustling waiters and waitresses. "But we're in France at the IEGs. Everyone will be watching the Games."

Dad's eyes smoldered. "Going deaf?"

"No, sir." I took a few paper napkins, went to the cold part of the breakfast buffet, and selected several types of meat, two rolls, and three types of cheese. I wrapped the food together like a sandwich and returned to the table.

Alex reached under the table and petted Thunder. "You're going to gain weight."

"It's my second breakfast like we used to make in Germany." I scooped Lightning off the seat. "Except we call it lunch. That leaves more money to buy snacks." I glanced at my watch and sped past Mom and Dad. "See you soon."

Five minutes after I entered the room, Alex walked in. "Are you in a hurry?"

I scribbled notes on a piece of paper and handed it to him. "Here." I packed my lunch into my backpack.

"That's a pretty full schedule." My brother tossed the paper back. "How do you know we can get to all those places on time? I don't see church on your schedule. And we'll have to ride a bus since the Elims are spread out between ten major venues."

"You of all people should value my organization." Satisfied with my backpack, I pulled clothes from the closet I would need to be outside in temps of twenty to thirty degrees Fahrenheit. "I want the meeting with Mom and Dad about schedules to be short so we can see Willie and enjoy the sports. We can walk to the church. It's about five minutes from here. We'll be back before nine-thirty."

"Considering Mom's attitude about G, that's a pretty big ask." Alex got his gear ready for the day. "She might make us come with them all day, every day."

"I tried to plan for places Dad would like to go. And Mom also likes hockey."

"We'll find out."

Mom and Dad occupied a suite on a higher floor than ours, decked out with more furniture. Old European-style tables, a desk, an embroidered love seat, and a few chairs filled one room. The other contained a King-size bed that looked like it came out of a castle.

"We're going to make this short." Dad told us to sit around a coffee table. I sat Lightning in my lap and Thunder lay beside Alex. Our father pulled out a brochure with schedules and times. "We've decided what we want to do." He pointed to circled events for today. "We'll meet each day to coordinate our schedules."

"Gabe made a plan for us." Alex motioned at me.

I laid it on the table. "I left two things out. Church and the meeting with Willie at nine-thirty."

Dad rubbed his jaw. "Pretty ambitious. You won't see a lot of these events because of the distance between venues."

I nodded. "That's okay. These are the events we both want to see. And we'll have the dogs with us."

Alex tapped the afternoon and evening events. "We'll see you at the Men's Ski jumping at Courchevel at three p.m. We can eat dinner and go to the evening USA versus Germany hockey game at Méribel."

Mom smiled. "I like that. You can do the Luge and Downhill events at La Plagne and Val-D'Isère."

"Don't forget Willie at nine-thirty." I scratched Lightning's head when he wiggled in my lap.

A cloud seemed to come over our mother's face for an instant, then cleared. She nodded. "I trust Willie. He's like your guardian angel." She tapped the table. "Make sure you are in contact with him or us before deviating from this schedule." Her lips formed a firm line.

"We will, Mom." I moved my hand over my chest. "Cross my heart and hope to die."

Her jaw dropped.

"Gabriel Zanadu." Dad glared at me.

I covered my mouth. "I take it back. Didn't mean it that way. I meant—"

Dad stood. "Don't say another word. Follow the schedule and stay out of trouble. Can you manage that for a day?"

I nodded.

"No dogs at church." Dad patted Thunder and Lightning. "It's smaller than the one near the Security Headquarters and in the opposite direction, but still old-style architecture and close to the hotel. You can retrieve the dogs and your gear after the service."

Alex and I grabbed the dogs, our packs, and hustled out of our parent's room.

In the hallway, my brother hauled me to the elevator, the dogs scampering ahead. "Are you crazy? You're like a sniper trained to shoot with the commands out of order: 'Ready. Fire. Aim.' You almost got us grounded for the day with your 'cross my heart' comment."

"I said I was sorry."

"After G's message, that was a disaster. Better let me do the talking next time."

At 8:05 a.m. we met Mom and Dad in their room. Bundled in our snow gear, we braved the frigid air and reached the church in time for the short eight-fifteen service. We began our return at 9:00 a.m.

"I loved listening to the service in French." Mom bubbled on. "The paintings on the walls—marvelous. The organ music and choir—heavenly."

Dad strolled with Mom's arm in his. "A wonderful experience."

Mom brushed her hand on Dad's. "Yes. It brought back the memories of our earlier time in Europe." She veered off the path back to the hotel, heading into a historic district. Our pace slowed to a crawl as she admired the French streets, architecture, sculptures, and on and on.

I checked my watch. Almost nine-ten. We needed fifteen minutes to get to the Security station from our room. And each step we took made the return even longer. We were out of time.

I glanced at Alex. He shrugged.

"Dad, this is a perfect walk for a couple." I flashed a brilliant smile. "Alex and I can see a lot of these things with our friends later today. Why don't we take off to stick with our schedule and let you both enjoy your walk together?"

Dad gave me a quizzical look.

Mom's arm tightened around Dad's. "That's an excellent idea. We'll see you boys later. Don't miss any of our meeting times."

"Yes, ma'am. Tata." I raced to the hotel with Alex trailing me.

We dashed to the room, snatched our bags, grabbed the dogs, whizzed through the lobby, and struck out for the IEG Security Station.

Chapter 5 – The Evidence

IEG Main Security Headquarters, Albertville
Sunday, 12 January 1992, 9:32 a.m.

The same female desk Sergeant lowered her eyes at us when we entered the Security Station. She stared at the dogs and shook her head. "Jil-bear." Sorting through papers on her desk, she called the man's name without turning.

Jil-bear walked us back to Willie's empty office, pointed to the chairs, and went to get us something to drink—coffee for Alex and hot chocolate with marshmallows for me. A few minutes later, after he delivered our drinks, Willie arrived. Taking a seat behind his desk, he pushed some papers to one side and dropped a report on top.

"G'day, mates." He grinned. "How's Colonel Zanadu and the missus? Guess they decided you're old enough to come alone."

I sat straighter. "We did bring our dogs. We also convinced our parents of the importance of this investigation and—"

"Hold on." Alex shook his head. "We almost didn't make it here. Let me set the story straight." He explained G's package and note, and what I said to Mom at our scheduled meeting.

"Cross my heart and hope to die?" Our friend scratched his head. "Be glad you're not here with chains on your feet."

"Not as bad as working with that Sergeant out there." I drew a finger across my throat. "She hates us."

Willie chuckled. "That's Greta Baumgartner. Born in Germany and raised in France. She thinks everyone's beneath her. I often have to dissuade her of that delusion since I don't work for her, but MI6. But, enough of that. What's your plan for seeing the Elims today?"

Tugging out a sheet of paper, I opened it. "Here's our schedule."

Willie motioned for me to hand it over, which I did.

He reviewed my paper against the program for the Games. "We can make this work. First, I have to tell you about the evidence you brought in. How much do you understand about the doping challenges the IEGC, that's the International Elimination Games Committee, has to contend with?"

I shrugged. "Nothing."

Willie propped his feet on his desk. "I'll summarize to make it easy. Since people want to win in the games, they'll often do anything they can, including taking performance-enhancing drugs that increase muscle mass and reduce fat. Because the body eliminates most of these short-lived drugs over time, the IEGC even tracks doping around the year using random athlete testing no matter where the athletes train."

"How do they find them?" I sipped my hot drink. "They can live anywhere in the world."

The chair under Willie squeaked. "Athletes have to tell the IEGC or their country's IEG Committee where they are and report if they move. The Committee can track them anywhere. Regardless, they still get tested before their events at the games and at surprise intervals."

Alex ruffled Thunder's fur. "What kind of drugs?"

Our friend opened the report he tossed on his desk earlier. "Steroids like dianabol, stanozolol, testosterone, human growth hormone, and the lot. Then there is blood doping. It increases the blood's capacity to carry oxygen to the muscles using blood transfusions and oxygen enhancing drugs like EPO." He closed the document. "The IEGC wants to protect athletes from the negative side effects of these drugs and ensure a level playing field for the competition."

I picked Lightning off the floor, let him settle in my lap, and scratched under his collar. "But isn't the testing expensive?"

Willie nodded. "We do blood testing, urine testing, and gas chromatography-combustion-IRMS. We're pretty thorough. Still, people cheat and falsify reports to help their teams get to the top."

Alex finished his coffee. "Wouldn't the athletes know they were taking drugs?"

A knock on the door startled the dogs. Their ears and heads focused on the sound. Jil-bear walked in, set a stack of papers on Willie's desk, and left without a word.

"Thanks, Gilbert." Our friend rifled through the pages.

When the assistant shut the door, I pointed after him. "Isn't his name Jil-bear?"

Willie chuckled. "You'll have to get used to French names and the English spellings. We spell his name G-i-l-b-e-r-t and say Gilbert in English, but the French pronounce it Jil-bear. Take your pick on how you want to say it."

"Back to European translations again." I shifted Lightning in my lap.

Willie flopped the paperwork in a pile next to an overflowing inbox. "We analyzed your evidence, twelve syringes, four pill containers, and the false reports. Next, my staff will match the blood samples for athletes in the competition, check for drug doping, and scan other testing reports to spot false leads. Great work."

My brother settled his dog back on the floor. "What about the athletes?"

"Right." Willie flipped the report to the side. "Some team trainers slip drugs into their athlete's diets without telling them what they are taking. In the case of younger competitors, they swear them to silence, forbidding them to talk to their parents. And in some countries, the governments force their athletes to take the supplements despite the dangers, threatening them if they were to say anything."

I scraped the inside of my cup with my wooden stirrer to get the last bit of marshmallow. Couldn't waste any of that good sweetness. "Sounds like a cut-throat business. Maybe the evidence we found will help."

"I reckon it will." Willie stood. "But you two need to get a move on if you're going to make the Luge at La Plagne. It's nine-fifty. Time for me to get back to pushing paper around. But I need your help, if you can."

"Sure." I jumped to my feet. "What can we do?"

Thunder and Lightning both darted over to Willie for a farewell petting.

Willie laughed. "Gotta love these ole' dish-lickers." His eyes connected with Alex and me. "I'd like you to keep your peepers open. Report anything suspicious. At the Downhill and Ski Jump venues, I can let your dogs into warm-up areas. Even at Final events." He paused. "Have fun but be careful. Drug runners are notoriously dangerous."

Chapter 6 – The Italian Girl

IEG Luge Venue, La Plagne, France

Sunday, 12 January 1992, 11:05 a.m.

Gabe and I speed-walked through La Plagne, a village about an hour away from Albertville. Surrounded by the snow-covered roofs of chalets, tourist stores, and mountain slopes, the setting made a perfect location to host the Luge event. Because we met with Willie, we were late for the second run.

While crunching through the snow to the reviewing stands, my stomach rumbled.

"I need something hot to drink before we get to the second Luge runs." Gabe carried Lightning in his arms. "If we go inside, that will give Thunder a chance to get warm."

"We need to be quick. The eleven-fifteen event already started." I dodged a man carrying skis. "I'm sure the festival seating area will be crowded."

"Dad should have reserved seats for us." My brother darted around a big lady to see better. "His special mission rates better than the general seating area."

Searching on the way to the venue, we found an indoor cafe that sold coffee to go. I went first, bought my coffee and a roll, and moved to the side to let Gabe order. Due to the tight space, I clicked on Thunder's leash and tucked my pastry in a pocket. While Gabe told the attendant what his drink would be, Thunder jerked my arm. My coffee spilled on the girl in the line behind Gabe.

"Oops." I grabbed several napkins. "Sorry to spill my coffee on you. My dog's fault…." I dropped to one knee and tossed the napkins on the puddle to absorb the liquid, brushing against her snow boots with the soggy paper.

"You Americans." She giggled. "So clumsy, yet charming."

I gazed at her from my lower position. Gorgeous girl.

"Don't worry about it. These snow pants and boots won't stain." She swished her long black hair back and adjusted her knit cap. She wore a bright red outfit with the Italian Flag sewn on her snow jacket.

I rose. My cheeks felt warm.

While we chatted, another girl brought her a drink. "I bought you something. We need to go."

"Thanks." She sipped her coffee and batted her eyelashes at me. "A pleasure to meet you. Addio." She giggled again and walked away with her friend.

Gabe stood next to me, put two creamers and two sugars in his coffee while holding his dog, and watched her leave. "Marvelous. I'll remember that technique for meeting girls when I'm ready."

"Thunder's leash jerked my arm." My eyes flashed.

"I'll teach Lightning that trick." Gabe set his dog on the ground and scanned the crowd. "Rats. No pretty girls around."

"Brothers." I shook my head in disgust and walked away.

The Luge track's grandstand surrounded the finish line at the bottom of the hill. Televisions displayed start and split times of each sled until the last turn before the finish. I loved watching them speed through the course. The competition kept me entranced.

We sat to the right side of the middle section; backpacks stuffed under our seats. Thunder squeezed between my knees and Lightning sat on Gabe's lap. About 11:45 a.m., halfway through the second heat, we left to see the Men's Downhill Elim Finals Race at Val-D'Isère, which started at 12:15 p.m. The fifty-two-minute bus ride meant we'd never make the first runs.

Outside the building, I heard someone call us.

"Gabe. Alex. Wait." A figure in blue snow gear ran in our direction. When he arrived, panting to catch his breath, he said. "Remember me?"

"Franco Giovanni." Gabe hugged his friend from our earlier time living in Germany.

He shook hands with me and hugged Thunder's neck.

"What are you doing here?" Gabe patted him on the shoulder. "You hate sports."

He nodded. "So true. But my father, our home-school science teacher, wanted to come to see the physics of each event."

"We're interested in the skiing events." I pointed at the bus stop. We've got to catch the next bus to the Men's Downhill, which starts in about twenty-five minutes.

"You'll be late." A figure glided next to Franco. She smiled.

I stared, recognizing her outfit instantly—the bright red snowsuit with the Italian logo.

Gabe set Lightning on the ground to let both dogs sniff Franco and the girl.

Franco's face swiveled back and forth between the young lady and me. "Do you know each other?"

The girl bent in a mock curtsy, extending the leg I spilled coffee on. "He is my American hero."

Looking away, I said, "I didn't mean—"

"No apology." She grinned. "What do you Americans say? You owe me one."

The corners of my mouth lifted. "Okay."

"This is Sofia Lamberti." Franco raised his hand toward her. "She is in the Italian Junior Games as an ice skater."

"Not a speed skater." She rubbed Thunder's fur.

Sofia listened while Gabe and I shared the adventures of the past couple of years with Franco. We told him about our passive mission from Willie to watch out for clues to any doping action. Then we talked about our schedule for the day.

Franco looked at his watch. "You need to go. You're already late for the start of the Downhill. But I can meet you at the Ski Jumping competition and I'll have another old friend of ours with me, Izabella Valentin. She's growing into a beautiful woman."

"I won't be able to see you at that time, but perhaps later." Sofia gazed at me. "I'm going to watch the Women's Freestyle Skiing in Tignes at four o'clock and the Mixed Pairs Ice Skating in Albertville at seven-thirty this evening. But I can get tickets for anyone who'd like to come to the skating event."

"Thanks." I glanced at her. "We'll see if we can change our schedules."

Gabe's eyes opened wide.

"I'm sure I'd enjoy your company." Sofia brushed Thunder's fur. "But no dogs are allowed inside."

I nodded. "Our hotel isn't far away. We can drop the dogs off and join you."

Franco tapped his watch. "Before you go, I think you should be at some of the evening parties after the events—that's where the action is." He jerked his head at Sofia. "She can get you into the parties you want to attend."

A smile crept across my face. "Sounds great. I'm sure we can make that happen."

We waved goodbye and hurried to get to the bus stop before the next one left.

"We're way late." Gabe increased the pace. "We're going miss the first half of the ski runs. And aren't we on restriction? How do you expect Mom and Dad to let us go out when—"

A man, weaving through the crowd at full speed, slammed into me, knocking me to the ground.

Thunder launched after the assailant.

"Thunder. Stop." I got to my knees.

The man kept running. Across the street, a tall man spewed rap-id-fire words in a foreign tongue at a thick-chested man wearing a green jacket. He nodded and took off after the first guy, brushing past several bystanders.

Gabe helped me to my feet. Thunder growled and Lightning barked.

I brushed snow off my waterproof coat. "Must not be my day. Wonder what caused that commotion."

"Don't know." Gabe shushed Lightning and set out for the bus stop. "Didn't that sound like Russian to you?"

"The guy who talked looked like a Russian." I held on to Thun-der's collar.

Gabe searched the crowd. "He disappeared. Maybe we should report this to Willie. That didn't look like normal activity at the Elims."

"True." I tugged on Thunder's collar to make him sit at the bus stop. "But maybe the guy was a pickpocket."

"I don't think so." Lightning climbed into Gabe's arms when the bus arrived. "The Russian acted calm, like a boss telling his worker what to do instead of a victim who lost money." He shook my head. "We'd better start studying Russian. Our adventure's growing into a pretty big snowball."

Chapter 7 – Spanish Connection

Downhill Venue, Val-D'Isère, France
Sunday, 12 January 1992, 1:05 p.m.

Val-D'Isère lay nestled at the foot of a mountain. Dark brown chalets and modern ski resort housing dotted the landscape. The sun glinted off the snow-covered buildings and slopes.

Alex and I slipped on our sunglasses while we exited the bus and followed the crowd to the circular stands surrounding the finish line for the Downhill event. The dogs jumped in and out of a few snow-banks as we got close.

"Wait." I dropped my backpack on the snow.

"What?" Alex motioned at the finish line. "We're pretty close."

I dragged out a can of suntan spray. "I need protection for the next four or five hours." My skin burned without protection, but my brother's tanned.

"Make it quick."

I sprayed some on my hands, rubbed them over my face, shoved the can back in the bag, and pulled out my second breakfast.

"Now what?" Alex watched me assemble a sandwich.

Glancing at him, I completed the task, closed my bag, and shouldered it. "Ready to go." I jammed the sandwich in my mouth.

We passed the entrance to the spectator area at the finish line.

I spoke around clumps of meat, cheese, and bread still in my mouth. "Where are we going?"

"To find Willie. We need to report that Russian."

The Security substation sat three buildings away from the event. We went to the receptionist and got nowhere. The woman spoke limited English.

"We've got to see Willie Gretzke." I raised my voice. "Doesn't anyone know him? He's an Aussie—"

"And he talks like an Aussie, right mate?" Our friend walked in from the back of the station. "Next time I need a megaphone, I'll have you say it for me."

I rolled my eyes. "The staff wasn't listening."

Willie beckoned us to the back. "They hear quite well. Don't be like the local tourist who gets louder and louder, expecting every person to understand English. You're in Europe."

Alex snickered. "And French happens to be the native language here."

I backhanded my brother's jacket, but Alex shrugged it off.

Thunder and Lightning sniffed at the waste basket in the back office. Thunder stuck his head in and pulled out part of a sandwich. Lightning tried to get some of the food, but the big Great Dane growled.

"When's the last time you fed the dogs?" Willie took a burger from a paper bag and put it in front of Lightning. "They seem famished."

Alex and I shrugged.

"We ran out of time this morning," I said. "I meant to feed them after church, but Mom took the scenic route back to the hotel. Which cut our time to meet you at 9:30 a.m. to almost nothing."

Alex stood next to Willie's desk since his back office contained a single chair. "You wanted us to report suspicious activity. At La Plagne, we saw a tall Russian man directing someone in a hunter green jacket to chase another guy."

"Can you describe them?" Our friend wrote while we poured out what we knew. "Are you sure he spoke Russian?"

Alex ran a finger along his jaw. "The tall Russian's brown hair stuck out of his hat. Dark eyes. Athletic build. His assistant—barrel-chested, green eyes, and about six inches shorter than the Russian giving orders—close to Gabe's height—five feet, eleven inches." A crease appeared on my brother's forehead. "The man who bowled me over appeared to be skin and bones but knew how to apply leverage. Lean and mean."

I tugged the chair away from the desk and sat backward on the chair, facing Willie. "I'm glad I didn't have to remember that much. The Russian used words like da and nyet. I didn't understand the rest, but he sounded like Russians Dad worked with in the past."

Alex gave a thumbs up.

"You're fortunate to find me here." Willie set his pen on the desk. "I move around quite a bit—like you chaps. When this event concludes, I'll head to Courchevel for the ski jump competition."

"Could we get a ride?" I patted Lightning's back. "If you have room for dogs."

"No worries. Meet me here when the Downhill event is complete."

We said our goodbyes and pushed through the crowd to see the finishing racers.

"Any sandwiches left?" My brother eyed me. "I saw you stick two rolls in your bag."

I rubbed my stomach. "I'll eat that before the ski jumping competition, but I could part with it for ten U.S. dollars." I held out my hand.

"Crook." Alex slapped my hand away. "I'd rather pay a vendor for my food. Besides, you didn't feed the dogs this morning. Mom won't be happy with that."

Lightning started barking.

"Quiet, buddy." I scooped him into my arms. Other people

glanced at us. He squirmed and Thunder poked his head behind us, inching away. "What's wrong with you guys?"

"Surprise!" A girl with black hair and aquamarine eyes danced into our presence.

Her Spanish accented voice sounded familiar. The dogs closed in, tails wagging.

The girl laughed, petting them while focusing on us. "You've forgotten me already? After homeschooling together for almost two years in Germany?"

"Izabella…" My mind churned for a second. "Valentin. Does your mom still teach dance on Friday afternoons for home-schoolers?"

She swirled in a circle. "Doesn't it show?"

Alex made a mock bow. "Indeed it does. Do you have a favorite Downhill racer?"

"I suppose not. I wanted to find you here to say 'Hi' before meeting at the Courchevel Ski jump competition. Franco told me about the investigation you're helping with and I wanted to introduce you to a friend who might help. He's French and knows some influential people here." She checked her watch. "Got to run. Find me at the bottom of the ski jump hill." She gave us both a quick hug and faded into the crowd.

"That's amazing." I collected Lightning into my arms. "Two old friends with connections."

Alex looked at the scoreboard for the Downhill. "G didn't mention any friends in his riddle. Or old acquaintances." At the end of their run, another skier arrived with a flourish, their skis digging in and spraying snow. "We've got three runs to go till the Downhill's finished."

Chapter 8 – Dogs on Alert

IEG Security Office, Val-D'Isère, France
Sunday, 12 January 1992, 2:05 p.m.

Willie glanced at us after we returned to the local security office. "You've seen me three times today. Give me a few minutes. Somebody's got to do the work around here." Flipping through a sheaf of papers, he dumped them in a box on one side of his desk. "I'll tackle that when I get back here. Let's move out."

Outside we climbed into a BMW SUV. Willie put it in gear and headed to Courchevel, the Normal 90-meter Ski Jumping venue. "Nothing new to report?"

"Not on the drug side." I rode shotgun with Lightning. "Nice. Heated seats." I punched a few buttons. "Ahh."

"Leave it to Gabe to find the comfort controls." My brother leaned closer. "We did run into another old friend from Germany you met when the human traffickers trapped us in the Salt Mines. Izabella Valentin. It's strange that we should meet two friends from Germany here."

Punching the radio, I found a rock music channel and cranked the volume higher.

"Turn that down." My brother put his hands over his ears. "I can't hear anything over that racket."

I lowered the volume to a whisper. "And before Alex continues, you should know that Izabella will introduce us to another kid who has some big influence at the Games. She didn't say his name. But he's French."

By creative driving and speedy maneuvering, Willie pulled into a reserved security parking slot near the ski jump course around 3:30 p.m. "Before you scramble out of my sight, I want you to listen. These drug dealers don't play games. If they catch wind that you're even helping me as part of my operation, they'll take you out. Be careful who you tell about me, even if they're friends. I'm not under-cover, but the fewer people who know what I'm doing, the better. I'll be at the bottom of the hill until the event finishes."

We stopped at a bistro. Alex bought a mid-afternoon snack. I bought the dogs something to eat and got them bowls of water. When our canine sidekicks licked their chops at the end, we trotted off to find Izabella.

I searched through the crowd of ski jackets and snow gear. "What color coat did she wear?"

Alex shook his head. "White." Hundreds of white snow jackets dotted the people-scape we surveyed. "The dogs can find her. Thunder—seek."

Thunder sat in front of Alex and tilted his head.

My brother chuckled. "Find Izabella."

Lightning loped over to me and waited for his instructions. "Seek Izabella Valentin. Cute girl, about my age, dark hair…."

Lightning rolled on his back, paws waving in the air.

"He's not buying it." My brother crouched in front of Thunder. "The last girl."

For a few seconds, neither dog moved.

I crossed my arms. "Go."

Lighting jumped on his feet and raced to my right. Thunder weaved his way between people. That got us more stares.

"Maybe we should have put them on leashes." I sprinted after Lightning. Europeans didn't like folks yelling at their dogs, but they disliked uncontrolled dogs even more. After ten or twelve steps, I stopped.

Izabella patted Lightning's head and scratched Thunder behind his ears. She raised her eyebrows at me. "Can't manage your dogs?"

"We told them to find you." I blew on my fingers and rubbed them against my chest as though I'd accomplished something.

She made a funny face at me. A boy stood next to her. He must have weighed about two-hundred and fifty pounds, most of it around his waist. "This is Bastien Dubois. He is French and his parents know my father and mother."

Alex and I shook hands with him and introduced ourselves.

"He knows about our past together. He's a friend of the French competitor in the Norwegian Combined skiing, Rolf Kristiensen. Bastien's father is Jacques Dubois, whom you may know trains many IEG athletes, has lots of connections, and a ton of money. Bastien can get us into many places others can't go."

Bastien gave a slight bow of his head at the introduction. A light French accent colored his words. "She is far too lavish in her description. My father is well-known but not a super-rich individual. However, I do have connections if they are helpful to you since you are American detectives and work with the security people employed by the IEGC."

I chuckled. "That description is also a bit grand. We like mysteries and solved several in the past few years."

"They are modest." Izabella reached out and patted me on the cheek. "They saved my life in the Salt Mines at Berchtesgaden, Germany. However, they need access to some of the exclusive athlete parts of each location to learn how the events work. Can you help?"

Bastien motioned at some snowmobiles on one side of the ski jump arena. "Let's take a tour of the ski jump facilities here."

"How will the dogs ride along?" Alex thumped Thunder on his side. "My dog's pretty big."

"We'll attach a small supply sled." Bastien trudged off at a good clip. We followed, walking for five minutes until we reached a small area with seven snowmobiles and several support sleds. Alex helped attach a sled. We settled both dogs on it with orders to stay until we released them. I piloted one machine with Izabella sitting behind me, tracking Bastien, who carried Alex and towed the dogs.

We dismounted at the top, parking the snowmobiles away from the ski jump tower and television cameras. Our French guide started the tour with the elevator to the top.

"No one is coming up the hill." Bastien watched as a ski jumper flew off the end of the take-off ramp. "We have a few minutes. Get in quick."

We squeezed into the glass elevator with the dogs crawling between our legs to fit in. The ride gave us a fantastic view of the mountains and valley.

"Gorgeous." Izabella's eyes widened. "What a spectacular experience."

Bastien grinned. "I love it each time I make the trip."

In a short time, the door opened at the top to a ready room with a few skiers waiting for their time to jump. We stepped inside the room, still somewhat cool, but warmer than the weather outside. A television camera on a tripod could cover the inside of the room or outside. Several chairs lined the walls.

A controller by the ski jump door called a man's name. The guy donned his goggles, sidling out the door and onto his perch. When he saw the green light, he would slide down the in-run track to the takeoff point. The other skiers ignored us. They kept their eyes closed or watched out the windows, focused on preparing for their jump.

Thunder and Lightning sniffed around the room. Thunder put his paws on a waist-high wooden railing to see out, but lost interest after a moment.

"Pretty spare accommodations." Izabella ran a hand across the back of one of the seats.

Alex went back to the elevator. "I'm ready."

"We wait for the next skiers to arrive, then depart." Bastien sat in a chair.

The elevator doors opened minutes later. Three skiers piled out. We climbed in and descended. At the bottom, Bastien grabbed Izabella's hand. "This way."

Behind the tower stood two small buildings built like chalets.

Bastien pointed to the left building. "That's the physical plant for the tower and support hut next door. Electrical, water, and a few heating pipes."

The dogs galloped over to sniff around but found nothing. We trailed behind Bastien to the hut. He opened the door and went inside.

"The hut is locked at night." He wandered around the inside, a basic rectangle. One wall included a microwave, a small refrigerator, a sink, and an enclosed bathroom. A padded bench deep enough to lay on lined most of the second wall. Wooden chairs, a desk, and a small coffee table graced the third wall, and the fourth wall we entered through contained a few posters.

"Is this a rest area?" Izabella wandered around the space. "An interior decorator might help make this place much more comfortable."

"From what I understand," Bastien said, "the building houses support staff that man the cameras upstairs, any monitoring equipment used in the tower for the jumps, and provides a backup gathering area for skiers if the staff encounters delays."

"I'm going to try the restroom to see if it works." I took three steps when Lightning whined. His alert signal. "Guess I'll wait."

"Thunder's got the scent too." Alex tracked his dog. Thunder gave a low growl but didn't stop. He paced in front of the padded bench.

"Where is it, boy?" I backed off a few steps to give Lightning plenty of room to work. He sniffed around the door jamb of the entryway and barked. "Outside we go."

Bastien opened the door.

Lightning shot outside, found the scent, and went behind the support building. Thunder followed suit, dipping his muzzle into the snow before streaking after his buddy. At a tree stump behind the hut, the dogs dug at a furious rate.

Alex and I dashed after our canine friends to keep them from ruining any evidence. They pawed through snow, hit dirt, and kept going. After they created a small mound of frozen muck, Lightning yipped. Thunder sat.

"Lightning got there first." Alex swept his hand in the hole's direction. "You can pull out the contraband."

"I'll ruin this brand-new jacket." Patting my jasmine green coat, I pulled out a tag. "See? I still haven't even taken the tags off it."

Izabella closed her eyes. "Wouldn't want to make a mess of your beautiful jacket, would we? I'll reach inside the hole."

"Not with that white coat." Alex raised a hand to stop her. "You'll trash it."

She grinned. "I'll take the coat off and—"

"Never mind." I took off my coat, handed it to Alex, and ran to the opening. Thunder and Lightning created a hole as wide and deep as my elbow to the tip of my fingers. In seconds I pulled out about twenty plastic baggies of a greenish powder in a brown paper bag." I brushed the dirt off my hoodie, donned my outer coat, and put on my gloves. "Still got your camera, bro?"

Alex lowered his backpack, fished out the camera, and took a few pictures. "I'll need to take pictures of that padded bench in the support chalet. The dogs tracked the scent there."

After Alex took enough photos for evidence, I found a bag and stuffed the other plastic bags inside.

"Good work." Izabella patted me on the back and leaned close. "I knew you could do it."

We shot to the hill's base on our snowmobiles, parked them next to the jump, and raced to the Security station.

Inside, I glanced around the open office area. "Willie." Most of the people in the room stared. I softened my volume and tried again. "Has anyone seen Investigator Willie Gretzke?"

A man narrowed his eyes at us. He jerked a thumb at the back office.

"Thanks." Alex waved at a few people as we worked our way through the desks.

"Don't be bashful." Willie sipped some coffee. "Cuppa?"

I set the brown paper bag of contraband on his desk. "Hot chocolate would be good for me." Everyone else gave their orders. Thunder and Lightning lay on the floor.

"Water for the dishlickers?" Our Australian friend rubbed Thunder's head.

"Sure." I leaned forward. "You should see the drugs we found." I motioned at the bag.

Willie poked his head out the door, gave a few orders, and returned to his desk seat. He checked the bag. Made a list. "Where did you find this?"

Alex handed over his photos. "Support shack behind the ski tower."

Willie counted the pictures. "That's six pics. I'm going to have the department buy you ten replacement packs. I don't want you to run out." He relaxed into his chair. "We'll have this analyzed by tonight. But your discovery brings about a new twist to our security focus."

"What's that?" I said.

Willie's eyes became hard as ice. "I've got to swear you to secrecy. Do you agree?" His eyes swept the room.

We nodded.

"I'm serious. This information is under the strictest confidence. And I need your full cooperation and verbal acknowledgment. If you break this promise, someone will get hurt and I'll have to lock you in jail."

"I agree." I raised my hand. The others did the same.

"All right, here it is." He hesitated. "We've identified a spy on the support team."

Chapter 9 – Russian Spotting

Highway N90 to Albertville, France

Sunday, 12 January 1992, 5:00 p.m.

Willie drove us back to our Albertville hotel in his personal car, a metallic blue Peugeot 605. I rode shotgun which gave Alex and Thunder lots of room in the back.

"You didn't tell us much about the spy you suspect on the team." Alex gazed into the rearview mirror to see Willie's eyes.

Our friend made a left turn, right into a mini-traffic jam. "Not much to say. I couldn't give out any real details because I don't know Bastien that well."

I adjusted myself and Lightning in the seat. "Why tell us about the snoop if you don't know more."

"Persistent anklebiters, aren't you?"

"We're not children." Alex poked his head over the back of my seat. "I'm going to be seventeen in May."

"Don't take it personally." He got free of the traffic jam and paused at a stop light. "MI6 wants me to do a deep investigation. I can't disclose some of those plans even to you. Or your friends." He pressed the accelerator when the light turned green.

I folded my arms on my chest. "I see. We're not considered real detectives."

Willie laughed. "You're much better than that. You're seasoned detectives. But even the best have to do the hard yakka. Like scouting suspects."

Alex sat back. "Like finding evidence. Thunder and Lightning did the hard work there."

"Right as rain." He pulled into the hotel car entrance and stopped. "Find the Russian. See what he's doing. And study the language."

I groaned. "That's gonna be a lot of hard yakka."

We walked and fed our dogs, and dropped them and our backpacks in our room. Alex failed to convince our parents to let us see the Mixed Pair Skating event with Sofia. Instead, we ate dinner with them at the Wild Boar Hotel restaurant on the ground floor and arrived at the USA vs. Germany hockey game in Méribel twenty minutes before the 8:15 p.m. face-off. Dad's connections got us seats ten rows lower than the nosebleed section, but a huge jumbotron let us see all the action. I loved watching players crash into the walls and move the puck around like National Hockey League players.

At the end of the first period, Alex elbowed me and pointed. "Franco."

I scanned the crowd to see him but failed. "Where?"

"Blue snow suit, remember?"

"Got a lock on him."

My brother leaned over to Mom. "Snack time?" He held out a hand for some cash.

Mom dug in her purse, slipped out some Francs, and tugged Alex closer. "You two come right back. No spying. No sleuthing. I don't care what happens. Comprende?"

"We understand." Alex stood. "But I saw Franco Giovanni. His dad, Alberto, taught us science in Germany."

"Cool." I jumped to my feet. "Can we go talk with him?"

She hesitated. "I suppose so, but I want you back here in fifteen minutes. And no snooping."

"Gotcha." I slipped past several people.

"Hurry." Alex slapped me on the shoulder. "He's leaving."

We dodged and darted, taking the stairs two at a time when we could, and still missed him. Twisting and turning, we made it to the concourse under the stands.

"There." Alex broke into a run with me in pursuit.

A security man blocked our way. "In a hurry?" His French-accented English and high voice didn't make him sound serious, but his hand hovering near his holstered gun made me slow down.

"Our friend." I looked around the Frenchman's head. "He went into the restroom."

"Ze toilette?" The man's face seemed tight.

Alex took a deep breath, relaxing his shoulders. "Yes." He explained how we knew him.

The security guard inspected us in detail. After a moment, he motioned us to the bathrooms. "Please walk. No hurry."

We thanked him, walked to the Men's room and split up. I went to the exit. Alex went inside. In the excitement, we'd lost track of Franco. A minute later, Alex came out with his hands in the air. "Couldn't find him."

"I'll double-check." I went in, used the facilities, and checked as many stalls as possible. I darted to the exit. "Nyet."

The security guard who stopped us walked past and stared. "American?"

I shrugged. "Practicing my language skills."

The guard scowled and left.

My stomach growled. "Snack stand is next."

We strolled to the first one we saw. I ordered a French pastry with a soda and Alex got a cup of coffee.

"We meet again." Franco stepped from behind a support post after we passed it. "I wanted to check your tracking skills. Not bad until you got the security guard suspicious." He laughed. "I enjoyed the show."

While we walked Franco back to his seat, we updated him on our visit with Willie and our current mission of spotting the Russian.

"Keep me informed." He paused by his row entrance. "I'll help. Sofia can also assist."

"Alex likes Sofia." I snickered.

My brother's hand poked me in the side. "Careful, little one." He shoved me in the direction of our seats.

Mom smiled at us. "I see you stayed out of trouble. Enjoy visiting with Franco?"

We both nodded.

The game ended with a USA 5-1 victory over Germany. The U.S. fans erupted in loud shouts and cheers.

When we departed, I grabbed Alex's arm to hold him back. "Look to your left."

The tall Russian man stood outside the hockey rink, waving his arms while he spoke to a blonde-haired woman. We couldn't get a good view due to the man's bulk and the fact she was a full head shorter than the Russian. She wore a close-fitting grey snow suit. We saw glimpses of her face, but she faced away from us most of the time to talk to our suspect.

"Get a picture." I shoved my brother at the couple. "I'll tell Mom and Dad you stopped to retie your snow boots."

"I don't have my camera." Alex held out his hands. "Too bulky."

Sneaking behind a knot of people closer to the man and woman, I peeked to get a better view.

"Gabe?" Dad tapped my shoulder. "What are you doing?"

I searched for my brother. "Trying to find Alex. I lost him a second ago."

He bumped into me. "Right behind you, bro."

Dad walked to Mom. "You two need to stick right next to us on the walk back. Our family time is critical. Now tell me about your day…."

We arrived at the Wild Boar Hotel after 10:00 p.m., said good-night, walked the dogs one last time, and crawled into bed. Lightning snuggled next to me. I didn't like his dog breath and settled him lower on my chest. Sleep took a while to come. My mind wandered over our second day at the IEGs. What a packed day. Meeting old friends and making new ones. Willie's guidance. The secret information he shared. Why did he do that? Finding drugs near the support shack. And the Russian talking with a blonde woman. Enemy? Spy?

We'd have to dig deeper. And use every trick we've learned.

Chapter 10 – Uneasy Partners

Albertville, France
Sunday, 12 January 1992, 10:30 p.m.

The delicious atmosphere of La Tanière du Lion's (The Lion's Lair) assaulted the senses as soon as one entered the restaurant. A bar lined the eatery's left side. The smell of steak, lobster, and beer drifted over the crowded tables. Boisterous conversations, back-slapping, and laughter filled the air.

"Genevieve, one moment." The tall Russian barged past me, ignored the raucous noise, and motioned the restaurant's host to lean closer over his podium. "The Bronze Medal table. Just the lady and me." Under his palm, he slid fifty Francs to the man.

My dinner companion treated me as though I wasn't there. Irritated, I brushed the side of his coat with mine, but he didn't even glance in my direction.

The host slipped the money into his suit's internal breast pocket. "One minute, monsieur." He disappeared for a few minutes and returned, a solemn frown on his face. With a heavy French accent, he continued in English. "Ze Bronze table is occupied. However, I believe ze Silver Medal table is available." He raised his nose. Gazed into the rear of the restaurant. His hand shifted forward on the podium.

The Russian scowled at the man. He slid another fifty Francs under the host's palm. "Very well. Make it spectacular."

The host pocketed the money and lifted a finger in the air. A hostess appeared with menus in hand. "This way, monsieur, mademoiselle." After taking our coats and seating us, she lit the candle on the table. The Silver Medal table faced the crowded room with the three other sides enclosed by a wall, like a semicircular booth, providing some privacy. "What would you like to drink?"

"Vodka on the rocks." The man's eyes dropped to the menu.

"Water with lemon." I flicked back a strand of my blonde hair and smiled.

The hostess left, stating she'd be back to take our dinner order.

"Does every Frenchman take out their dislike on Russians?" The man raised an eyebrow at me.

I laughed in a light-hearted way. "Dimitri Vasiliev, you slay me. Do you think all Frenchmen are against you?"

"Genevieve." He set his menu on the table. "As a French woman, you understand the ego of your people. Audacious. Bold. And often arrogant."

"I could say that of a few Russians I know." I winked. "Relax. We have much to discuss tonight."

The server came back and took our meal orders. I chose the Chef salad and Dimitri ordered a steak, medium-rare.

We indulged in small talk until the main course arrived. Dimitri shooed the hostess away and told her not to return for thirty minutes.

"Now we can talk." Dimitri cut a piece of steak and thrust it into his mouth.

"Why did you want to meet here?" I waved my fork at the restaurant. "Such an easy place to be overheard. Our plans are too confidential for this location."

Dimitri swallowed. "Mademoiselle Fournier. Notice the loud banter of conversation, the background music, and the lack of attention on serious matters of most people here. No one is interested in us." He cut another piece of steak. "Besides, we are in a corner of a sort." He placed the next morsel in his mouth.

"What kind of a fool do you take me for?" With a dainty motion, I squeezed my lemon and placed it on a paper napkin. "We're in a dangerous line of business. A part I'd choose not to play if you took my concerns in a serious fashion."

"But I do." He paused long enough to drink some vodka and take another bite. "The illicit business you do in France is safe because you know the country, the police, and the connections. I'm asking for your commitment to a tiny fraction of the same kind of work to reap millions more. Think what could happen. What if we could win more gold medals for the Cooperative or French Teams?"

I laid my salad fork beside the bowl though a quarter of my salad remained. This wasn't going my way. "Dimitri, I won't discuss this anymore in an unprotected environment." I gathered my purse. "Where did they take our coats?"

"Wait." Dimitri made a show of searching his sports jacket's pockets. "Ah, here it is." He retrieved a small device, which looked like a tape recorder, and set it on the table. "Meet a new invention of some friends of mine. An audio jammer."

My eyebrows arched. "How does it work?"

"When we finish our meals, we'll get one last drink, close the privacy curtains, and slide together close enough to whisper at the back of the booth." He smirked. "I'll increase the jammer volume louder than our voices. It won't bother the other guests but will mask any discussion we have. When we're done, I'll turn it off."

I dropped my purse on the table. "Agreed. But we must speak in generalities. You still have to prove to me I can trust you."

He ate some vegetables while I nibbled at my salad, marshaling my thoughts for the real conversation later. Making more small talk, we passed the time. Dimitri put his knife and fork on the plate and signaled the hostess. "Please bring my bill and another vodka. What will you have, my dear?" He tilted his head at me.

"Another water with lemon."

The hostess returned several minutes later. Dimitri paid in cash. The woman closed the privacy curtains at his request. Both he and I slid further back into our booth, almost touching.

Hitting the play button on the jammer, the Russian smiled when the sound generator started. White noise played in the background while a jazz vocalist floated in and out. "We're covered," he whispered.

I nodded. "Now tell me how we can get the drugs to the people without getting caught. This is the Elimination Games. They test athletes almost every day and at random to catch cheaters."

"Not to worry." Dimitri took a long pull on his vodka. "I have plants in the Security organization in the headquarters and the supply organizations. I can get falsified test results substituted for any event or nation."

"We have to stay away from the Australian detective." I moistened my lips. "He's here from MI6, which means they'll try to investigate anything he finds. Our operation isn't going to be easy."

"Don't get excited." Another sip of vodka. "I've worked in the KGB for many years. I know the procedures to block any attempt to break our logistics lines and eliminate overzealous officials. That's why you need me as a partner."

My anger flared, but I kept my face calm. How did I not know his KGB background? My researchers failed to give me a thorough report on him. "The KGB is too ruthless. They often use a hammer to kill a fly."

"Which reminds me." Dimitri set his empty glass on the table and stared at it. "Of two things."

"Don't keep me waiting. I have other business to conduct tonight."

"This might impact your business a little." He toyed with the glass while he talked, avoiding eye contact. "To remove the possibility of using a hammer when a flyswatter would do, I want you to sideline the two boys working with the Australian. The Zanadu brothers. They're snooping around, watching me."

I recoiled as though he slapped me. He couldn't be serious. I specialized in drug development, advertising, placement, and payment collection, not hiring thugs as enforcers.

"They found some drugs today that we planned to transfer tonight." Dimitri glanced at me. "I could handle it, but you're much gentler than me."

Eyes narrowed, I glared at him. "That's not part of the deal. You're supposed to handle security, not me."

"In a normal situation, I would agree with you. However, my men found something in Interpol's files that disturbed me." The Russian's eyes glittered. "When I saw the papers, I noticed your name on them. Perhaps I should return them?" Dimitri extracted several sheets of folded documents from his jacket pocket. "Copies for you. Read at your leisure." He handed the pages to me.

Stunned, I opened them and struggled to control my facial expression. I hated this man. Someone in my organization betrayed me and gave this back-stabbing Russian files I'd retrieved from Interpol years ago. I swallowed. Tucked the papers in my purse. With a flick of my hand, I smoothed my blonde hair. "You are resourceful, Monsieur Vasiliev." My lips curved upward. "Handling these two boys will be child's play." My smile widened. "In fact, dealing with security will become a priority for me, to squelch any attempt to bring unwanted publicity."

Vasiliev slid forward, parted the curtains, beckoned the hostess, and asked her to retrieve our coats.

I made a mental note to ensure my team provided an immediate report on the Russian's complete background. Two could play at this game. No man dictated contract terms to me. Tomorrow would be a different day. And I'd ferret out the traitor in my organization and eliminate them.

Dimitri turned off the jammer, put it away, and stood. We both donned our cold-weather outfits and headed to the front door.

"What a wonderful evening." Dimitri opened the door. "Will I see you tomorrow?"

A wicked smile crept over my face. "With pleasure, Monsieur. Adieu."

Chapter 11 – The Plot Thickens

Men's Downhill Venue, Val-D'Isère, France
Monday, 13 January 1992, 12:05 p.m.

A large crowd grew at the slopes of Val-D'Isère for the third day of the IEGs. Monday's temperatures hovered in the high thirties but would drop later in the day. White clouds speckled the blue sky. A perfect day for skiing. The Men's Alpine Combined Downhill started in minutes. With most people at the event, few pedestrians walked the town's streets. We hurried along the sidewalk to make it on time for the first ski run in ten minutes.

Alex pointed. "There he is."

Across the road and to our right, about four or five stores from us, the Russian spoke with two men, one taller than me. At least six feet in height. The other man, shorter by a few inches, slouched. The tall guy wore a red snow jacket. The smaller man's electric blue coat made him look like a plump blueberry.

"You need to take pictures. Quick." I motioned to an outdoor café. "We can hide around the corner."

We hustled over with Thunder and Lightning trotting beside us. We ducked around the side of the business, then reversed. I made the dogs sit.

"Where's Franco?" I peered over Alex's shoulder. "He's late."

My brother crouched, fiddling with his camera.

I replayed yesterday's conversation in my mind. "He said we would see him at noon, fifteen minutes before the race starts."

"Ready." Alex ignored me, slid around the corner, and knelt, resting his arm on his knee. He snapped two shots. "We're too far away, but I bet the tall man standing next to the Russian is the guy we saw on the first day under the stands."

I leaned out. "Let's move two buildings to the right."

Alex stood, camera in one hand. I tapped the dogs' noses and told them to be quiet. We adjusted our backpacks and sprinted around the rear of the building, taking the alley behind the store. Alex got in position with direct sight lines facing the Russian across the street. Thunder thrust his head out to see the road. I stood to my brother's right with Lightning in between my feet.

"Come on," Alex whispered. "Move it." He lowered the camera. An older couple paused in front of the Russian to admire the view, which blocked a clear photo. The man gazed in every direction like a lost tourist. He shook his head before striding forward.

The Russian, upset, raised his voice and jabbed the air. He slapped the blueberry man.

"I wish I owned a video camera." My brother got on one knee and raised his arms to take a picture.

Thunder's hundred-pound frame exploded from the alley, banging Alex's shoulder as he raced into the street with Lightning hot on his heels.

"Nuts." Alex's camera whirred and a picture popped out. "They ruined my shot."

The dogs raced to our left toward a figure clad in a green snowsuit walking in our direction. The person bent down and rubbed their heads when they jumped to greet him.

"Franco." I waved. "This way."

When Franco reached the sidewalk, the Russian shouted. His men flew at the dogs and Franco while he made a beeline for us.

"Run." I grabbed my pack, turned, and shot back to the alley. I made a few snow and ice balls while waiting for Alex, Franco, and the dogs to reach me.

"What are you doing?" Alex, backpack on one shoulder and camera in the opposite hand, whipped past me. When Franco and the dogs arrived, I whistled. The dogs skidded in the snow and flew to my side.

The blueberry man, trailed by the man in red, neared our alley.

"Attack." I threw the first snowball and hit the tall guy in the mouth.

The dogs galloped to the men. Lightning pounced on the blueberry guy while Thunder bowled over the man in red.

"Retreat." Alex called the dogs back. "Head for the Downhill crowd." He charged out of the alley behind me with Franco following.

The dogs returned, slid past the side of the building, gained traction, and raced toward Alex and Franco. Our pursuers rolled to their feet and kept coming. I nailed the man in red right between the eyes but missed the Russian. Out of ammo, I dashed through the alley at full speed. Using back streets, I joined the rest of our group about a block from the Downhill finish line stands. The men chasing us kept coming, drawing closer each second.

"Follow me." Franco plunged into the crowd that surrounded the stands. He worked his way under the seats to the concourse where we would be out of sight. He darted into the men's restroom. We followed.

A few people occupied some of the stalls. The cleaning man gazed at us when we rushed in.

"Hide." I headed for the last stall on the right with Lightning while Franco, Alex, and Thunder chose random stalls on either side. I closed and locked my door and sat on the toilet seat with Lightning in my lap. I whispered in his ear. "Shh. Don't make any sounds."

A blast of cold air let me know a door opened. A gruff voice asked something in a guttural language. The Russian?

"You speak English?" A thin response came back. "I clean toilets."

"Did you see three boys come in?" The Russian's voice was deep. Commanding. "With two dogs?"

"Monsieur, I don't understand."

"Their parents asked us to find them." The man cursed at the custodian. "We saw them come this way. Where are they?"

I couldn't see if he pointed to our stalls or out the door. Two new voices talked to the deep one in Russian.

Lightning licked my jaw, twisting to reach me. I grinned, imagining Thunder's massive frame shifting in my brother's lap. I didn't have it that bad. But I couldn't see a thing. I stood, braced one arm against a wall while the other held Lightning. Taking my time, I placed one foot on the toilet seat, followed by the other. The heavy plastic creaked under my weight. I raised my head to spy on the action, straining on my tiptoes.

The conversation between the men lasted about a minute. Then the Russian ended it with a nod. "Da." His deep yes filled the men's room. He gestured at the line of stalls, still staring at the cleaning man to pin him in place.

My heart sank. I dropped to a crouch.

Our pursuers would search each space. They trapped us.

"Iz everything alright?" A new voice entered the conversation. French accent.

I balanced with one hand on the wall, arm at full extension, and rose to survey the new situation. An IEG security man faced the Russian.

"Nothing's wrong, Officer Marchand." The Russian waved him away. "We are getting warm. It's freezing outside today."

The officer glanced at the cleaning man, who gave a slight shake of his head. Marchand's posture stiffened, his jaw tight. "Zis is not ze place to get warm. Find a café." His voice sharpened. "No loitering in ze Men's room. Please proceed now." He jabbed a finger at the exit.

I sank back into a crouch.

The Russian protested. "We've been here three minutes. Must we move on? I will have your superior put you on report, Marchand."

"Please." The officer's voice stayed firm.

Three sets of feet passed my stall. The exit door opened and shut.

In silence, I relaxed. Released a breath of air and stroked Lightning's head. I slid one foot to the floor and lost my balance, banging into the wall with a crash. Lightning slipped from my grasp. My knees hit the floor. I clambered to my feet, opened the door, and checked the area. The cleaning man casually wiped off a sink while the IEG security officer leaned against the first stall.

"Hiding?" The officer folded his arms. "I'd be interested in your story. The men chasing you have left."

"Thanks, officer." I scooped Lightning from the floor. He'd been wagging his tail at Marchand. I gazed around the room. "The coast is clear."

Franco and Alex came out of their stalls, Thunder heeling beside my brother.

Alex and I explained the situation, including Willie's request to watch for the Russian.

"Monsieur Gretzke told select staff members patrolling certain events that we may see you today." Marchand tipped his head at the janitor. "We have some connections like Girard who keep their eyes open for us. You are safe for now. Did you like my heavy French accent?" The man now spoke spotless English with no accent at all.

"Nice." I smiled.

Minutes later, the officer escorted us to Mom and Dad's seats. The Russian and his buddies were gone.

"You've missed the first four downhillers." Mom waved a French fry at us. "I see you connected with Franco per our schedule." She ate her fry. "Why did the officer come with you?"

Alex shoved himself in front of me. "To make sure we didn't encounter that Russian again. We met the security man at the Men's room."

Dad nodded. "Good. You boys better stay out of trouble."

Chapter 12 – An Upgrade

Men's Freestyle Venue, Tignes, France
Monday, 13 January 1992, 1:35 p.m.

After eighteen minutes on a bus, Alex and I arrived early for the Men's Freestyle in the village of Tignes. We threaded through the standing crowd section at the bottom of the hill to meet Bastien. He didn't show even though we waited at our designated spot for ten minutes beyond our agreed-upon time.

"Didn't we make it clear where we would meet him?" I searched in my backpack for a snack. Lightning stuck his nose inside the pack, sniffing for food. "They start in fifteen minutes."

Alex watched highlights of freestyle skiing on the jumbotron. "He'll make it. I bet he's schmoozing with his rich buddies. We're just the poor kids looking for help, remember?"

"I keep picturing what you and Thunder looked like in the bathroom stall." I laughed. "Must have been pretty tight."

Alex shifted to his right. "Be glad the officer sent the Russian and his henchmen out before you slipped and banged into your wall. We'd be black and blue by now if they heard you first."

I found some chocolate and bit off a chunk. "You're jealous because you didn't think of standing—"

"Bastien," Alex waved his hand over his head, "this way."

Our friend arrived out of breath. "I'm glad to find you. I've been searching for you for fifteen minutes."

"We agreed to meet near the south side of the bleachers." I swallowed more chocolate.

Bastien paused. Shook his head. "I am sure we said the north side."

"Doesn't matter," Alex said. "We're together. And we've tangled with the Russian and his men again."

Bastien nodded. "If we sit on the north side of the stands, we have a better view of the skiers. Great for helicopter flips and lots of rail action."

After we'd made our way to the north side and watched a few competitors, Bastien tapped me on the shoulder. "Want to see the facilities where the skiers launch for the freestyle event? Maybe we can find more evidence."

I nodded.

"Not me." Alex pulled his camera out of his bag. "I'm finding Willie and showing him these pictures. We're on a tight schedule. We might need to skip the hill recon."

I shrugged. "We can tag along to the security office."

Willie wasn't at the security station when we arrived. The dispatcher called him on his radio. We waited in his office. He strode in two minutes later and slapped us on the back. "Hey, mates. Would you like a bikkie?" He pulled out a round tin of cookies, opened it, and passed it around.

I took several, Alex one, and Bastien didn't take any. The dogs licked their lips.

"Nothing for the dogs today." Willie put the tin back on his desk and sat in a wooden chair. "Sit, gents. What brings you by?"

We each found a seat facing the desk. I glanced at Alex. He gave me the nod.

I gave an action-packed rendition of me snowballing the Russian's henchmen, our escape into the men's bathroom, the fear of being caught, and Officer Marchand's rescue of us.

Alex sighed. "He forgot the most important part." He lifted his camera out of his backpack and set three photos on the desk.

Willie inspected the pictures. "Pretty far away on the first two." He dropped them on his desk. "Were you trying a unique angle technique on the third shot? It's blurry and shows the top of the Russian's head along with a lot of blue sky."

My brother dragged Thunder to his chair. "Here's the culprit. He hit my shoulder when I took the picture."

Willie sat back in his chair. "I'm sure we can enhance these photos and get a good idea of some of the Russian's gang. I wish you carried a better camera."

"I bought it with my own money." Alex sat straighter. "The Polaroid SX-70 instant developing camera is a one of a kind."

"It's ten years old." I bit off a piece of cookie and chewed. "An antique."

Bastien shifted forward in his chair. "May I?" He hefted the camera, examined the device's body, and handed it back to Alex. He lifted a picture off the desk, examined it, and deposited it back on the desk. "I'll bring you a better camera you can keep. Last year's model, but I don't need it anymore. Bought a new one before the Elims."

Willie propped a foot on a chair rung. "Perfect. Okay with you?" He glanced at my brother.

"Are you sure?" Alex's eyes widened. "I don't have the money to pay for it."

Bastien grinned. "Consider it a gift. Anything to help with the investigation. The Kodak DSC 100 has a hard drive that can store 160 pictures."

Willie shifted his position. "That's a cracker. Don't want to miss out on that present." He nabbed a pen and jotted a note. "We need to discuss something more important than equipment. Do you recognize that the Russian man is upset with you two and your pets?"

Alex and I nodded.

"I can't spare the manpower to assign someone to follow you around this place, but I'll send out a more detailed alert to the security force to watch out for you and the Russian like Officer Marchand did today." He tapped his pen against his lips. "Maybe that will give me insight into another problem."

"What's that?" I leaned forward. "Something we can help you with?"

Willie's eyes flicked to Bastien, then back to me. "Not yet. The information's a bit dodgy. When it's more developed, I'll let you know." He stood. "Time to be on your way. As always, I've enjoyed our talk."

We exited the building and stopped outside to discuss the schedule. I checked my watch—2:25 p.m.

"Four o'clock is the Women's 600 Meter Speed Skating event." I lifted Lightning into my arms. "We have to get moving."

"Sofia and Izabella will meet us." Alex glanced at Bastien. "You coming?"

"I'm meeting a few other folks." He pointed at a woman who stumbled near us and fell into a snowbank. "First, let's help that lady out."

Trotting over to her, I saw she'd stepped off the cleared sidewalk into a hole.

"Are you all right?" I reached out with a hand to help her to her feet.

Alex stood beside me and took her other hand. The dogs squeezed between us to get close to the action. Bastien stood out of the way.

The lady wore a tailored white snowsuit that showed a slim figure. Her pretty face, blonde hair, and dazzling blue eyes seemed innocuous enough, but when she gazed into my eyes, my heart raced a little.

She smiled, but a slight grimace of pain crossed her face when she stood. "My right knee."

I moved closer to support her and held her right lower arm.

"Wait." She pulled me closer and put her right arm around my neck and over my shoulder. She let out a breath of air like she'd been holding it in. "Better." Her perfume filled the air between us, sweet and fresh.

I sniffed extra hard to take it in.

"Thunder and Lightning, get back." Alex helped steady the woman in a standing position.

"I need to sit." She hobbled as we walked her to the nearest café, went inside, and helped her sit at an empty table with four chairs close to the door. Her hand seemed to linger on my neck as she let go. Her blue eyes sparkled.

Bastien tried to keep the dogs back, but they proved too elusive, sniffing the lady's snowsuit and circling my brother and me.

"Is there anything we can do?" I sat next to her and lifted Lightning to my lap. "I mean…can we get you something to drink or call someone for you?"

Alex stared at me.

The lady laughed. "Oh, no." She glanced around the table. "I need a moment to collect myself and rest. I'll be fine." She rubbed her right knee. Her gaze lanced into my eyes. "Old skiing accident."

An electric tingle ran through my body.

Bastien checked his watch. "If you two are meeting Sofia and Izabella, you should go to the bus now. I can stay here with Miss…?" He raised an eyebrow at the woman.

"You can call me Genevieve." She gave us a half-smile. "No need to be formal with my heroes."

Alex tilted his head at the door. "Come on, hero. We've got some friends to meet." He pushed Thunder ahead of him. "We're late."

I struggled out of my seat, scraping the chair against the table, almost losing my balance. "Nice…very nice to meet you. Let's go, Lightning," I said and hurried out of the restaurant.

Chapter 13 – Party Time

Alex and I rushed to the bus stop, where a crowd jammed together to get on the coach to Albertville. Joining the tight knot of people, we managed to get aboard but became separated when we let some ladies sit.

I grabbed a safety bar overhead with one hand and rubbed my forehead with another. What was wrong with me? Genevieve made my head spin. I never let girls or women do that to me. I shook my head to clear my mind.

We arrived at our destination later than planned and hustled toward our hotel to drop off the dogs, using the path that skirted the speed skating event.

"Crazy encounter, wasn't it?" Alex glanced at me sideways. "I haven't seen you act like that since your crush on the Miller girl in third grade."

"How would you know?" I increased our pace. "You're always running away from girls because they get too serious with you."

"Isn't that what you're doing now?" He laughed and slowed a little. "She's at least twenty-something, and you'll be fifteen this summer." A grin plastered his face.

Lightning darted left. Thunder followed, making Alex stutter-step to keep his balance.

A snowball hit my shoulder. I swiveled to find my attacker.

"Can't you guys hear anything?" Izabella stood about ten feet away, hands on hips.

Sofia packed another snowball. "I'm trained in many sports." She cocked her arm like a pitcher and slammed her ammo right in Alex's chest.

He sucked in a breath. "That packed a punch." He rubbed the impact point.

"We've been calling your names. The race started five minutes ago." Izabella grabbed my arm. "Let's go."

I tugged my arm away. "We have to take the dogs to the hotel first. Can you hold our seats?"

Izabella nodded and pushed me away. "Don't be too late."

Alex and I hurried back to the hotel in a record five minutes, racing to a small park to let our dogs take care of business on our route there. We filled their food and water bowls in our hotel room and hustled back to the ice-skating venue.

I glanced at my watch—4:25 p.m. At the Women's 600 Meter Speed Skating race entrance, the tension mounted. "The crowd's cheering. Hope we haven't missed much."

Alex nodded. "There's still plenty of skating left."

I spotted the girls in the stands. We joined them and sat with the other American fans while fans of other countries cheered their competitors.

"The USA has a good chance at the Gold medal." Izabella gave us the details on the standings and the American skater. "Her name is Brenda Blossom."

"But the Germans and Chinese might have something to say about that." Sofia smiled. "The Chinese skater, Bai Ching, is quick, and the Germans, Ursula Ludendorff and Ingrid Fischer, are power-ful."

Chips of ice sprayed from the skates as the women, flying at incredible speeds around the track, jockeyed in a jammed cluster of competitors for the lead.

Alex tilted his head. "Isn't there more than one American competing?

Sofia patted his leg. "Yes. Tracy Tombaugh, Patrice Pepperdine, and Betsy Bastogne. But none of them is the American favorite to win."

The racers' hands brushed the frozen track inside the boundary line at the turns to keep from falling. As each heat passed, the flag-waving and cheering increased.

The skaters for the final medal event, including Blossom, crouched at the starting line. The crowd around us grew quiet. The gun sounded and everyone around us jumped to their feet. Ludendorff, Fischer, Bai, and Blossom battled for the finish line. We shouted. Yelled. My pulse pounded. The USA racer, Brenda Blossom, won by two-hundredths of a second, beating the German skater, Ursula Ludendorff.

Blossom did her victory lap, hands held above her head. The cheering continued for several minutes.

"Are you guys going to any parties tonight?" Sofia shouted above the noise.

Alex shook his head. "We didn't have anything planned. But if there's someplace to go, that would be great."

"Mom's tracking us like a hawk." I tapped my brother on the shoulder.

Alex shrugged me off. "I've got this." He gazed at Sofia. "What do you have in mind."

She glanced at Izabella and back at us. "If your Mom's curious, tell her you've received an invite to a teen event. Our section at the restaurant, Station de l'Europe, opens at seven tonight, but the party doesn't start until eight o'clock in the back room."

"But we don't have an invite," he said.

Sofia rolled her eyes. "I'm inviting you."

Alex hesitated.

I jumped in. "Got it. I'll work my magic on Mom. I'm her favorite son anyway."

Station de l'Europe crammed tables in every nook and cranny. The cheerful atmosphere and cozy lighting welcomed us in. The warm air carried the smells of roasted coffee, crepes, steak, and other sizzling entrees. Booths lined one wall on the street where people could watch traffic and pedestrians, and square tables filled the remaining floor space. A bar occupied some of the back area and European artwork decorated most of the wall.

Alex forged through the occupied tables, brushing past coats and typical winter clothing. I followed behind, sliding sideways to avoid knocking the cold weather gear to the floor.

The back room was a smaller version of the front. Sofia and Izabella waved us over with big smiles. Almost thirty people crammed their chairs around ten square tables shoved together. Other booths and tables overflowed, leaving many partygoers standing next to their seated friends to remain a part of the group.

"I'm happy you came before our arranged time." Izabella wiggled a chair next to her from the table and patted it. "Gabe, sit here by me. Alex can take a seat next to Sofia."

We tugged our coats off, tossed them on the backs of the chairs, and sat.

Sofia glanced at Alex. "Did you sweet talk your mother into the party or did your brother beat you to it?"

I sighed. "We tag-teamed both our parents at dinner."

Alex snorted. "That's not the way I remember it. I'm the one who mentioned the subject—"

"And I looked miserable and heartbroken when Mom thought we shouldn't come."

Izabella laughed. "You two haven't changed much over the years."

She passed a basket of bread. "Have some of this to get you started. And try this punch made with fruit and sweet soda water."

After several minutes, I noticed Alex and Sofia sitting closer together than when we first sat. I spoke facing Izabella, but loud enough for my brother to hear. "Before Alex and Sofia get lost in each other, can we meet some of the athletes and support people?"

Alex narrowed his eyes at me.

I twisted around. "What?" I shrugged. "We don't want to waste our time. Does Sofia know any of the competitors?

She arched an eyebrow, focusing on Alex. "Is your brother..." She smirked at me. "...always such a pest?"

He rubbed his chin and stared at the ceiling. "Most of the time."

"I happen to be more open and honest than others." I tapped my chest. "Honest Abe, they call me."

Sofia giggled and Izabella shook her head.

Turning in his chair to take in the partiers, Alex scanned the room. "Who do you know that might have some inside information on drug problems?"

The girls shifted in their chairs and glanced at each other.

"How much do you get out to parties?" Sofia's eyes twinkled, focusing on my brother.

Alex swiveled back to face her. "Well—"

"This is his first time." I grinned. "Unless you count Youth Group parties and gatherings at Pizza parlors. Isn't that right, bro?"

He swallowed. His face turned a little pink. "You're very helpful tonight, Gabe."

"What are brothers for?" I gave him a thumbs up.

Sofia scooted closer to Alex and put her hand on his shoulder. "Don't let his needling bother you." She stage-whispered. Maybe louder. "He's jealous."

Izabella snickered and focused on me. "She's got that right."

My eyes widened in innocence. "Who me?" I'm more interested in our investigation." I tapped my watch. "Almost eight-fifteen. When do we start asking questions?"

Sofia patted Alex's shoulder and faced me. "These matters are delicate. Didn't you tell me you've investigated many mysteries?"

"Yes, but—"

"Then listen to me." Her eyes bored into mine until I sat back. "You must build trust first to get the information you want from others. And it may not come to you but through me. To get others to share, I expect they'll have to meet you a few times before they feel relaxed chatting with you." She raised her chin. "Now, let me introduce you to my friends." Her hand slid around Alex's arm when they stood. She leaned in closer to Izabella and me, eyes twinkling. "And act like a couple, if you know what I mean."

Chapter 14 – Pub Advice

Le Stallion, Val-D'Isère, France
Monday, 13 January 1992, 8:30 p.m.

Le Stallion's clientele favored boisterous camaraderie at their famed bar while providing smaller rooms for private meetings and dinners. One of Val-D'Isère's favorite restaurants, Genevieve trusted the location for many clandestine meetings. She led Dimitri, climbing a flight of stairs to the second floor, continued down a hallway, and opened the third door of the right into a private room. The room's décor reflected a ski village motif. The floor of exquisitely polished timbers glowed, reflecting candlelight and the ceiling's dimmed fixtures.

"Should I use my audio jammer?" Vasiliev seated himself and reached toward his pocket.

She placed her jacket on an extra chair beside her. Surveying the empty room, she shrugged. "Perhaps it would be wise to ensure the surge of drunken brawls in this room don't provide an opportunity for someone to listen."

"You're planning to fight with me tonight?" Dimitri chuckled.

"Not unless you start it."

"How do we get a waitress here." He snapped his fingers. "I'd like a bit to eat and some vodka."

A tap sounded on the half-opened door.

"Come in." Genevieve slid into her seat while the waitress bustled in.

Both ordered a light evening meal. Dimitri requested his vodka at once, while Genevieve ordered water with lemon. The waitress curtsied and walked out the door, leaving it open.

"Non-drinker?" he said.

"During business meetings and workdays, which in this case means the IEGs." She drew her chair closer to the table. "I do enjoy a glass of wine, but that is rare. In our business, being alert is critical to success."

"An excellent business decision."

The waitress brought their drinks into the room.

"Bring me an extra vodka." Dimitri placed a napkin in his lap. "We don't want to be disturbed after our food arrives."

The waitress glanced at Genevieve.

"Bring me a pitcher of water to refill our water glasses."

She nodded and departed. Minutes later, the waitress brought in their food and the extra drinks. "Will that be all, Mademoiselle?"

"Merci."

The waitress curtsied and glided out the door, shutting it without a sound.

Dimitri and Genevieve ate without speaking for a few minutes, listening to the rumble of the noise from the first-floor patrons and light violin music piped into the room.

"Tell me you have made progress in our infiltration with IEG Security." Genevieve finished her salad and dabbed at her mouth with the napkin.

Dimitri, who chewed on a roasted potato, waited until he swallowed and sipped some water. "Our source tells me that the Australian alerted the entire force to my presence here. He even made a copy of a photo they have of me." He withdrew a paper from his shirt pocket and handed it to her.

"A blurry photo." She set the paper beside her dinner rolls. "I can recognize you, but they won't. What a terrible camera. Such shoddy work."

"The Zanadu boy's camera. An old Polaroid instamatic." He waved his hand in dismissal. "If that's the best the Australian can do through these boys, they're a mere nuisance and not a threat."

She selected a dinner roll, then split and buttered it. "I've made first contact with them." She smiled. "I'm sure the younger boy will be like putty in my hands."

"What did you do?" The Russian grinned" "Kiss him?"

Her eyes widened in shock. "A woman never reveals her secrets for influencing men, or in this instance, a growing young man." She bit into the roll and set the remaining piece on her side plate. "They're under my surveillance." She lifted her purse off the chair beside her and retrieved some papers. "I want to show you something. The plan prepared for drug distribution."

His wary gaze surprised her. "Plan?"

She stared back. "Yes. The plan. Like we discussed."

He placed his fork on the table and lifted his vodka glass to make a toast. He nodded at Genevieve to use her water glass. "Nostrovia."

"À votre santé." She clinked her glass against his to toast, drank a bit, and set it next to her plate. "Now that we have toasted each other for good health in our native languages, let me tell you about the distribution plan I've developed."

Instead of leaning closer to see her plan, he settled back into his chair.

"You're not interested?" She smoothed out the papers.

"Have you considered the targets we have in each country's team?" His eyes fixed on hers. "Do you understand the protocol for falsifying data?" His voice rose a little. "Does your distribution scheme include unseen delivery at specific times to my workers, some who sacrificed a great deal to infiltrate the depths of the competing teams?"

She glared at him.

"Nyet." He slammed his empty vodka shot glass on the table. "You have not."

Genevieve jumped when his glass hit the table. She vowed that wouldn't happen again. This wasn't the first time she'd dealt with men who bullied her. A fire started burning inside her. "Feel better?" She folded the papers and returned them to her purse.

"Drug deliveries take place when and where I need them."

"That might put my people at risk." She kept her voice controlled but firm. "My performance-enhancing drug business makes exceptional profits for me. I'm not risking it to save you money or resources."

His jaw tensed for a second, then relaxed. "I need more than performance-enhancing drugs. I need substitutes that will make athletes sick."

Genevieve stiffened. "You're planning full-scale drug warfare at an Elim competition? If the IEGC and police catch us, they will lock us away for decades."

"Who's going to catch us?" The Russian sipped his second vodka. "The Zanadu boys?"

Her stomach knotted. She wasn't going to let this over-grown gorilla ruin her operation. "The next thing you'll do is pull out machine guns and shoot a lot of innocent people. Find another distributor." She stood and grabbed her coat and purse.

"I wouldn't leave if I were you." Dimitri smirked. "It might not be healthy."

She bristled. "Are you going to have me gunned down?" She strode to the door.

"We have less obvious methods of eliminating loose ends."

She swung open the door.

A tall, broad man in a business suit stood outside and blocked her exit.

"You can return of your own accord or Stanislav can bring you back inside." The Russian's voice flowed in a soothing, pleasant tone. "I'd like to work with you." He grinned. "But more on my terms."

Genevieve's mind raced. Acid churned in her belly and she felt light-headed. But she clenched her jaw, eyes shooting daggers at Stanislav. Then, as though flicking a light switch, she swiveled with a broad smile on her face. "I must say, you are a charmer, aren't you?"

Chapter 15 – Distraction

Alpine Combined Slalom Venue, Val-D'Isère, France
Tuesday, 14 January 1992, 1:00 p.m.

I shivered in my coat while watching Alex and our dogs and friends a few feet away. Forecasters predicted Tuesday's cold temperatures, offset with clear sky and sunshine, would change into light snow in the villages and heavier snowfall in the higher mountain altitudes where the skiing would occur in the evening. I'd been outside for several hours, first watching the ski jumps at the K-90 hill at Courchevel in the morning, followed by a bus ride to our next event. Now, we waited. We arrived an hour before the Men's Alpine Combined Slalom second run at Val-D'Isère that started at two-ten in the afternoon. The crisp air made my nostrils tingle.

Thunder barked while chasing Lightning around another snowbank.

"Playful, aren't they?" Franco made a snowball and threw it at Thunder. The Great Dane mixed breed pounced on Lightning and ignored the splatter of snow on his side.

Alex and Bastien hustled over to me. "I think we've spotted one of our friends again." Bastien jammed binoculars into my hands.

"Sofia or Izabella?" I whistled for Lightning to return. He scampered back.

"Genevieve." Bastien smiled, placed a hand on my shoulder, swiveled me in the proper direction, and pointed. "Quick. Over there."

In an instant, I focused the binoculars, riveted in place. "Cool."

Alex held his hands out in a slow-down motion. "Whoa, cowboy. Act like you're scanning the whole area."

Franco trotted over. "Is the Russian with her? I don't want that gorilla chasing us into a bathroom again. He makes me nervous."

"Don't worry. We saw those two together just once." I swiveled the binocs, searching for him, and groaned. "Rats. He's here but on the other side of the slalom finish line. Genevieve's alone."

"She's got you hooked pretty well." Alex called for Thunder to come over. "They might not be together, but they're both here at the same time. A coincidence?"

Bastien snorted. "In my father's business, he doesn't believe in coincidences."

"I have a problem with them too." I plucked Lightning off the ground when he began to wander away. "Wait, that gives us an opportunity."

Alex groaned. "Don't tell me. You have an idea."

Franco chuckled. "You don't like his ideas?"

"Don't judge me yet." I swept my hands over the skiing event. "Willie hasn't given us any assignment except to keep track of the Russian, right?"

Everyone nodded.

I tapped my temple. "Why don't we go a little deeper?" I held up my hand to stop the reactions. "We haven't found any more drugs at the support sites. Let's go into a locker room for one of the countries to check for drugs."

Alex shook his head. "Aren't we here to watch the skiing?"

Franco and Bastien waited for more.

"Undercover detective work is tons more exciting than watching other people race downhill on skis." I knelt in the snow and drew a diagram. "Here's how it would work. I take Lightning past the Russian. I distract him. Maybe he'll follow me. When he leaves, Alex, Thunder, Franco, and Bastien find one of the country's support team rooms in Val-D'Isère."

Franco looked at the diagram. "The supporting staff rooms are here. Right, Bastien?" He poked his finger into the snow.

Bastien shifted his attention to the diagram. "Yes, that's the athlete's prep building."

"Then I draw the Russian away in the other direction." I lifted my eyes to the group.

Alex folded his arms. "And how do we gain access to the support team rooms? We look like visitors, not like competitors."

"We need a disguise." Franco pointed at Thunder and Lightning marking their territory at a tree. "One of us could act like it's an emergency to use the team's bathrooms. That part of town doesn't have public restrooms."

"That's not a disguise." Alex motioned at the finishing area for the slalom. "Let's follow Willie's instructions and keep an eye on our special friend."

I hovered over my drawing and slapped my leg. "That's it."

Franco squinted at my work. "What's it?"

I drew a circle around the support team area. "Does Girard ring a bell?"

"The cleaning guy?" Franco said.

"Yeah." I stood and faced Bastien. "Girard cleaned the Men's restroom and saved us yesterday. He wore regular clothes with a special IEG vest and a stocking cap bearing the same logo. Can you get one for Franco and Alex?"

"Why me?" Alex packed a snowball together and threw it at a tree. Bullseye. "It's your plan. You don't intend to pay Genevieve a visit, do you?"

A warmth spread across my cheeks. "You're the better choice because Thunder's taller and bigger in case you get in trouble." I narrowed my eyes.

"Excusez-moi, s'il vous plaît." Franco chuckled. "Let's focus on the plan. Alex and Thunder will be great. But we need some buckets and cleaning supplies." Franco's eyes gleamed with excitement.

Bastien thought about it. "I can use a snowmobile and be back in about twenty minutes."

"I knew you guys would do it." I grinned. "Let's talk about the rendezvous afterward...."

Armed with cleaning buckets stuffed with their disguises, Franco and Alex moved down the slope to the left of the finishing area for the slalom. In our meeting, we established thirty minutes for the total operation, planning on reuniting at 2:30 p.m. at a café on the north side of the village. The competition, halfway done, still planned a second run which meant neither athletes nor ticket holders would leave the finish area.

I headed to the right, straight in Genevieve's direction with Lightning in my arms. He could be flighty at times and the plan called for us to thread our way through a thick soup of people. Genevieve moved since I spotted her earlier. I managed to get close enough to be recognized, but a disturbance in the crowd to my right caught my attention.

The Russian shouldered through the people in my direction.

I angled away from him. Darted away faster than he could move between the groups of families and friends. As I neared the edge of the finish area, the knots of people thinned out. I bent and tossed Lightning onto the ground.

"Jog." We trotted for a minute together to a parking lot. When the Russian's head came into view, I burst into a sprint. "Race time."

I shot off with Lightning forging ahead to take the lead. I dodged moving cars, doors opening, tourists chatting, and a pair of slalom skis on the shoulders of a competitor. We threaded our way to a sidewalk and sprinted to the snow-covered main road. Minutes later, at the northern edge of the village, I spotted a few snowmobile paths leading to several ski resort lodges on a hill in front of us. I slowed, let a few snowmobiles pass me, and checked behind me. No Russian. I glanced at my watch—2:05 p.m. Twenty-five minutes to kill before our team meeting at the rendezvous site. Time enough to hide and get something hot to drink at a resort.

I lifted Lightning into my arms and cradled him while heading to a hotel. "Safe and sound, little buddy. We outfoxed that old Russian. He can't touch us now."

Chapter 16 – The Locker Room

Support Team Offices, Val-D'Isère, France
Tuesday, 14 January 1992, 2:00 p.m.

Alex, this way." Franco motioned for me to follow him near a supporting staff building at the ski hill base. Bastien's job entailed staying well behind us but on the lookout for the Russian or other people that might be trouble.

I peered over Franco's shoulder and saw the symbol for the Cooperative Team and several other teams on the entrance. "Perfect. Let's get our disguises in place."

We moved into an alley on one side of the building's entryway. The IEG vest slipped over my head and coat with ease like a reflective running vest. When I stuffed my knit cap into a pocket and jammed an IEG stocking cap on my head, I felt a lot safer. Franco finished donning his disguise a moment after me.

"One problem." Bastien surprised me, moving into the alley beside us. "Come here."

We trooped over to him. "What's wrong."

Bastien stroked Thunder. "I don't know any cleanup guys that bring along a black Great Dane. How will you explain that?"

I shrugged. "I'll think of something. We need him to sniff out the drugs. Maybe he'll be my seeing-eye dog."

"For blind people?" Franco chuckled. "You're out of your mind."

"You got something against handicapped people?" I rubbed my jaw to hide my grin. "In the U.S. we do a lot to help employ people that have handicaps. I'll put my sunglasses on, just in case."

I clicked Thunder's leash on his collar.

Franco, Thunder, and I ducked inside the entrance door. We found a long hallway. Moving quickly, we passed a vacant receptionist's office to the left, about ten closed doors, and followed the hallway, which made a ninety-degree turn to the left. The corridor opened into a large lounge room. A coffee bar, snack and beverage machines covered the far wall. Couches, chairs, and a ping-pong table filled the middle. To the right, a door with a male symbol indicated the men's dressing room, and the entrance on the left sported the female sign.

"I vote we go into the women's side." Franco tilted his head at the door with the skirted figure on it. "I'm a lady's man."

"Nice try, my Italian friend." I kept my volume low and pushed Thunder toward the men's locker room. "Let's hope Bastien's keeping a good eye on this place."

The men's locker room contained rows of back-to-back lockers with Team Logos on the side, benches in between the rows, and showers and toilets at the end. I headed to the back in case someone strolled in.

When we passed the third row of lockers identified with the Co-operative Team's logo, Thunder alerted.

I tugged on Franco to halt, snapped my fingers, and motioned for Thunder to search.

Nose close to the floor, he tracked the scent until he sat before locker 932. I jiggled the handle. Locked. Of course.

Two loud voices made me go still.

Franco ran into the row of lockers I occupied but across the central walkway. He pulled out a rag, polishing the bench and wiping off lockers. I did the same, whispering to my canine sidekick to be quiet and get under the bench seat. My pulse thundered in my ears.

The voices approached us, moving through the center aisle between the locker rows. Maybe they were headed to the toilets.

I knelt in front of a different locker, blocking the view of Thunder the best way I could. I focused on keeping my breathing steady. Regular.

Two men, both with dark hair, strode past without pausing.

I swallowed hard, stood, and headed for the center aisle to leave.

One of the men appeared in front of me. "Chto ty zdes' delayesh'?"

I cocked my head to one side, peering at him through my sunglasses. My pulse climbed, heart racing. What was I doing here? I didn't know enough Russian to respond. My mouth felt dry as cotton. I croaked out a one-syllable sound, trying to pronounce the words I heard. "Chew-toe—"

Franco brushed past the man in the aisle and yelled at me in Russian. He grabbed my arm and pushed me in the direction of the exit. Thunder heeled by my side. I fumbled for his collar and bumped into several lockers to keep up the disguise of being a semi-blind man, grazing against the exit's door frame when we left. Franco never quit yelling at me until we were back at the alley.

"Bastien." I slapped his shoulder. "You're on. Two guys. Dark hair. Delay them."

Franco, me, and Thunder sprinted down the tiny road, made a right at the next street, and took the next road to the left. Franco gasped for air. I got on my knees and gathered my dog in my arms. "Great work, buddy."

"Get out of these uniforms." Franco whipped off his hat and vest. He held his hand out for mine.

I yanked the clothing off and tossed the items to my friend.

Franco rolled them together, stuffed them in a skier's kit bag, tucked it in his coat, and straightened his hair. "How do I look?"

I gave him a half-smile. "Sort of okay. You'll need a sink and a mirror to get that hair to lay flat. Let's go find Bastien."

We left our cleaning buckets in the alley and walked back to the street. Bastien waited at the original street corner, where we changed into IEG outfits. Franco jogged to meet him and both strolled back to Thunder and me. We slid into the crowds at the finish line ten minutes later while the final competitors completed their combined slalom runs. We applauded with the rest of the spectators and left to meet Gabe.

"That blew our cover." I shook my head while we walked to our rendezvous location with Gabe—a café near the IEG bus stop on the north side of town. "That guy will recognize Thunder wherever we go."

"That won't be an issue." Bastien grinned. "I told the man you conducted an Interpol operation that required complete secrecy. If he reported it or reacted to seeing your dog at any time, I would have him arrested and locked in solitary confinement. I have his name and that of his friend as well." He extracted a notepad from his pocket to show us. "Not bad, eh?"

I slapped him on the back. "Awesome, as my brother would say." I checked the area around the café after we arrived. "By the way, wasn't he supposed to be here at two-thirty?"

Franco looked at his watch. "He's over five minutes late."

"He knows better than that." I patted my thigh. "Thunder, heel." I strode to the edge of Val-D'Isère to find the backup rendezvous site, followed by my friends. "Gabe thought this café might be compromised if he couldn't shake his pursuers. He said he'd go north to the hills."

"Knowing your brother, he's getting something hot to drink or a snack." Franco pointed at several resorts on the hill next to snow-mobile tracks.

"Perfect." I knelt next to Thunder. Ruffled his fur. Tapped his nose. "Track Gabe."

He sniffed the ground around us and sprinted up the hill.

Chapter 17 – Buried Alive

North Side, Val-D'Isère, France
Tuesday, 14 January 1992, 2:38 p.m.

Bastien, Franco, and I chased Thunder to the incline's summit. Snow flurries sprinkled our jackets, becoming a steady snowfall that collected on the streets and sidewalks. Some lamp posts already glowed in the dim light, although sunset wouldn't come for hours.

"Alex, go slower." Bastien huffed and puffed from the fast pace I set, steam rising from his breath.

I glanced at Franco, who stayed beside him, urging him to keep moving.

Bastien's forehead glistened from his sweat. "Are you sure Thunder knows what he's doing?" He wiped his face with a handkerchief.

"I'll meet you at the top." Focused on Thunder, I surged ahead.

We stood in front of the first of four lodges five minutes later.

"What's wrong?" Franco frowned. "Looks like your dog's confused."

"Could it be too much foot traffic here?" Bastien pointed at the hundreds of shoe and boot imprints in the area.

Thunder began casting in several directions. Soon he halted. His head swiveled, eyes locked on me. His throat rumbled.

"What's wrong?" I knelt by Thunder.

He snorted and shook his head. Growled.

"He doesn't like something." Bastien walked to the door of the Ski Lodge. "I can check inside."

I rubbed Thunder's neck. "Is Gabe in trouble?"

Another growl.

"Go get him. Full speed." I stood.

Thunder leapt forward, racing down a street. I dashed after him, Franco in tow. I didn't check on Bastien. Charging after Thunder took my full attention.

My buddy darted left into an alley. I rounded the corner seconds after he made the turn but didn't see him.

A bark sounded off to the right.

Franco and I rocketed forward. Three turns later, we arrived in a cul-de-sac containing several half-pipe drainage ditches. Thunder sniffed around a large mound of snow about four feet tall and twenty feet wide near one apartment building. No sign of Gabe.

"Dead end." Franco inspected the area. "Looks like a snowplow pushed most of the snow here into one huge pile. The place is empty. Why would Thunder bring us here?"

Bastien stumbled into the clearing and leaned against the wall, breathing hard. "You guys don't waste any time, do you?"

I focused on Thunder. "My dog works fast. He's an excellent tracker. I'm sure Gabe's been here."

"Maybe he smelled food." Bastien gulped for more air. "He's digging like he's found the motherload of doggie bones."

I flew to Thunder's side. "What is it?" I shoveled snow away from the little hill. The falling snow blurred the lines of my work.

"What if Gabe came here to hide but later went to the hotel for something to drink?" Franco watched me and my dog carve out a small cave in the snow pile. "Then we'd be—"

"Sh-h-h." I put a finger to my mouth. "I hear something."

I grabbed Thunder's chest and pulled him back from the hole. "Wait." I dropped to my chest, wiggled into the hole, and listened.

"I bet ..." Bastien's voice drowned out any other sounds.

Waving my arm, I silenced him and concentrated. The muffled sound came again.

"Franco." I tugged him closer to the opening. "What do you hear?"

My Italian friend got on both knees and stuck his head into the hole. When he lifted his head, he nodded. "That's a weird noise. Could be water, but it might be someone trapped. I heard a high-pitched sound too. Comes and goes."

"They're buried alive." I went back to work, joined by Thunder, throwing snow behind us at a frantic pace while we dug. "Franco." I paused for a moment, facing him. "Push that snow away to make room for more."

"What do you want me to do?" Bastien strode forward.

"Get us a snowmobile with a blade, some rope, flashlights, and some guys to help us out." I turned to the hole and glanced back. "Shovels would be nice."

Bastien lumbered out of the alley. Franco swept the snow back from the hole Thunder and I continued to make.

"Hurry." My brother's faint words filtered through the snow.

"We're coming, Gabe. Don't worry." I threw off my coat and dug faster.

In a short time, I struggled to keep going. My arms ached. We'd gotten less than a couple of feet deep.

A roar bounced off the walls when four snowmobiles appeared. Bastien, a passenger behind him, led a group of young guys. They parked on three sides of the hole, lighting the scene through the thick, falling snow. No snow blade. But when the guys dismounted, each held a shovel in his hands.

"His voice is getting weak." I climbed out of the hole and gathered the men together. "Understand English?"

They all nodded.

"Dig deeper to find my brother and his dog. Make the hole

wide enough to work from the sides. And keep the snow on the side packed firm. I don't want the snow to trap anyone else."

"This is terrible." A woman's voice caught my attention. "Your brother is under this snow?"

I faced Genevieve; her perfect face filled with lines of worry. "How did Bastien find you?"

She tilted her head. "Find me?" Her lips curled in amusement. "He burst into the hotel restaurant begging for help. Are you sorry I am here?"

Bastien rushed forward, standing beside Genevieve. "We're very thankful for her generous donation of these friends and snowmobiles. When she volunteered to assist, I told her Gabe was in trouble. She arranged for immediate assistance to rescue him."

I felt my face get warm. Her presence seemed pretty convenient to me. Did Gabe meet her in the hotel? "I'm...I must be confused. I thought—"

Hand on one hip, she tilted her head. "You thought—"

A man in the hole tapped his shovel, rapping something solid. "I've found something hard blocking the way."

"Excuse me." I jumped into the broader and deeper hole. Using my hands, I cleared away a layer of snow to find a board blocking the way.

"Gabe, can you hear me?" Something hit the board from below. I turned to the group. "They're still alive, but I bet their oxygen is low. Hurry."

Bastien and Genevieve clambered through the snow, searching the perimeter of the pile near the building with flashlights. In a few minutes, they came back to report.

"I called out to your brother. We heard him through a grate by the building." Genevieve pointed toward a wall.

"Almost missed him. He's super quiet." Bastien scratched the side of his face. "He said that someone tied his hands and feet and dumped him in the culvert. His attackers covered him with wooden planks crosswise, resting the boards on either side of the ditch. Like he's in a coffin. He's in the ditch connected to that building." He motioned behind him.

I clapped my gloved hands to get the men's attention and checked my watch. "Gabe's right under the wood. Whoever buried him did it a while ago, before our meeting time. Be quick, but don't poke him with your shovels."

Genevieve nodded. "Bastien cleared some snow away from the grate, which should give Gabe and his dog more air."

Though the men doubled their work, time dragged on. More than twenty minutes elapsed since they arrived. Snow flew in every direction. The men scraped off the boards revealing a four-foot square section of wooden planks.

I jumped into the hole, keeping my legs spread wide to either side to avoid pressure on the center of the wood. I lifted Thunder and dropped him onto the planks we'd uncovered. "Thunder, rescue." When he barked for confirmation, I slapped his side. "Go."

Padding in a circle, my dog halted at one end of the planks. Taking several delicate sniffs at the wall of snow remaining, he targeted a lower corner and plunged into the snow, digging, scraping, and clawing.

I borrowed a shovel. Sweating, I slaved beside Thunder. No telling what Gabe and Lightning's condition could be. We uncovered another plank.

I shouted in frustration. "How far do these planks go?" Snow pelting my face, I gazed into the sky and sagged to my knees. "Don't let him die."

Thunder stepped back and barked.

Arms exhausted, I heaved my shovel into the snow. The tool broke into a small pocket of air beyond the last board. "We've found the edge of the planks. Give me some help." I backed off and helped Thunder to the top of the chest-high snow pile. "Great job, buddy." I hugged him.

Two guys jumped into the hole I vacated, each taking one of the sides of the last board and thrust their spades into the open area.

"The snow on top is sliding, filling the gap Alex opened." Franco dashed to the area he saw shifting. "We have to dig from the top first."

The men renewed their work, working from the top first to remove the upper four feet of snow. They cleared a hole to the bottom of the concrete ditch, leaving about a foot-and-a-half gap in the culvert between the boards covering Gabe and Lightning and the wall of the hole in the snow pile.

I donned my coat and switched on the flashlight. "Gabe. Almost there." I lowered myself into the hole dug in the snow pile and stepped into the trench. Franco joined me.

Thunder barked, darting from side to side with excitement.

"Bastien, where is the rope?" Kneeling, I shined the light into the ditch and tried to spot Gabe's head, but the angle didn't work.

The coiled cord landed with a thump beside me. "Should be enough for fifty feet. Five-hundred-pound test." He smiled.

"Good work." I fastened a loop around my waist and handed the end to Franco. "One tug means I've made contact. If I tug twice, pull me out from under the boards."

Franco checked my knots. "Got it."

I crawled into the narrow gap under the boards, facing Gabe's direction while laying on my stomach. "I've got a visual."

Franco tapped my foot. "Good to hear."

The concrete ditch slanted downward at a shallow angle. I crept under the first board and trained my light ahead.

"C-c-cold c-c-c-concrete." The whisper of Gabe's voice came from in front of me.

"We'll free you shortly." I wiggled forward far enough to pat his shoulder. I tugged the line.

"We've got contact," Franco said.

While backing out, my coat bunched up, catching on one of the boards above me. "Stuck." I tugged the line twice.

"Hang on." Franco tightened the line. "Bastien, help me."

The rope squeezed my hips until I thought it would cut me in two. Seconds later, I jerked back to the opening, my coat scraping against the concrete culvert. I brushed myself off and sat up.

"Can you get a crowbar between those planks?" Bastien said.

I inspected the fit. "As long as the snow doesn't wedge the wood too tight. The attackers didn't nail the planks together. If we can separate them by lifting, I can put the rope around one of the boards. The snowmobile can pop it loose and the rest will be easy."

We scrambled to put the plan into action. Time flew while we dragged Gabe and Lightning out of the hole and cut the cords around my brother's hands and feet and his dog's legs, but not fast enough. I glanced at my watch. Three-twenty-two p.m. We'd be late meeting Mom and Dad. They'd be mad—big time. And that would kill our plans to meet Sofia and Izabella for the evening. If Gabe could even go out.

Genevieve laid out an emergency blanket. "Come. Lay here." She directed Franco and the men to lower Gabe on the cover and wrap it around him. "Coffee." She pointed at one of the guys. He got on a snowmobile and left.

Lightning curled himself on the snow next to Gabe's face, licking his cheek.

"You are hurt?" She placed a hand on his shoulder.

"B-b-b-bruised and b-battered." Gabe groaned a little. "Can I h-have another covering like an afghan or fleece?"

I got on the other side of my brother, Thunder sticking by my side. "Sorry, bro. We don't have anything except that Mylar sheet." I checked for broken bones. "Did the wood crush you?"

"D-d-don't think so." Gabe shivered and rubbed his side, his face scrunched in a grimace of pain.

Franco squatted next to Gabe. "Crazy place to take a nap. What happened?"

Chapter 18 – Fraternizing with the Enemy

Cul-de-sac, North Side of Val-D'Isère, France
Tuesday, 14 January 1992, 3:30 p.m.

Snow continued to fall, blurring the streetlamps near the resort area. The snowmobile lights kept the cul-de-sac brightly lit. To my right, Alex crouched near me with Thunder sniffing the emergency covering wrapped around me. Genevieve knelt on my left side. Lightning curled next to my head, using his body heat to keep me warmer. Bastien and Franco stood close by.

Franco approached me and dropped to one knee by my left ear. "Did you hear my question? Who did this to you?"

"I g…g…guess you could call it b…b…bad luck with the drug dealers." I shook a bit. Massaged my midsection, the easiest thing I could do wrapped in an emergency blanket. "I ran away from the r…r…Russian. Four bruisers came out when I got to the sk….ski lodge entrance, acting like they were tipsy. One of them y…y..yelled at me. 'Hey, American. Get out of France.' I b…backed away, turned, and ran."

A snowmobile roared close to Bastien and parked. The man handed out coffee in throw-away cups to everyone but me.

"Would you mind p…propping me on a snowmobile?" I groaned again. "That way I can drink coffee and t…t…take some painkillers for my headache."

"You are hurt in the head?" Genevieve directed Bastien and Franco to lean me against the snowmobile because the engine heat would warm me. After the guys helped me to the machine, I sat, still wrapped in the blanket except for one hand, and accepted a cup of coffee doctored the way I liked it.

Genevieve examined my head. Using a med kit from one of the snowmobiles, she cleaned a gash on my skull, inside the hairline on the right. She conducted a swift check for symptoms like blurry vision, nausea, tiredness, ringing in the ears, and other things. *Nice.*

"You act like a paramedic." Franco smiled.

"As a previous competitor, you have to know what to do for injuries on the slopes." She finished by pushing two painkillers into my hands and watched me take them. "You should be fine, but be careful for the next forty-eight hours." She pursed her lips. "You're still shivering. Allow me." She plucked the coffee from my hand, took off her outer jacket, and opened the emergency blanket. "Jacket off." With the Mylar cover beneath us, she pulled the ends together and wrapped her arms around my chest. "Lean into me."

I relaxed and let her warmth soak into my shaking body. The shiny Mylar reflected the heat into our space.

"While she's warming you, tell us the rest of the story." Alex smirked. "If you can focus."

I rolled my eyes at my brother. "The f..f…four guys chased me through these alleys until they cornered me. One left." I winced at a pain in my side. "The three other b…b…bruisers, no longer acting drunk, cornered me and threw some punches. I dodged their fists and knocked one of them to the ground." I shifted to a better position.

"Fewer details, bro." Alex looked at his watch. "We're late for the hockey game in Méribel."

"One of the guys popped me on the side of my face and I fell into the ditch. I hit my head on s…something and saw stars." Gabe grimaced. "They k..k..kicked Lightning into the ditch with me and tied my hands and feet and Lightning's legs. After that, the three guys threw some planks on top of us, dumped snow on the boards, and left us to die."

Bastien held out his hand and caught some snowflakes. "This storm will drop ten inches of fresh snow tonight. That would block your air hole in hours."

Genevieve shifted and pushed me to a more upright position. "You're warmer. I don't feel any more shaking. You'll be fine." She patted my shoulder and captured Bastien's attention. "Jackets please?" She slipped out of the cocoon on her knees, rewrapped me with my jacket, closed the covering, and looked around.

Bastien helped her stand. While she donned her jacket, he strode to a snowmobile close to us. "We owe your rescue to Genevieve. She corralled these guys in a couple of minutes."

"Thanks for rescuing me." I smiled. "And warming me up."

Genevieve smiled. "My pleasure."

Alex raised his coffee cup in a salute. "We appreciate the help. Couldn't have done it without you."

"Merci." The French woman seated herself behind Bastien on the snowmobile. "And my friends will give you a lift into town if you need one."

"Thanks." Franco waved when Bastien and Genevieve sped away.

"Let's get moving." Alex swallowed the rest of his coffee. "You'll have a lot of explaining to do."

"I'm trying to stay warm." I tightened the blanket around me.

Franco grinned. "It's not the same without the woman. Is it?"

Frowning, I flipped the blanket off, grabbed my coffee and finished it off, and dropped the cup on the ground. With internal jabs of pain, I got to my knees and stood, and tugged on my jacket. "Hey." I straightened it, noticing a jagged tear split the outside, exposing some inner lining. "I need a new coat."

Alex nodded. "As I said, lots of explaining."

I folded the Mylar covering, stuffed it under my arm, grabbed my empty coffee cup, and grabbed Lightning. "Let's get moving." I winced and crawled aboard a snowmobile with one of my rescuers.

"You guys are terrific." Alex climbed aboard another machine.

"Thunder, you're running." He tapped his driver. "Can you take us to the IEG Bus Stop?"

The man nodded.

When Franco mounted the last snowmobile, we roared off, Thunder racing to stay with us.

We made the 4:30 p.m. bus to Méribel, where the USA would play their hockey game against Luxembourg. Alex and Franco filled me in on their mission to the Cooperative Team's lockers in the support building, taking care to keep their voices low.

"Franco." Alex tapped him with his arm. "What did you say to those Co-op Team members in the locker room? They let us leave without a problem."

He laughed. "I called you nasty names and told the guys you were my idiot half-brother, mentally challenged and half-blind."

Alex chuckled. "At least it confused them a bit. Enough to get us out the door."

"Let's hope our escapade won't impact our other plans." I tucked Lightning inside my coat to keep him and me warm. "Mom and Dad could ground us for being late and for my ripped coat."

Alex shook his head. "That's the least of your worries."

Chapter 19 – The Brick

Ice Hockey Arena, Méribel, France
Tuesday, 14 January 1992, 5:40 p.m.

The Méribel indoor hockey arena loomed in front of us. I glanced at my watch. "Five-forty. We're over an hour late." I took Thunder's leash from my brother. "You go in first. I'll stay here with the dogs."

"No way." Alex whipped his dog's cord out of my hand. "You're the one who will have to smooth the way for us to get back to our snooping."

My body quivered. "Better for Mom and Dad to see you first. Nothing's wrong with you." I held out my hand. "But make it quick. I'm freezing again."

Reluctant, he passed Thunder's leash back to me. He disappeared into the building, returning in less than five minutes. "I told Mom a couple of American-haters shoved you into a ditch. She's upset and wants to talk with you right away."

I turned the dogs over to Alex, rubbed my aching head, and walked into the warmth of the building. The air temperature felt much better than the thirty-five degrees outside. I shivered again while I made my way to the fourth tier of seats. Spotting my parents, I made a beeline to them, sat on the open bench beside Mom, and chatted with my parents.

"Gabriel Zanadu." Mom examined me. "What happened to you?"

"A run-in with some bad people. I'm okay." I shivered. "A little c…cold."

Dad shifted to see me better. "Alex said people who hate Americans attacked you. Is that correct?"

"Yes, sir." I rubbed my side. "Threw me in a culvert and covered me with snow."

Mom's eyes got wide. "Alex didn't say they buried you. How did you get out?"

I lowered my eyes. "I couldn't do it." My body shook, fighting the cold. "They buried Lightning and me too deep. Alex and some friends rescued us."

Mom wrapped her arms around me. "You need to get warmer. The building custodian keeps the temperature at fifty degrees in here."

Dad inspected me. "You did well. I can still see the fire in your eyes. No damage some hot chocolate can't fix. But that jacket is ripped. We need to get you a new one."

I stirred, separating myself from Mom a bit. "That's a good idea. Alex and I could take the dogs and shop during the third period of the game and meet you before we go back. We have to stay outside with the dogs anyway."

Mom examined my eyes. "You have a gash on the side of your head that someone fixed for you. They did a good job. And I don't see any sign of concussion. How do you feel?"

"Other than cold, okay." I rubbed my side. "A little sore. But Alex can help me buy a new jacket and we can both enjoy the warmth of the stores."

Mom hugged and released me. "This is the end of the second period. You'll have to hurry. The game's end time is sometime after six-thirty."

After a quiet conversation, Dad passed some money to me. "I'm sure this is too much, but prices are higher right now. Don't spend it all but get a quality coat. The temperatures are brutal outside."

"I will. Can you keep this while I shop?" I handed her the emergency blanket.

She nodded and gave me another hug. "Stay away from bullies. Be back here no later than seven."

"Thanks." I rose and wedged my way past the seated fans, went past the concessions area, and met Alex outside. "Shopping time." Smiling, I patted my pockets. "Lots of money to spend."

We made it back to the arena with fifteen minutes to spare. Alex stayed outside with the dogs. I watched the last few minutes of the game with Mom and Dad and cheered for the USA team. We collected Alex and the dogs outside and left for Albertville, forty-five minutes away.

My brother and I dropped Thunder and Lightning off at our hotel room and hurried to our parent's place.

Mom inspected my new jacket like a detective looking for clues in a murder mystery, making sure it fit well, used the correct material and fabric, and would withstand the cold. "Not bad."

Dad held out his hand.

I dipped into my pocket, counting out the bills and the coins.

Dad chuckled. "Nice." He handed me five dollars and pocketed the rest. "That's hot chocolate money."

"We have another invite to meet with our friends." I twirled around one more time to show off the coat. "No parties. We want to get together and talk. But we would need a few bucks to spend on sodas and a little food."

"What about the spending money we gave you for this trip?" Dad crossed his arms.

"Wasn't that for daytime snacks and souvenirs?" Alex shrugged. "We didn't get any money for the evening."

Mom sighed. "They do need to make friends. That anti-American attack scares me."

"We'll talk about it while we ride to our next event." Dad motioned to the door. "We're behind schedule. We'll miss part of the Mixed Pairs free dance, which starts at seven-thirty. Check on the dogs in your hotel room before we go there."

After some family time watching the skating, Mom and Dad gave us enough money for evening activities for the entire IEGs. With an eleven o'clock curfew, they let us go about nine o'clock. We raced to meet our friends.

The Brick, an American-style pizzeria and variety bistro, looked like a combo pizza packed with toppings. Customers dressed in festive colors crowded around tables, blended with the red and white uniforms of the staff. Spotting Bastien near the back, we hustled inside. Izabella and Sofia sat opposite him on a wooden picnic-style table, with one end of the table facing us.

"Alex." Sofia scooted to one side and patted the wooden bench next to her. "I saved you a seat.

Alex smiled, waited for Izabella to let him in, and settled next to Sofia.

"Gabe." Bastien mimicked Sofia's action, patting the open space next to him. "Here's your seat.

I sat next to him. "Where's Franco?"

Izabella hesitated, grabbed her coat, and slid in beside me. "Franco said he would meet us around ten. Not a bad idea since we need to give Alex and Sofia room to breathe."

Bastien, me, and Izabella packed one side of the table. Izabella's jasmine perfume attracted my attention.

A waitress came by, took our order, and brought water and sodas.

Sofia threw her hands in the air. "This is terrible. You're in France but eating American pizza. Disgusting. You should try some of our great European recipes."

"I like the pastries." I rubbed my gut.

"You're hopeless." Sofia breathed deep and inched closer to Alex. "It's a little cool in here."

My brother shifted his shoulder next to hers to share a little warmth. "I couldn't agree more."

"Cool?" I sipped my soda. "You have no idea what that's like. This afternoon I recuperated in an emergency blanket after being buried alive."

The girls stared at me.

"What?" Izabella took a deep breath. "How? Is that where you got that gash?"

Alex rolled his eyes and explained in a quick summary what happened.

"You're kidding." Sofia tilted her head. "The Genevieve bombshell helped you?"

Izabella adjusted her position to hear better and put at least two more inches between us.

"How do you know about Genevieve?" I set my drink on the table.

"No wonder boys have difficulty with relationships." Izabella giggled. "They think we live in a vacuum." She glanced at Bastien. "We have our sources."

The corners of his mouth curved a little. "I did mention our first meeting with Genevieve to Sofia and Izabella after we met her."

The pizza and Quiche Lorraine arrived.

I worked through my pizza in record time. "But we're not here to talk about food. Tell us how the Women's 7.5 Kilometer Biathlon went. Did you see any smugglers?"

"Nothing at all." Sofia wrapped her arm around Alex's and gave it a squeeze. "We had a calm day."

The server brought Bastien another serving and he dug into the Quiche Lorraine. "I'm not sure if there is a connection, but I hear that one of the skiers had a severe accident today near Val-D'Isère. I don't know the details." He swallowed another bite of quiche and whispered, "A possible connection to our search for the drugs."

Sofia dabbed her mouth with a napkin. "Why don't we meet some skaters after the show?"

I rubbed my head. "Not me. I need to get some more painkillers and go to bed."

"It won't take long." Izabella sipped her drink from a straw. "It's almost ten."

"Made it." Franco squeezed past a group in the walkway and dropped into the open seat by Alex. "Are we going to a party?"

Alex interlaced fingers with Sofia. "Maybe. But I need to tell my parents about the change of plans. Let's walk back to our hotel. With everyone there, Mom and Dad will be sure to say yes."

We paid for our food, got our cold-weather gear on, and strolled back to our hotel.

At the hotel, Mom's eyes lit up when I told her I didn't want to go to the party. She gave me pain capsules for my headache and patted my shoulder. "Good decision to get some rest, honey."

Dad cleared Alex to go with our friends to the party.

Izabella squeezed my hand. "Get better. I'm praying for you."

Sophia waved at me. "I'll be praying too."

I watched the others go before making my way to our room. Every muscle and joint ached. I brushed my teeth, washed my face, undressed, and crawled under the covers, waiting for the pain pills to take effect. Genevieve came to mind. How did she come to my rescue that fast? Did the Russian know her? He chased me, but she found me later. I remembered seeing them together for the first time outside the hockey arena on the second day of the IEGs. Did he bump into her and she told him off, or did she run into the Russian that day for another purpose?

20 – A Moral Dilemma

Wild Boar Hotel, Albertville, France
Tuesday, 14 January 1992, 10:24 p.m.

I took Sofia's gloved hand while walking away from Mom and Dad's room. Bastien and Izabella followed a few feet behind us.

"Alex." Bastien increased his pace. "Is Gabe all right?"

I shrugged. "Not sure. We'll see in the morning. You've seen him in action, though. He always wants to be the center of attention. Skipping parties is a big deal to him."

We left the hotel behind, walking through the snow, which continued to coat the ground in soft mounds. Streetlamps lit the walkways. The town's streets glowed from the lights of the restaurants and bars while the conversations and music around us infused a vibrant spirit into the evening air.

"We've arrived." Sofia entered the back of a building and climbed a stairwell to the second floor.

"Is this a ghetto?" Izabella pointed to crumpled papers scattered on the first-floor landing.

Sofia laughed. "No. It's an apartment complex." She reached the second-floor hallway, went past three doors, and knocked.

A low male voice inside said something in French.

"Oui." Sofia added a few more words in French and said her name.

The door opened until it reached the indoor chain's entire length. "How many?"

"Four."

The voice asked a question to someone inside the room. The young man got his answer, unhooked the door, and ushered us in. "That's the limit. Come in."

Sofia led the way. I followed with Bastien and Izabella behind me.

Handsome men and pretty female skaters hung out dressed in fancy T-shirts and shorts, collared shirts—both long and short sleeves, jeans, boots, and other expensive clothes. I felt like my snow boots, cheap jeans, and T-shirt might not fit in.

"Coats in the bedroom." The door-guy pointed the way.

"I'm not dressed for this, Sofia." I dropped my coat on the bed's growing pile of jackets, scarves, and parkas.

Bastien tossed his coat on the bed. "Don't worry, Alex. No one here cares about what you wear. They're relaxing."

Izabella tapped my shoulder. "Let's get some hot chocolate while Sofia makes her presence known."

"Good idea." Sofia's eyes scanned the living room. "I'll introduce you to some friends in a bit. Hang out in a corner somewhere. I'll get you at the right time."

Bastien wandered away, leaving me with Izabella. We went into the kitchen, snagged two cups of hot chocolate, and went outside on an enclosed, heated balcony. Music flowed around us. Chatting couples came and went. Izabella and I sat in two corner chairs with an end table in between, overlooking the bright streetlights backdropped by dark mountain shapes. Snow kept fluttering to the ground.

"Amazing, isn't it." Izabella set her hot chocolate on a coaster.

"The mountains?" I sipped my drink. "They're beautiful, even at night."

She giggled. "No. I meant us."

I glanced at her. "What do you mean?"

"We've grown a lot in a few years. You act differently than when we did homeschool together. You're less antagonistic to your brother. More confident."

"The same for you." I smiled. "Model. Dancer. Much taller and more graceful. And more assured. Even though you're Gabe's age, you act much older."

"Your adventures keep getting more dangerous?" Izabella touched the cross on her necklace. "I've prayed for your safety many times. Jenna, your old German girlfriend, keeps me informed."

"Our homeschool group is still close." I rubbed my jaw. "The mysteries we solved together created a pretty strong bond. And Jenna keeps writing letters."

"Now you're drawing close to Sofia." Izabella grinned.

A smile crept across my lips. "Can't hide anything from you. But this is dreamland, a make-believe place where wishes might come true. Europe. The IEGs. Glamorous people with extreme talent. Sofia seems wonderful, but this is a special place and time. And I have a close girlfriend at home."

"Sofia's a nice girl." Izabella shifted in her chair. "She's level-headed and strong in her faith. I would know."

A noisy group of friends wandered into the room, admiring the view.

"What's your friend's name in the States?" Izabella scooted closer.

"Emma." I set my drink on the table. "But I'm not sure where we stand. She's a good friend and a mentor in my spiritual growth in Christ.

"Nice."

We both sank back into the cushions of our chairs, listening to the chatter around us.

I rubbed my chin, thinking. How did Emma fit in my life? She taught me a ton of fool-proof investigation methods. She spent hours with me reviewing research she and our Youth Pastor completed to prove Jesus lived, died, and rose again.

"Alex."

Startled, I straightened in my chair. "Ah, Sofia." I shook my head. "Lost in thought."

Her eyes danced. "That's good. I like deep thinkers."

Izabella stood. "Did your friends provide any information we can use?"

"Not tonight." She sighed. "Maybe another time."

Bastien appeared by her shoulder and chuckled. "We get to do this tomorrow as well?"

I rose from my chair. "Sounds like fun to me." We went to the bedroom, got our coats, said goodbyes, and left.

Walking back to the Wild Boar, Sofia's arm in mine, I glanced at Izabella and Bastien trudging beside Sofia. "Gabe and I will meet with Willie in the morning and fill him in on today's events."

Izabella peered around Bastien's bulk. "He might have found leads to tell you about."

I nodded. "I sure hope so because this day's been a bust."

Chapter 21 – Ramped-Up Security

IEG Main Security Station, Albertville, France
Wednesday, 15 January 1992, 9:00 a.m.

Five days into the IEGs. About a half-foot of snowfall from last night lay fresh in the fields and glistened in the light. At a frosty thirty-one degrees, I dragged my sore body to the Albertville IEG Security Station at a painful jog. Alex loped ahead of me without difficulty. Inside, the Desk Sergeant glared at us when we entered.

I waved and smiled.

She shook her head and slashed at the papers in front of her with a pen.

Gilbert led us to Willie's office. "Nine o'clock. Right on time." He grinned.

We settled into chairs while Gilbert provided hot drinks and waited for Willie to finish his paperwork.

"How ya going?" Willie pushed back from his desk, eyes roving over Alex and me. "You look a bit knackered." He lifted his coffee, waving it in my direction.

"Not tired." I touched my chest. "A bit sore."

"You should stop all the sit-ups." Willie sipped his drink.

Alex chuckled. "He absorbed lots of body blows yesterday to strengthen his abdominals."

Our friend sat straighter. "What?"

Alex and I covered the attack yesterday by American-haters who buried me in the snowbank at Val-D'Isère.

Willie jotted a few notes and studied us while we talked.

"The French woman slid into the emergency blanket with you?" Willie pointed his pen at me.

I shrugged. "Yes, she helped me get warmer. Is that bad?"

He scribbled on his paper. "Did she say anything about the Russian?

"I didn't ask her." Alex set his coffee cup on an end table. "Her voice and facial expressions appeared shocked when I asked about her even being there."

"From our previous contact," I said, remembering when we tried to take a picture of them, "we don't know if she told the Russky to take a hike or if she met him to talk." I rubbed my side. "She might not know him at all."

"Says the guy who spent several minutes with her in a warming blanket." Alex rolled his eyes. "You're a biased witness."

The twinkle in Willie's eyes made me grin. Our friend sank into his chair, put his hands behind his head, and rocked the chair a bit. "Let's suppose that she is part of the underground ring and wants to keep an eye on you. Do you think a friend-based approach would work better than an antagonistic one?"

"You mean she tricked me into liking her?"

"Makes sense to me." Alex tapped his temple. "I'm more objective about this than you."

"Don't tip her off that she's under suspicion." Willie pulled a sheet of paper off a clipboard, writing on it. "I'm filing a report that requests we search the database for anyone whose first name is Genevieve and has dealings with the drug industry. I'll also ask for photos." He set the paper aside. "As for you," he pointed at me with his pen, "you need to stay away from IEG events for today."

"But we planned to watch the Women's Alpine Combined Downhill in Méribel at twelve-fifteen followed by the two-thirty 15 Kilometer Cross-Country race at Courchevel." I shifted to the front edge of my chair. "How will we keep investigating if we take a day off?"

"You can find lots to do here that doesn't pertain to the IEGs." Willie cracked his knuckles. "What about going ice skating? Or hitting a ski slope somewhere that officials didn't close for the IEG games? Or you could go to movies, shop or see museums and local attractions."

"We don't know how long we'll be here." Alex lifted his cup, saluting Willie. "Missing a day could mean we don't have enough time to solve the case."

Our Australian friend scanned his office. "Shut the door."

I got to my feet, made sure the door clicked shut, and refilled my cup from Willie's personal coffee pot.

"Watch it, mate." Willie glanced at the ceiling.

"What?" I paused in front of him.

"You little anklebiter." He raised his eyebrows. "That's *my* coffee pot. You're stealing my coffee."

"Oh." I looked at the coffee pot, then back at him. "Do you want me to put it back?"

Willie slumped back in his seat. "They don't pay me enough for this." He gathered himself, gripped his mug's handle, and motioned to me. "Bring the pot over here, fill 'er up, set it on the burner, and take a seat." He grinned at me. "I'll give you a lesson on manners later."

I gulped, did what he asked, and sat.

"Time we got down to business." Willie doctored his coffee. "At this point, we've let you know the bare minimum about our efforts here. Now we're going deeper, but you can't spill this info to anyone else. I'll tell you what you can share before you leave. Understand?"

Alex and I nodded.

"We look at our special area of law enforcement like the military might— in three sections. The tactical side consists of the actual legwork and hands-on investigation. The operational part concerns itself with the drugs impacting the IEG Games. Finally, the strategic piece covers the political impact of illegal drugs on the IEG Committee and future games, including criminal activity penetration from Russia into France. With me so far?"

"Didn't we know this in the beginning?" I drank some coffee. "This is general stuff."

Willie grinned. "Now for more important information. As I said before, I can't reveal it all. But you can get a higher level of detail now. Ready?"

Alex gave him a thumbs up. I raised my cup.

"The Russian you are tracking is an ex-KGB agent by the name of Dimitri Vasiliev. He's interested in creating issues with the IEG games and he's trying to infiltrate the French underground with the ultimate prize of placing himself or others in a position of influence over French political affairs. We don't know his entire history, but he's a dangerous man. The KGB doesn't pull punches when they go after the good guys."

"What about the drugs we've found?" I drained my drink.

"We have plants in each team and support staff." Willie tapped the report he made. "Your discovery of drugs in locker 932 of the Cooperative Team is too old and tentative to do a raid. They could have moved the drugs overnight. But we'll be ready for the next credible evidence we get."

Alex stiffened. "Thunder is never wrong. After he finished his training for tracking drugs, he's alerted without error every single time."

"We need more evidence." Willie put his hands on the desk and rolled forward. "The good thing is we caught three drug-users from the Cooperative team already. We're jailing two and leaving one without any knowledge we've made him. He might lead us to others. One last thing. After you've told me your stories about yesterday, I'm assigning a bodyguard detail to both of you, even though I can't afford the personnel drain."

I leaned forward. "But—

Willie held up a hand. "Due to those attacks, I can't leave you unguarded. The team may be male or female, but they will stay out of sight. I want two people on the team; however, if personnel restrictions require, it might be one person."

"How will they know what we're doing?" Alex shifted in his chair.

Our friend opened a drawer and pulled out two round objects like silver dollars. "Each of these is a transceiver with a special code." He handed both of us a coin. "Each coin's unique number will be your code. Whatever your plans, we'll find and follow you."

"What if we need help?" I flipped my coin in the air, slapped it on the back of my hand, and peeked to see which side showed on top.

"The bodyguards carry walkie-talkies and have access to whatever transportation they require." Willie smiled. "You should be reachable in a few minutes and our agents can report your position if they need backup."

"Cool." I flipped the coin another time and guessed the outcome, heads or tails. I won again.

Willie tapped the desk to get my attention. "Keep the coins in your pocket since they're high-tech instruments. We don't want them to break or let someone steal them from you." Willie checked his watch. "I have to go." He briefed us on what we could share. "Have a safe day today." He rose, patted both of us on the shoulder, and left.

Chapter 22 – Accident Investigation

That ruined our day with useless info." I stuck my gloved hands into my coat on the walk back to the hotel.

"Why do you say that?" Alex kept pace with me. "We did learn a few new things and we got to see Willie again."

"I still think we aren't getting the intel we need." I scowled. "And now we have a bodyguard that will babysit us every day. What are we, children?"

When we arrived at the hotel, a clerk waved us over. "A Bastien Dubois left a message for you." The clerk dropped an envelope into my palm. "Have a nice day."

As we walked toward our room, Alex snatched the message out of my hand and ran.

"Give it back." I chased him.

Alex smirked at me and opened our door. "We need to be quiet for the other guests." Thunder brushed against my brother's pants to welcome him home and Lightning leaped at my legs, begging for a hug, which I gave him after closing the door.

We dropped our coats on the beds. Alex opened the note and read it out loud.

"Let's meet after lunch at one o'clock as a group. Invites are out to Sofia, Izabella, and Franco. We can meet in the lobby of your hotel. I have arranged a skiing afternoon if you're interested. See you soon. Bastien."

"That's crazy." Alex passed the note to me. "How would he know that Willie offered us the option to go skiing instead of the IEGs?"

I reread the note, petting Lightning and sitting on my bed. "Right. Does he have a connection with Willie we don't know?" I tossed the message on my pillow. "What about ice skating instead?"

Alex rubbed his jaw. "Sofia would hate that. She competes in that sport."

"Okay." I flopped on my bed. "I haven't skied in a while. Could be fun. Maybe it will be a top-notch course."

We informed Mom and Dad about the invitation while we ate together at noon. They agreed after telling us we had to leave the location for them in a message at the front desk. After lunch, we went to our rooms, fed and petted the dogs, told them goodbye, got our backpacks, and waited in the lobby.

Bastien strolled in like he owned the place. He wore a light jacket instead of heavy snow gear. "Can you go?"

I gave him an okay sign.

"I'm driving my four-wheel-drive Mercedes SUV. It can hold us all."

Alex dropped a note at the front desk for Mom and Dad with the name of the ski run. After throwing our backpacks in the trunk, he and I piled in with the rest of the crew—Izabella, Sofia, and Franco, who sat in the front passenger seat. I crawled in next to the car's left rear door and sat by Izabella, with a drink and a snack I had taken from my backpack. Alex took the right-side door next to Sofia.

Bastien started the car and drove away. "We're going to do a little investigation before we get to the top of the mountain."

"What kind of investigation?" Sofia, wedged in the middle between Alex and Izabella, shifted to make herself more comfortable.

"An accident investigation on the upper lift of the backside of Val-D'Isère. It's a commercial venture not connected with the IEG ski runs."

"What happened?" Izabella said.

"The police aren't sure, but the fallout was bad." Bastien turned left onto the main road. "Rescuers transported at least ten people off the hill for treatment yesterday. No deaths, but a few serious injuries."

"I heard that one of the support stands fell over." Franco mimicked the event by slamming one hand into the other.

I set my bottled water in a cup holder. "Kersplatt. What new evidence can we find now that the investigators couldn't find?"

"Due to the late hour it happened and the snowfall, the investigation began this morning." Bastien weaved through slow traffic. "I know the lead investigator and told him we had a team that could sort out what went wrong if we got the opportunity."

"With six more inches of snow, how can we figure it out?" Izabella shook her head.

"We've got company." I faced Alex. "Did you see our tail?"

Alex stretched his arms and twisted his head back and forth several times. "BMW?"

"Dark grey." I stretched my neck, took a bite of my sandwich, and tilted my head left and right while I chewed.

"What are you guys talking about?" Izabella tapped me on my arm. "What's a tail?"

I swallowed. "A person that's tracking us." I shrugged. "Willie wants to keep an eye on us in case someone attacks."

"Attacks?" Sofia scooted closer to Alex. "Why?"

I rubbed my chest. "Based on the incidents yesterday afternoon, Willie thinks the K—"

Alex narrowed his eyes at me.

I took a swig of water and cleared my throat. "I bet the Russian guy arranged to have some men bury me alive."

Bastien peered into the rearview mirror at me. "You know more than you're telling. Spill it."

Alex sighed. "Here's what Willie told us earlier." He talked about the different levels of the investigation; tactical, operational, and strategic; some details about why his office couldn't investigate locker 932; and their suspicions about Genevieve. He left out the ex-KGB info and the fact that we had transceivers on us the tail could track.

"Don't worry." I scanned the faces. The guys didn't care, but Izabella frowned, and Sofia tightened her lips.

"We have a babysitter." I finished my little sandwich. "From past adventures we've taken, they might be an A+ at what they do or maybe a C-. Willie's team is stretched pretty thin."

"Nice job." Alex shook his head. "You want them to worry more?" He patted Sofia's knee. "We've beaten the crooks in Germany, Austria, Okinawa, and in Texas. We'll be okay."

"Let's focus on how we can find the cause of the ski lift failure." Bastien made a left toward the mountain. "If something happens along the way, we'll think of a plan."

We wrestled with a list of possible causes, our conversation flowing back and forth until we reached the ski resort. After exiting the SUV, we retrieved our backpacks and rented our skis, poles, and other equipment at the rental shack. I rented my favorite, short trick skis, while everyone else got regular ones. Bastien led us out onto the slopes. "We have to take an alternate route to get to the site. When we get off, follow me."

The first lift dropped us off a third of the way higher on the backside of Val-D'Isère. Bastien led us to another working set of ski chairs to our right, which converged with the broken machinery on the left near the top of the mountain where the most challenging slopes began.

The second lift consisted of chairs seating four people. At the top, we gathered together behind Bastien.

"Our babysitter must have stayed in his car." I pointed at the empty chairs ascending the slope.

Alex smiled. "We're on our own."

Bastien skied to a blue trail marker. "For this mountain, blue is beginner, yellow is intermediate, red is advanced, and black is expert."

"Challenge us a little." Izabella pointed her pole at a red trail. "Can we get there faster on that trail?"

"Let's have some fun." I started forward to the marker.

"Wait." Bastien's voice rang out. "Not all of us can ski the hard trails. I can handle a yellow."

We found the intermediate trail and sliced around trees, darting back and forth. Sometimes I wished I wore the standard skis since they were faster on the straight parts. But I could make quick stops and changes of direction better than those with regular skis.

In less than five minutes, we encountered the top of the damaged ski lift. Three police officers stood at strategic points around the yellow-tape enclosed space. Four other individuals roamed back and forth across the cordoned land, about the size of a football field, studying the slope and looking at the twisted poles of the lift.

"Halt." A police officer skied over to Bastien. "This area is off-limits."

Switching to French and waving his arms at the officer, our friend and guide made several forceful points. The official raised his arms and voice, unhappy with Bastien's words. Sofia translated for us.

"The police officer said we cannot come into the taped-off area." Sofia raised an eyebrow. "But Bastien says he has permission from the Chief of Police in Albertville to investigate with us. The officer protested that his boss didn't notify them and he doesn't take orders from Bastien."

One of the individuals not in uniform came over to the policeman. After a heated exchange, the plain-clothes individual raised a walkie-talkie to his ear. He waved his arms to punctuate each point he made, glaring at Bastien, then at us. After a few minutes, he reholstered his walkie-talkie at his waist.

Sofia's face betrayed a mix of emotion. She covered a laugh when the plainclothes man turned away. We could see the sparkle in her eyes.

Alex side-stepped near her. "What's so funny?"

Sofia lowered her voice. "The detective's boss overruled his objections to us coming onto the site. He called us several names, including privileged, pompous, and pampered. But we're allowed into the cordoned area against his best judgment."

The ski lift looked like a T, with a single column in the middle and a square metal top that contained cables on both sides. Somehow, two towers had lost their tops. The chairs, steel-wire ropes, and T-tops lay in the snow on one side of the towers.

Bastien waved us over to the yellow tape. We crossed the line and made our way to one of the fallen tops, now jammed into the ground. A detective moved around the mangled wreck. Several lift seats, bent and tossed at odd angles, covered the landscape. The wire rope connected each chair to the next.

"How tall is the tower these bench-seats fell from?" I inspected a fallen chair near me.

The plain-clothes detective near us heard my question. "This tower is fifteen meters above the ground."

"That's about forty-nine feet." Sofia moved near the detective. "Was that the height of the benches or the tower head that held the sheaves and ropes?"

The detective came nearer. "I see you know a little about chair lifts."

Alex skied next to Sofia. "We each know a little bit. Like the seats on this lift are quads because they carry four people." He placed his hand on the clamp at the top of the chair. "The bench-seats are detachable, not fixed."

"Wire cables, called ropes, run the length of the hill." Izabella pointed to the tower head. "And rubber-wheeled sheaves support the haul rope."

I slid to the top part of the ski lift that had driven itself into the ground. "Do you have a forensics team here?"

The detective's eyebrows knit together. He lifted his walkie-talkie to his lips.

Bastien held a finger in the air and spoke French.

The detective didn't respond but lowered his connection to the primary inspector. "Since you have permission, how can I assist you? Our forensics team will arrive in thirty minutes."

Izabella pointed to the metal pole sticking into the air. "This supported the tower head. The separation point appears pretty smooth, with jagged edges on one side."

I inspected the metal. "Alex, would you bring your backpack here?" While my brother skied to my position, I removed my skis, laid my poles on the snow, and shucked off my pack. Digging inside, I found what I wanted.

"What?" Dropping his backpack near me, Alex stepped out of his skis and planted his poles in the ground.

I stood on top of one of the sheaves support poles, tweezers and plastic bag in hand. "Take some close-up pictures of this severed area on the metal pole that held the tower head."

"Quit trying to boss me around." Alex dug around in his pack. "I know what to do."

After my brother used the new camera Bastien gave him, I twisted tiny metal fragments from the edge of the pole. I tugged out another plastic bag and sterile swabs wrapped in plastic. Using one swab, I ran it around one side of the damaged pole's sharp edge.

Izabella skied near me. "Something interesting?"

"Residue from either an explosion or maybe det cord." I placed the swab in a plastic bag, sealed it, and put both baggies in a leather pouch. Sliding the container in my backpack, I stepped back.

Alex inserted his camera in his backpack and lifted a small bottle with white powder and an eye dropper into the air.

The detective objected. "That will ruin the entire crime scene."

Alex glanced at Bastien for help.

"What procedure are you doing?" Bastien opened his palms wide.

"Dusting for fingerprints." Alex opened the bottle, sucked a little powder into the eyedropper, and gazed at the detective. "I'll test this side of the pole at the break. You have the other tower head and half of this one for further investigation."

Bastien nodded and spoke in rapid French, gesturing in firm motions while pointing to the other pieces.

The detective gave in. "You must do no more." He glanced at his watch. "Our team arrives in five minutes."

Alex squirted the powder from the eyedropper, covering one-half of the mutilated pole. He rubbed his chin, grabbed his camera, clicked several shots, and stowed his gear. "We should head out."

My brother and I got our skis back on, gathered our poles, and settled our backpacks over our shoulders.

The detective smiled when his walkie-talkie beeped. He held it to his ear, speaking in a quiet tone a few times. "Our forensics team is on the way."

"We're done here." I checked with Bastien. "Which way do we go?"

"I'll lead." Our French buddy led us to the right of the broken lift. "Lots of interesting runs on this side of the mountain."

We skied beside the broken lift as a group. Bastien slowed our progress when he fell within the first minute. He regained his feet and faced sideways to the hill. His eyes widened. "Here comes trouble."

Four skiers in camouflage slid into view, cresting a hill that hid the broken chair lift. Each of them carried a pistol holstered on their hips.

Chapter 23 – Four Skiers – Six Targets

Closed Ski Lift, Val-D'Isère, France

Wednesday, 15 January 1992, 3:17 p.m.

Glancing at my trick skis, I grinned. They were the perfect choice. Alex and the rest of the group wore long skis, which might be faster but less maneuverable. I'd have the advantage if we raced into the trees and skied the most demanding trails, like the black diamonds.

Bastien waved at the girls. "We'll take the intermediate yellow trail through the trees to the chair lift in use. Those gunmen won't dare use their weapons there." He jerked a thumb at the other side. "The harder trails are on that side."

"Hurry." Alex's jaw tightened. He shoved off, heading straight into a black trail.

I stayed in his tracks for a few minutes. Making quick turns through the trees, I noticed two pursuers behind us. "Two bogies."

I slipped past my brother on a small jump, shouting over the wind whipping past me. The trail split ahead. "I'll take the right."

"Got it." Alex flew into the pines on the left.

A black square with three diamonds emblazoned the tree next to the trail I entered. My pulse quickened. I jumped a rock in the path, sliding right but turning left. I glanced behind. The man pursuing me wore a black knit cap on top of his head. His olive-green goggles and black beard left me no reference to his age, but his quickness and longer skis helped him gain on me rapidly.

The trail narrowed. Tree branches slapped me in the face. Another check. Twenty feet away. Without the twists and turns, the guy could shoot his pistol at me anytime with ease.

A quick right, followed by an immediate left, gave me a little cushion, but it wouldn't last long. Negotiating the tight turns gave me the advantage. I widened the gap between us. Sweat trickled under my eyes inside my goggles, making them a little foggy. Unzipping my coat halfway, I let the air cool me off and soon stopped sweating. My googles cleared. Too many clothes for a breakneck sprint away from an armed man. I ducked under a pine branch and found myself on a straight, clear path. I twisted to see my pursuer's position.

He burst from the trees. Pulling his pistol, he aimed.

I swerved.

He fired.

Darting left, the trees gave me some cover. The hitman might draw closer, but maybe the thick trees and small side trails would confuse him. When he dropped out of sight behind me, I stopped.

Quiet blanketed the area. Selecting a fallen branch thick as my wrist from the snow, I crouched on the downside of a tree with an immediate drop and clear skiing behind me. The man would have to come from above my position. I listened.

My heart surged in my chest. "Breathe deep." My Dad's training helped me settle. A few seconds and the pulse pounding in my ears gave way to crystal clear focus. A few birds chirped downslope. The wind moved the tops of the pines. I adjusted my goggles, letting tiny bits of sweat drip onto my cheeks, and resealed.

Was that a sound? I couldn't let the man take me by surprise. I'd be dead.

A metal edge scraped snow to my high side. The man came closer.

I tensed, backing up a fraction.

The chaser burst through the pine branches of the same tree where I hid and its closest uphill neighbor. Like a Big Foot, the guy's height and bulk made me react instinctively.

I rammed the end of my branch right below his ribcage into his solar plexus.

The guy bent in half, sucked in a breath, and toppled over.

I threw the branch in his face and shot away on the slope, weaving through several trees back to the triple-black diamond. But though I gained at least four or five seconds with that maneuver, the guy righted himself and kept coming. Rats. His abs must be like iron.

Rocketing past a warning sign that showed a cliff and falling stones ahead, I prayed the trick skis would let me turn fast enough to avoid going over a huge drop.

My pursuer flew out of the trees and gained ground. The man couldn't pull his gun and negotiate the back-and-forth turns.

I dodged trees, working on getting rid of him. Skiing to the right, I gambled with the cliff. Left and right. A jump. Miss a rock. He could almost grab me. I kept a low posture, like a racing skater. Sliced my skis into the ground.

A space opened in front of me. The man trailed by a ski length. The path veered to the left, but there wasn't enough snow to make the complete turn. We moved too fast.

I dug in hard, throat clenched tight.

Snow under my skis gave way on the slippery rock.

My aching legs jammed the skis sideways, searching for any traction to stay on the trail. I flung myself at a bent tree. And missed.

Chapter 24 – Calculated Risk

Closed Ski Lift, Val-D'Isère, France

Wednesday, 15 January 1992, 3:17 p.m.

When Gabe split off to the right, I took the left black trail. An advanced route, but not too hard. Equipped with standard-length skis, I couldn't execute the tight turns as fast as I wanted.

The man behind me kept pace but couldn't seem to catch me. I darted through the trees, branches clawing at my clothes. Trees blurred, flashing past my face at top speeds. After tight turns, my speed dropped enough to keep tabs on him.

A crack sounded.

Snow dropped from a tree limb that jiggled in front of me. *He shot at me. What's wrong with these people?* If I didn't make this more difficult, he could get lucky. The thick trees meant he needed to close the distance for an accurate shot. *I need more speed.* I got into a ski jumper's crouch, dug in my ski edges on the turns, and flew down the mountain. For a moment, a clump of pines and undergrowth camouflaged me. I slid into the trees and waited.

The man flew by me but realized I'd pulled off the trail when my tracks disappeared. He skidded to a stop, cursing in Russian.

I darted onto a second trail, another black diamond.

Scanning the trees, the guy tracked my movement and slid on a parallel path by me. Trees whipped by. Gaps opened and closed in an instant. He streaked closer. Twenty feet. Ten. Five. I crouched lower. He matched me. I leaned back, slowing, and slipped through a gap to trail him on his path.

I switched trails again, going with a yellow. My chaser took a shortcut. Could I win against his experienced tactics? The skin on my back tingled, knowing he could catch me soon. A second later, the crack of another shot made my muscles jerk. A branch crashed from a tree and fell on the path behind me, blocking the trail. At last, a break went my way.

My skis stabilized me on my feet while swerving through switchbacks, dropping down a steep slope, shooting past trees like a slalom skier goes through gates, and letting the limbs and branches slap my legs and face. The pursuer lost precious time—time I'd use to take him out.

Rounding a blind corner brought me between two firs very close together. One tree's branches hung on the snowdrifts. The distance between one tree for concealment and the skinny tree on the other side appeared to be less than three feet.

I stopped and rapidly stepped out of my skis, gambling. The guy chasing would have me in his crosshairs soon. Crawling under the bigger tree's branches, I lay on the ground, ski poles hidden by the limbs and snowfall on the tree. I poked a hole in the snow to see the trail above me.

The swoosh of skis cutting through the snow warned me of the attacker's closeness. My muscles tensed. Despite the chill that penetrated through my snow coat, I focused on my upcoming critical actions. "Lord, need a little help here."

A flash of a metal edge caught my attention. *Now.* I thrust my two poles across the gap to the skinny tree trunk for bracing, lifting them about a foot off the ground.

The man's snow boots struck the rods, bending them and jerking them out of my hands. He flew forward on the trail, tumbling, his poles flailing to either side. One caught a tree limb, twisting him to the left. His shoulder slammed into the ground and his head hit next, bouncing off something hard in the snow. He sprawled on the trail.

I grabbed my bent poles for defense and approached the guy. He lay motionless. I nudged him with my boot. Nothing.

Keeping one pole ready to slam into him, I slid his pistol out of the holster. Rotated the selector lever to safe. Dropped the magazine into my hand, pocketed it, and ejected the round in the gun's chamber. I collected his poles, discarded mine, and tucked the pistol into my belt. With caution, I backed away, silent as possible.

I snapped my boots back into the skis. Skirting the unconscious pursuer, I zipped over the trail to the edge of the woods. I could see the ski resort below, the first ski lift, and crowds of people moving. Too far away to pick out individuals, I found another trail and worked my way to the top of the first ski lift. When I saw Bastien and the girls scanning the slopes above them, I raced to their side.

"Alex." Sofia moved higher on the hill to meet me first.

"Made it." I slid beside her.

"We were worried about you two." She hugged me and checked the uphill slope. "Where's the guy in camouflage?"

I explained how I got rid of him. Lifted the bottom of my coat to show the pistol tucked under my belt. "More evidence."

"We took a simple trail." Izabella rushed to my side. "At first, the two guys got close, but when the trail led us back out into the open area under the broken ski lift, I got nervous."

"That's when a few of our detective friends joined us." Bastien smiled. "The men in camo clothes must have recognized them. They peeled off onto another trail and we haven't seen them since."

"Why did the detectives leave their project at the ski lift?" I said.

Sofia grinned. "They left to have a coffee at the resort."

"Good timing." I scanned the slopes and frowned. "Where's Gabe?"

Chapter 25 – Mountain Survival

Ski Trail Cliff, Val-D'Isère, France
Wednesday, 15 January 1992, 3:42 p.m.

The tree branch I hung from creaked with my weight. Smaller than the one I missed, this pine tree's branches hung over the cliff. My gloves slipped on the needles. Exhaustion from yesterday's burial drained my muscles, but my heart raced with each lost inch of grip. "Alex. Anyone." I shouted again. "Help me."

My throat felt raw from calling out. I glanced skyward. "Can we have a good ending here?" A cold breeze filled the void left by God's lack of response. "I'm not going down without a fight."

I couldn't see any ground right under me. About ten feet below, behind my dangling body, a snow-covered ledge nearly six feet wide offered the single possible solution. But if I dropped straight down, I'd miss the outcropping and tumble into space. I'd tested the branch for flexibility. No dice. I'd have to be further out on the limb for any hope of success.

You're not going to make it. The thought permeated every part of my body, encouraging me to quit. I rebelled against the negative. "Not true," I yelled out loud. "I'm gonna survive. Somehow."

My arms and abs ached. Tiredness seeped into my bones. Rest. I needed rest.

Watching the man that chased me shoot into open space earlier, wrenched at my gut. He didn't make it. Remembering his shouts caused a shiver to run through my spine. *Not me.* I fought gravity to get a better grip on the branch. It trembled in my hand.

With a crack, the branch dropped another foot. My grip loosened. I slid further out to the edge of the limb. I clamped onto it hard.

A wind blasted me from above. I lost more inches on the branch when the whole tree swayed in the frigid air. When it swung forward, I clung to the wet pine, but my aching muscles almost lost their hold. The wind died. The tree whipped in the opposite direction. The limb supporting me flexed backward, snapped, and fell. Adrenalin cleared my fog of tiredness. I flailed to maintain some type of balance in the air.

My back slammed into a snowdrift. The impact forced a grunt out of me. I gasped. The blow shot jolts of pain throughout my sore chest. My feet hung over nothingness. I lay tilted on an angle toward my feet. Anticipating another fall, I closed my eyes and waited.

Minutes later, still lodged in the same place, I sucked in air and gazed at the blue sky above. "Thank you, thank you, thank you."

I flexed my hands, finding the poles still attached via straps to my wrists. My left ski remained on my foot, but I'd lost the right one. Other than being sore, I found safety. For now.

Exploring my position with easy, cautious moves, I could touch the cliff on my right but discovered emptiness on my left except for the edge of the outcropping. I clenched my jaw. To squash the nagging voice of fear, I encouraged myself out loud, "I've got this."

Desperation gnawed at me. Scary situations made me hyper, filling me with tension and adrenalin. All my senses were on alert.

I needed to get closer to the cliff face to avoid falling off. My poles might help. I could create a level hole to crawl into with some careful digging. Without my right ski, I could move more freely to that side. The left ski release mechanism's failure to pop open might pose a problem even though they were short skis. "Not a problem for Gabriel Zanadu."

Without sitting or changing my prone position, I dug into the snow between me and the cliff. A tough crust covered the snow's top layer, but I broke through to softer snow beneath. After what seemed an eternity, I rolled myself closer to the cliff and into the new ditch I'd created in the snow and sighed. A little safer.

The wind carried the sound of voices. "Yes." I shouted and pumped my fist. A rescue party.

I yelled to attract attention while lying on my back. But the voices drifted away. *Please. Someone help me.* The cliff and snow must have absorbed my calls. I wiped away a tear.

Cold crept into my back, hands, and lower legs. Stiff joints and sore muscles throbbed. I spiraled downward. Life's miseries piled on top of me.

"Don't quit." I punched the snow to break the negative cycle. Dad trained us to be tough in the gym, at Karate practices, and when we hiked and camped. "Never let your feelings control what you can do," he told Alex and me.

I breathed deep several times. "I will win." I calmed my mind. Slowed my speech. Still talking to myself out loud, I emphasized each word. "I will overcome."

Gripping a pole in one hand, I poked it over my head on the ledge into the snowdrift to loosen more snow. Scooping the snow away gave me more headroom. I wormed my whole body onto my safe haven. I braced my remaining ski against the cliff and jammed a pole into the release mechanism several times until it popped open. "Yes." I raised my fist in the sky. "Gabe does it again." I removed the ski, stored it beside me, and rotated until I could get on my knees, making my survival job a lot easier. By packing the drift near the edge with the extra snow, I built wind protection and shelter.

I examined my handiwork. Pretty solid. If no one rescued me soon, it could get dark and the rescuers would have to call off the search. I tugged off my backpack to inventory my survival gear. A couple of flares, a hundred feet of rope, five carabiners, a hammer, some food and water, a Swiss Army knife, a flashlight, several glow sticks, and other miscellaneous odds and ends for detective work.

I ate a roll and some cheese. Drank a little water. As the strength from the food warmed me, I heard voices again. This time stronger.

I whistled through my teeth as though calling Lightning to come home. I yelled and shouted.

The voices got louder. I could hear Alex.

"Here." I breathed deeper. Shouted again. "Alex, over here."

"Gabe, where are you?" Sofia said. "We can't see you."

"I'm on a ledge by the cliff."

About ten feet above me, the height of a basketball hoop, Alex inched his head over the lip of the dropoff to see me. "What's happening, bro?" He laughed. "Did you decide to camp and make a snow fort?"

"If you drop down a grill with some steaks and BBQ sauce, this would be a great vacation spot." I craned my neck to see the heads of the others creeping into view. "But since there's no bathroom down here, drop me a line and pull me out."

"Still being bossy?" Alex's head disappeared. The end of a rope fell to the cliff. "Can you strap in or do you want to climb out?"

I knotted the rope in a few places. "Climb out." I threw the left ski to Bastien, ensured Alex kept the cord tight and climbed the wall. Near the top, Bastien and Alex grabbed my arms and pulled me to safety.

"Where'd the chaser go?" Bastien glanced around the ski trail. "There's no sign of him."

I pointed at the edge of the cliff. "He missed the turn."

Chapter 26 – Russian Entanglement

IEG Main Security Office, Albertville, France
Wednesday, 15 January 1992, 6:09 p.m.

Willie's office buzzed with activity. I waited almost an hour with Sofia, Bastien, and Alex to see him.

"Mates, what do you have for me?" Willie's feet were on his desk, his chair lounged back, and his fingers woven together.

Alex pointed at me. "Why don't you start with Gabe?"

I opened my backpack and deposited two plastic bags on our friend's desk. "Other than this, not much."

Willie raised an eyebrow. "And these are…?"

I set the backpack by my chair. Lifting the first bag containing the metal shard, I settled it near a folder. "Your forensics crew should test this piece of metal for stress and fatigue." I plucked the second bag off the desk. "Also for forensics." I placed the bag next to the first one. "We decided to get a sample of the residue from one of the tower heads where an explosive cut the metal."

"That's it?" Willie's laid-back manner made me wonder what he thought about our work. As a general rule, he showed more interest in our finds.

Alex handed our friend eleven pictures printed by the police staff while we waited. "The photos show several parts of the severed pole, a fingerprint shot, and some of the quads on the ground."

"Quads?" Willie glanced at each photo. "You mean the four-seater chairs?"

"Right." Alex sat in his chair.

"Does this have anything to do with the IEG drug runners?" He leaned back and folded his hands together again.

I sipped my hot chocolate. "The catastrophe connects straight to the Elim Games. By sabotaging a ski lift, maintenance crews will have to close IEG lifts until they reinspect them."

"Distraction." Alex shifted. "More work for your staff and less you can commit to the main problem of fighting drug trafficking."

Wille grinned. "Why would the drug runners work that hard to distract me?"

"Not just you." I stood to stretch my legs. "The entire International Elimination Games Committee might be distracted by the news. And the effort used to make this happen is like a military organization."

"Like a KGB operation." Alex dug into his backpack and drew out a pistol. "Does this look familiar?"

Willie accepted the pistol from Alex. "A Makarov .38 caliber. Good on ya, mate. That's a Russian make and model. Where's the lad who carried this ancient weapon?"

Alex shrugged. "Not sure. I left him unconscious on the trail." He produced the ammo and set it on the desk. "But he's Russian without a doubt. I heard him swear in Russian while he chased me."

Willie glanced at me. "Did they chase you too?"

I laid out the whole story. "When I made that hard turn near the cliff, I thought the guy flying after me would grab a tree, but he didn't. I doubt he made it." I lowered my head.

"No worries." Willie left his chair, came around the desk, and put a hand on my shoulder. "You can't stop what the enemy will do."

I took a deep breath. "Right." I swallowed. "Anyway, back to the ski lift sabotage. My theory is that they used det cord to separate both tower heads from their concrete columns, making them both fall in the same direction." I demonstrated with my hands.

"Whoever laid the cord must have failed their explosives training. They took off their snow gloves to do it." Alex drank some coffee. "The photos show their fingerprints."

Willie rubbed his chin. "And how would they get access to the towers unseen? Someone must have noticed them."

I nodded. "Could the crew do maintenance work at night?"

Willie leaned forward in his chair, scribbling a note. "I'll be checking that out." He tapped his watch. "I'm running a bit late. Meet me in the morning with the rest of the crew. I'll have breakfast here. Eight o'clock. We should have results to review."

Chapter 27 – Clandestine Orders

Hotel Conference Room, Albertville, France
Wednesday, 15 January 1992, 9:30 p.m.

Genevieve rode the elevator to the third floor of a posh hotel in Albertville. Plush carpet covered the floor. The trim, beige walls sported paintings and pictures of mountain scenes. Next to each door stood polished wooden end tables with fresh flowers. She found room 421 and knocked.

Dimitri Vasiliev opened the door dressed in knit slacks, a white collared shirt, and a smoking jacket. A vanilla scent made a poor cover for the cigar odors. "Punctual." He waved her into the room.

"It pays to be on time in my business." She glided past him into a living room area. Three vanilla candles burned on a coffee table next to a couch in the middle of the room. The sofa faced two over-stuffed chairs accompanied by end tables and a wall of windows that provided a view of the mountains. The open space on the left held the kitchen and a small dining nook. A hallway to the right led to other rooms.

She dropped her purse next to a plush chair, doffed her coat into the other, and eased into her seat. "What's on your mind at this hour?"

He went to a small bar, poured himself a vodka, and wandered over to the chair where her coat lay. "Do you mind?" He deposited his drink on the end table, snagged her jacket, and placed it on the couch. "I'd like to meet on a cordial basis, side by side, as opposed to a face-off between each other."

Genevieve knew the tricks of the trade. Relax your guest, charm them if you have to, and if they don't agree to your terms, get rough, ugly, or both. She would not underestimate him again. "I prefer this seat better."

He pulled out a cigar, cut one end, and laid it next to his drink while he slid his hand into his pocket. "As you wish."

When he pulled out a lighter, Genevieve wrinkled her nose. "Must you?" She opened her hand at the candles. "The aroma is perfect as it is."

He eyed her with a bit of suspicion but placed the lighter next to the cigar. "As you wish." He glanced at her. "Would you like water with lemon?"

She raised an eyebrow. Dimitri remembered the restaurant. She'd rather leave any man she worked with a little off balance. "I'd like a glass of wine, Sangria if you don't mind." She brushed a hand through her hair. "It's after nine-thirty. My last meeting of the night."

"Excellent." Dimitri went to his bar. "I don't have Sangria, but would you like Moscato instead?"

"Merci."

He poured her drink, brought it to her, and motioned at the end table. "Enjoy the snacks."

A wooden bowl divided into three parts contained cashews, chips, and crackers. A separate bowl held a cheese dip.

"You go all out for your guests." Genevieve imagined Dimitri having quite a social life. His rugged looks, good physical condition, and overpowering presence would attract many women.

After a few minutes of small talk, Dimitri got to the purpose of their meeting. "Did you hear about the chair lift fiasco on the non-IEG side of the Val-D'Isère mountain?" He raised an eyebrow.

Genevieve furrowed her eyebrows. Could the question be a trap? She couldn't remember anything except the morning's news reports. "Yes. French officials started an investigation. Someone tampered with two tower heads yesterday, causing them to crash on the ground and injure ten people." She selected a cracker and dipped it in cheese sauce. "But no one died."

"I'm referring to the events of today, not yesterday." His eyes were like dark pools of water. "Did you track the two Zanadu boys today?"

"Of course." Tension coursed through her body. She'd sent one of her enforcers to check on them in the morning. "They met with the Special Investigator from Australia in the morning and went for a ski trip in the afternoon." She nibbled at her cracker and sipped her wine.

Dimitri leaned on the arm of his wicker chair. "Their ski trip turned into an investigation of the ski lift disaster."

She swallowed hard. Cleared her throat. "My contact left when they got to the slopes."

"Incompetence." Dimitri bared his teeth. "Do not use this contact again. We cannot afford a mistake at this juncture. In two days, we falsify data for other country competitors. In the meantime, our performance-enhanced athletes will compete over the next four days to win events. Pending their performance, we can make a lot of money and impact for our nations." His knuckles whitened as he gripped the chair arm. "We must eliminate these boys."

Genevieve held her tongue. Stalling, she dipped another cracker into the cheese and locked eyes with Dimitri. "But these children— they are harmless. No threat." She waved her hand dismissively. "Their detective credentials probably come from cereal boxes."

Dimitri snorted. "Bah. You don't understand." He stood, taking his drink with him. "We lost an operative today, one of the better ones. A second will also be out of action. Because they chased these harmless children."

While Dimitri stomped to the bar to pour another vodka, Genevieve sucked in a breath. That man drank like a fish. She ditched her frivolous prejudices and honed in on the problem with the boys, chewing on her cheese and cracker. In a moment, she'd thought of an idea.

"We cannot eliminate them." She stiffened her back at Dimitri's glare from the bar. "Their father's position is too high in the military intelligence community."

"All the better." Dimitri set his drink on the dining table. "We can teach the Americans that no one is off-limits."

"Instead, we can scare them." Genevieve did not waiver. If she showed any weakness to the Russian, she would lose her entire business. "What is precious to them that they cannot lose? Let's ransack their rooms and steal their dogs."

Dmitri scowled. He grabbed his drink and strode to his chair. He rocked the chair when he sat. "The dogs are the children's concern, not the parents." He raised his glass to drink and paused. "We must strike to put fear in the parents' hearts. Then they will leave."

Genevieve backpedaled in her mind. Soon Dimitri would be murdering people to satisfy his goals. She couldn't allow that. A stain of that magnitude on her record would topple her business and discredit her in the industry, even in the criminal world. Whatever plan Dimitri proposed, she decided to agree on the surface and ensure that the outcome didn't include a fatal result.

"What do you have in mind?" Genevieve swirled her wine, watching the pink Moscato glisten in the low-level lighting.

"Something a little more permanent." Dimitri's teeth appeared again when he nodded. "We will erase one of the boys from the canvas. A loss like that will send the family packing."

Genevieve wrestled inside to understand the Russian's plan. "What does that mean?" She sipped the wine. "Do you want them to go missing?"

Vasiliev drained his drink, stood, and offered Genevieve her coat. "I have business to attend to in a few minutes. For your part, you can punish the boys for their meddling by ransacking their room. Take something valuable to them. I'll take care of the other arrangements."

She nodded. "Consider it done."

Dimitri grabbed her wrist before she left, swinging her back from the door. "And keep an eye on the Zanadu boys' every move. Be ready to execute my plan."

She jerked hard to free her hand, fire in her eyes. "Watch your step with me, Vasiliev. Don't touch me again." She clenched her teeth, seething. Turning, she left the apartment, racking her brain for a way to minimize his influence in their partnership.

Chapter 28 – Terminated

IEG Main Security Office, Albertville, France
Thursday, 16 January 1992, 8:00 a.m.

Willie's office smelled great at eight in the morning. Hot coffee aroma mixed with the smell of sweet pastries and a platter of sliced cheese and meats.

"Come in, the lot of you." Willie directed us over to the food. "Let's start with a little breakkie."

Izabella mouthed the word to me and lifted her shoulders.

"Breakfast," I whispered. "Aussie language."

I sat next to the coffee, hot chocolate, water, and assorted food. To my right sat Izabella, Sofia, Alex, and Bastien, next to the door. Willie sat at his desk.

We snagged paper plates, ate first, and discussed how we liked the IEGs.

"If I could see a few things, I'd be happy." Alex shook his head. "The drug runners have kept us busy."

"That'll end today." Willie rolled his chair closer to his desk. "After our discussion this morning, I'm taking you off the case."

"You're kidding." I edged to the front of my seat. "After the crazy things they've done to me and the rest of us? We should have justice."

Willie smiled. "Indeed, you should. I reckon justice means a reasoned approach to the evidence and a thoughtful ruling based on what we find." He scanned the group, eyes lighting up when he came to me. "We can't enforce the law based on retaliation or emotional revenge. Right, Gabe?"

"But they fired pistols at us, chased us downhill on skis, and buried me under a pile of snow." My pulse raced. "I have the right—"

Willie raised his hand. "You, none of you, has a right to any police information or ability to aid in the investigation." He pushed himself out of his chair, rounded his desk, and sat on a corner facing us. "You're not here to be investigators. You're here for the Elim Games. And you should enjoy them."

Alex scratched his chin. "Are we detracting from your investigation?"

Willie threw his arms wide. "This whole thing is a dog's breakfast. Unscrambling one team from another is hard on both the good and bad side."

Izabella looked at me again.

"He means a mess." I kept it low, but Willie laughed.

"I still have me old vocabulary." Our friend gazed at each of us. "Alex and Gabe can be my interpreters."

"What about the evidence we left with you yesterday?" I munched on some cheese and ham.

Willie reached behind him, shuffled through some reports, and selected one. "Forensics confirmed the pistol is a Russian make and in use now, though a new model is planned for release next year. No identifying marks on the gun, including fingerprints." He scanned the room. "It's clean."

He dropped that report and grabbed another. "The residue on the scrap of metal and from the pole that held the tower head is from two sources: det cord and C-4. Since the explosion occurred during the workday, the crooks used timers to activate the bombs. However, no physical evidence remains of the timers." He searched for another report.

"Where did they hide the timer?" Bastien crossed the room, filled his second paper plate with food, and returned to his chair. It creaked when he settled in.

"We're having the detectives check the top of the sheaves, where the rubber wheels move the haul rope, which is invisible from the ground."

"What about the pictures Alex took?" Sofia tilted her head.

Willie gathered several pages, skimmed them, and ran his finger under a line. "The pictures were great. Camera detail excellent."

Bastien grinned. "Better equipment makes for better evidence."

"The fingerprints are with Interpol. No results yet. The other shots do show a specific cut pattern to the metal. The suspects meant for both tower heads to fall in one direction."

I tapped a finger into the center of my open palm. "That makes my point." I gestured at the reports. "With the info we gathered, you'll have a strong case against whoever caused the accident."

"The local police didn't like how you obtained authority to look at the site." Willie pointed at Bastien. "How did you make that work?"

Bastien widened his eyes and put his hand on his chest in surprise. "A mere coordination issue. I told them my father talked to his friend, the Chief of Interpol French operations, and I could enter the site with my detective friends as long as we didn't damage the area."

Willie nabbed a notepad from his desk and a pen. "No wonder this has been a headache." He glanced at Bastien. "The local police consider the site compromised because of the amateurs who contaminated one of the poles by touching and dusting it."

Alex and I shrunk back in our chairs. Izabella crossed her arms and Sofia pressed her lips together.

Bastien's chair creaked as he leaned forward. "We did not expect this to be a large problem." He focused on Willie. "I will stay away."

"What say the rest of you?" Willie's expression was open, honest.

Sofia, Izabella, and Alex glanced at each other and nodded.

I sighed. "If we have to, I'll do it." I stuck my chin out a bit. "But if they mess with me one more time, they'll be sorry."

"Good on ya." He pointed at Alex and me. "I'll feed any additional information I think you need to know through you two. And I'll still put a tail on you for your protection." He winked. "It's a different cop. Her name is Laura Schofield, from England."

"I hope she's better than the last one." I drained the last of my hot chocolate and tossed the cup into the trash. "I don't need to go cliff camping in the snow today."

After some goodbyes, we left and went to our hotel.

I tossed out our plan for today to see if anyone might be interested. "We're going to Tignes for the eleven-thirty Women's and Men's Moguls Elimination Finals. Who wants to go?"

Franco shook his head. "I'm a little tired. I'm saving my strength for the hockey game in Méribel later today."

Izabella held a hand to her stomach. "Not feeling well. See you tomorrow."

Sofia slid her arm around Alex's. "Count me in."

Bastien checked a sheet of paper. "I can't be there at the beginning, but I'll join you later."

"Let's take the ten o'clock bus." Alex glanced at Sofia with raised eyebrows.

"Sure." Sofia squeezed Alex's arm and smiled. "See you at the bus stop."

Chapter 29 – Demolition Derby

Shuttle Stop, Albertville, France
Thursday, 16 January 1992, 10:00 a.m.

The bus to Tignes left on time. We arrived with Thunder and Lightning, met Sofia, and boarded. Alex sat with Sofia on the left side of the bus, with Thunder next to the aisle. I sat behind them with Lightning.

The bus departed and drove on the outside lane of a cleared four-lane highway surrounded by snowy fields. Off the road's paved shoulders, tips of rocks pierced the snow.

I felt bored. Left out. Alex and Sofia sat close. She giggled and he smiled while she bubbled over with unending chatter, including how well she knew Tignes and Val-D'Isère since both nestled next to the Italian border three miles away. Thunder stationed himself on the floor, swiveling his head to check out new people who boarded. I didn't have anyone to talk with but Lightning.

"What did you think about the skaters who raced?" She twisted to see his face better.

Alex rubbed his chin. "I liked the—"

"Watching the girls, I bet." I tugged myself closer, ruffling Lightning's hair and thrusting my head next to theirs. "I tracked the monitor information to see their country of origin. The stats they showed were amazing for the USA. In fact—"

"Out of my face." Alex gave me a deadly glare.

Sofia rolled her eyes.

Alex's sharp reaction would have stopped most people, but not me. I knew how to push my brother's buttons. At least he recognized me instead of ignoring me. Thunder wasn't even bothered.

"I'm not in your face." I widened my eyes. "I thought we were all going to Tignes as a group, to build our camaraderie."

Alex shifted to face me better. "Can you—"

"Gabe." Sofia pointed at a mother in the aisle, grasping a plastic loop from the ceiling while a young girl clung to her side. "We can talk at Tignes, but would you be a gentleman and let that lady and her daughter sit?"

I stole a glance. "Of course." I slid out of the seat, cradled Lightning, and motioned for the woman and child to sit. She said something in French and seated her girl first before sitting.

For a few moments, I hung by the plastic strap, rotating back and forth, watching the scenery. Lightning licked my cheek. I squeezed him. "Love you too, little one." My mind wandered while the bus accelerated. Until a garbage truck banged into the bus's left rear corner.

Heads turned to the rear. Riders yelled. The truck behind us weaved and took the inside lane of the four-lane highway on our left. The mother drew her daughter into her arms.

The garbage truck slowed and the gap between us widened. If we wrecked while speeding along at forty miles an hour, lots of people could be injured.

"That guy's nuts." Alex, sitting next to the window, peered back at the truck. "When he hit the corner of the bus, we could have spun off the road."

Thunder wiggled until his forepaws were on the seat and he could see out the window.

"Settle, boy." My brother stroked him.

Sofia got on one knee to see above the people's heads behind her. "Is the truck driver drunk?"

Our bus slowed.

The garbage truck's driver braked, keeping his vehicle behind us and to our left.

I swiveled on my plastic strap to watch. Lightning's ears perked up.

"Is it gone?" Sofia's concerned face stopped the wisecrack I wanted to make.

The vehicle stayed half a bus length behind, like a race car drafting to conserve fuel.

"No." I bent lower to see inside the truck's cab. "And the guy driving isn't drunk. He's focused on the road and talking on a radio of some sort."

Alex stood and pivoted to the see behind the bus. "Our tail is two cars back. A blue Fiat with an antenna. And she's on her radio."

The truck increased its speed, passing the rear end of the bus.

"That guy's one of the four from yesterday." Sofia pointed.

"His beard and face are the same." My jaw tightened. "Those guys are relentless."

The man driving the truck scanned the bus. When his eyes caught sight of me, Alex, and Sofia, he nodded. Got on his radio. Then launched forward.

Moving close to the median in the middle of the road, the truck swerved right, smacking into the bus's front end near the driver. The collision threw the passengers into each other. Several fell into the aisle.

Thunder slid into Alex, his paws clawing for footing on my brother's lap.

I tightened my grip on Lightning.

The fasten seatbelts sign at the front of the bus illuminated.

I chuckled. *Good timing.* Anyone in the aisle, like me, didn't have that option.

The passengers in seats scrambled to find their seatbelt straps and put them on. The woman in my previous seat frantically searched, but couldn't find a seatbelt.

The bus driver tried to stabilize the vehicle. Powered through the slides and skids. Tires screeched. Smelled like burning rubber. Passengers whipped back and forth. Grabbed for handholds. A little girl cried.

The traffic behind us slowed.

Our bus driver wrestled with incredible strength. The bus stayed on the road.

"Brace yourselves." I gripped my strap and prayed it would stay attached to the roof.

The garbage truck slammed into the bus driver's seat area again. The truck's driver kept contact, shoving the bus toward the road's shoulder.

The wheels dropped off the pavement, jerking the bus. People screamed. When we plowed into a field, one yelled, "Lord, help us" in German.

For a second, I thought we'd be fine. The bus clumped straight over a few rows of the tilled field. But we hit a soft spot. The right front wheel of the bus jammed into the dirt, throwing everyone forward. The vehicle changed direction and bounced forward. Off balance, it tilted right. The shouts got louder. More urgent.

"Hold on to something." Alex gripped the seat in front of him with one hand, Thunder's collar with the other. Realizing he might choke his dog, he let go. "Stay low."

Thunder dropped to his belly, his paws searching for purchase on the smooth floor.

Sofia's hands grabbed the seatback like Alex. But the lady who took my old seat tucked her daughter next to her and clutched at the back of Alex's seat with one hand.

I jammed my feet against the seat supports. Released the overhead strap. I clamped one hand on the seatback behind the lady, gave Lightning a quick hug, bent over, and set him on my left shoe. "Hang tight, buddy." With a split-second to spare, I slapped my right hand on the seat top in front of the lady.

The woman's eyes widened in fright, mouth and jaw tight.

"Stay calm." I nodded to emphasize my shouts. "Lean toward the window."

The bus reached its tipping point, lurched, and ground to a halt.

The din of voices made conversation impossible. The bus flopped onto the ground, the right side resting on the ground, making it the new floor. The original floor became a wall, and the left side transformed into the roof.

I stood on the seat supports now below me. The woman and her child crashed into my wide-open arms. She wrapped an arm around one of my shoulders. I bent backward under the strain, praying I wouldn't drop them.

Thunder slid straight down the floor, now vertical like a wall, getting tangled with the people piled against the bus's right wall, which rested on the ground.

The bus rocked for a micro-second and stabilized.

The woman's arm slipped from my shoulder. Balancing, I released my grip on the back of her seat, twisted, and gently lowered the girl.

"Slow motions." I released some of the pressure against the woman. "Lower your feet next to mine.

She said something in French I didn't understand.

Sofia talked to the woman in her language. The lady nodded. She extended her foot, tracing my leg to the seat support I stood on. With one foot secure, her eyes brightened. She repeated her actions and stood on her own.

With the weight of the woman and her daughter off my arms and back, I checked the seat below me. Thunder, on his feet, barked at Alex. Both passengers below him were out of their seat belts. The two women stood close to the bus windows to distance themselves from Thunder and give me room. One of them rubbed her head.

Lightning yipped.

"Jump." I let my buddy hit the new floor of the bus first, followed him when he leapt out of the way, then assisted the woman and child.

Several passengers groaned. Alex, Sofia, and I, along with our canine escorts, moved around to see if we could help. The right-side windows became the walkway between the top of the seats and the bus's roof. Most windows remained intact even when we walked on them. We discovered several people with broken arms, a shoulder injury, and many with bumps and bruises on our search.

"That's not good." Alex pointed to the front three seats.

Five people, groaning, lay piled near a window. One was an older gentleman whose head lay on top of a shattered window where a large rock poked inside the bus.

Thunder whined. Lightning tried to reach the man, sniffing the area.

"Back." I gathered Lightning in my arms.

Alex pulled Thunder away from the injured people. "Stay." Thunder lay on his belly. I set Lightning next to him. "Wait." My buddy snuggled next to Thunder.

The driver shouted in German.

"The ambulance is coming." Sofia translated the bus driver's announcement. "Should be here fast since we wrecked not far from Albertville."

"Sofia, ask the driver if he has a first aid kit and blankets." I worked with a person lying on top of the old guy while Alex checked the one by his side. Sofia translated when we helped a few people out of the way.

"Is there a doctor on the bus?" Alex shouted while moving a woman to the side with me. Sofia translated, but no one came forward.

A loud banging came from the rear of the bus. Both dogs raised themselves to see the back door.

The driver pushed a button and the emergency door in the middle of the back clicked open. Passengers strained against the door but couldn't open it more than a few feet. With our vehicle on its side, the hinge to swing the door open occupied the upper part of the rear panel, making the door about five feet off the ground.

A woman's voice came through the crack. "I'm Detective Schofield, with the Albertville police. An ambulance is on its way. Do not panic. We have the situation under control."

A guy yelled, "My friend needs medical attention. Now."

Alex and I kept working and cleared the rest of the people away from the old man.

"He's breathing." I slid to one side.

Sofia held his wrist. "Pulse is strong."

Alex surveyed the situation. "We can't move him. Could have neck or spinal issues."

"Does anyone know this man?" Sofia glanced at the passengers without results.

The exit door creaked open. A female in a police uniform stood on something outside the bus, lifting the door to its open position and locking it. She sounded like a tour guide with her British accident. "The ambulance and paramedics will arrive in three minutes. If you can move to the bus's rear, I'll assist you in exiting. A new bus is coming. I recommend every passenger talk to the paramedics for medical screening. If you cannot exit in this way or need more medical attention, stay where you are." She repeated her announcement in French.

"We have a critical injury in the front." I stood, waving my arms. "An old man, weak breathing, pulse strong, head injury with glass, and maybe neck or spine injuries. We can't move him."

She disappeared. Returned in a minute. "I've notified the ambulance. They'll arrive in one minute."

When the ambulance crew arrived, they told the riders still on the bus to stand between the seats and allow them to have a clear path over the windows to the front of the bus. Climbing in the open emergency exit door, the crew rushed in with a backboard to move the man and relieve us.

After collecting our dogs, we exited the bus, talked to the paramedics, and plodded to Detective Schofield's car.

"Novel idea." Alex tapped the car hood. "Using your car as a step stool to open the exit door and get us out."

She peered over a clipboard at me. "You Yanks say that necessity is the mother of invention. I'm brilliant, I guess."

"Can you help us contact a friend?" I used my best 'I'm helpless' smile. "Bastien Dubois could give us a lift. You know him?"

She rolled her eyes. "Of course. I've studied your junior detective group. I'm not surprised a bus ride isn't good enough for you." She radioed her police station with the request. "Next thing you'll want is a meal and a free lift ticket."

I rubbed my hands together. "Can you do that?"

"You're incorrigible." She answered her radio when it squawked. "Your ride will be here in five minutes. Try to stay out of trouble for the rest of my watch. I go off at five this afternoon." She tore a sheet of paper off her clipboard, eyeing us close. "Think you can do that?"

"Is that a hidden threat?" I crossed my arms.

The radio went off again and I didn't get an answer.

Chapter 30 – Kidnapping

Accident Site, Thirty-five Kilometers from Albertville, France

Thursday, 16 January 1992, 11:03 a.m.

Bastien arrived on time in his four-wheel-drive Mercedes. Thunder, Sofia, and Alex went in the back seat. Lightning and I rode shotgun. On the way to the event at Tignes, we grabbed sandwiches and drinks at a café and watched the last of the mogul competition. We strolled away, going through the town to Bastien's car.

"You don't mind driving us to Women's Combined Slalom at Méribel?" Sofia adjusted her knit hat.

"Not an issue." Bastien motioned for us to cross the street. "I have business to do there and the hockey game is in the same town later."

I used a store window for a mirror when we crossed. "I can see our detective babysitter is still on duty." Schofield's reflection showed her meandering along, gazing at store windows.

"She still has three-and-a-half hours left on her shift." Sofia stopped at an Italian Ice shop. "I'd love an ice cream before we go."

Thunder faced away from the store and growled.

"Wait." Alex focused on the window and did a one-eighty, inspecting the opposite side of the street. "Check out the alley."

Across from us, in a small gap between the stores, wide enough for two people to walk side by side, two men struggled with Schofield. The tall man wrapped his hand over her mouth and the second knocked her legs out from under her. They pinned her to the ground. The smaller man jabbed something in her neck and she went limp.

"We've got to help her." I dashed to the street, my dog beside me, but a car aimed at us. "Lightning, heel." I darted back to the sidewalk. "Run to the car."

We raced in the direction of Bastien's parked car, the dogs in the lead. At the first intersection, three burly men headed our way.

"Option two." Alex whistled for the dogs and spun me around.

We sprinted in the opposite direction.

Bastien gasped for breath. "Slower."

Sofia tugged at Alex's jacket. "We can't leave Bastien behind."

I reversed course, dropped back to Bastien, and patted his back. "You can do it." A glance further back showed the men tracking us at a casual pace. "Our pursuers must be confident we're trapped. They're walking."

"If we go into a store, I bet they won't attack us." Sofia pointed at a sports clothing shop. "Too public."

Alex kept pushing ahead. "If they used a needle on Schofield, we'll suffer the same."

I paused at a store entrance. "In here." I pointed at the snowmobile sign. "Let's see if there are any we can rent."

We darted inside. The sales rep turned in our direction. "Can I help you?"

Rushing to the counter, the words spilled out of my mouth. "We need two snowmobiles. Fast."

"Will that be rental or for sale?"

"Rental," Bastien said while gasping for air. "We're in a hurry."

The clerk opened a wooden key cabinet behind him. "I'll have to do paperwork. Do you have a license? And what brand do you like? We have a wide price range. I have—"

Bastien fired some rapid French at him. The boy's mouth shaped a wordless 'Oh,' and he whipped two keys out of the box and pointed to the back. "I'll lock the door."

As he moved to the front, I scooped the keys with one hand. "Let's ride." We grabbed helmets and dashed for the door, jamming the headgear on and tightening the chin straps.

The dogs galloped with me when I burst out the back door. The snowmobiles sat on the snow base, lining the backside of the shop, facing out.

I threw a key to Alex.

"The clerk said the first two snowmobiles on the right are ours." Bastien pointed.

Sofia climbed on the first one, Alex behind her. "Up Thunder." He sandwiched Thunder between the two of them. She tried the key without luck.

"Change keys." She handed the key to Alex. He tossed it back to me and I reciprocated. Sofia's second attempt resulted in a mighty roar.

I settled into the driver's seat and fired up my machine. I unzipped my coat a little, leaving a breathing opening, and stuffed Lightning inside. "Let's roll."

Sofia, Alex, and Thunder took the lead, charging to the tree line. I dropped my machine into gear, racing to catch them.

Bastien pounded me on the back. "They've got snowmobiles too. And they're gaining on us."

I gunned my engine, staying in Sofia's track to gain on them. When our snowmobile closed in, I yelled to get their attention. Alex turned around.

"Go for a mountain trail." I waved at the backside of the mountain range.

He tapped his ear and shook his head. Leaning next to Sofia's ear, he said something. Their snowmobile reduced speed.

I whipped sideways and pulled alongside them.

"Italy's to the right." Sofia motioned to me. "Follow us."

Bastien waved his arm. "We should stay in France and go left. I know my home mountains. The paths can be tricky."

I peeked at the side mirror while we barreled ahead. The bad guys were gaining.

"Break into two teams." I tapped my chest and pointed left. "Call when you're safe."

Alex tapped his chest and pointed right. "Stay safe." He told Sofia what to do.

We diverged in a Y.

Chapter 31 – Snowmobile Trick Track

Tignes, France

Thursday, 16 January 1992, 1:03 p.m.

We played the cat and mouse game with our two pursuers for an hour. Being the mouse wasn't fun. The chilled air made my arms and face numb, but Lighting kept my chest warm and Bastien's heat protected my back.

"Gabe, go left." Bastien tapped my shoulder.

I veered in that direction, slicing through the snowy crust. Over the sound of our engine, I could hear the other two engines bearing down on us when I slowed for turns. They sounded close.

"We've done this trail before." I followed the tracks from our earlier drive through these trees. "Those guys almost caught us last time."

Our pursuers weaved from side to side, trying to scare me off of the course to upset our snowmobile.

"Look out." Bastien grabbed tight when one assailant flew out of a stand of trees in front of us and almost clipped our front end.

"They're splitting up." I flew around a right turn, getting onto a less-used path. "We have to leave that trail behind."

"Dangerous." Bastien tapped my helmet, yelling in my ear. "Beware of dropoffs. It's an old trick racing track."

"That should teach them to chase Gabe Zanadu." I rotated the throttle to accelerate. Lightning yipped at me. "That's right, little partner. We're an unbeatable team."

A roar came from behind us. I glanced at the side mirror but couldn't tell the distance of the pursuer. And I couldn't see the second guy. I twisted around to check.

"Whoa." Bastien's arms gripped harder when the snowmobile drifted left.

"I'm on it." I corrected our direction, spotting the chasers two snowmobile lengths behind.

"First trick is ahead." Bastien pulled even closer. "You have to be at full speed to make it. About sixty-five miles-an-hour."

I checked behind me. One snowmobile length separated us. I twisted the throttle harder to max speed for our machine, about seventy miles an hour with the two of us.

"What's the trick?" I imagined a small jump or a tight curve.

"A loop-the-loop."

My insides turned to jelly. "Are you kidding?"

The snowmobile behind us closed to half a length away. With all my strength, I tugged at the throttle for more speed, but I'd already maxed it out.

"No joke." Bastien's voice seemed sharper.

I ducked under an overgrown tree branch to stay on the course. The trees fell away except for small pines lining both sides of the trail. The chaser lost a little distance avoiding the tiny pines but shifted back on track, his machine creeping near our left side.

I risked one last glimpse.

Inches separated us. The guy could wreck us any number of ways.

"Center line." Bastien patted my left shoulder. "Center line."

A blue line appeared in the packed snow ahead. I put the blue line between my two front skis.

Bastien tapped my helmet. "The dotted blue line means it's safe to veer away. When it's solid, you'll crash if you decide to abort."

The chaser raced beside us, kicking at our machine, and causing us to buck and sway. He kicked one last time and pulled away. Five dashed lines remained.

I went for it. Leaned into the machine. "Go, baby, go."

Bastien's bear hug got even tighter. Crushed my ribcage.

Engine whining, we hit the ramp at seventy. Max speed.

My body vibrated with the machine. My stomach balled into a knot. "Geronimo."

The ramp provided the start of the loop. Like a roller coaster, we flew up one side, became inverted at the top, and screamed down the other side, our tread and skis spitting snow and ice on the down ramp.

"We made it." Bastien sounded ecstatic. "I can't believe we cleared it!"

My throat relaxed. The tension in my arms eased. "Great. What's next?" I checked to our rear. The pursuer behind us lay next to the trail, the machine's windshield and front demolished by a pine tree trunk next to the jump. The man wasn't moving.

The second chaser didn't stop to check on him. He ripped through the snow, coming off a steep hill right at us.

"Keep going." My French friend patted my back. "There's more fun ahead."

"He's going to ram us." I cut an arc off the trail to avoid the collision.

Lightning squirmed, yipping.

"What's wrong, little one?" I drove us to the top of a ridge. "Did you lose your balance?"

The enemy knew the terrain better than me. He stayed below me on a trail that joined with mine ahead. We met at the intersection. I veered off, but we still made contact and bounced right. Enough to tip us over the edge of a fifty-foot drop. The man maneuvered his machine to a stop where he could observe our crash.

I disappointed him.

The sheer drop gave way to a steep slope that slanted a fraction and curved like the side of a bowl. We flew to our right over the edge. I yelled to Bastien. "Lean left."

When my French buddy put his two-hundred and fifty pounds to work, he flattened the trajectory and sideways lean to match the hill. The rear track hit first and our skis plowed through the top layer of soft drifted snow. The powder blinded me for precious seconds. When I could see, the packed layer of snow underneath the powder gave us enough traction to keep moving without getting stuck. In minutes we were on our way out of danger.

"He's still on us." Bastien pounded my back.

I checked the mirror by reflex, but the image blurred, masked by snow. Disgusted, I turned to get a visual.

The man flew after us at incredible speed.

"Must be nice to have a newer, faster model." I pointed straight ahead. "Any more tricks?" Minutes later, after entering a narrow trail lined by pine trees, I got my answer.

"One scary place ahead," Bastien shouted. "An accident waiting to happen."

"What?"

"A condemned bridge over a ravine." My friend cleared his throat. "Twenty feet across. Built of wood."

"Wood?" A shock went through my system. People built wooden bridges for snowmobiles to be tough. "Who condemned it? When?"

"The park ranger. Five years ago." Bastien leaned closer. "Rotten support beams."

The engine screamed when we flew over a hill. A jagged, black line indicated the ravine about half a football field from us. A snow-covered bridge, with red rails on both sides, spanned the gap.

"How wide's the ravine?" I struggled to keep us on line.

"Forty-seven feet." Bastien adjusted his position. "The bridge is rickety. You'll have to slow a bit. Don't freak out when the skis chatter and shake the snowmobile. You can handle anything, right?"

"Right."

The bad guy crested the hill behind us. He'd gained a lot of ground. I estimated we'd reach the bridge a few seconds before him.

Wrong.

We hit an exposed root. I wrestled to keep us on the path, slowing to less than thirty-two miles per hour to correct the steering. My French buddy hung onto me like a heavy magnet bonded with steel. His crushing grip made me breathless.

"He's going to catch us." I increased the throttle when I regained control.

Bastien tapped me on my helmet. "Stay left. No matter what."

The bad guy tried to pass me on the left, but I swerved in front of him. Like race cars battling for position during the straight section of an oval track, we maneuvered for the best path on the bridge. I stayed in front until the trail widened right before the bridge. I swung to the left. The enemy took the right.

He pulled alongside me when we hit the red engineer tape at the bridge.

My skis chattered, sending shocks into my exhausted arms and back. I winced when jabs of pain shot through my back. The red tape fluttered to either side of me, sticking on the windshield.

The guy raised his leg to kick our side.

I focused and stayed left. Sweat trickled to my chin. I strained to keep the skis straight. Instead, the snowmobile bucked and jittered like a runaway jackhammer.

A piece of wood splintered at the center of the bridge. On the right side.

The hit man's machine careened toward the edge of the bridge.

My heart jumped when the back of our machine slipped. With arms like rubber, I struggled to stay on course. Each move brought a new lance of pain. My wrists seemed locked in a vise grip, unable to shift or steer without superhuman effort.

The crack of splintering wood refocused me, energized my body. Tilting right, the bridge began to collapse.

Twenty feet to go. Bastien's grip crushed my chest. Couldn't breathe.

The other snowmobile slipped to the right. The rider gunned his throttle to keep traction, moving in front of me.

Fifteen feet to go. Our machine's track slipped at first, finally gripped wood, and jerked forward. The other guy's day got worse.

He struggled to correct the tilt to the right. He failed. His forward momentum carried him into the right four-by-four support post anchored by wires. The snowmobile hit the post dead-on, ejecting him.

Our machine hit solid ground right when the bridge twisted in the air. Thrown sideways, our forward momentum rammed us onto the snowy pack base. Our tread caught and we jolted onto the path.

I slowed, turned around, and went back near the destroyed bridge to find out the fate of our pursuer. I stopped and shut off the engine.

Bastien dismounted first, wandering to a tree for support. He sat back against the tree and put his head between his legs.

"You all right?" Walking like a cowboy who rode too long in the saddle, I approached my friend. He waved me away. I set Lightning on the ground and walked to the bridge. At that point, I heard a retching sound come from behind.

I crouched, stroking Lighting's back. "He didn't take that very well."

Lightning yipped and trotted to the right of the bridge. After going into the trees several paces, he wagged his tail and barked.

I checked out his find. The hitman lay on the ground, moaning. He was a wreck. His right shoulder and arm didn't look right, his left leg bent at an awkward angle, and lacerations covered his face and neck.

"He's a mess." Bastien ambled over to my side, his face paler than usual. "If he makes it, that will almost be a miracle."

"The injuries don't look critical, but the cold might kill him." I hoisted Lightning to my chest. "We need to tell Willie what happened." I headed back to the machine.

Chapter 32 - Avalanche

Mountains near Tignes, France
Thursday, 16 January 1992, 1:07 p.m.

Sofia drove our snowmobile uphill with daring that would have made any racing skier proud. She darted in and out of trees like they were gates on a slalom course.

"Watch out, Thunder." I yanked my dog's head close to my chest, afraid the branches whipping past us might poke out an eye.

A rumble sounded in the distance. Oh, great. The last thing we needed— a snowstorm to battle through. I searched for the clouds or darkening skies. The pines around me blocked any decent view.

Sofia's deft moves kept us out of trouble. Reaching a short straightaway that broke into an opening for almost a football field length, she turned an ear to me. "Alex, uphill or downhill?"

"Downhill."

She nodded and took the left path. With fearless abandon, she created a trail through tiny gaps between the trees. A downed tree forced us onto another track twice the width of our machine. The path ahead curved around the mountain, a steep dropoff on our left and a rock cliff face on our right. We surged forward, keeping the two criminals several seconds behind us.

The rumble grew louder. Sofia tensed. She said something over her shoulder, but I didn't hear it.

The trees below us on our left became an open field. The cliff on our right smoothed out to a gentle slope. I glanced right to find the dark storm clouds.

Snow exploded over us.

Avalanche.

The micro-slide poured over the trail.

Sofia clung to the snowmobile handles. Snow slammed into our snowmobile, sweeping it off the trail.

The flood of snow knocked Thunder and me off the back. I held my dog tight. My helmet hit a rock, dazing me. But I kept my grip on my buddy, locking my legs around his body. Like a surfer in a wave, I swam with my arms. We stopped moving after I counted to thirty.

I took a deep breath, inflating my lungs to the max.

Thirty seconds of sliding. We could be thirty feet under or have traveled hundreds of feet.

Thunder struggled against the snow. I sensed his legs churning, which meant the snow hadn't set yet.

My mind raced through the previous avalanche training and checklist in my brain. Swim to stay close to the surface. Passed. Get rid of backpacks or other nonessential gear. Failed. But maybe the backpack's extra weight could mean I faced the sky.

I continued through the list. Take an avalanche beacon. Nope. Didn't have one of those. Inflate your avalanche airbags. Out of luck there. Expand your lungs to total capacity and carve an air pocket in front of your nose before the snow sets. I did take a deep breath. But I needed to create that air pocket. Count to track time and keep calm. I worked on it.

Thunder thrashed around, trying to get out.

"Thunder, take it easy." My legs wrapped around him tight. I doubted he could hear me because the snow packed between his head and mine killed the sound. I called out again anyway. "I'm here." I needed to get him to stop twisting or we'd exhaust what little oxygen remained.

Trapped. In a dark, cold tomb. My throat tightened. Panic struck. I gasped and sucked in snow.

Coughing hard, I struggled to control myself. *Stop it*, I mentally yelled. *Just stop it.*

I clawed at the snow, compressing it into the softer snow and clearing a space in front of my nose and mouth. The tiny air pocket helped. Breathing deep, my mind settled. I wiggled my hands through the snow to connect with Thunder. I *needed* to touch him. When my left hand hit his ear, I stroked him using tiny finger motions, which calmed me. Kept my claustrophobia away. And my canine buddy's drastic squirming lessened.

Forcing myself through relaxing Karate mental exercises returned me to a peaceful state. *Breathe.* When I found I couldn't get enough air for a deep breath, I prayed. "Need a little break here, Lord."

I continued pushing with my right hand, determining my orientation in the snow. My left side felt heavier than my right. Could right be up?

Seconds later, my right hand hit an air pocket. I jammed my hand further and broke into the space around Thunder's muzzle. His body relaxed. I patted him with my left hand.

My arms ached. I sucked the air I could, trying to get enough oxygen. Exhausted, I closed my eyes. I couldn't see anyway, could I? Maybe a short nap would help. Make me feel stronger. What difference would it make? A few seconds here or there. No big deal. I'd dream about....

I jolted awake.

Thunder's nose poked my right hand.

A trickle of fresh air flowed from the space around his head to where I lay. My heart pounded. That's twice I'd lost control. My left hand squeezed my dog's fur. I needed to concentrate or we'd just be another statistic of those who didn't make it.

The air pocket allowed me enough freedom with my right arm and hand to compact the snow into a wider channel around Thunder's head. The fresher air cleared my head. "Thanks, bud. You saved my life."

Were we facing the sky or the ground? Complete darkness enveloped us.

The snow packed tighter with each passing minute until it seemed like concrete. I investigated the space of the air pocket. My right hand moved with ease in a circle, brushing the sides of the pocket. "We might have another seven or eight minutes of good air."

Thunder responded with a deep growl.

I smiled. "Hate to tell you this, bud, but you have doggie breath."

With nothing else to do, I checked the sides of the air pocket again. A hard side made me think I'd touched a boulder. Another part felt soft, like snow. Some tiny pebbles and rocks came off a third area, and I felt the edges of a straight hard object on the other.

"Hey, bud. Found something we can use." I dug around it. Tugged and pushed hard until one end came free. Long, slender, twisted, and hard. Maybe a broken piece of a branch.

Wiggling the object back and forth for close to a minute, it popped out into my hand. That gave me an extra foot or so of reach. I poked it around in several directions. Solid snow.

I heard the sound of a snowmobile, like a distant roar.

"Sofia. We're over here."

The sound faded. We might have a minute or two left.

Fear crept back in. Each statement made my heart beat faster.

We wouldn't make it.

I swallowed.

The odds were against us.

I clenched my hands, and my imagination engaged.

Carbon monoxide poisoning....

I screamed, "Stop it. Fear is a liar."

Fighting back, I returned to my calming routine. Minutes later, I could think straight again. The snowmobile sounded like it came from above me. Maybe my face pointed toward the sky. I poked the stick up using that strategy. No dice. Solid. I pushed to the right and got movement.

I flexed my shoulders. "Focus," I said. My mind sharpened a fraction. I thrust the stick to the right once more and something gave way. Must be the direction of the sky. I punched with the stick several times, causing fresh air to flow inside our snow cave.

"We did it, Thunder." I laughed. "Sofia will find us."

I widened the hole above us.

The snowmobile's roar penetrated through the hole. Sounded near. I thrust the stick as far as I could into the hole and shouted.

"Over here." I wiggled the stick. "This way."

The snowmobile engine died. Something tapped on the stick.

"Sofia." I grinned. "You found us."

Chapter 33 – Rescue Surprise

Mountains near Tignes, France

Thursday, 16 January 1992, 1:35 p.m.

A tap-tap came on the stick. "Sofia might not be able to hear us, bud. We'll have to wait."

In silence, several minutes went by until something hard made a shh sound while it drove into the snow. The tool cracked the signal stick in my right hand.

"Be careful." I withdrew my arm a bit. "If you're shoveling to find me, you almost cut off my arm."

A little light trickled in from the opening made by the digger.

My gut tightened. Why didn't Sofia say something? Couldn't be the guys chasing us, could it? My jaw tightened.

"Thunder, be ready." I touched his fur. "Play dead dog. I'll yell attack when it's time."

I got the normal ruff of agreement.

Two hands grabbed my exposed right arm and tugged hard.

"Ow." The snow above my body didn't give way. "Dig me out."

The airflow improved enough that I sucked in deep breaths. The clean air cleared my thoughts. I needed a plan to defend myself if the person digging wasn't Sofia.

The shovel worked around my body, freeing my head first. The backpack might have acted like a buoy and kept my head higher in the snow by a foot or so. The digger cleared the snow around my torso area next. While that work went on, I used the broken stick to scrape out space around my upper right leg. I removed enough snow to allow Thunder freedom of movement when I climbed out of my hole without giving away his position. The digger would never see him if I could extract my legs without any assistance since he lay with my legs around his body. He could get out on his own.

The digger's precise spadework kept me injury-free.

"You. Get out." Something whacked my helmet while a deep male voice gave the order.

I wiggled. Took my time, all the while knocking more snow away from Thunder. Edging out of the hole sideways, I propped my hands on the edge of the hole to push myself out. Crawling on my knees, I shaded my eyes with my right hand from the sun.

"On your feet." A hand slapped me on my helmet.

I took my time, using deliberate motions to regain my balance and scout out the situation. Acting stunned after being buried, I raised myself one leg at a time and surveyed my predicament.

One of the guys chasing us stood before me; rifle leveled at my chest. "Lay on sled." The rifle's muzzle swung from me to a snowmobile parked under a nearby tree. The machine might fit two, but he towed a sled behind the snowmobile. "Facedown."

I stalled for time to let Thunder dig out. "But I have to rescue my dog. He got buried with me."

"No dog." The rifle swung back to me.

"I know he's here somewhere." I spread my arms wide. "Can't I look?"

"Sled." He cocked the weapon, placed it on his shoulder, and aimed through the sight.

I edged my way nearer to the parked machine, raising my hands in the air. "Don't shoot."

My slow progress bothered the man.

"Move." He came a few steps closer.

I reached the sled and hopped to the other side.

"Stop." The man gave a sharp command. "On the sled. No tricks or I shoot."

Lowering myself into a crouch, I paused. Grabbed the branch of a pine tree to steady myself. I scraped snow off the limb, pretending to lose my balance, and packed it into a snowball behind my right thigh. I cocked my ear at a noise. Snowmobile engines sounded in the distance, getting closer. "Are your friends coming to help you?"

"In sled." The man motioned the weapon. "Now."

Behind the man, Thunder's eyes and ears peered out of the hole. "Attack."

Thunder barked and charged while I dropped flat on the ground.

The distracted man fired and swiveled his head.

I jumped to my feet, brushing aside the branch the pursuer shot off the tree.

Thunder raced at the man.

He raised his rifle.

I threw my snowball and smacked him in the head.

The rifle went off.

Thunder lunged at the man and knocked him to his back. The rifle fell to the side.

I leapt on the snowmobile, switched it on, and gunned the engine. I aimed for the man's head, turning at the last instance. "Sled." I pointed.

Thunder growled at the man and raced past him to jump on the sled.

The man rolled to his side and searched for the rifle.

I gunned the engine and drove straight downhill through the pine trees, following an animal trail.

After three minutes by my watch, I stopped near a major snowmobile trail. With the thick pines surrounding us, the man wouldn't have a shot for a while.

The sound of a full-throttle machine came from the upper part of the trail in front of me. I tweaked my snowmobile throttle and pulled behind a pine tree, facing the path like a police speed trap on a highway. The sound grew. Soon it became a roar.

I goosed the throttle to get me closer to the trail.

The roar died to the regular buzz of an average speed. Sofia sped past my position.

I jammed the throttle on the handle back to full, jerking the sled. I checked on my buddy.

Thunder, who stood when we stopped, flopped back on his belly and came close to spilling out of the sled basket.

"Sorry, boy." I faced forward, raced until I pulled close to Sofia, and yelled at her.

She glanced in her mirrors to see what caused the commotion. Went to full throttle.

We flew across the mountainside for a few minutes, leaving the pines behind and running through open fields of snow.

I slowed. Didn't she recognize me? Or maybe I'm too scary to hang around. I sighed, stopped, and got off the snowmobile to check on Thunder. I hugged him and let him lick my face. "Great job, buddy."

A snowmobile approached us from Sofia's last location. I recognized Sofia when she slowed and halted, hopped off, and hugged us both.

"We made it." She swept her helmet off her head, took off her goggles, and buried her head in my shoulder. Her arms wrapped around my chest. "You're all right."

I hugged her back, glad that she came back for us. "That might be the last time I ride with you. You're a daredevil."

When she released me, I removed my helmet, set it on the snowmobile, and put the goggles on top of the seat. I opened my arms. "One more hug?"

She smiled and gave me another embrace. We clung to each other for a minute before separating. Sofia knelt and stroked Thunder. "I didn't know what happened to you."

"We got buried." I sat on my snowmobile while she kneaded Thunder's ears.

"Alex, I'm sorry." Her hand covered her mouth. "I thought you could hold on...."

"No problem." I grinned. "A little help from upstairs made sure we survived." I pointed to the sky.

"I forgot to pray." She swallowed hard. "I tried to lose that other snowmobile for over thirty minutes." Sofia's hands clenched and opened. "When I drove to the hilltop, the other guy cut me off. I knew if I went around the corner or took a different trail, he'd trap me."

"How'd you lose him?"

She shrugged. "I went on what could be considered a black diamond for snowmobiles. Serving around trees, hugging cliffs, going down forty-five-degree grades, I went through a series of switchbacks. Then I took a mountainous cliff-side trail where my snowmobile barely fit on the ledge." Her lips trembled, eyes moist. "I stayed on the trail. He went off over the cliff." She looked away.

I stood and enfolded her in my arms. "Hey, it's not your fault. These are hitmen who came to take us out."

She cried, soft sobs racking her body. When Thunder nuzzled her leg. she stroked his fur. "Good boy." She sniffled and glanced up at me. "We'd better get to town and report in."

"Yep." I separated from her and grabbed my goggles. "Wonder how Gabe and Bastien did."

Chapter 34 – Lightning Alert

IEG Main Security Headquarters Albertville, France
Thursday, 16 January 1992, 4:00 p.m.

Willie's eyebrows shot into the air when Bastien and I walked into his office in Albertville. "G'day, mates." He rolled his chair back, stood, and waved at the seats by the coffee machine. "Have a cuppa."

We shed our coats and gloves, and I dropped my backpack on the floor. Bastien got a cup of coffee while I chose some Swiss hot chocolate. Drinks in hand, we sat and faced Willie, who already had seated himself. Lightning settled by my feet.

"I take it you're here on business." He leaned back, twirling a pen.

I smiled. "Of course."

"Right." He pointed the pen at me. "I'll let master storyteller Gabe Zanadu bring me up to speed. About how you tried to stay away from the criminals trying to wreck our Elimination Games."

"We did our best." I set my hot chocolate on the coffee table. "However, the drug sellers sent out some hit men in Tignes."

"Two of them took out Schofield." Bastien sipped his coffee. "They put her out with a drug and hauled her away."

Willie jumped to his feet. "We need to get to the trail while it's still hot."

Bastien and I stared. Lightning danced around on the floor.

"We haven't told you the whole story." I pushed myself out of the chair and slurped one last gulp of chocolate.

"Tell me on the way." Willie grabbed his gear, including his gun, and strode out the door.

Bastien and I grabbed our stuff and darted out of the office to catch him. Lightning trotted by my feet.

With Willie's lights and siren on, the ride to Tignes sped by ten minutes faster than expected. I sat in the front seat with Lightning. Bastien leaned forward to be part of the conversation. When I got to the part about the snowmobile trick track, he stopped me with a finger.

"Tell me that again." He pointed at me. "You did a loop-the-loop in a snowmobile?"

I tried to describe it and Willie shook his head.

Bastien cleared his throat. "That particular snowmobile event didn't last long. After several deaths, the county magistrate closed the trail."

My eyes widened. "Did you say deaths? You didn't tell me that before we hit the ramp."

"I figured those crazy men behind us would spur you on." Bastien raised an eyebrow. "You're the second person in the history of that trail to make the trick work."

I paused for a second, letting that sink in before finishing the story of how we got back.

"And where are Alex, Sofia, and Thunder?" Willie dodged a few cars.

"We don't know." I pointed to an alley. "That's where the men took Schofield."

Willie got on his radio and ordered a backup team to our location. He got out, dug in his trunk for a few things, and motioned us over. He handed me rubber pylons and Bastien a spool of yellow tape to keep pedestrians out of the area. Willie gripped a small leather pouch. "Let's go protect the crime scene."

"Did you know about the bus wreck caused by these guys?" I jogged to stay beside Willie. Lightning and Bastien trailed me.

"What?" Willie shook his head. "First things first, mate. Let's cordon off the crime scene, check out what we have, and follow that with chatter about that accident."

We restricted the area using rubber pylons and yellow tape barriers. In the process, I found a gold earring next to a wall.

"Willie." I motioned for him to come over. Lightning sniffed the earring while Willie examined the security of the space inside the pylons and tape.

"Find something?" He grinned.

I pointed. "Docs Schofield wear earrings?"

"I don't know all her clothing habits, but she might."

"If Lightning gets a good whiff, maybe he'll find other pieces of clothing you might recognize."

Willie rubbed his jaw. "I reckon. But," he wagged a finger back and forth, "under no circumstances can he touch, move, or disturb the evidence."

I called Lightning over and gave him the alert-only command. After smelling the earring, he worked the cordoned area. Five minutes later, he barked.

"Hang on." I finished with Bastien and speed-walked to where Lightning sat.

Willie answered a call on his walkie-talkie before joining me. "Did he find something?"

"Yes." I crouched over the snowy ground near Lightning, who began to dig.

"Stop." Willie's sharp command startled my canine partner.

Lightning looked at me.

"Wait." I motioned for Lightning to sit. After he followed my instructions, I stood facing Willie. "Why not dig?"

The Australian detective rubbed his chin. "This is a crime scene and my investigators will be here in a few minutes. If we disturb the scene, the crime analysis division may not reach solid conclusions. You already disturbed that ski lift site yesterday."

"Schofield needs our help now." I patted Lightning on the head. "Lightning may be able to track her scent to help us find her."

"If she wasn't whisked away by a car." Bastien checked his watch. "I have to leave for an appointment if that's okay."

"No worries." Willie's eyes roved over the site. "My guys will be here in no time. We've got it covered."

Bastien trudged away.

My Australian friend rubbed his jaw.

I waited.

After a couple of taps of his finger on his lips, he nodded to himself. "Right. Here's what we're going to do." He removed a can of spray paint from his pouch, sprayed a blue box around the area that interested Lightning, and grinned at me. "Have at it, lad. Stay within the box and show me anything you find." He handed me a few baggies and some plastic gloves. "Follow standard procedures."

"Got it." I knelt next to my dog, pulled on the plastic gloves, and sifted through the snow in the outlined box. Lightning decided to get more involved, sticking his nose in my way. "Sit." At the command, Lighting went back to his starting point and sat.

The team arrived while I worked. They erected cameras, boxed off sections of the alley, and began their search.

"Found the matching earring." I lifted the gold jewelry out of the snow and bagged it.

Lightning barked and jumped. He sniffed the ground and barked again.

I wiped snow off the spot, finding fringe material from a knitted scarf. A few strands. I put them in another bag.

My canine partner stretched and yawned. He'd done his part.

I walked over to Willie. "Maybe these guys came from the Cooperative Team's area. I bet Lightning could track Schofield from this evidence."

Willie, distracted by the other investigators, shrugged. "They could be from any team or none at all."

Lightning yipped and circled a small area outside the taped-off alley.

I joined him. "Another clue?" I studied the ground he sniffed. Two tracks like heels drug in the snow appeared for a short distance—maybe less than a foot.

"Willie." I waved him over. When he arrived, I showed him the depressions in the snow.

"That could have been anything, like a cart or suitcase wheels."

"But Lightning alerted." My canine partner spun in circles, spouting little yips while he turned. "He's excited. We should investigate."

While Willie rubbed his jaw, his walkie-talkie beeped. He snatched it from his hip, listened, and replaced it. "Your brother, Sofia, and Thunder are fine. They're on their way to the office now."

"We still have to find Schofield." I crossed my arms. "You know Lightning can find her. You're acting like most of the other cops. You don't trust us anymore."

Willie arched an eyebrow at me. "You'd better not be wrong."

Chapter 35 – Private Discussion

Val Claret near Tignes, France
Thursday, 16 January 1992, 4:22 p.m.

Sofia and I drove into the town of Val Claret, on the opposite end of Tignes Lake. I found a good place to park near several other snowmobiles. Sofia pulled in next to me. We shut off the engines. I got Thunder out of the sled and met Sofia by her machine.

"Have you ever been to Val Claret?" I glanced a Sofia and around the building.

"No." Sofia pursed her lips. "The name is familiar, but I've never visited. And before we go to the police station, I need to find a restroom. Something better than this."

"France is like Germany, right? Restrooms are set apart for paying customers." I studied the street. "Maybe we're close to a restaurant or hotel. Let's go this way." I pointed to my right.

We hustled to the sidewalk, and in ten minutes we'd located a hotel and 'freshened up' according to Sofia. By asking a few people where we could find the police station, we got the general direction, which we followed for a few more minutes. We found a white Peugeot police car marked with blue and red outside the small station. Inside, we found three desks facing the entryway.

"Excuse me." Sofia waved at the person at the first desk. He wore a blue epaulet with two white chevrons on it. "We need to make a call to Willie Gretzke at the IEG Security Headquarters."

The man stiffened his back. "Why?"

At that point, the conversation went to French. After a heated discussion for a few minutes, the man referred us to the next desk. This guy wore a blue epaulet with a red stripe. Sofia started again. The conversation ended with a referral to the last desk.

I whispered to Sofia while we waited for an audience. "Hope this is going well."

"Not bad." Sofia shrugged. "They don't want us to use their phones unless it's official business."

The third man we saw wore a blue epaulet with a red stripe surrounded by two white pinstripes, with a white stripe above that. He listened, expressionless, to the last man Sofia talked with and waved us forward.

"You wish to speak with a detective named Willie Gretzke, located at the IEG Security Headquarters?

Sofia smiled at him.

The man shoved a phone on his desk to me.

I blinked. "We don't know the number."

The man growled and jerked the phone back to himself, extracting a small booklet from a desk drawer. He flipped through the pages, studied the contents intently for a few moments, and slammed it shut. He seized the phone's receiver and hit three numbers on its base. "Information? I would like you to connect me with the IEG Security Headquarters." In seconds, he handed the phone handset to me. "It's ringing."

I held the receiver to my ear but motioned Sofia to lean close. It clicked. A thin woman's voice in French came next. I handed the receiver to Sofia. She talked for several minutes and dropped the receiver in the base's cradle.

The French policeman glared at her.

"They will call us back in a few minutes."

The policeman, a Major, went back to routine paperwork on his desk. When the phone rang, he snatched the receiver from the cradle. He spoke his name and rank, listened, and handed the phone to Sofia. More French flowed. After several sentences, she hung up.

She thanked the policeman and headed to the door. I followed with Thunder in tow.

Outside, she grabbed my arm, brisk strides whisking us across the street. "Willie is out investigating Schofield's disappearance with Gabe and Lightning. Bastien's okay. They'll send a crew to meet us at the police headquarters in thirty minutes. The dispatcher will notify Willie on the double."

The pressure of her arm guided me to the next place we needed to stop. A restaurant.

"I'm starving." She moistened her lips. "We can get a quick bite to eat here."

"Great idea." I patted her arm in mine. "Follow me."

Thunder settled on the floor between our feet. We draped our coats over chairs. Sofia sat to my right at a round table for two near the front. The plate-glass window gave us a full view of the street and traffic. I set my backpack near Thunder.

I glanced at my watch. A quarter to five p.m. I sighed. Safe for now.

We ordered sodas. I got a sandwich and Sofia selected a salad. I let the waitress know we were on a tight schedule and needed the food brought without delay.

Sofia edged her chair closer to mine until our shoulders touched. "Do you mind?"

I smiled. "Not at all."

She let out a deep breath. "I guess I'm still shaking from that chase."

"Pretty scary." I draped an arm over the back of her chair and rubbed her shoulder.

"But you don't seem scared." She flicked her eyes at mine. "You seem confident, unmoved by what just happened. Don't you care about the men who trailed us?"

The waitress brought our drinks.

I peeled the wrapper off my straw, stuck it in the glass, and gulped some soda while I thought. "I'm an internal processer." I reached under the table, pulled a pen from my bag, then took a napkin from the holder. I placed the napkin flat on the table and drew a diagram. "When information comes into my brain, I analyze it, organize it, and take action."

"You don't have feelings about anything?" She tapped the napkin. "I don't see a heart on here."

I drew a heart pierced by an arrow around the word organize. "For me, I think about things first. The feelings come later. I guess I'm a logical thinker."

She took the pen, drew a diagram of her thought processes. Everything flowed through the heart. "I start with feelings and think about them. Out loud. After I test a couple of possible courses of action, I take the one that feels right." She frowned a little. "Except for skating. That's all automatic."

I chuckled. "We may have opposite personalities."

The waitress brought our meal orders.

I closed my eyes and bowed my head to pray, folding my hands over my plate of food.

Sofia's hand crept into mine. "Pray for us both."

I thanked the Lord for our safety and the food. When I lifted my head, Sofia stared at me.

"You pray at every meal?" Her eyes sparkled at me.

I bit into my sandwich, chewed, and swallowed. "Most times. Sort of a habit."

Munching on her Italian garden salad, she considered that for a second. "My fear…when those guys chased us and you were swept away by the avalanche…." She swallowed. "I hoped you would be okay and that I would make it out alive."

"Yeah." I quickly ate my food and checked my watch. In about ten minutes, we would need to leave.

"I'm thankful that we made it."

"Me too."

We ate in silence for a few beats.

"I can't believe you're not phased at all about what happened." Sofia shook her head.

"But Sofia, I've gone through this at least five or more times." I set my sandwich on my plate and explained the terrifying traps, chases, and encounters that Gabe and I overcame around the world. "I do get scared, but I've found that God's got it under control. He's helped me every time. He even uses a guy named G to send us messages before an adventure begins. And now my Youth Pastor and Emma are teaching me that there's evidence that Jesus' claims about Himself were true and can be verified."

"Emma who?"

I sipped some soda. "Emily, nicknamed Emma, Polkowski. I call her Em. She's a pretty good teacher and a close friend." I got hold of my sandwich, took a big bite, and polished it off. Another glance at my watch. "We need to leave in five minutes."

"Okay." Sofia played with her salad while I talked, taking a few bites. We spent a couple of minutes talking about G and his messages before she excused herself to use the bathroom.

I paid the waitress. When Sofia returned, I asked her to guard my backpack and watch Thunder while I went to the restroom myself. When I returned, we tossed on our coats, I slung my gear on, and we walked out the door, Thunder by my side.

Halfway to the police station, Sofia's voice became thoughtful. "This Emma friend of yours, is she a friend who is a girl or she is a girlfriend?"

I laughed. "She's a friend. You sound like my brother trying to figure out if I'm attached to anyone."

"I didn't mean to pry." Sofia stopped walking.

"Hey." I veered to a store window, out of the other pedestrians' paths. "That's okay. I didn't mean to upset you. I don't have a girlfriend right now. Except for this investigation, though, I'd like to have fun and enjoy this experience at the Games. And that includes being with you." I smiled.

She brushed back her long dark hair. "Of course. Being with me is always fun." Putting her arm in mine, we strolled the rest of the way to the police station. Sofia told me about her extensive training schedule and lack of time to make friends or relax.

We walked into the station to find three men waiting for us.

"Willie couldn't make it?" I probed the senior man of the three.

"He's engaged in finding Detective Schofield." The man inspected Sofia and me. "You're unharmed?"

I gave him a thumbs-up.

"Please show me the two snowmobiles." He stretched out his hand. "I'll take the keys. Both will have to go into police custody for now."

"You know that the one I rode is one of the criminal's machines?" I handed him the keys. "You'll have to do a good search for knockout drugs since that's what happened to Detective Schofield."

After relinquishing the snowmobiles to the men, the senior guy herded us into a medium-sized car. I sat next to a window with Sofia beside me. She leaned on me, head on my shoulder, and closed her eyes. Thunder gazed out the window for a while and lay beside Sofia to doze.

My thoughts swirled. I prayed that they could find Schofield. Next, my mind wandered to Mom and Dad. Mom would be furious that criminals ruined our day out. I dreaded even telling her because her typical response would be pulling the plug on our IEG vacation. But that might be fear speaking because I didn't want this adventure to end. Willie would lecture us about not staying out of trouble. Dad might do the same. And he might send us away.

I gazed out the window. The people on the streets seemed happy, glad to be here. Smiles, laughter, knots of people greeting each other, hugging, and enjoying their wonderful IEG dream.

I shook my head. Our dream vacation seemed more like a nightmare.

Chapter 36 – Discovery

Tignes, France

Thursday, 16 January 1992, 5:37 p.m.

Lightning searched back and forth, sweeping the street for any smell of Schofield. In a few minutes, he acquired the scent and loped along, stopping to confirm from spot to spot.

"Gabe, don't let him get too far ahead." Willie inspected the ground for any other clues while we trailed my dog.

I glanced back. "Sure." When I swung my eyes forward, I couldn't see him. "Lightning, where'd you go?" I sprinted ahead, glancing at each alley I ran past.

A yip got my attention after I passed three side streets. I ducked into the alley. Lightning worked his way back until the street ended in a snow-covered field.

"Looks like a dead end." Willie pointed at the field. "The little dishlicker ran out of petrol."

Lightning skirted the last building and disappeared.

"He might be tracking." I waved at the end of the building. "He didn't go into the field."

A sharp bark came from around the corner. I raced to see what Lightning may have found. He sat in the snow, a few feet from a wooden building, about the size of a large shed. The side's wooden slats were worn. On one end was a door, but my dog wasn't sitting there.

"That about settles it." Willie looked at the wall. "No door here. Maybe they carted her away in a car."

"No." I walked to the shed. "She's in there. Check out the snow by this part of the wall." I stepped back to let Willie see. "No tracks, like it's been swept clear."

Willie tapped his lips, pacing back and forth. "You may be onto something."

A ray of the sun glinted off a nail head on the shed. "That shiny nail is one of the best clues." I crouched and moved forward. "All the rest of the nail heads are rusty. Old. That one—" I pointed above my head. "And that one—they're both brand new."

"That's a ripper." Willie got on his walkie-talkie, alerting others to come with equipment to dismantle a wall. "You may have done it again."

In fifteen minutes, the wall was open.

"Need an ambulance right now." Willie barked orders on his walkie-talkie. "We've found Detective Schofield, but she's suffering from cold exposure. I want a medic here in three minutes or less."

Following Willie's directions, I outlined a square around the end of the building for a search area. A female officer, schooled in forensics, checked Schofield over. She used plastic gloves and baggies to finish her once-over before the medic arrived. She handed the evidence to Willie.

"What have we here?" My Australian friend held out three baggies: one with a lock of hair, one with scraped skin from under the detective's nails, and one that held a program for the event we went to at Tignes.

With Willie's siren going, we reached his security office by 6:30 p.m. We walked in to see Alex and Sofia relaxing on chairs with a hot drink in each of their hands.

"At last, we're back together again." The Aussie dropped his gear on a stand behind his desk and sat.

Thunder and Lightning's tails wagged when they greeted each other, sniffing and licking each other's faces. They lay next to each other while we settled in to talk.

"First order of business." Alex set his coffee on the side table. "We left one of our pursuers on the mountain. The other didn't make it." Alex told Willie the approximate location where he left the man.

"I'll have a policeman get on it." Willie motioned Gilbert into the office and sent him scurrying away. "I'm already checking on Gabe's pursuers. What I need to hear from beginning to end is the details of your chase."

He propped his feet on his desk.

Sofia and Alex took turns. At the end, our Aussie friend brought his feet off the desk.

"These are dangerous, hardened criminals." He scooted his chair closer to his desk. "Because of your earlier efforts, you're each a target for the Russian and French woman." He placed his forearms on the desk, eyes roving over the scattered papers. "Here." He snatched a memo, scanned it, and dropped it on his desk. "The briefing I'm about to give you is essential for your safety. It's not a lecture, but it may come off that way. When I'm done, we'll talk."

Our Aussie friend read directions for staying safe when pursued by criminals, including reporting, checking in at regular intervals, evasive actions, and taking cover under fire. He paused, took a drink, and explained when and how to engage an enemy with a captured weapon. "That assumes you're unarmed to start with." He raised an eyebrow at me.

"I brought a slingshot." I patted my backpack.

Alex pulled out a knife with a lock blade. "For emergencies."

Willie glanced at Sofia.

"Nothing for me but a purse or some skates." She smiled.

"Glad to hear that." The Aussie pressed his lips together before he spoke again. "Serious shenanigans with these hit men and all. Do your parents know about this?"

"Not yet." Alex sighed. "But they will tonight. We were supposed to meet them in Méribel for the U.S.A. hockey game. It's too late for that."

"Mom's gonna have a heart attack." I sipped some hot chocolate.

Sofia glanced at me, shifting to focus on Willie next. "My dad serves in the Italian police force. Our family doesn't tolerate these types of criminals. They would support me."

"Sofia, you haven't been brought in as deep as the Zanadu boys." The Aussie corralled a pen, twirling it in his right hand. "But now you need to know a little more. The Russian man, ex-KGB, must be at the heart of the matter. Since KGB agents never retire, he's creating a scandal. A diversion for creating confusion. His true purpose is to infiltrate the criminal element in France."

"But what about the French woman?" Sofia moistened her lips. "Isn't she more dangerous than the Russian?"

Willie shook his head. "From what we've learned of her activities, she's a drug seller who avoids resorting to fatal actions to resolve issues. She tries to maintain a tight but clean dirty operation." He grinned. "If you know what I mean."

"She breaks little laws, not the big ones." I noticed the donuts on the coffee table. My stomach rumbled.

"Yes." The Aussie tilted his head at me. "Hungry?" He pointed at the donuts. "Go ahead. They're from the morning but should still be good."

I grabbed two and tore into one.

"We have pictures of Genevieve now." Willie set his pen on his desk. "The Frenchwoman will use softer ways to gain information or remove you from the game but consider her like poison. The Russian may control her enough to cause her to break some major laws." Our friend sat back. "Tomorrow, we'll have a new bodyguard on task. Meet me at nine o'clock. Eat first. It could be a long day."

I stuffed the rest of the donuts into my mouth, swallowing them in four bites, guzzled my hot chocolate, donned my coat, and grabbed my backpack. Alex and Sofia got their coats, hats, and gloves on. Alex shouldered his backpack. The dogs followed us out.

After a short walk full of discussion, we reached our hotel.

"You must be starving." Alex squeezed Sofia's gloved hand. "You didn't have a donut in Willie's office and picked over your salad after our adventure. Can I take you out to eat?"

"That would be nice."

"Gabe, why don't you stay here with the dogs. Sofia and I will find a restaurant close by to get some food." Alex widened his eyes at me.

I knew he wanted me to leave them alone, but I wasn't about to be left behind. "Where are we going?" I ruffled Thunder's fur. "I'll take the dogs upstairs and be back in a few minutes."

"Gabe…" Alex's voice got tense. "Sofia and I would like to finish our earlier discussion."

Sofia laughed. "It's okay." She put her arm through Alex's and leaned on his shoulder. "I've never dealt with a little brother before. He'll be cute."

Alex's eyes shot daggers at me.

I trotted away with the dogs, gave them some food and water, and returned in five minutes.

We stayed out until eight o'clock. Alex thought Mom and Dad might be back from the hockey game around eight-thirty. We walked Sofia to her hotel first before trudging back to ours.

"Not sure this session with Mom and Dad is going to be any fun." I kicked some powder snow into the air.

"Mom's not going to be happy." Alex frowned. "We have to let them know what's going on. Maybe Dad can get some support from his military contacts."

We entered the hotel lobby about 8:15 p.m., left a message for our folks to let us know when they arrived, and took the elevator to our room.

I unlocked the door, pushed into the room, and stopped after two steps.

Alex bumped into me. "What—"

I surveyed the upturned beds, drawers lying on the floor, and clothes torn out of the closets.

I dove to check under the beds. "Thunder. Lightning. Where are you?"

Chapter 37 – Canine Catastrophe

Wild Boar Hotel, Albertville, France

Thursday, 16 January 1992, 8:58 p.m.

Two forensics analysts were on their hands and knees in our room, checking for clues when Mom came out of the elevator. Spotting Willie, Alex, and me in the hallway, she knew something was wrong.

"Hey, Mom." I walked over to her.

"What's going on?" She raised her chin at Willie. "What's your detective friend doing here?"

An analyst stuck his head out our door. "Detective, you need to see this."

"We wanted to talk with you about that…." Alex motioned for her to come to the door.

I fell in beside her. "Somebody's taken Thunder and Lightning."

"Not again?" Mom reached the door and peeked in. "Is any place in the world safe anymore?"

"Mrs. Zanadu." Willie came out of the room into the hallway. "Sorry to meet under these circumstances."

"Willie." Mom closed her eyes and breathed in. She opened them, pinning our Aussie friend under her gaze. "We'll need you to give my husband and me a full understanding of the situation. Upstairs." She turned on her heel and left.

After she entered the elevator, Willie shook his head. "She's mad as a cut snake. We'll be lucky to live through the night."

"We need to get this over with." I tried to fake a smile but grimaced instead.

"You lads go ahead." Willie pointed at the room. "I'll follow soon."

Alex and I padded over to the elevator, rode to our parent's floor, and went to their room. Dad opened the door when we knocked.

"I can't...it's impossible to believe." Mom stomped around the room. She stopped and clamped her hands on the back of a chair. "Less than six months ago, some crazy boy kidnapped Thunder and Lightning."

"Honey, this isn't the boy's fault." Dad waved his hands in the air. "The boys didn't start any of this."

"It's that crazy G person who keeps sending notes and clues." Mom shook a fist in the air. "I don't know what he's trying to do, but it feels like he's creating a no-win situation for the boys. Even though he gave them seven keys for seven adventures, they're not adventures. More like dangerous trials."

Alex and I stood to the right of the door and watched. This conversation teetered on the edge of a precipice—a disaster in the making. A storm ready to explode with fury.

Dad grimaced. "Yes, but—"

"No buts." Mom's eyes blazed. "Every time we get a package, the boys' lives are at stake. Why? To stop terrorists, human traffickers, a madman, the mafia...." She paused, breathing fast. "On and on it goes, doesn't it? Who knows what will be next? Maybe chase scenes, maybe hit men, maybe...."

Dad stepped toward her. "I know it's upsetting—"

"Upsetting?" Mom glared at him. "My heart's beating like a runaway freight train. My pulse is pounding in my head. I want to tear this chair apart."

Dad stopped. "Hon?"

She nodded to herself. "I can take the boys to Germany to visit our friends." She kept nodding. "You have to stay here because of military duties, but I… no… we don't have to be here."

Dad scratched the side of his jaw. He wandered to the couch and eased into a comfortable position. "Sure. That's all possible." He shrugged. "We just have to work out the details."

"You're not going to try to talk me out of it?" Mom's eyes darted to his.

"No." He motioned her to sit next to him. "But I don't want you to leave upset like this. We're together now, and with hotel security, we're not in danger."

"I have a headache." Mom let go of the chair, her white knuckles returning to a neutral color.

"Why don't you take some medicine for that?" Dad pointed to the bathroom. "I took a few pills earlier and left the bottle next to your regular meds."

"Okay." Mom went into the bathroom.

"Boys." Dad waved us over. "Your mother and I have a few things to talk about. Come back in a half-hour."

"We've got to get Thunder and Lightning back." I stood by his side, whispering. "I know Mom doesn't want us to stay, but they're our dogs."

Alex kept his voice low. "We need to find them. They're counting on us."

"We'll talk about it when—"

Someone knocked on the door.

"I'll get it." I sprinted to the door and opened it. "Oh, hi. Didn't expect to see you here."

Bastien walked into the room. "I went to your room. They told me to come here. I got your parents' room number from the desk clerk."

"They gave you our room number?" Dad focused on Bastien.

"My mom and dad do a lot of business in the Savoie area." The French boy gave a disarming smile. "I know the woman behind the front desk. Or my mom does. She met her at an interior design class several years ago."

Mom walked back into the room. "Bastien? How are you?"

After a few pleasantries, Bastien looked at me. "Did you forget?"

I racked my brain to remember anything. "Not a clue."

He chuckled. "No matter. We talked about going out to a party to find more information." He side-glanced at Mom. "You know."

Another knock on the door.

"My turn." Alex strode to the door and opened it.

"May I come in?" Willie waited out of courtesy until Alex said yes.

I motioned to the couch. "Might as well sit. We're all gonna want to hear what you've found."

Willie sat on a chair. Bastien seated himself on another chair. Alex and I plopped next to Mom, who positioned herself close to Dad.

"First, we're not done with our analysis of your room." He narrowed his eyes. "But we are doing a thorough search. We have recovered some hair, blood samples, and a dropped ampule of fluid. Nothing to lead us in any specific direction." He shrugged. "We have to talk with the crew on duty here at the hotel to determine if unusual activity took place."

"Professionals?" Dad straightened to focus on Willie.

"Without a doubt." Our Aussie friend leaned forward. "In all likelihood connected to a certain Russian we suspect who is trying to create suspicions about the drug-free environment here. However, I recommend we move the boys to a different room since their current room is a crime scene."

Dad sighed. "I thought you might say that."

"You might consider changing rooms also." Willie looked around. "I know you're comfortable here, but changing locations is one way to stop any immediate actions from these criminals."

"You would be welcome at my parent's hotel." Bastien looked at me. "My parents have many rooms reserved for special guests. Some couldn't make it. They would love to meet you."

Mom bit her lower lip. "That's a lot of work. We have two weeks of clothes and luggage. I couldn't be ready for two hours."

Dad sat back. "The distance would be longer for my work, but that's of no consequence right now. Safety is most important." He glanced at Bastien. "Why don't you call your dad to see if he has rooms for us."

"Of course." Bastien stood. "May I use your phone?"

Willie escorted Alex and me to retrieve a few clothes and personal items from our room while he watched to ensure we didn't disturb the rest of the crime scene. After we collected our items, we went back to our parents' room. Dad opened the door to let us in while Mom packed her stuff for the move.

Willie glanced at Dad. "I'll have a meeting at nine tomorrow morning to update you on what we've found. Can I count on you to be there?"

Dad patted Willie's shoulder. "Count me in."

At 11:30 p.m., we unloaded the last bag from the van and rolled it to Mom and Dad's room in our new hotel, the Vue sur la Montagne (Mountain View) Hotel.

"Boys," Dad walked us into the hall to send us off to our room, "After we all get a good night's sleep, we'll talk again. Come back to our room about seven-thirty in the morning."

Alex and I left. When we reached our room, Alex went straight to the bathroom. He got ready for bed, followed by me. We both lay in double beds near each other.

I wrestled with the covers. Punched the pillow. "We need to stay here and find our dogs." I missed having Lightning curl up next to me at night.

"I agree." Alex rolled toward me. "We need to rescue them and let Willie finish the investigation. Mom's devastated and scared we'll get hurt again."

"Yeah." I propped myself on an elbow. "But those people need to be put in jail. I bet we could nail them with some evidence."

"Maybe, but we can't do anything right now." Alex stared at the ceiling for a few minutes. "Thunder's the best dog anyone could have. We've got to save them. Now."

I slapped the bed. "We can't let the kidnappers torment them as they did in Texas last fall."

Alex shook his head. "We can't waste any time. The last kidnappers planned to kill our dogs. Without us taking action on our own, they wouldn't be alive today." He shut off his light, plunging our room into darkness.

"I bet Willie will help find them." I plopped back onto the bed, pulled hard on the covers, and wrapped myself in a cocoon. I tried to sleep, imagining Lightning's soft hair tickling my face. My eyes leaked tears.

The rustle of Alex's tossing and turning kept me awake.

I tugged my pillow tight over my ears and drifted to sleep.

Chapter 38 – Nighttime Rendezvous

Genevieve stood in her kitchenette, fixing a cappuccino for herself while Dimitri sipped a cognac opposite her in the living area. Her apartment wasn't high-tech or trendy like Dimitri's, but a modest skiers' retreat from a day at the slopes. A couch and two armchairs, with a coffee table in front of them, filled most of the open space, with a dining table and chairs next to the sliding door and balcony on one side. A pair of snowshoes mounted in a crossing pattern hung over the fireplace, which warmed the room with a glowing, crackling fire. A light music track played in the background.

"Bad news again today?" She finished preparing the cappuccino and carried the coffee along with a tray of crackers and chocolates out to the coffee table. She sat in one of the armchairs near Dimitri, who lounged on the couch.

"That would be quite an understatement." Dimitri swirled his drink in the large glass. "Four operatives gone or captured. The children still free to do whatever they want." He tilted his head at her. "What is your assessment?"

Genevieve mixed her coffee one last time with a spoon and placed it on the tray with a click. "I must admit these young boys create a difficult environment to work in."

"Difficult?" Dimitri snorted. "Impossible." We can't make a move without them destroying the results we want. We have to end this."

She slipped off her shoes and tucked her stocking feet beside her in the chair. The informal atmosphere she created would throw off Dimitri's business mindset, making her seem like a frivolous woman instead of a lethal enemy. Plus, she'd dressed in clothing that showed off her figure, redid her makeup before he arrived, and looked fresh and alert. She smiled, knowing she'd done an excellent job preparing for this conversation. "I've been rethinking my earlier estimate of the situation. You're right."

He stared into the fire, sipping a drink. "I have a final solution for them, but it will take part of a day to arrange it. The Elimination Games will become a reality for those boys." He smirked at her. "Can you handle them for a day?"

"I thought we could split them apart." She glanced over the top of her cappuccino. She pushed harder against his authoritarian attitude. "I've already won over the younger boy. Now it's time to work on the older boy while you handle his brother."

"How would we know they've separated?" Dimitri deposited his cognac on the coffee table. "They aren't staying at their original hotel. They are at the Vue sur la Montagne Hotel, owned by Jacques Dubois." He shook his head.

"There are two ways to know what is going on." Genevieve sipped from her cup and placed it on the tray. "You have a few plants in the IEGC's Security Headquarters. Also, I can work on the son of Jacques Dubois, Bastien. I'm sure he has a weak spot I can exploit."

Dimitri snatched a few chocolates from the tray and tossed one into his mouth. "The kids travel together in a group. If we can erase the two Zanadu boys from the equation, the other kids and the security team's investigation will return to a less intense effort."

"If they don't split up, you have the manpower to make that happen." She sipped her cappuccino, enjoying the warmth and the aroma. Her plan would rid them of the older boy on her terms, not his. "I'll plant some drugs on Alex Zanadu and use your man in the security office to blow the whistle on him."

Dimitri laughed. "Impossible. With their Australian friend, you'll never make it stick."

Genevieve smiled back. "I'll manage that part. I can slow his investigation for at least one day. But you'll have to keep the younger boy occupied."

The Russian drained his cognac, stood, and stepped over to her chair. He grabbed both chair arms and leaned within an inch of her face. "The young one may not survive another day. Don't put yourself in the same category. I'm tired of losing men."

He didn't wait for a response. He shoved himself back from the chair and strode to the door. Seconds later, the door's click announced his departure.

The smile on Genevieve's face widened. Perfect. His anger primed him for a significant mistake. One she would exploit to the fullest.

Chapter 39 – Insufficient Clues

Vue sur la Montagne (Mountain View) Hotel, Albertville, France

Friday, 17 January 1992, 7:30 a.m.

The clatter of dishes became louder when Alex and I approached the main dining room. Aromas of cheese, eggs, French Toast, and bacon poured through the open doors of the dining room.

Bastien waved us over to him. "You're family's sitting with us for breakfast. Everything's on the house." He sat with his parents, Jacques Dubois, an influential man in the athletic circles, and his mom, Yvette.

"Thanks." We filled our plates from the buffet and began the meal. Mom and Dad arrived shortly and I went back for seconds. When I got back to the table, Alex tugged at my shirt.

"What?" I speared a piece of ham and wolfed it down. "Delicious."

"Mom and Dad talked about their plans." He whispered while passing me a roll with butter. "Dad told me she's going to visit their friends Karl and Frieda Schultz while he helps us find the dogs. But we only have two days."

I sliced open the steaming roll and slathered some butter in the center. "Got it, bro."

Yvette invited Mom to see the interior decorations she'd done at the hotel. Mom agreed and all the adults stood and left.

"We need to make plans for tonight." Bastien drank from his glass of orange juice. "When's a good time?"

I glanced at my watch and dropped my fork on the table. "It's eight-forty. We're going to be late."

"Right." Alex glanced at Bastien. "Meeting with Willie at nine."

I jumped to my feet. "If we hurry, we can tell Dad and meet him there."

"Be careful." Alex pushed back his chair and stood. "Just a routine meeting. Don't make any waves."

"Got it." I motioned at Bastien. "Let's meet at the speed skating event at four this afternoon. We'll get our other friends and walk to some place we like after the race."

"That's good for me." Bastien waved. "See you later."

The Security Headquarters hummed with activity. Franco, Izabella, and Sofia waited in chairs near the entrance.

"What are you guys doing here?" I said. "Didn't expect to see you until later today. We were going to contact you for lunch."

"Willie called us in." Franco lifted his shoulders. "I guess he didn't want to say things twice."

A few minutes after Dad arrived, Gilbert entered the lobby to take us back to Willie's office, then exited the room. Willie put his phone receiver in the cradle. "Busy morning. Sorry to keep the lot of you waiting."

"Not a problem." Dad sat. "However, Rachel is leaving on a plane this afternoon. I need to leave in a few minutes."

Willie grinned. "Let's get to it." He slipped a report out from a stack of paperwork, gave it a once-over, and handed it to Dad. "The details don't help much. We're analyzing the blood, hair, and fluid which resulted in negative hits on the Interpol database."

"Nothing yet?" I sat on the edge of my seat. "Our dogs are gone. We've got to find them."

Willie's jaw tightened. "We haven't quit. The team's doing more in-depth research."

Dad finished with the report and handed it to me. "Check out the tests."

"Next topic." Our friend tapped a paper on his desk. "We did find evidence on the snowmobile Alex and Sofia brought in. Interpol found prints of two male suspects involved in drug smuggling between Russia and Germany."

"Good." Sofia's eyes narrowed. "What else can be done to get rid of these drug runners?"

"I'm glad you asked." Willie played with a pen while he talked. "Some athletes performed better than expected, especially on the Cooperative Team. We've decided to increase drug testing. We can't allow you to enter due to IEG Security protocols. When we finish today's round of tests, we'll plan the next steps."

Dad checked his watch, stood, and snagged his coat. "Thanks, Willie." He turned to Alex and me. "If you keep your eyes open today, maybe you'll find a clue about the dogs."

"I guess so." I hung my head. Nothing seemed to be going right.

Dad stepped in front of me. "I'll also work to find Thunder and Lightning in my free time. Don't give up." He squeezed my shoulder and left.

Alex got another cup of coffee in a cup to go. "We'll let you get back to your work."

"Don't try anything crazy." Willie pointed at me. "Which includes you, mate."

I collected my coat, threw it on, and chuckled. "Who? Shy and retiring Gabe Zanadu? Not on your life."

Laughter broke out in the group. We left Willie's office and stopped in the lobby.

"What's next?" Sofia glanced at Alex.

"My plan," I said, "is to investigate different venues to find clues about the dogs' location."

My brother smiled. "I suppose you'll find the Russian, ask him where they are, and he'll tell you right away?"

I shot him a nasty face. "At least I'll be doing something. I'm not going to hang around some Security testing site to see if anyone's tested positive."

Izabella shrugged. "That sounds like a good plan to me. Where are we going?"

"I want to see the Luge competitions." I pulled a program from my pocket. "They're at La Plagne, starting at 10:30 and 11:30. We won't make the first run on time, but we'll see the beginning of the second run."

Sofia whispered into Alex's ear. She listened to his reply and announced it to the group. "We're going to Les Saisies for the Women's Biathlon and later to the Men's Ski Jumping teams at Courchevel starting at 2:30 p.m."

"See you later." I walked to the door. "We might see you at the ski jumping event. If not there, we can meet at the Women's Speed Skating in Albertville at four o'clock." Franco joined Izabella and me. We headed out the door to catch the bus to the Luge events.

Several minutes later, Franco tapped me on the shoulder. "Did you see the guy in the red snow jacket? He seems to be following us."

"Let's cross the street." I led Izabella and Franco to the other side, pretending to like some food I saw in a restaurant.

"I'm not hungry yet." Izabella checked her watch. "We need to get to the bus station."

In the reflection on the glass, I saw the red-jacketed man cross the street behind us.

"Let's hurry." I speed-walked to the bus stop, catching Izabella's arm to hurry her along.

At the bus stop, we jumped inside the vehicle's doors right before they closed, and we sped away. I looked out the back window and saw the red-jacketed man standing on the sidewalk, looking disappointed. But he pulled a walkie-talkie out of his pocket, lifted it to his ear, said something, and nodded. He turned, strolling on the sidewalk without a hint of worry.

I bumped into Franco to get his attention. "Our tail contacted headquarters or somebody else. Maybe they'll assign another spy to watch us."

Franco sighed. "I'd hoped we would have some time to enjoy the games without any other excitement."

Izabella brushed her hair to one side. "I'd rather travel on an adventure than sit in a confining crowd."

I wondered what the man in the red jacket did that caused him to walk off. Maybe he got other orders. Or maybe his boss sent him to follow Alex and Sofia.

"Gabe?" Izabella raised an eyebrow at me. "Aren't you happy?"

"Sure am." I laughed. "Can't wait to see people rocketing down an icy slope in a race." I stuffed my concerns into a distant corner of my mind and enjoyed the moment.

Chapter 40 – Cryptic Conversation

Woman's Biathlon Venue, Les Saisies, France
Friday, 17 January 1992, 11:00 a.m.

I enjoyed wandering with Sofia through the crowds in the Women's Biathlon stands area, looking for anything that might lead us to Thunder and Lightning's location.

Behind and underneath the stands, snack shops, restrooms, and memorabilia stores filled most of the area. But under some seating sections, empty cargo areas for loading and unloading left dark nooks and crannies to explore. These areas, protected from the winds, felt warmer than the seats above.

"Let's check underneath the stands for any clues." I pointed at an exit.

Sofia went first and I followed. She wore her white snowsuit. My dark-blue snow jacket kept me comfortable on top. I wore jeans with long-johns underneath to stay warm.

"We've got to find the dogs fast, or they could get hurt." I strode to the closest end of the stands. "I'd like to search from one end to the other."

Sofia captured my arm in one hand and walked close to me. "Slow down. We've got to be thorough. Besides, it's warmer this way."

I smiled.

We strolled. I kept my eyes focused on the details surrounding us, looking past the store customers and folks walking, paying particular attention to the darkened corners and unusual spaces.

"Tell me what happened during your last investigation." Sofia turned her face to mine, a twinkle in her eye.

"I don't want to bore you." I glanced around. "Someone tried to frame me for crashing roller coasters around the country. We found out the culprits and caught them."

"If that's the single bit of information you told me, I would be bored." Sofia gave my arm a playful tug. "Tell me about the excitement. Tell me about...."

When she didn't finish, I stopped looking around and focused on her. "About?"

She pursed her lips. "I'd like to know a little more about the methods you used at the end. You know, the ones that other girl told you about."

I rubbed my jaw. "You mean Emma?"

She shrugged. "Sure."

"The methods we used came from some investigations Emma researched. Using the eyewitness evidence, verifying the reports through corroborating evidence, and checking the scientific methods, we found clues that led us to the real criminals."

"But I thought Emma's case revolved around Jesus claiming to be the Savior."

"Yep. But the methods worked for solving any case, like for a courtroom. She even talked about the use of psychology to crack the mystery."

"I guess everyone uses their own methods to believe the evidence in front of them." Sofia maneuvered me past the girders at the end of the stands, turning us back the way we came.

I glanced over at the side we'd just examined, realizing my focus was terrible. I stopped.

"What's wrong?" Sofia pushed a little closer into my side. "Am I bothering you?"

"Yes."

She pulled away.

"I mean...no." I drew her back by my side. "It's difficult...I can't concentrate well on checking for clues when recalling details about a previous investigation. My mind wanders from what I should be doing."

"I'm a distraction?" Her head tilted, eyebrows rising.

"Sort of."

"Only sort of?" She laughed. "I'm not exciting enough for you?"

"Hey." I grinned. "We're supposed to be finding clues about Thunder and Lightning. Instead, we're talking about the process of investigation."

"Maybe you are." She smiled. "I'm investigating you. I want to know more about you."

"Okay." Next to a slightly recessed area by the woman's restroom, I pulled her off the main path. We stood, arms linked, watching people amble by. A few children ran from one shop to another or raced to the snack stands for a treat. I turned a bit. "What more do you want to know?"

Her eyes widened a bit and an impish grin stole over her face. "I'll be a little more direct."

"You mean I'm dense?"

"To be determined." She patted my shoulder. "Don't sweat the small stuff. We talked a little about this before, but I'm not sure where you stand on the issue."

"Of?"

"You're faith." She smoothed her hair. "You spout a lot of facts and figures. Like there's five thousand copies of the Greek New Testament, way more than other famous ancient documents including the *Iliad* by Homer."

"True."

The corners of her mouth curved in a half-smile. "And some apparent contradictions in the Bible are often different perspectives of the same event."

"Correct." I raised my eyebrows a bit. "People see events differently and report details others missed. If people see one side of a story and don't consider other views, they're not seeing the whole picture."

She glanced away when a couple strolled past, then bored her eyes into mine. "Some people say Jesus was crazy."

I shrugged. "Either that or He told the truth. If he acted psychotic, the disciples would have left him. And he appeared to hundreds of people after the Romans hung him on a cross until he died. He rose again just like the Jewish scriptures said." Releasing her arm, I held her hand and faced her. "What's made this so important right now?"

She moistened her lips. "Oh, not much. Gunmen chasing us on snowmobiles. Detectives, friends, and dogs getting kidnapped." Her eyes began to redden. "It's dangerous out there right now."

I pulled her into my arms, hugged, and released her. "Bullseye. Without God, it might even seem hopeless."

She swallowed. "I like you. A lot. The criminals we're fighting scare me. I need someone strong to help me weather the storm. But we can't build a closer connection until I know you have a strong faith in Jesus. No reservations."

I gazed at her. "We're building a closer relationship?"

She narrowed her eyes. "You're being evasive."

A shock ran through my system. Several thoughts rattled through my mind. Beautiful girl. Interested in me. What do I believe? Have I made a decision? More than my parents' faith? More than going to church?

"Buongiorno." Blonde hair spilled out of a knit cap onto a powder-blue ski jacket. The speaker's blue eyes, clear and commanding, demanded a response.

"Good morning." Sofia beat me to the punch. Her tone made me feel like she hated the intrusion. "How amazing to meet you here."

"Oh, am I interrupting something?" The blonde placed a hand on her mouth.

Sofia and I faced each other. The blonde crashing our conversation stood to my left. I raised my right eyebrow for Sofia to see. "Genevieve?"

She stepped close, wrapped her arms around my left arm, and squeezed. "You remembered my name."

Chapter 41 – Dancing with the Devil

Woman's Biathlon Venue, Les Saisies, France
Friday, 17 January 1992, 11:30 a.m.

Sofia drew closer to me, sliding next to my right side and tugging my arm around her waist. "How marvelous." The icy tones might have been colder than the freezing weather around us.

Eyes focused on mine, Genevieve didn't seem to notice. "How is your brother?"

"Gabe is doing well."

"What a terrible thing for people to do, burying him in the snow." Her eyebrows knit together. She held tight with one arm and patted my chest with the other. "I'm glad I could warm him enough to keep his body temperature stable."

My internal heat index rose. An aspiring girlfriend on one side and a dangerous woman on the other. I extricated my arm from hers and touched her on the arm. "We are thankful for your generous help."

She glanced around, checking for something. "I have critical information to help you. We can't speak here, but a small restaurant I know in the local village will be a safe place." She lowered her voice and leaned closer to me. "May I take you there?"

Sofia squeezed my arm. Hard. "We'd be happy to go, but we have plans for the day."

Genevieve smiled. "A short lunch is better than no lunch at all. Let's go." She stepped into the concourse and tugged my left arm, swung Sofia and me away from the stands, and walked toward the village.

After a few steps, I relaxed a bit. Sofia still held my right arm in a vise grip, but Genevieve hooked her arm into mine and maneuvered me with a light touch. We walked and talked about the weather, the Elim Games, and the winners of various events.

Genevieve held the door at the restaurant, shooed us inside, and followed us into the warmth. "Wait here." She forged into the lunch crowd, spoke to a man behind a counter, and soon returned to escort us to a table in a side room.

"Are you Sofia Lamberti, the Italian Junior ice skating champion?" A woman, near thirty, stopped our group.

"Yes." Sofia smiled. "That's me. Can I help you?"

The woman pointed across the restaurant. "My ten-year-old daughter would like to meet you and get an autograph."

Sofia's eyes lit up. "Of course. However, may I do that when we finish lunch? In a half-hour or so?"

The woman grabbed Sofia's hands in hers. "That would be wonderful." She rushed off, looking over her shoulder. "Marvelous. Thank you."

Genevieve led us to our dining area. "You'll love this quaint restaurant."

"Great." I smiled.

Our spacious room looked out on the Biathlon event mountains. The snow scene made the comfortable warmth of our enclosure even more inviting. The décor of our spot included signed team pictures, other ski events, and winter scenes. A U-shaped bench seat surrounded the table on the window side with chairs opposite the window.

Genevieve, still on my left, removed her powder blue jacket and hung it from a coat rack on the wall opposite the table, inside some privacy curtains where we entered the room. Acting like a hostess, she extended her hands for our coats. "May I?"

I shrugged my jacket off and Sofia did the same. Sofia and I sat next to the window while Genevieve hung both coats on the rack and seated herself around the corner from me on my right, facing the other diners.

A waiter entered, took our order, and closed the curtains to reduce the restaurant noise.

Genevieve started the conversation. "Sofia, tell me about your competitive events in the Junior competitions."

While we waited for our food, my Italian companion grudgingly discussed her career. After the waiter returned with our order, Genevieve told him not to return for half an hour. She handed him several bills in French currency, telling him it included his tip.

"How's your soup and sandwich?" Genevieve stirred her cup of soup.

Both Sofia and I had ordered French Onion Soup and half-baguette sandwiches stuffed with deli meats and cheese.

I tasted my sandwich and swallowed. "Mine is excellent." I skimmed some of the cheese off the French Onion soup to avoid burning my mouth, a trick I learned as a young boy.

"Good." Sofia nibbled at her meal. "I eat salads for lunch most days, but we're in a hurry." She stared, eyebrows raised, at Genevieve.

"You make such a cute couple." Our blonde adversary scooted a bit closer to me and leaned over the table toward both of us. "You must keep the following information close hold, even from your Security friends at the IEG."

"Why would we want to do that?" I jammed another bite of sandwich in my mouth.

Genevieve's eyes twinkled. "Insightful question. You would blow my cover."

My mind reeled. What could this be about? A game within a game?

"Explain." Sofia's dark eyes became deep pools of doubt. "You're buying us a meal, trying to butter us up. Why? To keep you out of trouble?"

Genevieve placed a finger on her ruby-red lips for quiet. "Whisper, please." She glanced around the room. "Beware of possible eavesdropping." She refocused on us. "We are a small organization attached to Interpol, but it's a hush-hush operation. Even your Australian friend, Willie, doesn't know about us." She pressed her lips together. "Our intentional lack of coordination made it seem like we're the enemy."

"And?" I edged a little closer.

She tapped on the tabletop. "We've got one objective. To put Dimitri Vasiliev behind bars. I have evidence of what he's done in the past, but now we understand he wants to break into the drug-enhancement business starting at the IEGs."

"I've heard enough." Sofia stood. "I don't trust you."

I remained seated. "Anything else?"

Sofia's eyes seemed like smoldering volcanos. "I'm going to meet with my fans. When I get back, I'd like to leave."

"No problem." I turned back to our blonde adversary, thinking of a way to trap her. "Go on."

With Sofia gone, Genevieve became more open. Her eyes got red and glistened. "I'm in terrible danger. The Russian has threatened me twice, even hinting that he might hurt or kill me if I don't follow his instruction." She scooted closer, her face inches from mine. She moved my drink to one side with her left hand, grabbed one of my hands with her right, and slid around the corner next to me. Her perfume wafted over me, her eyes riveting me in my seat. "Someone needs to know if I go missing what happened."

"Why?" I gripped her hand tight. "Do you need protection?"

Her lower lip trembled. She swallowed. Her breathing quickened. Her face came closer. "What I need is—"

"What you *need* is to back off." Sofia flung the curtain wide.

Genevieve squeezed my hand and pushed away. She pulled a tissue from the inside of a sweater sleeve and dabbed at her eyes.

"Alex, we need to get going." Sofia glanced at her watch. "Our time is gone."

I plucked my glass off the table and drained the remaining soda. "I need to make a pit stop first. Don't let the waiter take my sandwich." I stood.

"I'll wrap it for you." Sofia threw on her coat.

Genevieve slid out from behind the table. "I'm sorry to be an imposition like this, but you needed to know." She sniffed, walked over to the coat rack containing her coat and mine.

"Let me help you with your jacket." I reached for her coat.

"Alex." The steel in Sofia's voice caught me off-guard. She snapped off a glare that made me wince.

"Thanks for the meal and your generosity." I reached out my hand to shake hers.

"No problem, Monsieur." She dodged the hand and pecked me on the cheek. "Farewell."

I thought better of reciprocating the typical French custom of a kiss on the cheek with Sofia around. Her anger already made the air thick with tension. I noticed Genevieve drop her gloves on the floor by the coat rack during my exit, but I left the room without assisting her, even though she seemed pretty upset.

When I returned, only Sofia remained, sitting and looking out the window. She didn't acknowledge my presence until I donned my coat.

"Hey, I'm back." I zipped my jacket. "Ready to go."

"Don't forget your sandwich." She tossed it at me. It bounced off the table once before I caught it. Those smoldering eyes and compressed lips sent her message loud and clear.

"I guess it's off to the Ski Jumping competition." Though I said it with a light tone, the comment fell flat when she strode past me to the door.

Chapter 42 – Spanish Disappearance

The Luge Venue, La Plagne, France
Friday, 17 January 1992, 1:12 p.m.

The village at La Plagne sprawled over the mountainside. I waded through the people with Franco and Izabella behind me into a restaurant near the center of town. "I wonder how Alex and Sofia are doing at the Women's Biathlon event."

"Do you think they're totally focused on finding Thunder and Lightning?' Izabella grinned.

"Now that you mention it, probably not." I plopped onto a chair near the window, looking onto the street. "But we struck out again. No clues to find our dogs and we haven't found the Russian yet."

Izabella played with a menu. "We discovered our shadow watching the luge event."

I rubbed one of my eyebrows. "Why did he have to follow us instead of Alex and Sofia? I think he's cramping our style."

"Gabe. Quit being a sourpuss." Franco motioned for a waitress to come by the table. When she arrived, he said, "Cappuccino for me. What about each of you?"

Izabella and I ordered something to drink.

I pressed my lips together. "We're not quitting. We need to go back to the luge site one last time."

The waitress arrived with the coffee and hot chocolate.

I slurped at the whipped cream on top of my hot chocolate. "Clues of Thunder and Lightning's kidnapping should be at the hotel in Albertville, but I'm looking for the Russian."

Izabella raised her eyebrows. "And how would that help?"

My jaw tightened. "I'd give him—there he is." I leapt from my seat. "Pay the bill and follow me." I raced out the door.

My friends stood, dishes clattering when they set their cups on their saucers, but I focused on a single figure disappearing around the corner.

The sidewalks, cleared of snow, gave me a quick path to chase the man. When I rounded the corner, he'd passed several buildings. I accelerated, sprinting after his broad back. Less than a minute later, I grabbed the sleeve of his long, black coat.

"Excuse me." I panted a little. "I need to talk with you."

The man looked down at me. He might be half-foot taller than me, but I didn't care. I knew he stole my dog.

"Where is my dog?" I studied his face for a twitch.

The man jerked away. "What do you think you're doing?" He brushed his coat like wiping the dirt from a filthy garment. His face didn't show surprise or fear, just annoyance. "You're the little fly who's been bugging me."

Motion behind the Russian caught my eye. Franco and Izabella flew around the corner. Our tail appeared a moment later.

"You, or someone you hired, stole our dogs from our hotel."

"Is that right?" The man shook his head. "If you don't leave me alone, I'll call Security to take you away."

Izabella waved at me to join her and Franco where they had stopped a building away. Our shadow crossed the road and ducked behind a parked car.

I crossed my arms. "That would be a waste of your time. You don't know who you're dealing with. I've got connections."

"As do I." The man smirked, his voice dropping to a low volume. "Tell your guard my men detected his location. If he tries anything funny, they'll take him out." He slid his hand inside the long coat right where a shoulder-holster for a pistol would be.

I didn't back off. "You're bluffing. Any bloodshed here would put you in jail as a suspect."

The man withdrew his hand from the coat. He put a small device to his ear. "I'm ready." He shoved the device in his pocket. "I'm sure we'll meet again."

A Mercedes pulled up beside him. The passenger door opened. He slid into the seat, snickered at me, and the car drove away even before the door slammed shut.

Franco and Izabella dashed to me.

"What happened?" Izabella fell in on one side and Franco took the other.

I rubbed the side of my face. "Mexican standoff."

"What?" Franco lifted his shoulders, hands spread wide.

"Walk with me." I stomped off, telling them about the short exchange. "Neither one of us held an advantage, which made it a standoff. His men covered him and our shadow watched us."

"Where are we going?" Izabella pointed straight ahead.

"Back to the luge area for one last look." I pointed ahead. "The shuttle is right there."

"I need to make a stop at the Ladies Room first." Izabella broke off to her right, heading to a public restroom.

"We'll do the same." I turned toward her. "Meet you here in a few minutes."

I studied the area while we walked to the Men's Room. "Where'd our tail go?"

"Perhaps taking a short break now that we're out of trouble." Franco went inside first.

A few minutes later, we waited for Izabella in the cold. I checked my watch. "We've given her several minutes. She should be here by now."

A woman skirted Franco and me to go into the restroom.

"Excuse me." I waved.

The lady stopped.

I nudged Franco. "You know French better than me."

Franco explained we'd lost our friend and asked the lady to check for Izabella in the restroom.

Several heartbeats later, the woman opened the door and spoke to Franco.

"We can look inside." Franco led the way.

The search took no time at all. Five stalls. All empty.

Franco thanked the woman. We rushed around the back of the building and found a deserted alleyway.

"We've got to tell the local Security office." I raced, Franco following.

The local Security desk sergeant acknowledged us as special support for Willie's investigations but couldn't contact Willie because of his involvement in today's drug testing. I gave the officer an old homeschool class picture that included Izabella, providing her full name and description. They copied the photo and gave it back to me.

"Why are you carrying our class photo?" Franco said.

"You don't do that in Italy?" I shrugged. "I like to remember my good friends."

Franco shrugged. "Great idea."

The sergeant put the picture's copy in a folder on his desk and smiled. "We'll check it out."

"You've got to find her now." I pointed to his radio. "Send out an alert."

"Gabe." Franco tapped his watch. "The shuttle leaves in two minutes."

"We're taking the bus to Albertville to find Willie." I tossed that statement out while we ran to catch the bus.

Willie still wasn't at his office, but I convinced his assistant to call him at the testing site.

"He tells me you must go to him." Gilbert shrugged. "Sorry. Do you know the site's location?"

We nodded.

"Hurry." Gilbert motioned us away. "He must start another round of testing in ten minutes."

I glanced at my watch. Franco and I raced through the Security Headquarters, causing a few papers to scatter off desks and a few angry shouts that echoed around the room. We sped through the labyrinth of streets to the IEG Testing Center.

A guard stepped in front of us. "Testing is active now and no one is allowed to enter." A red light flashed on top of the door.

I sucked in big breaths. "Seven minutes ago, we talked to Willie Gretzke and he told us to see him now."

"That's impossible." The guard remained resolute.

Franco spoke to him in French. When he finished, the guard lifted his walkie-talkie and spoke a few terse words.

"What'd you say?" I stepped away from the guard.

Franco smiled. "I told him that if a girl died because of him, he'd never be a security man again. I emphasized he'd better call Gilbert again."

When the guard's walkie-talkie beeped, He listened and waved to the door. "You may enter."

The entryway housed a tiny cubicle of an office, allowing about four people to stand inside at one time. A desk blocked most of one side with a door next to it.

Willie popped his head into the office. "Have you lost Izzy?"

I slapped the top of the desk. "Not my fault. That Russky kidnapped her."

"Sure about that?" Willie lifted a finger to a person on the other side of the door. "I'll get some investigators to do a sweep at La Plagne. I have one last test to do. After that, I can talk with you at my own office. See you in thirty minutes."

He shut the door.

I glanced at Franco. "We can't win today." I slapped the wall, startling the guard.

Franco held out his hand to the security man. "It's okay. We're leaving."

Outside, we retraced our steps to the IEG Main Security office.

I stomped around and kicked the snow banks while we walked. "I'm so amped I could punch a hole in the wall."

My buddy listened. "You've gone through bad times before."

"That doesn't change what's happening now." I weaved past a clump of pedestrians. "Before this adventure, other people trapped us underground, we almost drowned once, and terrorists, human traffickers, and the mafia chased us. Not only that. We lost the dogs once before. They could have died."

Franco kept silent for a block while I stewed. "Willie's team will help find them."

I scooped some snow into my hands, packed it, and fired away at a road sign, making it wobble. "We've got no clues. Anything could be happening. They might be dead. And Izabella's gone too. We're sliding down a slippery slope into a pit of darkness. Complete disaster."

Chapter 43 – Arrested

Shuttle Stop, Courchevel, France

Friday, 17 January 1992, 2:25 p.m.

Getting off the bus at Courchevel to watch the Ski Jumping competition, I felt like a convict released out of prison. Since we left the restaurant where Genevieve treated us to lunch, Sofia said less than ten words to me.

"Why don't we find Gabe, Izabella, and Franco?" I waited while Sofia dismounted from the bus.

"Good idea." She stepped past me, giving me a wide berth, and examined the town.

"That's them." An IEG Security guard spoke to his partner about ten feet away. He pointed in our direction. They sprinted toward us.

"Sir, please move over to the side and let the rest of the passengers off the bus." The dark-haired, chisel-featured security guard prodded me with a short black stick. "Make it quick."

I stumbled several steps to my right.

"Ma'am, you'll have to join him." The second officer, a potbellied man with grey hair, motioned Sofia to join me.

"What's going on?" I crossed my arms.

Chisel-chin ignored me for a moment and glanced in his book. "Confirmed. He read off our descriptions. "Traveling together as reported."

Sofia, no longer consumed by her anger, raised her eyebrows at me. She faced the grey-haired officer. "Why have you stopped us?"

"No questions allowed at this time." Grey-hair motioned to a vehicle parked behind the bus. "Follow me."

I stood firm. When chisel-chin poked me with his stick, I knocked it away. "I'm an American citizen and haven't done anything wrong. We're not going anywhere." I spread my feet apart and leaned forward on the balls of my feet.

The guard facing me smiled. "I guess you forgot you're in France. You're not in a consulate and I have no papers proving you're American. Even so, I don't need proof of anything to arrest you." He gave me a once over. "I suggest you relax and come without a fuss or you'll end up in handcuffs with bruises on your head and your ego." He smiled.

Sofia's anger upset me. I clenched my hands and released them. Tension rippled in my muscles, making me like a fine-tuned, fuel-injected car ready to race around a track. Adrenalin pumped through my veins.

"Alex."

Sofia's voice caught my attention. I gave her a brief nod, flexed my biceps, and curled my right hand into a fist. I felt great. I could take on both security officers without a problem.

"Alex, you're not thinking straight." Sofia's voice rose in pitch.

I shook it off, like water sliding off my shoulders. My smiling security man needed to learn a lesson or two.

"Alex, no." Sofia ducked past the grey-haired guard and flew into my arms. "Stop." She shook me several times. "Calm down. Relax." She rubbed my arms. Took my hand and pried open my fist. "Settle." Turning to chisel-chin, her back to me, she took a protective position between us. "We'll come with you."

I felt pumped. Ready for action. I let Sofia guide me to the car.

A glance behind confirmed chisel-chin's eyes drilled me from behind. He kept patting his baton.

The car ride to the station made me mad.

Sofia held my hand the whole way. "What's wrong? Did you eat something bad?"

I racked my brain for an answer. "I'm not sure. The soda I drank tasted sweeter than normal and bitter at the end, but that could be the syrup mix in France."

She held my hand, squeezing it to help me maintain control.

When we arrived at the station a few minutes away, my anger simmered below the surface.

Chisel-chin opened my door, motioning with his baton for me to get out and go inside. Sofia exited on the other side of the car, going into the station first. Inside, we stood in front of the desk sergeant.

"As requested." The grey-haired officer poked his thumb at Sofia and me. "We caught them when they got off the bus."

Chisel-chin, grey-hair, and the desk sergeant chattered in French for a short while. Sofia glanced at me, but I couldn't follow what they said.

"We know Willie Gretzke." I interrupted their conversation. "Call him and he'll clear us."

Sofia shook her head. "You're under suspicion of taking drugs and being a drug carrier."

"Investigator Gretzke is unavailable for now." The desk sergeant spoke in English, peering over thick, black-rimmed glasses. "He's incommunicado doing drug testing at our main building in the IEG Village. I'll leave him a message."

"Not good enough." I stepped closer to the desk sergeant. "Do I have to make the call?"

Chisel-chin positioned himself between the sergeant and me.

"Alex, be calm." Sofia reached out and pulled me back. "If not for me, then for you. You're acting strange."

"We'll need to search you and take a urine sample from both of you." The desk sergeant pointed a finger at me. "Cause me trouble and I'll lock you in the local jail. These men will take you to the back. A female officer will administer the girl's testing and one of the apprehending officers will handle you."

Chisel-chin smirked.

"You won't find anything." I clenched my jaw and shot the officer a challenging look. "I know my rights. Why did you arrest us? These tests aren't normal."

"I can do whatever I want." The desk sergeant glanced at chisel-chin. "Give the boy a blood test too. That will be all." He dismissed us and went back to his paperwork.

Twenty minutes later, Sofia found me in a holding cell. "What are you doing here? I've been searching for you."

I sat on the bench in the cell with another guy, head down, kneading my fingers back and forth through my hair. "Drugs in my jacket. How did that happen? Either you or I kept it in sight the whole time. And my test came back hot for steroids."

"I'm not sure about the coat, but the bigger question is how you tested hot on the urinalysis." Sofia hesitated. "You aren't taking any anabolic steroids to build muscle, are you?"

"Dad would kill me if I did that." I flexed my arms. "Natural development. Nothing extra. Never."

"Maybe somebody faked the test." Sofia raised an eyebrow.

I swept a hand through my hair and sat back. "I'm not sure what's going on, but I feel like this is a setup. Maybe Willie can help us figure it out."

Sofia took a deep breath. "I'm going to try the IEG Security headquarters again. It's almost three o'clock. Maybe Willie's available now."

Chapter 44 – Drug Test

Security Station, Courchevel, France
Friday, 17 January 1992, 3:01 p.m.

I prayed, regardless of the men held behind bars with me. I didn't know what else to do. Sitting in a holding cell, now packed with three other men, wasn't my kind of fun.

"Alex, I got hold of Willie." Sofia's voice broke through the chatter of the men. "He's having a policeman from the Security station drive us to the IEG testing site in Albertville in a few minutes." She paused and looked at the ground. "Since I'm riding in the back with you, you'll have to wear handcuffs."

My muscles tightened. "I'm not going to run away."

"I didn't have anything to say about it." Sofia bit her lip. "But I have more bad news—"

Chisel-chin stepped in front of Sofia, unlocked the door, and motioned me to come out. He spun me around, locked my wrists behind me, and led me past her outside. The freezing wind chilled me in a second. "Can't I have my coat?"

A smile creased Chisel-chin's face. "Evidence." He opened the other door for Sofia to slide into the back, closed it, and got behind the wheel. Wasting no time, he roared out of the parking lot, onto the highway, and drove like someone chasing an ambulance. Sofia kept me from bouncing off the vehicle's interior while we darted and dodged past cars to reach the Station.

He grinned at me in the rearview mirror when we swerved into the curb. "Must be a record time."

"I'll bet." I waited until he opened the car door, stood, and brushed my shoulder into his chest while I passed him.

He shoved me forward, making me lose my balance outside the entry door of the Testing Site. The door guard watched me fall to my knees and topple onto the ground.

Willie swung the door open. "What's going on here?"

Chisel-chin laughed. "The prisoner tried to escape. I made sure he didn't get any more crazy ideas."

"That's a lie." Sofia's eyes narrowed. "Do you get your jollies pushing handcuffed people around?"

"Officer Fornet, I'll see you later tonight." Willie dragged me to my knees and lifted me to my feet. "Unlock this suspect. He's not a flight risk."

Fornet obeyed.

"Where's his jacket and the evidence?" Willie sent me inside with Sofia to wait while Chisel-chin gave him what he needed. In moments, he joined us in the square entry room.

"Sofia, wait here until I run a few tests." Willie grabbed my arm and propelled me into a narrow hallway.

After several rights and lefts, a Private led me into a small bathroom for another urine sample. He accompanied me into the bathroom as an observer to ensure I didn't try to falsify the test somehow. Afterward, he guided me to another room, where a med-tech took blood.

With all that completed, Willie met me in the hall and escorted me to the small entry room.

"Crazy day." Willie beckoned Sofia to join me. "I'll have a guard take you to my office. Gabe and Franco are waiting. We have lots to talk about." Willie disappeared back into the testing site rooms.

Not long after, a guard appeared. "Alex Zanadu?"

I raised a hand.

"I'm your escort to the Security Headquarters building." The man pointed at Sofia. "You're together?"

She gave a quick nod.

"Follow me."

Gilbert led us into Willie's main office at the IEG Security Head-quarters. He waved at the coffee table with a few snacks. "I heard you might be thirsty."

"Thanks." I sat next to Sofia in the two chairs by the coffee table.

Gabe pointed at my jeans. "You have holes in your pants at the knees. You haven't been proposing to Sofia, have you?"

"Nice to see you again, bro." I rubbed my knees. "A security officer decided to push me onto the ground."

"And you let him do it?" Gabe laughed.

Sofia's eyes blazed. "Gabriel Zanadu, back off."

"Bingo. Pretty serious, huh?" My brother sat forward in his chair. "Did you get stopped for something?"

I rolled my eyes. "A setup." I relaxed into the back of my chair, lifted my coffee, and enjoyed the warmth sliding down my throat. "Genevieve, your French crush, figured a way to trap me."

"My French crush?" Gabe sighed. "It's the other way around. She would die for me, I'm sure. But we have no deep connection."

"What happened?" Franco patted Gabe on the shoulder. "Without the barbed comments."

Sofia stole a glance at me. "Genevieve shocked Alex and me by inviting us to lunch. I don't remember anything strange going on."

I shook my head. "But you weren't there the whole time."

"And what did she do while in my absence?" Sofia narrowed her eyes.

I sat back and stroked my chin. "She told me some secret information." I straightened and slapped my hands together. "That's it. She surprised me by crying, scooting close to me, resting on my shoulder, and leaning in as though her lips would kiss mine."

Sofia stared at me. "Secret? What secret?"

Willie strolled into the room. "Another drama to unfold?"

Gabe stood, went to the coffee bar, and made another hot chocolate. "You've nailed it." He motioned at Sofia and me. "Soap opera episode twenty-one. Sofia's ready to blast Alex for keeping secrets from her."

Gilbert walked in. "Cuppa?"

"Sure." Willie draped his coat on a spare chair behind his desk. "Set it on the coaster."

"Reports per your direction." Gilbert set the coffee down and flopped the papers next to the cup. He left, shutting the door on the way out.

"When did he learn Australian lingo?" Gabe wandered back to his seat, peeking at the stack of paper on Willie's desk.

Willie nabbed his cup, rocked back in his chair, and sipped. "Doesn't take long around me." He surveyed the room. "Tension's a bit high in here. Our enemy wants us to badger each other. To split our home team into fragments."

Sofia and I shared a glance.

"The first tactic of the enemy is to divide and conquer their opponents." Willie set his cup on the desk and captured a pen. "If they can sow discord and disharmony on our team, we won't be able to trust each other and work together."

Gabe tapped Franco. "No trouble here."

Willie twirled the pen in his hand, spinning it several times while he talked. "Gabe, who's responsible for Izabella disappearing? Weren't you watching for traps?"

He ducked his head a little. "I guess…"

"You're the hotshot expert for investigations, aren't you?" Willie tossed the pen on his desk and rolled forward. "Didn't you tell me you're better than the rest of the detectives?"

Gabe's eyes lowered to the floor.

Willie swiveled his chair toward Sofia and me. "How would someone make you two mad at each other? What if a woman tried to act in a way to make you doubt the relationship you've started?"

Sofia pressed her lips together.

I breathed deeply, glancing at the ceiling.

Elbows planted on his desk, Willie faced the four of us at once. "And why don't we plant drugs on Alex that makes him positive on a drug test?"

"I knew it." Gabe pumped his fist in the air. "Bullseye."

Willie sighed and pointed at Gabe. "Focus." He shook his head. "We are missing Izabella and your dogs. We've got some hard yakka in front of us."

"The work isn't too hard if we take it one step at a time." I rubbed my jaw. "Did you get new reports on what happened to me?"

Willie rifled through the reports on his desk. "Yes. You're hot for DBOL, which stands for Dianabol, an anabolic steroid. Your interior coat pocket contained several packets of stanozolol, Furazabol, and DBOL." He flopped the papers on his desk. "They want us to think you're a mule for the IEG Games."

I shook my head. "A mule? I don't carry drugs for anyone. How did she get them into my inner coat pocket? She never touched my coat that I can remember."

Sofia lifted a finger in the air. "While you went to the men's room, she dropped her gloves by the coat rack." She took a deep breath. "She ticked me off so much that I turned my back and watched the street until she left."

"She played you pretty well." Gabe snickered.

Sofia's eyes shot daggers at my brother.

Willie slapped the side of his desk. Our heads snapped in his direction.

Retrieving his pen, our Australian friend directed it at Gabe. "That'll be enough of that, mate. We're a team. Don't be a wanker. Handle your share of the load and support your teammate."

Gabe gulped and sat back in his chair. "I didn't mean—"

"That's another thing." Willie poked the air with his pen. "No excuses, mates. We're people. We make mistakes." He leaned forward. "That drug-runner wants us to bicker and fight."

"Everything all right, Willie?" I tried to lighten the mood. "You sound mad as a cut snake."

His head whipped in my direction. But in a fraction of a second, he smiled. "They're getting to me too." He dropped his pen on the reports. "I'm a bit knackered."

"Tired?" Franco sighed. "I'm exhausted too. I could use a nap."

I shifted in my chair. "Genevieve suckered me in. My drink did taste weird, but if she drugged it, I didn't notice. Her eyes were hypnotic."

Gabe's eyes brightened. "She sounds like a trained scam artist or pickpocket from a big city."

I rubbed my chin. "Her whole spiel must have been fake. According to her, she's an undercover agent with Interpol. When Sofia left to meet her fans, Genevieve told me Dimitri Vasiliev threatened her. Even planned to kill her." My eyes darted to Sofia. "She grabbed my hand, pulled me close, and started to cry. I thought I'd gotten to the bottom of the story."

Sofia's lips became a firm line.

"I know." I held up my hands in surrender. "She duped me."

Her face softened a bit.

"That last part might have been true." Willie scratched his chin. "The tears might have been fake, but the Russian is trying a power grab and she's losing the battle."

"And I'm sure the Russian took our dogs and Izabella." I sat on the edge of my seat. "We need to get them back now."

Willie rocked forward in his chair. "Here's what has to happen." He checked each of us to make sure we were listening. "Alex, you're on probation due to the testing."

I opened my hands in front of me, pleading. "But Willie—"

Willie pushed out his hand like a stop sign. "That's what I'm putting out through official channels. You're still part of my team.

But you can't leave now until the investigation is over, and I'll have to limit your access to Security Headquarters support."

Our Aussie friend leveled his finger at Gabe. "I expect you to cooperate with everyone and not act by yourself. You're in charge of finding the dogs."

His finger swung to Sofia. "We need your support and help. You have connections to lots of skaters and key athletes. I'd like you to take Alex and Gabe to meet your friends. Take Bastien too. He has a lot of influence. Find out if anyone knows about the plans for drugs or the abduction of the dogs. Can you do that?"

A smile crept across her face. "No problem. We're supposed to meet Bastien at the speed skating event right now." She stood. "We're late."

Willie rose, chuckling. "We're almost back to normal. See the lot of you at oh-seven-thirty in the morning tomorrow."

Chapter 45 – Debrief to Dad

Speed Skating Rink, Albertville, France
Friday, 17 January 1992, 4:45 p.m.

Alex kicked at the snow. "The event's almost over. I bet Bastien's already left."

Sofia walked beside him, an elbow's length away. "The crowd's still here. Maybe we can find him."

I let Alex and Sofia drift away, ahead of Franco and me. "It's serious." Grinning, I poked Franco in the ribs.

Franco swung his arm into my side. "I'm gonna bury your head in the snow for that." He gave me a friendly shove. "Of course, it's serious. Izabella's gone. And Thunder and Lightning are missing."

"Not that." I pointed at Sofia and Alex. "Those two are serious. See how Sofia's getting closer to Alex while he pouts about being on probation." I chuckled. "I bet by this evening they'll be laughing and smiling."

Franco peered through the crowd. "I guess his German girlfriend, Jenna, is out of the picture now."

I shook my head. "I've seen my brother go through this a couple of times. Love's good, but love hurts. A continuous cycle I plan to avoid until I'm in my twenties."

"Good luck with that." Franco pointed to the stands where U.S.A. supporters stood. "We need to hurry to get inside before the gold medal elimination run. Does the U.S. skater have a chance?"

"Brenda Blossom can blow away the competition." I led the way to join the Americans. Alex and Sofia weren't too far in front of us.

The crowd in the American section held signs for Brenda. The thousand-meter race wouldn't last long. Most of the group stood cheering, chanting, or waving U.S. flags. When we reached some open seats, the official raised his pistol in the air.

With the crack of his gun, the racers dug into the ice and flew into action. The U.S. section roared when Brenda took the lead. I noticed Alex and Sofia a few rows in front of me, standing right next to each other.

I tugged on Franco's jacket and pointed. "See? Already back together."

Franco laughed. "Watch the race. History in the making."

Brenda swept around the corners, but the Chinese competitor named Bai nipped at her heels. The skaters rounded the final corner and the noise became deafening. They flew to the finish line. Neck and neck. With a final surge, Brenda crossed first. Bai tripped and slid across the line in second place. The American's rocked and shouted. People slapped hands, hugged, and yelled. Blossom beat Bai by sixty-five-hundredths of a second with a time of 1:24:37.

"That will be the best score going into the World's next month." I slapped Franco's back. "She'll probably take all the skating events."

While the U.S. section celebrated, I scanned the crowd and found Bastien waving at us. I waved back and pointed to the area behind the stands. I prodded Franco out of our seat area. When we got to Alex and Sofia's level, I motioned for them to follow. Alex gave me a thumbs up.

"Bastien." I waved at him to get his attention. "Over here."

After we connected, I suggested the five of us talk outside the skating rink area. We walked to a nearby park and stood out of the primary traffic way.

"Exciting race for you." Bastien shrugged. "Not good for France; however, the U.S. wins another medal."

"The whole day's been exciting—or disastrous." I filled him in on the action Franco and I encountered, including losing Izabella.

We huddled tight together while people flowed around us. Alex and Sofia shared their information together. Alex ignored the fact that Genevieve got past his defenses but mentioned his probation until we solved the case.

"Willie thought we should get out on the night scene to find information on the dogs or Izabella." Alex looked at Bastien and Sofia. "Can you two get us into places to socialize?"

Bastien gazed at Sofia. "I can get us in, but I think she knows the better crowd."

Sofia shrugged. "Yes, I know several places to go. We should leave around seven-thirty tonight."

Franco shook his head. "Not me. I have homework to do."

My eyes widened. "Homework? You're at the IEGs."

Our Italian friend sucked in a lungful of air and let it out. "Mother has her plans. I'm free tomorrow."

I patted him on the shoulder. "We'll see you then."

"Sofia and I will meet you at the entrance of the hotel." Bastien turned to go. "I'll provide the transportation."

Alex waved. "We'll be ready." After Bastien departed, he lowered his eyes and spoke to Sofia next. "Thanks for understanding about lunch."

She giggled. "Boys don't always realize what they're getting into." After giving my brother a quick peck on the cheek, Sofia joined a crowd of other skaters coming out of the arena. "I'll get our evening line-up organized."

Alex and I headed in the hotel's direction, but he didn't walk fast.

"Come on." I checked my watch. "Are you afraid of telling Dad what happened? The sooner we get it over with, the better."

"I guess you're right. Race you." He shot forward on the sidewalk.

After getting warm in our room for half an hour, we met Dad at six for dinner in the main dining room. He sat at a table in the back of the restaurant.

"Crazy day at work for me." Dad reviewed his menu. "Your mother got off to our friends without a hitch and is staying at their house. She'll feel a lot better when you boys join her day after tomorrow."

Alex's jaw got tight, and I kept quiet.

Dad lowered his menu. "Silence tells me you know something I don't." He sighed. "Let's order first. Whatever it is, I want the truth."

I ordered steak, Alex got a chicken dish, and Dad requested salmon. We made small talk about Mom until the entrees arrived.

"I'm ready." Dad ate a forkful of his entrée.

Alex's laydown sounded like a spy novel.

Dad tilted his head, listening and eating at a steady pace until the part about probation. "What does that mean?"

My brother set his fork on the table. He lifted his shoulders and raised his eyebrows. "Willie said I can't leave until the case is solved."

Dad straightened in his chair. "We'll see about that. The case may take longer than a day to solve and I'm not breaking a promise I made to your mother."

"Just giving you the truth." Alex readjusted himself. "That's what he said."

I sipped my water. "That's not the worst."

Dad rolled his eyes. "You can top that?"

I slapped my hand on the table. "Yes. Alex fell into a trap from a woman who tried to play him for a sucker. My team lost a teammate searching for the dogs."

Our father didn't get upset much. But when it happened, the signs were clear. Lowering his fork with his bite of fish still on it signaled his anger.

"Details. Now."

When I finished, he pointed his knife at me. "Never threaten a suspect in public." He leaned closer and lowered his voice. "When you shame them in front of others, they retaliate. They make your position worse. And you endanger the rest of your team. Didn't Willie teach you that?"

"Yes, but—"

"No buts." He sat tall. "I have to go back to work. What are your plans tonight?"

Alex pushed his plate back a bit and placed his napkin on top. "We're going to a few parties with Sofia and Bastien." He glanced at the clock on the wall behind Dad. "We leave in about twenty minutes."

I scanned Alex's plate for any tasty, left-over chicken tidbits I could eat. I reached over for one and he slapped my hand.

"Hey." I jerked my hand back.

Dad closed his eyes for a second and shook his head at me. "Sometimes, I wonder about you." He tilted his head. "Here are my rules for the night. The four of you must stay together from party to party. No drinking, drugs, or dangerous games. And you have to be in bed by midnight."

"Got it." I pointed at his salmon. "Can I taste your salmon? I might want some tomorrow night."

Chapter 46 – Italian Connections

Wild Boar Hotel, Albertville, France
Friday, 17 January 1992, 7:30 p.m.

Sofia waited with Alex and me outside our hotel entrance. I stomped my feet, shifting around to stay warm. We showed at seven-thirty, but Bastien arrived late.

"How do we get Gabe into these parties?" Alex waved a hand at me. "He looks like a twelve- or thirteen-year-old."

Sofia raised an eyebrow. "We should let Bastien take Gabe around and introduce him to folks as a guest from his relatives." She slid her arm under one of Alex's arms. "We can go in like a couple. Besides, the two of you are strangers to these people. No one will reveal anything to you, but you might distract them, which would allow Bastien and me an opportunity to unearth some info."

"We're window dressing?" I slapped a hand against my face. "The dogs are our loss, not yours."

"Right." Sofia grinned. "You're still emotional about it. That's why we can handle it better." She brushed her black hair with her fingers. "Besides, Izabella isn't yours to lose either, or is she?" An impish grin crossed her face.

I felt my face get warm. "I was in charge when we lost her. She... she's a good friend."

"Right." Alex grinned. "Who happens to be a girl."

A dark red BMW rolled into the driveway entrance of the hotel. A bell hop opened the front car door and Bastien rose from the driver's seat. "What are you waiting for?"

We climbed in, Sofia taking the front passenger seat to provide directions.

"Before we hit any parties, I want you to see how this car performs. I borrowed it from a friend for tonight." He revved the engine.

"We're supposed to stay safe tonight." Alex buckled in. "Our father's orders."

Bastien nodded. "Okay, short spin on the highway. Top speed is 155 mph or over 250 kph." He eased the car from the hotel, threaded through the nighttime traffic on Highway D990.

Even though an IEG hockey game was in progress, people packed the bars and restaurants, celebrating the festive atmosphere in the town. The drive to N90, the high-speed divided highway, chewed up fifteen minutes or more. The entryway to the onramp contained no traffic.

"Zero to sixty in six point nine seconds." Bastien floored the gas pedal and the pressure pushed us back in our seats. "We'll take it to a hundred miles an hour before I slow down."

We cheered and laughed during the trip. Bastien drove the switchback mountain roads on the way to the party, giving us a demonstration of handling. I loved the ride—smooth, powerful, and intoxicating.

A smile creased my face until we reached the first party's location. "BMW 850csi. I'll remember that for my first car." I extricated myself from the back seat. "Awesome."

But while I smiled on the outside, I focused on the inside. We needed info to rescue our dogs and Izabella. The fun ride didn't erase our mission from my mind.

Alex got out. "Remember the plan. We're eye-candy Americans."

"If they have food and music, I'll have no problem." I sidled next to Bastien. "My host will take great care of me."

"The primary group of the first party is skaters, but the two after that will be gymnasts first and Bastien's friends second." Sofia's eyes narrowed. "Don't cause a ruckus. I plan to ask some pointed questions. After being almost killed in a snowmobile chase, I want to rid our IEG Games of these criminals."

Bastien pointed at my brother. "Need to keep her in a party mood tonight or we'll get nothing."

The Italian team's private party filled a hotel lounge room and a guard at the door let us in. Sofia led Alex into the crowd. Bastien and I headed for the snack bar. We grabbed non-alcoholic drinks and circulated in the room.

The jabbering and animated gestures got me in the right mood. I laughed, listened, and told stories to people interested in my background. I even spouted some Italian, French, and German to let them know I understood a little.

About eleven o'clock, we'd been at the third party for almost a half-hour. Alex came over to me without Sofia and motioned for my attention while I wowed a small audience with the story of our adventure in Salzburg, Austria.

"Give me a second." I waved him away, but he stayed in my peripheral vision. Five minutes later, still wowing the crowd, I paused to sip my soda. Alex grabbed my arm and dragged me away.

"Sorry, everyone." Alex smiled. "My brother and I have to meet some friends."

Several people wanted me to finish. I tried to break free of Alex's grip, but he didn't let me go. "No scenes, remember?" When we got to the edge of the crowd, he faced me. "We have to figure out a place where we can meet alone and discuss anything we found out. Before we meet Willie tomorrow."

I straightened my shirt sleeve. "I've got to get back and finish my story. I can't leave my admirers hanging."

My brother glared at me. "Our purpose isn't storytelling." He turned away, and his eyes landed on Sofia talking with a few girls her age.

"You get Sofia and I'll get Bastien." I stepped in the direction of my new friends.

"No, you don't." Alex put a hand on my chest. "Wrong direction. We're in enough hot water with Dad. We don't need to deviate from the curfew he set."

I swept his hand away. "I'm not a baby."

Sofia spotted us and drifted our way.

"I hope she's got some info on the dogs." I fidgeted with a coin in my pocket.

"Good news." She checked the area around us. "But we need to get away and talk."

Alex grinned, his 'I told you so look' shining in his eyes.

Bastien appeared at the far side of the room.

"I'll get him." I plowed past them and into the crowd. We rejoined them in minutes.

"Take us to a local dessert place close to the hotel." Sofia placed a hand on Bastien's arm. "A place where we can get a table."

Settled into a Bistro table near the back of the restaurant, each of us enjoyed a late-night snack. Bastien and I munched on French pastries. Alex drank black coffee and Sofia sipped on a French vanilla cappuccino.

Sofia beamed. "I made contact."

"For what?" I got excited. "Thunder and Lightning?"

She gave a shake of her head. "Drugs." She motioned us in closer and whispered. "I have arranged to buy some performance-enhancing drugs tomorrow."

Alex frowned. "Our goal was information on the dogs and Izabella. How will that help?"

Sofia's eyebrows furrowed. "The main problem is the drug-ring these criminals use to scam unsuspecting top competitors. I'm going to entrap them as Genevieve did to you."

Bastien wiped his mouth with a napkin. "Pretty dangerous. Does Willie know?"

Sofia's lips firmed into a straight line. "He will tomorrow morning. The Games are over in eight days and we have nothing. We need to get evidence we can use now."

Alex sipped his coffee. "I guess that logic makes it the right course of action." He breathed deep. "I'll be praying for you."

She smiled. "Thanks."

"I have a lead on the dogs." Bastien finished his dessert, wiped his lips one last time, and lifted his cappuccino. "I talked about black Great Danes and orange fluffballs that were the Shih-Tzu breeds. No takers on that end. But one of my friend's acquaintances saw something."

"Don't keep us hanging," I said. "Spit it out."

An expression of fear flickered through Bastien's face. He gulped like a fish gasping in the air. "Later. We must leave now. Back way. Quick." He pointed at the entrance.

Dimitri stood outside the store's front window, motioning to two brawny men near the entrance to go inside, his eyes locked on us.

Chapter 47 – Death or Detention

Hotel Conference Room, Albertville, France
Friday, 17 January 1992, 11:39 p.m.

Genevieve entered the conference room, a typical high-cost private hotel layout. The table could hold eight people on the sides in executive chairs, with a ninth chair on one end and a blank wall with a screen on the other. A waste of money for this meeting, but typical for his style—big and boorish.

Dimitri glanced at her and ceased reviewing some reports when she arrived. He sat at the head of the table and gestured for her to sit next to him on his right.

Ignoring his invitation, she strode to the left side, sliding into the second chair from his seat.

He frowned. "I told you that Detective Gretzke wouldn't fall for the Zanadu boy as a drug user or carrier."

She set her face, grim and determined. "Probation will be enough. Alex Zanadu will be out of the picture for several days, if not the rest of the IEGs. That's what you wanted."

"You don't know what I want." He tapped the table. "I want him and his brother eliminated. Permanently. Plus their friends if they get involved."

Genevieve held her tongue for a second. Her words and tone must convey the proper message. She wasn't his messenger, his lackey, or his stooge. *I'm a full partner.* If he couldn't accept that, she'd make him regret it, despite his impressive KGB career and criminal background.

Pressing her back into the executive chair, she focused on the glowing lights of Albertville below. Without fanfare, she threw out her first point. "You've tried to kill or eliminate the boys at least twice. Without my agreement." She swiveled to check out Dimitri's reaction.

He snorted and drew a cigar from his suit jacket.

Now for the next jab. "I'm interested in detaining the boys and some of their friends for insurance and leverage, *not* for liquidation." Genevieve swiveled in her chair, stood, fixed some hot tea, and returned. She sat poised for battle, stirring her tea with deliberate strokes and facing Dimitri.

"My incompetent comrades are no longer with me." He sneered.

"Dead?" She gritted her teeth. A subtle threat from him, perhaps. But two could play this game. "Or taken out through failure in pursuit?" She flipped her blonde hair for emphasis. "I know how to win with finesse instead of foolish heavy-handedness. My smooth, artful weaving of the web entraps the enemy without wasting energy."

"Enough." Dimitri slammed his fist on the table, making it rock. "Don't question my methods. In the end, a dead enemy is no longer a problem."

"You fool." Her detached manner and frosty tone chilled the air. "Kill the boys, and our operation is over. Every possible police organization, the news hounds, and the governments involved will pursue us in a relentless hunt."

"Let them try." He cut the tip off his cigar, lit the end, drew in a breath, and released a puff of smoke into the room. "They've never captured me."

"There's always a first time." She tapped her spoon on the China cup. "Let's drop this worthless conversation and get to the bottom line. What's tomorrow's plan?"

"Today's plan, now." Dimitri pointed to the digital wall clock, which read 00:03 a.m. He walked to the bar at the end of the table and poured himself a drink. "First, the positive test results start to come out in the morning. We now have control of the random testing process and the paperwork records. This removes several French and Italian competitors in medal contention. Second, we eliminate the Australian in a tragic motor accident in town. Our plant in the Security office will provide details on the man's route."

The Russian sat again, facing Genevieve. "Third, our newest associate, a well-known Frenchman, will assist us in capturing the boys. And fourth, we support our current drug constituents and start working recruits for new users and drug runners." His face relaxed.

"Murder the Australian?" Genevieve exploded out of her chair. "Impossible." She didn't agree to any of this. And the Australian held a chief investigator slot. His accident would cause heightened controversy and a high-level effort by the Australian, British, and French governments.

She leaned on the table. "We still have to hammer out the details." Who was the Frenchman he mentioned? When would they capture the boys? And who were the recruits? "I'm exhausted. Can we pursue this in the morning?"

"Some actions are in motion now." He shrugged. "Wasting time is not one of my failings. Expedient operations are a must." He sent her a dismissive glance.

"Very well." She straightened, regaining control of her emotions. "Shall we meet here at nine?"

"My pleasure." He stayed seated. "I'll have breakfast available."

Striding to the door, she thought of one last question. "Your plan for the dogs?"

He scribbled on a notepad.

"Dimitri?"

He glanced at her, acting startled. "Oh, you're still here." He grinned. "We'll release them in a few days. You see, I do have a heart."

She slipped out the door, clicked it shut, and whispered to herself.

"Liar."

Chapter 48 – Bugged

IEG Main Security Headquarters, Albertville, France
Saturday, 18 January 1992, 7:25 a.m.

Dad walked with Alex and me to the IEG Security Headquarters. Gilbert ushered us back to Willie's office. Franco lounged in a chair inside, sipping a hot tea.

"Mates, come on in. Get your drinks and we'll start."

Dad and Alex grabbed a hot cup of coffee.

"No hot chocolate?" I glanced at Willie.

His eye twinkled. "I'm sure that's a crime in this country. But you'll live."

Settling for a cup of coffee, I stirred in lots of cream and sugar. After removing our coats, Alex and I stored our backpacks under our chairs, and Dad set his briefcase on the floor. We settled in our seats. Franco sat by the door, then me, Dad, and Alex.

Our Aussie friend stood and motioned for Gilbert to lower the blinds in the room.

"We've run a check on our offices here and at the Drug Testing Station." Willie fiddled with a projector on his desk and clicked to the first slide. "This presentation will be the quickest way to fill you in." We've found twenty different bugs in the Testing Site and five in here."

I sat forward and spilled my coffee on the floor. "What? You mean the crooks have been listening to us all the time?"

Dad tapped me on the shoulder. "Get some paper towels and wipe that clean."

I jumped out of my chair, grabbed some napkins from Willie's coffee table, and scoured the floor. I trashed the wet paper and tapped my shoe on the floor to check it.

Willie waved me back into my seat. "Gilbert will clean the floor later. And yes, the criminals have been listening, but—"

He flipped to the second slide.

"We knew about it for three days." The Aussie lifted a wooden pointer and indicated where the spies hid each microphone. "Killed the connections here in a flash. Faked information for the other locations."

Alex cocked his head. "They'll know you're on to them."

Willie shook his head. "We leaked an upgrade to our countermeasures against spying before we cut them off. Now their listening experience consists of a loud buzzing sound."

Franco sucked down some coffee. "Is that why Sofia isn't here? Or Bastien?"

Willie moved the extra chair in the office to sit next to Alex and the coffee table. He handed Gilbert the clicker for the slide projector and called out, "Next."

The slide changed and a list of bullet points filled the screen.

"Cool." Franco studied the slide. "You found a lot of info on the dogs."

The Aussie chuckled. "Leads, for the most part. Bastien talked to a support team member for the Italian skate team. He happened to be near your old hotel when a commotion arose outside the building. A couple of men carried two muzzled dogs, a huge black animal and an orange hairball, to a panel van parked in the hotel's service entrance."

"Lightning, the hairball." I grinned. "Not a bad description."

Willie shrugged. "Both dogs seemed drugged, but the informer said the black dog snarled and barked when the man tossed him into the van. The men wore uniforms and the van's logo advertised one of the hotel's cleaning companies called Nettoyants Savoie."

"When will your men investigate this information?" Dad's gaze swept over our Aussie friend.

"They started last night." Willie stretched his legs in front of him and motioned to Gilbert. The next slide popped into view.

Franco's eyes widened. "You found the van."

Our Aussie friend smiled. "Correct. Bastien stopped by to talk about what he knew. We researched the company, which reported a truck missing, and located the abandoned vehicle on the west side of town. We found dog hairs, black and orange, but nothing else yet. Twenty minutes ago, a fresh team initiated more detailed forensics and went to talk with the company. I'll get an update by noon unless they find something earlier."

"Did Sofia tell you her plans for today?" I finished my coffee. "She planned to buy some drugs."

"A gutsy sheila, she is." The Aussie drew his legs back to his chair. "I don't know many blokes that would attempt to be a buyer. She told me a girl at the party last night knew how to get drugs if she wanted them for her Junior IEG competitions."

A troubled expression crossed Alex's face. "The girl told Sofia that she would arrange a drop for her tomorrow at the Women's Downhill Elim Finals event at Méribel."

"I reckon that's right." Our friend stood, went to a map on his wall, and tapped it with his finger. "Sofia's friend told her most of the drops take place in Méribel or Val-D'Isère because the sellers could disperse with ease if Security made an appearance."

Dad's voice rose in pitch. "She's not going alone, is she?"

Willie turned from the map. "No, not in the beginning. We didn't have her come to the Security office in case our unknown enemy had us under exterior surveillance. When she called last night, I told her not to come in. A trained agent will meet her in town, follow her to the drop, and watch her. She will also have a transponder and a hidden wire and camera to catch the transaction."

I pulled out my transponder from a pocket. "Like this?"

Franco held out his hand. I dropped the gadget onto his palm. He examined it and glanced at Alex.

My brother patted a pants pocket. "Yep. Me too."

"When's the drop?" I grabbed a donut from the coffee table.

Alex sat straighter. "Yeah. I'd like to see her before she tackles this mission."

Willie dropped into his office chair, sliding it forward to his desk. He shuffled some papers, grabbing one. "The drop is at one this afternoon. At Méribel. The friend who gave her the information and arranged the meeting acted scared. She'll take Sofia to the area, point out the general location, and wander away. We have cameras in most areas. We're analyzing different feeds now to find Izabella and the dogs."

"How can we support her." Franco narrowed his eyes.

Willie swiveled his chair to Alex. "Sofia's schedule needs to look ordinary. Connecting with her this morning is a perfect cover. But she'll separate about noon to prepare. You'll meet her after and walk her partway to the drop with her friend."

I touched another donut. "Oops. Another one bites the dust." I munched on one side and waved the donut at Willie. "That's a perfect fit with our plans." I swallowed. "I want to see a famous American baseball player named Rodriguez compete on the Bobsled runs at La Plagne. We can see the nine o'clock run, but we'll need a car to get us over to Méribel in fifty minutes for the eleven-fifteen start."

Willie shook his head. "Sorry. Limited resources, you know." He searched for and found a pointer, stood, walked to his map, and traced the route from La Plagne to Méribel. "Looks to me like we have the regular IEG shuttle that can make the run in an hour." He raised an eyebrow. "Unless you'd like to contribute to our police budget?"

I grabbed a ten-dollar bill from my pocket. "Here."

Our Aussie friend took the bill, examined it, and tucked it in a desk drawer. "That'll get you a toy car, mate. But considering my coffee and donut bill for feeding you, I believe we'll call it even."

My eyes widened, the obvious shock registering on my face.

Dad laughed. "Serves you right." He checked his watch. "Willie, I need to run. Here's the laydown you wanted from me on Dimitri." Dad retrieved a folder stuffed with paper from his briefcase and passed it to him. "You can see he has quite a history with the KGB, Interpol, and he's known on the U.S. networks. He's crafty, cagey, and an intense personality. Pretty high in the KGB retired population. Many others that have stood in his way disappeared."

Franco gulped. "And he's got a bead on us."

I patted his shoulder. "We won't let that happen to any of us."

Dad squared his shoulders. His eyes bored into Willie with the force of a laser for the next point. "Dimitri's men have chased and attempted to remove my boys and their friends from the IEG venues. At this point, I think Vasiliev is trying to scare my boys and their friends, but if danger tips the scales much further against us, I'm pulling my sons out."

Willie cleared his throat. "Mr. Zanadu, we can stop this all now."

Dad shook his head. "No. These men violated my household. I believe God will work this out like He's done in the past. They have clues and a key from a Mr. G who hasn't been wrong yet. But don't forget, these criminals, with special emphasis on the Russian, can be cut-throats." Dad stood and plucked his coat from the coat rack. "I've got a U.S. mission to run. If I obtain more background on Dimitri, you'll be the first to know." He glanced at Alex and me. "Don't overcommit. Stay in contact. Let the Security team do their work. You're assisting—nothing else. Got it?"

We both nodded.

Dad left with a wave at Willie.

The Aussie stared at the door after our father walked out and quiet descended on the room.

I jumped to my feet, reached the coffee table, and grabbed the last donut. "One for the road. Gotta keep strong."

Chapter 49 – Drug Deal Prep

Bus to La Plagne, Highway N90, Southeast of Albertville, France

Saturday, 18 January 1992, 8:19 a.m.

I sat by Sofia with Gabe and Franco behind us on the bus to La Plagne for the Bobsled runs. Bastien caught us before we left Albertville. Because he planned to do business in Méribel after the Women's Downhill event, he decided to drive and meet us in the town around eleven-thirty.

The bus heater cut the air's sharp chill, but the temperature remained cool to ensure riders didn't sweat on the fifty-five-minute ride to La Plagne. Sofia and I took our coats off. Gabe and Franco, both skinnier than me, left their coats unzipped but on.

"Scared?" I nudged Sofia while the background noise in the bus grew from all the conversations.

Her lips squinched together. "Nice weather we're having here. Sunny. Cold. But beautiful. What's the weather like in Texas right now?"

Weather talk? That boggled my mind. She must be frightened. Or maybe careful. I scanned the bus but didn't see anyone that looked suspicious. "How many friends did you talk with last night? I lost track during the second party."

Her eyes glowed. The rest of the bus ride conversation went back and forth about our friends—what they thought and did. After learning that she couldn't stand pink, wanted to become Italy's number one skater, and wanted to travel around the world, I understood her better. I explained that I wanted to go into the military like my Dad, travel the world, and become an engineer. In the end, the ride felt short.

"Come on, bro." Gabe tapped me on the shoulder. "You and Sofia can't ride the bus back to Albertville."

Sofia and I smiled. I followed her when she exited the bus and we searched until we found the Bobsled Run stands.

Gabe pointed to the American section. "I'm getting a seat now. The baseball player's team might be one of the first runs."

"Take Franco and save us seats." I waved him away. "We're going to get something to drink."

Gabe drifted forward. "Get me a hot chocolate, will you?"

"Sure." I touched Sofia's arm. "Let's find a quick-stop eatery."

She took my arm. "I couldn't talk about it on the bus."

"It?" When the word came out of my mouth, I knew what she meant. "Right." We strolled and I listened.

She shook her head, talking with me but not looking at me. "Dangerous." She tightened her grip on my arm. "I'm going to disappear for a moment with no one watching me. I'll bet wherever we're meeting, the crooks have disabled the cameras and kept the lighting low."

I glanced at her.

She pressed her lips together. "Surprise will be their tactics. Maybe they won't recognize me. But they might. We've spent a lot of time together the past few days. They could know I'm attached to you." Sofia squeezed my arm.

"I'll be praying for you."

She blinked her eyes and accelerated our pace.

I let her guide me to the coffee shop. "You don't have to go through with this."

"I *have* to help." She swallowed. "Drug dealers spring up wherever we go. It's personal for me. Junior IEGs officials in Italy barred my fifteen-year-old brother, Lorenzo, from competing due to drug use. Now the dealers took your dogs. Your friends. Chasing us with guns. It'll get worse if we don't take them down now."

We reached the coffee shop and made our order: cappuccinos for her and me, and hot chocolates for Gabe and Franco. After paying for the drinks, we retraced our path to the stands.

"The dealer's bosses, Dimitri and Genevieve, will make us pay for interfering." I balanced the drinks while she pulled me around three kids dashing through the crowd. "Promise me something."

"What?" She gazed in my direction.

I stopped. Looked deep into her blue eyes. I felt myself getting lost as we locked onto each other. "Promise me that at the first sign of trouble, you'll cut out and run."

She clenched her jaw.

I cleared my throat. "Gabe and I have survived our first five adventures because God kept us safe. We walked into trouble. Failed to see the warning signs." Breaking eye contact for a second, I returned to her unrelenting focus. "Be smart. Getting hurt by them doesn't help anyone. Leave if the operation falls apart."

Seconds passed. Her jaw muscles twitched. She dropped her eyes to the ground. She whispered something.

"What?"

She drew in a breath and let it out slowly. "Okay." She wiggled her neck back and forth to loosen the muscles. "I don't want to let you and Gabe down."

I wanted to hug her but didn't want to spill the drinks. I smiled. "You won't."

We continued to the stands. Gabe and Franco waved at us to join them.

I led the way through the packed metal stairway. Near the top, we side-stepped our way into the two open spots Gabe held for us and sat.

"Couldn't find seats farther from the exit point, could you?" I needled my brother while handing him his drink.

Gabe narrowed his eyes at me. "I doubt you could have done any better—"

Franco jabbed a finger at the track. "There." He banged on Gabe's shoulder. "The man on the left."

My brother shifted a bit, stood on his toes. "Yep. That's him." He pulled out a baseball trading card." Manuel Rodriguez. Six foot-three, 241 pounds. All muscle."

"He doesn't look happy." Sofia watched the man and his driver glance at the run time. "Not the best run on the track for them today."

I shrugged. "Four runs total. Two today and two tomorrow. He still has time to redeem himself."

Gabe poked me. "Get a picture of him for me, will you?"

I handed Sofia my drink and dug in my backpack. By the time I got the camera in my hand and ready, the baseball player had disappeared. "Maybe next time."

"We have to leave before the next run starts." My brother shook his head. "You're getting slow."

Sofia tilted her head at Gabe. "We did get you a hot chocolate. Besides, we're here to watch competitors from each nation."

Chapter 50 – Options

Méribel, France
Saturday, 18 January 1992, 10:56 a.m.

Bastien met us at Méribel next to a concession stand. A blanket of snow covered the streets and sidewalks, though little remained on the walkways. Bastien brought us a note from Willie, which we passed around while we ate lunch and munched on hotdogs, fries, and French pastries. I read it last and pondered his message:

> Team – Here are three plans for the operation. Either it's a cracker, muddle, or dog's breakfast.
>
> Plan A – Cracker – Best plan possible. The deal goes through with no hitches, Sofia returns with the drugs, and cameras capture the exchange.
>
> Plan B – Muddle – The exchange doesn't oc-cur, the dealers don't show, no drugs trans-

ferred, or we don't get camera footage of the deal. Sofia's threatened.

Plan C – Dog's Breakfast – A disaster. The dealers keep the drugs, take the money, hurt Sofia, and escape.

Assisting Sofia. Agent Renee Dupree – French

Watching Agent Dupree – Sam Rutherford – American

Backup to capture fleeing dealers. Two snowmobiles behind the ski shop next to drop off.

Several Drug Test positives this morning. Could affect medal standings. I can't make it out for a while.

Willie

"Restroom break?" Sofia pointed at the public toilets nearby.

Gabe and I slung our backpacks on. "Meet you in the front." We used the facilities and about ten minutes later, Sofia joined us by the entrance. As a gaggle of teens, we strolled to the stadium seats for the Women's Downhill event and settled into our seats.

Sofia's friend, Natalie, joined us around twelve-thirty. While the two girls separated themselves at the end of our row to chat, we cheered for the competitors and joked around. About fifteen minutes before 1:00 p.m., Sofia and her friend stood and walked out of the stands without saying goodbye.

Bastien tugged on my coat and pointed.

I grabbed my pack and hustled to the stairs behind Sofia and her friend. They passed the edge of the stands, the stadium exit, and headed for some businesses on the closest village street.

"Wait for me." I jogged to catch them.

The girls paused and Natalie checked her watch. "Did you want something?"

"I thought I would…uh…spend some time with Sofia and you?"

Natalie raised an eyebrow. "Girl time. No guys allowed."

Sofia giggled. "Boys—can't keep them away, can we?" She smiled, turned her head so that Natalie couldn't see, and winked.

I stood in my spot, planted like a tree. "I could walk you into town."

Sofia widened her eyes at me before resuming her smile. "Maybe later."

I knew she wanted me to leave, but I struggled with that. Thoughts exploded through my mind at a dizzying rate. If I didn't let them go, Natalie wouldn't be able to take Sofia to the drop. That would ruin the plan. But I didn't have a choice. "Okay. See you in a bit."

Natalie stared at me until I reversed course, trudged back through the pedestrians, and rounded the corner of the stadium.

I counted to thirty and peeked around the stadium's entrance at the roadway. I couldn't see the girls. But I did see Agent Dupree. She strolled half a block away on the far side of the street. She gave herself away when she whirled around, dug her compact out of a purse, and powdered her nose in a mirror, a common technique of inexperienced female professional investigators to keep track of their targets.

Gabe sighed. "Willie guaranteed an experienced operative, not a klutz." He, Franco, and Bastien gathered beside me.

My brother tapped me on the shoulder and pointed. "Let's window-shop at that ski shop. We'll keep an eye on you and look for Agent Sam."

Dupree resumed her ambling on the village sidewalk, frequently checking Sofia's location.

I stayed on the opposite side of the road of the agent, the side the girls must be on. When we neared the general area of the drop-off point, I strained to see past the tourists to catch a glimpse of Sofia.

When Dupree stopped, I did the same. She hesitated and pulled out a tourist map. Made a big show of taking a few steps one way, unfolding the map, shaking her head, and going back in the original direction. The lost tourist act seemed silly but an acceptable disguise.

I spied Natalie walking away on my side of the street. She quick-walked to the far side using a crosswalk and increased her pace to the next traffic light. Sofia's friend wasn't sticking around. Did something terrible happen?

A snowmobile appeared from an alley on my side of the street.

Two bulky men held a woman between them with her hands tied in front. Sofia. I clenched my fists, mad that I let her get caught in a trap.

"Hey." I waved across the street to Gabe, Bastien, and Franco. "Snowmobile."

I dashed to the vehicle. The other guys recognized the problem and sprinted.

Dupree raced into the street, holding out her hands to stop the snowmobile. A black Mercedes sped forward, slid on the snow-covered road, and smacked into the agent. She crumpled to the ground. Agent Sam burst out of a store and rushed to her side. He jerked a walkie-talkie from a pocket and shouted commands.

"Plan C." I waved the guys to cross the street to a ski shop on my side, where two parked snowmobiles waited.

When we arrived, Gabe darted to one of the machines. A man bolted outside the shop, yelled, and tried to stop my brother from mounting the snowmobile. Franco rushed to Gabe's side.

I zig-zagged around him to the other snowmobile and jumped on. The key turned without a hitch and the motor roared to life. Since Franco and Gabe tussled with the man from the shop, I shouted at Bastien. "Get on behind me. We're losing time."

Bastien said something in French to the man, which made him pause, calming him a little. Following that, he threw his bulk on our machine.

I opened the throttle to maneuver through the snarled traffic on the street, glancing in the mirrors for safety. I caught part of the action behind me.

Gabe pushed the man back into Franco, scrambled on the second snowmobile, and eased into the street. Franco argued with the guy while he shook a fist at my brother.

Bastien slapped my shoulder. "Watch the traffic ahead. A policeman has stopped cars in both directions to allow Agent Sam to aid Agent Dupree."

"Got it." I gunned the engine, steering around the motionless vehicles. "The men with Sofia are getting away." I risked one last glimpse in the mirrors.

Gabe's snowmobile dodged around people and vehicles, speeding to close the gap between us.

"We're losing them." I gunned the engine.

"Go right." Bastien thumped my back.

I opened the throttle and we skittered past a curb, snow flying when the tread re-established itself on the snow-covered street.

"Hurry." Bastien leaned forward into my back. "Gabe's almost caught us."

We raced at full throttle through the empty side of the street.

"Left turn." Bastien tapped on my left. "See the tracks?"

I did. An oncoming car approached at close to 50 kph, the speed limit downtown.

"Say a prayer." I whipped the snowmobile to the left, losing a little traction on an icy spot in the snow.

The car went into a slide, careening sideways at us.

I cranked the throttle wide and hoped we would make it.

Chapter 51 – Frozen Pond

Mountain Trail near Méribel, France

Saturday, 18 January 1992, 1:27 p.m.

Gabe zipped around Bastien and me. "I'm faster. I'll take the lead in the chase."

The prayer rushed from my lips. "Lord, protect Sofia." I followed Gabe and the kidnappers on the slopes outside of town.

Extra snowmobile tracks told me at least one or two more snowmobiles were in the mix besides Gabe and me. I couldn't see my brother anymore. We were on our own. I gritted my teeth. *Not again.*

After several minutes of flying over the trails, dodging branches, and finding shortcuts to catch Sofia and her kidnappers, we slowed to negotiate a tight left turn that brought us to a frozen pond. I opened the throttle and sped across the surface—about a quarter football field wide and almost half a football field long.

Thick woods surrounded the oval pond, growing to the edge on both sides except at the trail entrance and exit on either side of the pond. Several small streams flowed into and out of the pond from the sides.

When we approached the middle of the pond, my heart pounded. Popping and splintering sounds accompanied the appearance of cracks in the windswept ice. "Hang on." I gunned the engine, hoping we wouldn't break through the ice.

The cracks lessened the closer we came to the edge of the pond. The snowmobile slid onto solid ground on the far side and I released the breath I held.

"Turn around." Bastien patted my shoulder. "I'm sure someone's following us."

I whipped the snowmobile to the right behind some tall pines to hide.

"The ice is weak." Bastien dismounted. He rushed to grab a thick, broken branch, about half my height and twice the thickness of my biceps. "Maybe I can break it with this branch and put the guys chasing us into the water."

"Great," I said. "Do it."

Bastien gripped the log in his hands and lumbered onto the ice about ten yards. He raised the log over his head and slammed it into the ice.

Little clicks and cricks told me Bastien needed to hit harder. "Not enough." I searched for anything in the snowmobile storage compartments that might help us and glanced at my friend's progress. "Go out farther. Hurry." I found a rope, a flare gun, several flares, a couple of screwdrivers, a small socket wrench, and a multi-tool knife.

Bastien hustled forward several more yards. He pounded the ice again. The popping sounds got louder. I pocketed some screwdrivers, took the flare gun, and sprinted to the right of Bastien for a good angle to shoot at the person trailing us.

Engine sounds alerted me to the approach of the chaser's machine. At the left turn, his snowmobile slid sideways into a tree and surrounding bushes, bringing him to stop.

Bastien pounded the ice one last time, turned, and darted to me. He slipped and crashed onto the ice.

A huge crack appeared, snaking under Bastien on our side and across the pond to the other side.

The guy wrestled with his machine, freed it from the entangling bushes and tree, and roared onto the ice.

"Stay low, Bastien." I leveled the flare gun at the snowmobile and fired.

The flare flashed into the rider, catching him on the chest. He released his machine and fell, flailing to get rid of the burning flare. His machine slid to a stop a few feet away from him near the middle of the pond.

Bastien scrambled on his knees to get off the ice, which groaned with each move.

I threw the flare gun at our snowmobile, dashed over to him, tugged him to his feet, and crashed into the ice myself. I waved at my friend. "Get off the ice."

Snaps and clicks sounded from the ice like firecrackers going off. Bastien retreated to the edge of the pond while I rose to my hands and feet, about twenty yards from the guy's machine.

The chaser got to his feet, dashed to his ride, and yanked a rifle from its holster.

I climbed to my feet.

"Hands in the air." The man faced me, his rifle going to his shoulder.

Before he set his firing stance, I flipped a screwdriver out of my pocket and threw it.

The man side-stepped and slipped on the ice.

I raced to the log Bastien dropped earlier. Straining, I whacked it into the ice near the big crack at least three times before the man yelled at us.

"Stop." The man stood tall, rifle aimed at my chest. "Enough games."

I dropped the log and raised my hands in the air, edging back in tiny increments to solid ground.

"Stay right there." The man tilted his head to see through the scope of the rifle. "One more move, no matter how small, and you'll be eating a bullet."

I held my position a few feet in front of Bastien.

Satisfied I wouldn't budge, the chaser back-pedaled to his

machine and climbed on without hesitation. He glanced at the ignition, dropping one hand to start the engine. Distracted, he didn't see me move back at first. But his head snapped around when I took my second step. He smirked. "I told you not to move." He swung the rifle to his shoulder. Sighted on me.

Two big does broke from the trees on my left, pounded a few feet onto the ice, and darted back into the treeline.

Startled, the rifleman lost his focus. The ice creaked beneath him.

I eased back another step.

Three smaller deer appeared and disappeared on the same path. But the distracted rifleman refocused and aimed again.

"Down," Bastien said.

I tried to turn and run but lost my footing. I dropped to a knee, facing the man's snowmobile.

The ice cracked like the snap of a whip.

Losing his balance, the rifleman fired a quick shot and fell on his machine.

I felt a burning sensation in my left arm but focused on my opponent.

The force of his impact on the snowmobile spelled disaster. Screaming, the man and his machine disappeared beneath the ice.

Chapter 52 – Joining Forces

Mountain Trails near Méribel, France
Saturday, 18 January 1992, 1:51 p.m.

I parked my snowmobile to see if Alex and Bastien followed me. But I didn't stop for long—another snowmobile driven by one guy barreled over the slopes at me.

Why didn't Alex follow me? I knew the right course of action. The snowmobile carrying Sofia disappeared in front of me a few minutes earlier, headed to my right. Should I follow them or find my brother? I shook my head, made my decision, and swung my snowmobile around, launching straight at my pursuer's machine. I could play chicken with the best of them.

At first, the man didn't react. I guess he reasoned I would lose my nerve.

"Come on." I opened the throttle wide. Speeding downhill, I aimed directly at his machine and searched for a slight bump under the snow to use as a ski jump.

He kept on course. In seconds we'd collide if he didn't veer off.

A faint shadow in the snow ahead showed the bump I needed. "Faster. Roll, baby." I rose from my seat, preparing for the impact.

The other snowmobile slowed.

I hit the bump and flew through the air, my track aimed at the man's head.

He veered left and plowed into some brush on that side.

I landed my snowmobile and cranked the throttle more. "Take that, little man." I neared a spot where I thought Alex and Bastien went another way. But a second set of ski tracks crossed the first set and went through the trees. I stopped and let my machine idle. "Which way did they go?"

I studied the tracks. One set was deeper than the others. That would be my brother and Bastien, assuming a single man chased them. I heard the roar of a snowmobile and turned to check it out. The man chasing me raced across the hill. I chose the deeper tracks and gunned it.

Minutes later, with my pursuer gaining on me, I found where my brother turned right through the trees. I slowed, made the turn, and twisted the throttle for more speed. Bouncing over some brush and tiny trees, I jiggled and jumped to another trail. Two sets of tracks covered the ground. I swept to my left to follow. The guy chasing me crashed through the brush. I might have three or four seconds on him.

I slowed and negotiated a tight left turn. In front of me, an icy pond marred by a hole in the middle caught my attention. Bastien stood on the opposite end of the pond, waving me to my right.

I stopped and scanned the woods. I yelled. "There's no trail." Raised my hands and shrugged.

Bastien stomped his foot and pointed.

I glimpsed a slight opening, like an animal trail, to my right. I swerved into the gap, wiggling my machine through the trees. The snow wasn't that deep, but I navigated over fallen limbs, past a few rocks, and around many bushes.

The man chasing me closed the distance.

When the trail widened halfway around the pond, I goosed the gas and sped through a wider gap between two trees with bushes on both sides. The path widened out and I rounded the far corner of the pond. Bastien raised a hand for me to stop.

"What?" I backed off the throttle when he stepped in front of me.

Bastien pointed at a clearing in the woods behind me.

The guy following me shot through the wide gap between the trees and flipped in the air.

"Lucky man." Bastien stepped around my machine. "Alex's rope almost caught him in the neck."

Alex stood by one of the trees and darted away from us.

The man rolled, his snowmobile shutting off and sliding into a tree. He jumped to his feet, searching for the person who set the trap.

I revved my engine, turned my snowmobile around, and waited.

The man neared the trees where the rope lay. Drew his revolver.

"Oh, no, you don't." I jerked forward, passing Bastien, and gained speed.

The gunman fired into the bushes on one side and stepped closer.

I flew at top speed at the man trying to kill my brother.

Alex rose from the brush pile on the other side and threw something at the man.

The gunman clutched his shoulder and dropped the weapon into the snow.

Like a knight on a horse, when I passed the guy, I kicked out with my right foot, knocking him into a tree. His helmet bounced off the trunk.

He shook his head, got on hands and knees, and swiped snow away from where he lost the gun.

We had to keep him occupied. If he found that weapon, we might not live to tell about it.

Chapter 53 – Recon Work

The Frozen Pond near Méribel, France
Saturday, 18 January 1992, 2:33 p.m.

Gabe." Alex pelted the man with rocks and snowballs from his side of the trail. "Make another run."

I turned my snowmobile around, snagged some broken branches thick enough to be clubs, wedged them between my leg and the seat, and rocketed back into the action.

On his knees, the attacker groped for the weapon he'd dropped. He stilled for a second, leapt to his feet, and whirled to face Alex, gun in hand.

Rats. My muscles tensed. *Now he's armed and dangerous.* I raced closer.

He swung the gun in my direction. Fired.

Heart pounding, I ducked and swerved. His bullet missed me but went through the windshield.

Alex smacked him on the helmet with a snowball, distracting him.

Close enough to attack, I realigned my machine. About two car lengths from the guy, I yanked out a branch, stood, and threw it at his head.

He raised an arm to block the club-like wood but kept the gun trained in my direction.

Like a one-two punch, Alex hurled a rock the size of a baseball into the man's face shield, cracking it. He staggered, aim wavering.

I kicked him in the gut when I flew by, connecting with his weapon hand on my follow-through. The gun went off. The force of my boot knocked it into the snow again and the man crumpled to the ground. I slowed and turned for another run.

Alex charged out of the bushes and jumped on the man, wrestling to gain control.

Bastien ran to me, huffing and puffing. "What can I do?"

"Find some rope to tie his hands." I waited. Bastien returned in seconds and slid behind me. I roared back to Alex.

Alex twisted the guy's wrist backward until he stopped struggling. "Tie his legs together first."

I jumped off, took the ropes from Bastien, and tied the man's feet and hands. "We have more people chasing us on snowmobiles." I stood. "We should turn the tables on them."

Bastien gulped for air. "I'd rather have a nice dinner and let the Games Security Team handle this."

"We still need to finish with the man who fell in the water." Alex motioned to the other side of the pond. "The guy who tried to kill me."

I glanced at my brother. "You've been busy. What's that bandage on your left arm?"

Alex smiled. "Nothing. A flesh wound from the man chasing me. We need to get him in an emergency blanket, though. He's like an icicle."

Bastien lifted his hand at my snowmobile. "Can you give us a lift to our machine?"

"Sure." I sat forward. "It's a short distance. I can take you both."

We crowded around the man who went through the ice after reaching Alex and Bastien's snowmobile, dismounting, and trekking to his position behind a tree. Alex released the rope wrapped around the man and the tree. The wet guy fell sideways. Shivered. His pale skin appeared waxy and his hands and lips showed a bluish tinge.

I scanned our captive. "Hypothermia. Let's get his wet clothes off and wrap him in a blanket."

Alex and I dragged him back to our snowmobiles. Bastien dug through storage compartments for supplies. Our French buddy found an emergency blanket in my machine, a sleeping bag shell and thermal blanket in Alex's, and zip-ties in both sleds. My brother and I stripped the wet guy to his undershorts, zip-tied his hands and feet, and wrapped him in the thermal blanket.

"Put him inside the sleeping bag shell." I helped Bastien while Alex zip-tied the other man's hands. We propped both men against a tree.

Alex wrapped the rope around their pursuer first, tied it off, and looped it around the second man, going through the arms and the legs. When he finished, he stepped back to check his work.

I strode to the man in the thermal blanket, adjusting his head in the sleeping bag shell. "He needs to breathe into the shell and thermal blanket to retain the warmth of his breath. That will gradually increase his body temperature." Satisfied, I approached Bastien. "Why don't you take my pursuer's snowmobile?" I handed the man's key to Bastien. "Keep it for evidence. Now they won't have a quick way to leave if they get out."

Our French friend accepted the key. "Good idea. But we need to inform Security in the next couple of hours. The sun will set by 6:00 p.m. and the wet man will freeze even with the blanket."

We climbed aboard our machines and revved them.

"First, we need to locate Sofia." Alex pointed along the trail. "We can cut them off continuing past this pond."

I shook my head. "Whoa." Bastien and Alex stared at me. "I saw them take a different trail before reaching this water hole. If we go in your direction, we'll never find them."

"I'm sure they followed this path." Alex sat back. "I watched from the hill, checking out which way they might take."

"But I saw them in front of me." I tapped my ruined windshield. "I watched them get away. You—"

Bastien made a slashing motion with one hand. "Quit arguing. I know these mountains. Look at the tracks leaving this pond." He waved his hand at the snow. "One set of tracks. If we check out Gabe's direction, we lose maybe ten minutes. Several tracks led off to the right. If we go in Alex's direction, we may be following a decoy and never find Sofia."

I raised my eyebrows at my brother. He hesitated and motioned for me to lead. "Go for it." I skirted the pond, going back the way I came in, and found the place where the snowmobile tracks diverged.

We could still trace the tracks of the other snowmobile with Sofia. Ski ruts deeper than Alex and Bastien's that led to the right.

About thirty minutes later, I stopped. Bastien and Alex drove to my side. I drew a hand across my neck.

We shut off our machines. An engine roar came from the woods in front of us. We dismounted. Alex snuck forward on the left side of the trail. Bastien and I crept along the right. In thirty feet, the forest ended.

A crack sounded. One of the trees in the woods across the open field in front of us fell, sending powdery snow flying in the air. A man carrying a gas-powered saw stomped his way out of the woods to the tree. He cut it up.

To our right, a large two-story house occupied the center of the clearing, positioned at a slight cattycorner to us. Smoke rose in plumes from the chimney. Light shone from each window. An attached garage completed the side opposite us. A separate woodshed or shop of some sort poked out from behind the home. A plowed driveway extended from the garage to our right. The snowmobile tracks we followed went behind the house.

Alex made the fallback sign. When we reached our snowmobiles, he said, "We need to make a plan."

"First, we need to make sure Sofia is here." I pointed to the tracks. "I'm sure these are the right tracks, but we can't make mistakes."

"Right." Alex shook his head. "You know everything."

Bastien tapped me on the shoulder. "Once we're sure they're here, one of us should leave to tell Willie what's happening in case we can't get inside or we need to wait to attempt a rescue."

Alex and I exchanged a glance.

"He's right." Alex pointed to the snowmobiles. "While that guy's cutting wood, we can park these machines for a quick exit.

After backing the machines into the woods, we regrouped.

Alex drew a diagram of the house, garage, driveway, and woodshed in the snow. "We approach on a diagonal to the back corner of the house near the woodshed. One at a time."

"Why not from behind the woodshed?" Bastien indicated a direct approach from the treeline in the back with his finger. "It's quicker."

"More exposure." I tapped the corner of the house. "No windows facing this direction. The windows we can see have some kind of drapes, which limits the vision even more. But if you come directly from the back trees, the second-story windows have a great view to see our approach."

"Ah." Bastien sat back.

Alex drew a line to the corner of the house, looping it behind the building to the middle. "Since a woodshed sits at the building's rear, there's a high probability the house has a back door. We need to flatten ourselves to the house wall, creep under any windows, and peek into the back door. Based on the front door, which has a window in it, the rear door should also have a window."

I poked my finger by the door, twice on one side and once on the other. "I'll cross over the doorstep or concrete pad to the other side, leaving you and Bastien on the side closest to our current position." I raised a finger. "I'll take the first look, slide back, and tell you both what I saw. If Sofia is there, we prepare to enter."

Our plan felt good. I pumped my fist. "We'll get her out."

Alex grinned. "A piece of cake."

When Bastien didn't smile, I studied his face a little closer. He seemed nervous. A few beads of sweat glistened on his forehead. "Something wrong, Bastien?"

His eyes widened a bit. "When you enter the house, that's when I leave?" He licked his lips.

Alex patted his shoulder. "Yes. Gabe and I know how to get into the house, even if it's locked, subdue the staff without making a sound, get Sofia, and return here. You'll be gone, but we can call you when we reach the town to let you know we're safe."

"You're sure you can do it?"

I rose to my feet and tapped my chest and motioned at my brother. "We're bona fide rescuers. Experts that never fail."

Alex smiled. "We have lots of experience."

"Tons." My jaw tightened. "With Thunder and Lightning, we couldn't lose."

Bastien pressed his lips together. "You miss them?"

Alex looked away. I took a deep breath. "Like I'd miss my right arm. They're family." I swallowed. "Let's get back on task." I demonstrated the hand signals we would use for this minor operation to Bastien. "Time for a protein bar and water."

Ten minutes later, refreshed and focused, we weaved our way through the trees to the diagonal point we selected.

"What about the man with the saw?" Bastien motioned across the field.

"Good question." I tilted my head at logger. "He's got three-quarters of a tree to saw and about an hour or two of daylight. He won't stop until he's done. But if he does...."

Alex patted his backpack. "We have tools to restrain him and leave him in the woodshed."

"And if the door's locked?" Our friend swallowed.

I grinned. "Not to fear. Alex can pick locks and I have G's key for this mystery around my neck. We'll get in."

Alex lifted a finger to his lips. We went to silent mode. Like a sailor directing a jet to takeoff from an aircraft carrier, he swung his finger at the house.

I glanced at Bastien. With his chunky frame, he wouldn't run well or for a long period of time. "You'll have to crouch while you run to the house." I demonstrated the position.

He tried to copy me, but his form looked uncomfortable.

"Forget it." I waved my hand away. "Run as fast as you can. When I reach the house, I'll signal for you."

He sucked in a deep breath of air. "Got it."

This would be risky. I glanced at Alex's raised hand for the "Go" signal.

Chapter 54 – Deception Plot

House on a Hill near Méribel, France
Saturday, 18 January 1992, 3:50 p.m.

The walkie-talkie's green light in Dimitri's hand glowed brightly. Incoming call. He raised the device to his ear and listened. Smiling, he clicked off and laid it on a table beside him.

"Genevieve, the kids are in the woods, watching the house."

Dimitri and Genevieve sat in the comfortable sitting room on the second floor, monitoring the situation around the home. The room, decorated in the latest fashion, contained comfortable chairs, a sofa, coffee and end tables, complete with plates of snacks, mountain paintings on the wall, and a beautiful scenic view. She occupied a chair, hot tea on the end table beside her, and a report in her hand. The Russian, seated on the opposite end of the sofa, fiddled with his latest gadget.

"Am I supposed to be surprised?" She set down the report from her dealers outlining the impact of the positive results coming out from the testing today. "Of course, they would follow us. The bait's irresistible for the older boy, Alex." She smiled. "He's found love."

Dimitri snorted. "What do kids know of love?" He withdrew a cigar from his pocket, cut the end, and puffed while he used a lighter to get it going. "We have some time to review our plans."

"Must you smoke those filthy things?" She narrowed her eyes at him. "The smoke gets in my hair, on my clothes, and in my nostrils, making everything I wear stink."

"You are a fiery woman." A grin appeared. "Let's go over our actions. Tell me what you remember."

She fumed. His arrogance and continuous desire to control made her stomach churn. *Who was he to tell me what to do?* But she quieted herself, knowing she would cut him out of the operation after they'd removed the threat of the children. She stood and paced.

"We agreed that when the boys reach the back of the house, the lights and the music stay on." She made a mental note to change the music to something louder. At the moment, soft violin music filled the air. "Your man in the woodshed will click his walkie-talkie twice to let us know they're present." She plucked her tea cup from the end table, sipped, and lowered it to the coffee table. The warmth made her throat feel good.

"And?"

She snorted at the man. He annoyed her at every turn. She continued. "We descend to the first floor, past the blindfolded girls, opening and shutting the front door to make the girls think we've left. We hide in the kitchen, let the boys in, and at the right moment, we appear with guns and capture them."

Dimitri blew a ring of smoke. "Perfect. I'll handle the disposal of the loose ends."

After another sip of tea, she tapped the report on her end table. "Have you read this?"

The Russian shrugged. "The highlights. We'd made lots of progress. The authorities haven't caught anyone important using our drugs yet. Our Cooperative Team should take a gold medal and the Italian team can take the silver position in another event." He checked the walkie-talkie. "The false positives we've tried to create have failed. That detective, Willie Gretzke, is hard to beat. We have to discredit the IEGC. They need to pay for ruining Russia's reputation on the world stage in previous world-wide games. And I will make them pay. We still have time left to achieve our goal."

"Russia's reputation is of no consequence to me." She shifted in my chair. "Your goal creates more work."

Dimitri's eyes narrowed. "The goal is important. And we will work to make it happen." He shrugged. "And I appreciate your help setting this in motion because now I will have a network in France."

"This is not a permanent relationship." She let the heat of her anger sharpen her gaze on him. "We are partners for the Elimination Games. Nothing else. France is my territory."

His smile widened.

A chill ran down her spine. Maybe she'd left him too much control of their arrangement. But he couldn't do anything to her. Without her, he would have no capability to supply dealers and set up contacts at the Games. She owned the network, not him. She slipped a cracker from a plate on her end table into her mouth and chewed. *I must eliminate his influence after the IEGs.*

The walkie-talkie clicked twice.

Dimitri stood and squashed his cigar in an ashtray. "Let's get to our hiding spot in the kitchen pantry."

Chapter 55 – Sneaky Entry

House on a Hill near Méribel, France
Saturday, 18 January 1992, 4:18 p.m.

I raced across the open field, crouched low. Gaining the cover of the house, I slid around the corner. Clear. I reversed direction, peered around the corner, and waved them up. Bastien lumbered across the space, followed by Alex.

Backs against the house, Bastien, my brother, and I paused for a count of ten. I crept forward, ducking under two windows to reach the back door. Climbing two steps, part of the small concrete porch, I scurried under the door's half window to the other side.

The others followed. When in place, I stepped close to the door's window and peered inside through lace curtains. The door led into a dark kitchen. Beyond the kitchen area, the house opened into a sunken living room. Sofia sat next to Izabella, both on wooden chairs. The kidnappers blindfolded them, tied their wrists to each chair's back spindles, and secured their feet to the chair's legs. A set of stairs in the background led to the second floor.

A man guarded the girls, lounging on a maroon couch to one side, reading a magazine, and taking swigs from a beer bottle.

I completed my survey of our targets, crept back to Alex and Bastien, and whispered the results of my recon. "Izabella is here too. We've got two girls to rescue." Alex motioned to Bastien. He jogged back to the corner of the house, forgetting to duck under the windows.

"He's gonna get us caught." I glanced at Alex and tapped the side of my head.

Bastien disappeared to our snowmobiles. Alex and I flattened against the house, waiting for the back door to open.

After waiting three minutes without being discovered, I rolled my shoulders to relax them, climbed the two stairs to the rear entry, and prepared to try the doorknob. I took several deep breaths to calm myself. Gliding over the stairs, I placed my hand on the knob and twisted. The door handle didn't rotate. I glanced at Alex and shook my head.

He started to climb the stairs. I raised my hand, he stopped.

I reached inside my shirt and pulled out the latest key from Mr. G. Examining the keyhole, I slid my hands over the cold metal of the key to see if it matched. It might work. Inserting the key without a sound, I turned using light pressure. The key resisted. My jaw clenched. I twisted harder. The key moved. A fraction of an inch at a time, I increased the pressure. A slight click sounded.

I ducked away and Alex pulled back. I tensed, getting ready to use my Karate skills.

Seconds ticked away.

A minute later, Alex raised his thumb.

Hyper-alert, I set my feet by the edge of the door to slow it from opening if the guard wanted to pounce on us. Setting my other foot in a balanced stance, I peered inside. I waved to Alex for him to join me. I raised two fingers to my eyes. Pointed at him to indicate he should check out the setup inside. He copied my earlier move and crouched low.

"Go." His lips moved, but I didn't hear his whisper.

I opened the door.

Chapter 56 – Betrayal

House on a Hill near Méribel, France
Saturday, 18 January 1992, 4:30 p.m.

I slid through the door first, Alex right on my heels. He closed the door, staying low. Without a sound, he scrambled to my side, hiding beside the kitchen's stove, out of the guard's sight.

The man watching our friends shifted in his chair, checking both girls for any changes. By focusing on them, he faced away from us.

I tapped Alex.

My brother found a cutting board on the counter and dropped it.

The clatter brought the guard running, his gun in his hand.

I stayed low. Alex crouched several feet behind me, per the indoor plan. When the guard reached the stove, he threw his glove against a lower back corner cabinet.

The distraction made the man swing his gun away from me.

I leapt at him and drove my fist into his solar plexus.

The man collapsed on the floor, his gun skittering to one side.

Alex raced to the weapon, snatched it off the floor, and pointed it at the guard.

Moaning and rolling on his side, the man curled into a ball.

Plucking some zip-ties from a jacket pocket, I knelt over the man and secured his hands and feet. A handkerchief and wad of cloth served to gag him. Leaving him, I rushed to the girls and whispered, "Gabe here. Don't talk." I motioned Alex to go upstairs.

Alex crept up the stairs, gun aimed in front of him. Carpet on the stairs helped.

While he checked the second floor, I freed the girls. After they hugged me, I put a finger to my lips. I whispered, "We wait."

In minutes, Alex appeared on the stairs. He kept the gun directed at the ground and gave me the all-clear signal.

"We can talk now but need to keep it low." I swept my hand around the house. "We don't know if someone else might arrive or the kidnappers bugged the house. Let's not take chances."

Sofia shrugged.

Alex joined us and tucked the gun in the small of his back. "Did you girls see anyone else in the house except the guard?"

"No." Izabella thought for a moment. "But I heard two sets of footsteps descend the stairs. The guard put blindfolds on us before that."

Sofia edged in closer. "Right after the footsteps reached the bottom of the stairs, the door opened and closed. Whoever is in charge left."

"We need to leave before they get back." Alex turned to the kitchen.

'Not yet." I tapped his arm and faced the girls. "Did you hear a motor start or a garage door opening?"

Both shook their heads.

"Neither did I, which means—"

"That we've caught you in our trap." Dimitri's voice made me pause. I swiveled around to see him. He pointed his Lugar at our group. Genevieve stood by his side in the open kitchen area. "Move and I'll shoot." He motioned to Alex. "Lift the gun by its handle and toss it over here."

Alex threw the gun like an underhand softball pitch. The weapon skittered on the wooden floor near the Russian.

Genevieve knelt, cut the zip-ties off the guard, and rose.

The man sprang to his feet, a grin on his face. "How'd I do, boss?" He didn't wait for an answer to retrieve his gun and aim it at me.

Dimitri glanced at Genevieve. "I'd give him a five-star rating out of five."

She smiled. "Give your guard a bonus. The kids had no idea we were here."

"Stanislav, get the SUV ready." Dimitri holstered his gun, plucked a cigar from his pocket, prepared it, and lit the end. "Call in our other team members, the Frenchman in particular. We need him now." He withdrew his gun again, resuming a watchful stance.

"Right away." The guard left through the front door.

Genevieve waved at the couch. "Sit." She reclined in one of the plush chairs.

The four of us plopped on the red couch, Alex furthest from the door on one end, Sofia next, Izabella, then me.

"Pretty comfortable." I stretched and fluffed a pillow. "Is there any chance we could have some hot chocolate? I'm pretty thirsty."

A laugh exploded from Dimitri. "I almost like you. But I'm afraid not."

"You have a nice kitchen back there. I'm sure—"

"Shut up." Dimitri snarled. "You will be dead in a few hours, but I can make it happen now if you'd rather go earlier."

Alex shifted. "Be careful what you say, Dimitri Vasiliev. Willie and the IEG Security team will arrive in short order."

Genevieve straightened in her chair. "You're bluffing. No one knows your whereabouts."

Sofia and Izabella's faces brightened. "They're coming?"

"Let me clarify." I scooted forward to tap on the coffee table in front of me. "Bastien is notifying Willie. He left a while ago." I glanced at Genevieve. "They'll be here any minute."

The Russian shrugged. "If they arrive, we would have a hostage situation, I suppose. Assuming your facts are correct."

The front door behind us clicked open.

"But you may want to revise your conclusion." A wicked grin crossed Dimitri's face. "Bastien, I'm glad to see you're on time."

I twisted in my seat. Our French friend stomped his boots on the floor to get the snow off and came into the living room. The guard entered simultaneously, ignoring our friend and casually walked to the kitchen area, opened the fridge, and got a drink.

Bastien shook hands with Dimitri. "Got delayed." He glanced at us. "I wanted to make sure the Zanadu brothers didn't suspect anything."

"Well done." Dimitri puffed several times. He waved his cigar in the air while he spoke. "To make your death less messy, I've asked Bastien to obtain sedatives from a local veterinary he knows. Why waste good bullets on kids? A gentle death, dying from frostbite and exposure, might be better, don't you think?" He chuckled. "A fitting end to your Elimination Games." He roared with laughter, stepped back, and patted Bastien's shoulder.

"You're a marked man, Dimitri Vasiliev." I narrowed my eyes. "Willie will never let you live if you take us out."

Bastien motioned to the guard. "Zip-ties on hands and feet."

Dimitri aimed his gun at us.

"Too bad you're not closer or I'd wipe you out myself." I wrinkled my nose at him.

The guard zip-tied me first. He made me stand and turn around to secure my hands behind me. The plastic cut into my wrists. "Don't make them that tight." I wiggled my arms and growled at the guard.

"That's for the punch in my gut." He spun me back around, shoved me on the couch, and zip-tied my ankles. He completed his task and resumed guarding us with his gun.

Dimitri put his weapon away and sat on a dining table chair across the room.

Bastien prepared our shots. He talked like a disinterested doctor administering medications. "Oldest first." He grinned and rolled up Alex's sleeve. "This will knock you out for a little while."

"Traitor." Alex clenched his jaw.

"I don't want to hear it." Bastien smirked. "I have my reasons."

Sofia protested. "But you hid this from us and acted as a friend?"

He swabbed her arm, checked the syringe, and injected the fluid. "You are detectives, correct? Even though I arranged for meetings, high-priority seating at IEG events, and I even coordinated for you to stay at my dad's hotel—free of charge, did you notice? No. And my absences during the games for business…well, let's just say it wasn't all legal business."

He moved to Izabella. Tears wet her cheeks when he prepared her arm. Her eyes found mine. She whispered. "Gabe, you're my hero."

That put me in shock. Hero? What kind of hero? Like a personal hero? And what did that mean? My brain short-circuited.

Bastien rolled his eyes. "Too late for love now. That hot Spanish fire will freeze soon in our icy pond." He shoved the syringe in her arm and pushed the plunger.

"You'll never drown us." I strained to break the zip-ties on my wrists. "I still have faith in Willie."

"Gabe," Alex said with fuzzy words, half asleep. "Shut your trap. You're making this worse."

Dimitri grinned. "He's right, you know, but you're not going to drown. You'll freeze to death."

Bastien agreed. "First, we'll dip you in the pond, then leave you in the snow near a tree." He shrugged. "But you'll be too sleepy to notice. A pretty easy way to go, if you ask me."

Sofia's eyes slid shut, but Alex's eyelids drooped at half-mast. He stared ahead, moving his head slightly as though listening to our conversation. Izabella's eyelids fluttered. She struggled against the drug.

"What changed?" I glared at him. "I thought you were our friend."

He gave me a lopsided grin. "You could say that what I'm doing is the underside of a good business decision. I'll be set for life."

I bounced off the couch and head-butted him.

He fell back and dropped his needle, crushing it under a shoe. He clutched his bloody nose and blood oozed from his cut lip. "That's what you deserve."

"Bastien." Genevieve ran forward to help him.

"Don't shoot." Dimitri signaled his guard and glanced at his watch. "If we weren't on a timetable, I'd keep you around for a little fun." His eyes smoldered. He strode over to me and slammed a hand in my gut.

I crumpled on the couch; the air knocked out of me.

Genevieve fixed Bastien's nose and gave him a dish towel for his lip. He grabbed another needle and jammed it in hard. "You'll pay for that."

The room became fuzzy. Bastien checked everyone's eyes with a bright light. He could tell I wasn't entirely under when he got to me. "You and your brother seem to have a higher resistance to this drug, but the effect is sufficient."

Dimitri spoke with an edge in his voice. "Give them more sedatives. We don't want any glitches."

Bastien stood and raised his hands. "I don't have anymore. But it will be fine. The guys' systems must be more resilient. They can't get away or resist."

"You'd better be right." The edge in Dimitri's voice cut through the fog. "Now get them in the SUV."

Chapter 57 – Decision

The Frozen Pond near Méribel, France
Saturday, 18 January 1992, 6:23 p.m.

The pain exploded on the side of my face. My body jerked, eyes flicking open. What happened? Like a coal-fired engine on a train chugging to a mountain's peak, my thoughts searched for answers, slow and steady. My eyelids worked, but I kept them partially closed to hide my wakening senses. White snow filled the blurry vision in my right eye, but I noticed the back of a white coat with my left. I knew that coat from somewhere. My mind flitted around. I couldn't move but wanted to grin when I remembered Gabe head-butting someone. My brother never quit.

Sounds of grunting came from over my shoulder. Two voices came from farther away. One possessed a harsh accent, the other almost melodic. French.

Why did my brain feel crippled?

I tried to move, but my legs and arms wouldn't obey. Sensations were dull or not there at all. My back twitched involuntarily and my head shifted, bringing my right eye out of the snow. But I still lay on my side. Legs lower than my head. The person in the white coat and I lay on the slope of a hill.

"Throw him over there." The Russian voice came closer.

How did I know he spoke in Russian? I racked my brain, but no answers came. Maybe I should go to sleep. I'd feel better in the mo-moron-morning.

That made me laugh inside. Was I a moron?

Two men appeared in my peripheral vision, with someone slung between them. A familiar person. A boy. They lowered him partway, dropping him the last foot or so. His head twisted in my direction. I saw his face with blurry vision.

Brother.

Like a jolt of electricity, my mind snapped into clarity.

Gabe.

The French voice shouted. "I'm moving the snowmobile on the ice closer to the hole. The anchor to the rope for my buddies." The snowmobile roared to life, ran for a minute or two, and stopped.

Bastien. The picture took shape, piece by piece. Did he call us buddies or bodies? My mind struggled like a cold engine trying to start. I wasn't friends with him anymore.

I felt a mild thud in my side. The blow didn't sting but left a slight ache. Whatever the cause, my body rolled on its back, my head canted to the right. I glimpsed the pond below me before I clamped my eyes shut in case someone thought I'd become alert.

"Americans." The Russian voice carried contempt. The man cleared his throat, making a spitting noise. Wetness hit my nose. "No more meddling for the privileged youth of a U.S. Army officer." The voice receded.

"How brave of you." French voice. Pretty woman. We shared lunch. "Spitting on Alex. A drugged and bound teenage boy. You're a pig. We need to leave." The door of a vehicle slammed shut.

Chuckling, the man said, "For the glory of Russia." A stab of despair hit me when I recognized the man's voice. Dimitri. The head of the drug-smuggling operation.

"Bastien, you're in charge." Dimitri kept speaking. "Finish this with Stanislav. Meet Genevieve and me at the house in thirty minutes." A second car door shut. An engine turned over, revved a few seconds, and dropped in volume until the sound disappeared.

I peeked to figure out my situation.

Bastien trudged over to the guard from the house. He must be Stanislav. They stood several feet away from me, enough that I could catch some snatches of their conversation.

I opened my eyes wider. The snowmobile sat on the ice, blocking my view of the hole where we would be dipped. I tried to feel my hands, my feet, my face. Nothing. I felt warm and comfortable, but the temperature must be dropping. The light faded. Twilight.

"…drop them in the water." The guard argued with Bastien. "The bodies disappear and no evidence remains."

"That's not what Dimitri told us to do." Bastien raised his voice. "We're going to do it the exact way he specified."

I realized the four of us would die tonight. Because Gabe and I failed to understand we couldn't do everything. Our dogs, the best friends we'd ever have, also became our greatest vulnerability.

"…I don't care if I'm the newest member of the team. I'm in charge." The French boy yelled at his partner. "You heard Dimitri."

My throat felt dry. What happened when I died? Alex Zanadu – the great detective, gone. Murdered by a villain. Did I become a ghost? My pulse ratcheted higher and thrummed in my ears. Did I disappear from existence? I struggled to move, to get away, but my body didn't respond. I imagined hell, the fire, the pain, the suffering. Shallow breaths robbed me of strength. Panic seized my thoughts. I'd messed up so many times in my life. *Lord, help.* I…

"…I don't like it." The guard shouted back.

"Would you like a bonus?" Bastien said.

Silence followed.

How did that happen? The shouting stopped my runaway train of thought. At precisely the right moment. An answer to prayer. A calm swept over my mind. I remembered a few calls for help that God answered in the past. He always made things work out in the long run.

"How much?" The guard's voice got quiet.

"A hundred thousand French Francs."

"How can you afford that? Is this a trick?"

Money. I realized people tried to make it paramount, but life wasn't really about money, power, or stuff. Relationships mattered most. With others. And with God. Things people can't touch or see. Important things.

That settled it. Lots of people, my parents most of all, told me about Jesus. I heard, but I didn't understand until now. If I had to die tonight, I needed to make sure I knew my final destination. Heaven.

I ignored the argument between Bastien and the guard. Clamped my eyes shut. If I died in this world, I wanted to keep living in the next.

God, thanks for showing me my failures, making a way for me to tell you I'm sorry and turn-around, and then providing a path through Jesus to accept your forgiveness. He died and rose from the dead to save me and give me everlasting life. Jesus, you're my Lord and King. I'll live and serve you forever with everything I've got—no matter what.

"Settled?" A silkiness returned to Bastien's tone.

"Yep." The guard wandered over to me.

I blinked at him.

"This one's awake."

Bastien's face appeared. "Let me get a light." He left and returned. He pointed the tiny light into my eyes. "Let's try a needle jab to see if he reacts to pain. If he does, I need to sedate him again."

"I don't have a needle."

"Give me something sharp. Like a knife." Bastien frowned at me. "I don't know how you've recovered this much." He looked over his shoulder. "Thanks."

A survival knife appeared in my vision.

He smiled. "If you jump, we'll kill you right now."

I sensed a dull ache in my left side, but only my face could feel anything with clarity. Like the wetness from Dimitri's spit. The movement of my eyes. I tried to smile. Maybe the corner of my mouth moved. That was it. I couldn't control anything else.

Bastien moved from my sight. In a bit, he returned, checking my face. "No pain reaction either in his leg or his face. He won't get any feeling back for hours."

"Let's dunk him first." The guard now peered in my face. "He doesn't look that drugged."

"You can punch him if you want, but make sure he can breathe." Bastien stood. "I'm getting the rope."

"Okay." The guard swung a fist and knocked my face to the right.

No pain, but a sensation of more wetness.

"That's enough." The French boy gave the man a rope. "Thread the rope under his armpits and knot it in the back. I'll double-check your work."

"Where do you want him after he's wet?" The guard worked the rope as directed, turning me on my face in the snow for a count of forty.

I held my breath at the last second, not wanting to inhale snow. Concentrated. *Don't breathe.* Seconds dragged by. I felt my lungs burning. Ready to gasp involuntarily. I sucked in—.

The guard rolled me over. "Were you having trouble breathing?" He snickered. "Time to get you to the pond for a bath."

Chapter 58 – Breathe

The Frozen Pond near Méribel, France
Saturday, 18 January 1992, 7:13 p.m.

The guard staggered under my weight. "I could use a little help here."

"Alex isn't that heavy." Bastien strode into view.

"Hands in the air, mates." Willie's voice rang out.

The guard froze for a second, dropped me, and pulled his gun.

I fell forward. Two shots rang out. I hit on my right shoulder, bouncing left on impact. My face went back into the snow.

God, help. I started counting, holding my breath.

"Don't shoot." The French boy pleaded. "I'm innocent."

"Any others here with you?"

Ten, eleven, twelve....

"No," Bastien said. "We're alone."

"Where are the others?" Willie's voice came closer.

Twenty, twenty-one, twenty-two....

The crunch of Willie's boots on the frosty snow told me he walked near me.

Bastien must have shifted. I could hear heavier crunching in the snow. Thirty-two, thirty-three....

"I need answers." Willie threatened. "Now."

Thirty-seven, thirty-eight, thirty-nine.... My throat tightened. Seconds remained before I would gag on the snow. I'd choke to death.

"Sir, these kids are drugged," another voice said.

"Is that why Alex isn't moving?" Willie's voice changed. "Bastien, did you drug these guys?"

Forty-seven, forty-eight...I couldn't hold my breath any longer.

Someone lifted my face from the snow, flipping me onto my side. My body convulsed a fraction. Fresh air filled my lungs. Relief swept through my body. *Thanks, God.*

"Alex." Willie's voice washed over me. "If you're okay, open your eyes."

My body jerked one more time when I gulped in more air. I blinked. Let my eyelids close again.

"Don't lose it, mate." Willie braced my head. "Rock up. Don't be a no-show to the party."

I opened my eyes. The edges of my mouth twitched in what I hoped was a smile.

Chapter 59 – Questions

The Frozen Pond near Méribel, France
Saturday, 18 January 1992, 7:45 p.m.

Willie, the Russian forced me to do this." Bastien swallowed hard while one of Willie's men handcuffed his hands behind his back. "I didn't intend to kill anyone. I planned to sneak back here and free everyone."

I glanced at Gabe, Sofia, and Izabella. My arms and legs tingled like they were numb from a deep sleep. My brother acted alert, blinking his eyes. His head shifted a bit. The girls seemed to be sleeping.

"Sir," one of the security men flipped a thumb at Bastien's SUV, "we need to move these teens before they freeze to death. If we tuck them together in that vehicle, the heat will warm their bodies."

Willie nodded. "Good idea, Sergeant Grimes. Send someone to keep an eye on them since they can't move." He barked more orders and studied the area. "Bring a chopper in for the Russian I wounded. Near that house on the hill. Get this man in a rescue basket. Drag him behind one of our snowmobiles."

Sergeant Grimes wrestled with Gabe. Another man lifted Gabe's feet, taking him to the SUV.

"Alex." Willie knelt beside me.

I made a croaking sound.

"No worries." He placed a hand on my chest. "Do you know where Dimitri is?"

I struggled to nod.

"Good." Willie walked back to Bastien. "If you want leniency, tell me where Dimitri is."

Bastien's lips pressed together in a firm line.

Willie tapped him on the chest. "Alex will tell me in ten minutes, but they might have moved by that time. I might consider your earlier comments if you help me now."

Bastien gazed at the ground. "I know where they were, but Genevieve didn't tell me where to meet them."

"Where were they?"

"That way." He pointed. "In a house at the end of the trail thirty minutes away." Bastien sighed. "That's where we captured Gabe and Alex."

"Keep talking." Willie's eyes tracked the other activities.

Bastien straightened, looking into the trees on the right. "Dimitri told me to leave the SUV at the house, set it on fire, and drive away on a snowmobile using this trail. He didn't tell me where they were going, but mentioned he'd contact me later to dispose of the dogs."

"When will that happen?" Willie stepped within inches of his face.

Bastien licked his lips and looked away. "I'm not sure. Tomorrow? The Russian's henchmen hid the dogs where no one would find them. Thunder and Lightning might not be alive anymore. But I don't know where they are."

Grimes and his buddy were ready to move me. When they raised me off the ground, I winced at the pain in my left side where Dimitri kicked me. Right where I injured myself from a roller coaster fall last year. I'd need some pain meds.

Chapter 60 – Abandoned Building

I glanced around the building, amazed I could stand on my feet and search for our dogs. Bastien drugged me, Alex, Izabella, and Sofia less than twelve hours ago. Willie drove us to a hospital for a checkup. After they patched up Alex, we explained our latest battle with the Russian and Frenchwoman to Dad. He ensured we slept, ate, and went to a short church service before meeting Willie in this derelict structure.

Each step I took echoed in the hallways of the abandoned office building. Holes in the ceiling tiles, sputtering florescent lights, and writing on the walls told me the cleaning company, Nettoyants Savoie, used the place years ago. A condemned sign hung on a chain near one of the entry points into the structure. The place felt cold but not like the temperatures outside, which hovered a little above freezing. I pulled my coat tighter to stay warm.

Alex shuffled into a room, searching for Thunder and Lightning.

"Find anything yet?" I approached Willie, who followed another man with his German Shepherd on a leash.

"Gabe." Willie waved me forward. "The tracking dog hasn't found any scent yet. Stick close to your brother. He's limping a lot. Help him look in the offices we pass by."

"Why are we here in this building?" I stuck my head through a doorway into a room. Empty space. "Wasn't the abandoned truck that carried our dogs found more to the west side of town? We're on the north side right now."

Willie shrugged. "Call it a hunch. While you attended church earlier this morning, my team explored the different possibilities for your hidden dogs. That truck could be similar to the fake positives we identified at the IEG drug testing facility yesterday meant to lead us astray. A false lead. Because the kidnappers used a Nettoyants Savoie truck, they could have driven here without drawing any suspicion. Some company drivers come here to take breaks."

Alex plucked on our friend's sleeve. "Does that guy know what he's doing?" He whispered the question. "He keeps his dog on a leash. Without the freedom to follow his nose, the dog isn't directing the search—the man is."

Willie raised his eyebrows. "Don't drug dogs in airports work while on a leash? The man might not do it as you would, but the dog's nose is still on the ground. Patience."

I trailed behind Willie, who observed several doors back from the man with the dog. "What did the dog get for his search? Yesterday's evidence? The dog hairs?"

"Yes." Willie stopped and faced Alex and me. "Tell you what. You should explore the building. I'll meet you on the first floor. We'll see who finds your dogs first."

"Deal." I grinned. "What floors can we search?"

Willie scratched the side of his face. "This is the seventh floor. We've already done floors ten through seven. Can you cover four through two in twenty minutes? We'll do five and six and meet you on the ground floor."

Alex tapped me on my arm. "We'll split apart. You take three and four. I'll take two."

"Can you make it that far, Alex?" Our friend's eyes ran inspected my brother's stance. "Feeling unsteady yet? Those bruised ribs might be a problem."

My brother waved him off. "No worries." He grinned. "The prescriptions for pain will allow me to go for a while."

Thirty minutes later, we met together on the ground floor. The man with the tracking dog shook his head at Willie. "No dice. My dog can't find anything."

"What's his name?" I knelt before him.

"Spike."

I let the dog sniff my hand and rubbed his ears. "Spike, we have two extraordinary friends we want to rescue. Did you smell them?"

The dog whined.

"Better leave him alone." The handler checked his watch. "He gets moody when things don't work out." Directing his voice at the dog, he tugged on the leash. "Time to go."

The handler and his dog moved to the employee exit at the back corner stairwell, Spike's nose close to the floor. Spike's head veered to the right before they reached the exit. He tugged hard enough to get his master to stop.

"I said we're done." The handler yanked Spike back to the door. He swatted his rear and dragged him outside, raising his voice and spewing lots of French.

"Did you see that?" I whirled around to Alex and Willie.

"See what?" Willie whipped out a notepad and tapped it with his finger. "We're done here. The next place to visit—the basement of your old hotel."

Alex rubbed his side. "Something bothering you?"

I pointed at the exit. "Does this place have a basement? Spike got excited near the right side of the hallway by the exit." I glanced at Willie. "But the handler dragged him away from the spot. I bet the dog found something."

"The handler knows Spike." Willie tilted his head. "Don't you think he'd recognize his dog alerting?"

I shook my head. "The man doesn't care about finding our dogs. Our best friends. He ran Spike through the building for money. He wanted to leave because of the time."

"He may have another scheduled appointment." Willie stuffed the notepad into his back pocket. "And it's almost noon. Time for lunch."

"Come on, Alex." I waved for him to follow me. "Let's see what excited Spike."

Alex lumbered after me, going slow and holding his sides while walking. Willie followed us.

I examined the place where Spike moved to the right earlier. An open doorway led to a back stairwell. "Must be a way to the basement, but it's pitch dark."

"I can go to the bottom, but I'm not going on the higher floors again." Alex leaned on the wall. "Between the German Shepherd and us, we've covered everything above this floor."

"Deal." I dropped my backpack on the floor and got my flashlight.

Alex hobbled to the railing. "Willie, you've taught us to be thorough no matter the circumstances. Gabe saw something from Spike." He took off his backpack and rummaged in an exterior pocket. He tugged his flashlight from the bag.

"Five minutes." I clicked my light on. "If we don't find anything in five minutes, we leave."

Willie sighed, back against the wall. "You'll be the death of me."

Alex went first, holding his ribs. Willie carried Alex's flashlight for him.

I went last, but I darted past them in the hallway at the bottom. I waved my hand in front of me to clear the cobwebs. "It's like a spider's nest." I glanced inside a few doorways. More empty rooms.

Alex called after me. "Is this necessary? Each open room has no furniture. It's a bust."

"The last four doors at the end are shut." I swung my flashlight around. "You may need to pick the locks."

Alex knelt in front of the first locked door a few minutes later. He retrieved his lock-picking kit from his bag. In a flash, the first door opened. Nothing. The second room proved no different.

The third room was a challenge. "Something's jamming the keyhole." Alex poked around but couldn't clear it. We bypassed the place.

"Try the last door." Willie passed Alex. "We'll come back."

The last door wasn't locked. Various desks, tables, rolling chairs, cabinets, storage closets, and other furniture filled the space. I crawled underneath and around it all. "No dogs."

We went back to the third door.

Alex spent five minutes trying to unjam the lock. "No dice." He stood and grabbed his ribs. "I need a bed to lay flat for a bit."

"Understood." Willie faced the exit. "Let's go."

Alex shuffled to his side.

My anger flared. "I can't believe after four hours of searching we couldn't find them." I kicked the door with such force the wood near the latch splintered a little.

"Happy?" Willie faced me. "Getting mad—"

Something fell on the other side.

My brother's head snapped to the door. "Did you hear that?"

We listened. Silence.

"Break in." Alex returned at a snail's pace and stood opposite the unopened door, hand on the wall. "Gabe, kick it again."

Willie crossed his arms. "We're going to have to pay for that door."

"Our dogs are more important than money." I took a few steps back, crouched, and launched at the door. I slammed my foot with maximum force. The wood made cracking sounds but didn't give. After several attempts, I quit.

"Willie, we need help." Alex limped to the door. "I bet Thunder is in here. That German Shepherd, Spike, alerted at the stairwell. I believe his sense of smell confirms your hunch."

Our friend paused. When he realized we weren't leaving, he smiled. "Right, mates. I'll have a crack crew of door destroyers here in half an hour." He pointed at Alex. "You need to lay on the floor." He slipped his coat off. "Here's some more padding. Give those ribs a little rest."

Twenty minutes later, a fire department crew arrived along with a veterinarian. Using a sledgehammer, the first responders broke the lock. The door swung in partway and stopped. The bulky firefighters couldn't squeeze through the gap, about a foot-and-a-half wide, but I slid through it sideways.

"What's in there?" Willie said.

"Several old desks, cabinets, and boxes." I coughed. "Lots of dust."

Alex talked next. "Where's my dog?"

"Don't rush me." I swept my light around the room. "The room is stuffed with cabinets, boxes, and desks. About the width of our living room at home and one-and-a-half times the length. Maybe twenty by thirty feet." I wiggled forward to get a better view. The room seemed neat except for one stack of boxes in the back which seemed disorganized. That caught my attention.

"Let the other men in." Willie banged on the door.

I threaded my way back to the door. A desk sat lengthwise behind the door. I grunted, raising the piece of furniture onto its short side. That allowed the door to swing in several more inches. Willie, Alex, and a young fireman squeezed into the room.

The fireman went under the desks and to my left. Willie went to my right. Alex leaned against the wall, face tight.

"Gabe, check out those fallen boxes on the back wall." Alex pointed past me.

"Already noticed them." Working straight to my goal, I bypassed the neat stacks of cardboard boxes. The tallest stack of six sat by a desk at the back wall. The top two containers looked like book boxes. The other four seemed to be about three-foot square each. Next to that neat stack lay the disorganized pile of boxes. I opened each of those with no luck. I eyed the neat stack of containers that remained. The fourth box from the top, slightly damaged, stuck out two or three inches to the right from the others. Small irregular holes poked out through the cardboard on the side. I shoved the heavy box back to keep the stack from falling. "Six to go."

"Top box—empty." I tossed it aside.

Packing paper filled the second and third. I tossed them behind me.

"Careful." The fireman threw one of the boxes behind him. "You hit me with the box. I'm trying to help, not get knocked out."

"Sorry." I paid more attention to my next one, the damaged container, which held something heavy. "Box number four—Styrofoam bits. Peanuts."

I dug my hand into the white packing material. My hand touched something soft. Fur. A gentle movement pressed against my hand.

"I found them." I twisted and called out to the fireman. "Over here."

The young guy scrambled over the desks and other furniture, scattering cardboard containers aside. We both dug into the box, tossing Styrofoam peanuts on the floor.

"It's Thunder." I dug into the peanuts to finish uncovering him.

Alex's dog breathed lightly. Thick grey tape kept his muzzle closed. Tape wrapped his front paws together. A zip-tie bound his back legs. He lifted his head and opened one eye. He made a low whine.

"We've got you now, Thunder." I stroked his neck. "You'll be fine."

He relaxed.

"Let's carry the whole box." The firefighter tugged, twisted, and dragged the box between him and myself until we reached Alex.

My brother's eyes reddened. "Thunder. I've missed you." He wrapped his arms around Thunder's neck and hugged him.

After several squeezes, I pushed Alex out of the room. The man and I lifted his weakened dog out of the box, carried him out the door, and laid him by the veterinarian in the hall.

The vet kneeled by Thunder's side before I dashed back into the room.

Racing through the door, I shouted. "Lightning, you're next."

Chapter 61 – Wise Up

Nettoyants Savoie Building, France
Sunday, 19 January 1992, 12:41 p.m.

I scrambled through the mess of cardboard containers strewn throughout the room to the last two unopened boxes. I ripped the tape, keeping the fifth box shut. Brown wrapping paper filled it to the brim. No dog.

"Lightning, where are you?" I tore into the last box. Styrofoam peanuts spilled out. "Come on. Be there." I scooped the filler out, digging in frantic haste to find my friend. He wasn't there. I slammed the box into the wall. Peanuts went everywhere, spilling onto the floor.

"You're raising the cleaning bill, mate." Willie waded through the mess. "She'll be right."

I glared at him. "Really? It's an abandoned building." I kicked the box into the wall. "And no, it's not all right. We've found one dog. Not both of them."

My friend sat on an upside-down desk near me. "Quit your

spewing." He glanced at me and swept his arm around the room. "I've searched each cabinet. Empty." Pointing at the young fireman, he raised his eyebrows. "Our first-responder mate crawled under all the desks. No results." He tapped me on the shoe. "You've ripped apart any box you found in here and scored once."

"Lightning's my best buddy." I sat next to Willie, tears streaming. "But he isn't here. We've checked everywhere." I put my arms around my bent legs, pulled them tight to my chest, and lay my head on my knees. "He's gone."

Willie scooted closer and patted my back. "We found him the last time someone stole him."

Alex popped his head in the door. "The vet wants to take Thunder for treatment."

"Give us a sec." Willie sighed. Rubbed the back of his neck, swiveling it around. "Gabe, we have to leave. I've got other duties." He tucked his chin, craned his neck back, and stretched it out. He stared at the ceiling. "But before we go, let's put things in perspective." He tapped my shoulder. "What did it take to figure it out on your last adventure in Texas?"

I sniffed. "Deduction. Good detective work."

"Didn't you have some higher help?"

"You mean the FBI? Yeah."

"Maybe someone a little higher."

I wiped my nose on my knees. "You mean God."

My friend sighed. "I reckon. When you get stuck, maybe you should look for the highest wisdom, leaving things you can't control in His hands."

I swallowed. "But I want my dog back." I brushed tears off my cheeks."

"He knows that. Give Him time to solve the puzzle." Willie pointed at the ceiling with his flashlight. "Keep your eyes focused up."

I let go of my knees, sat straighter, and stretched my neck back to relieve the tension and regain my composure. "Okay." Willie's incredible coaching helped Alex and me forge ahead in spite of the crushing blows we encountered.

My eyes swept across the suspended ceiling tiles lit by his flashlight. Something caught my attention. "Willie?" I rose to my feet.

"Yes?"

I tapped his shoulder. "Would you shine your light in the corner at the ceiling with mine?" I flicked my light on and focused on the ceiling tiles in the front corner of the room.

"Sure." His light joined mine.

"Does that corner tile look the same as the others?"

"No. It's a bit discolored."

"Guys," Alex called from the hall. "Are you taking a nap?"

I jumped to my feet. "Not yet. Send the firefighter back in. We need a ladder."

"They already left."

I clambered back to the front. "Willie, can you get me near that ceiling tile?"

We hurried to the front and stacked two desks on top of each other. Willie gripped the legs tight to steady the desk while I climbed on top.

I shone my light on the corner ceiling tile. "It's yellow and brown. It's gotta be Lightning." I took a deep breath to calm myself. I stretched but couldn't reach the tile. "Must be a twelve-foot ceiling. How about giving me that coffee table?"

Minutes later, I stood on the coffee table and pressed on the tile, but it wouldn't budge.

"Try another one."

I pushed on the next one. The acoustic tile popped out. "I can't see anything."

"Keep working at it." Willie steadied the desk. He turned his head to the door. "Alex. Get the vet and come in here. We need your help."

When they arrived, he asked Alex to hold the top desk to keep it from shifting and scaled the two desks and coffee table to stand next to me. "I'll lift you. Shine your light and check it out."

Seconds later, Willie lowered me to the desk.

"Lightning's there." I gripped an arm. "But he's taped to the tile.

We need scissors to cut him loose. The tile is stuck to the grid. We can't bust it loose without hurting Lightning."

The vet let go of the desk. "I've got you covered." He returned quickly with scissors and handed them to me.

I climbed back on the coffee table and let Willie lift me high enough to cut Lightning free. Cradling him, I leaned on Willie to clamber to the floor safely.

"We got you, buddy." I rubbed my cheek against his soft orange hair. "You're safe now."

Lightning's matted hair smelled. Thick grey tape covered his legs and mouth.

The vet examined my orange fuzzball and sucked in a deep breath. "He won't have much hair left when I'm done, but he seems okay."

Willie took us to the vet's office and dropped us off. "Make sure the vet gives them the royal treatment. I'll be back."

The veterinarian removed the tape and the attached, entangled hair, giving us directions on the safe method to remove the sticky residue from the tape with olive oil or rubbing alcohol. He gave each dog an IV treatment to infuse them with fluids they'd lost.

"Your dogs are young and healthy but malnourished and dehydrated. The cool temperatures in that building made a difference in their survival. No overheating. They should be back to normal in a week if you feed them well and offer them plenty of water. They'll act tired and weak for a few days." We told him about our travel plans. "Make sure you visit a vet in Germany to check for any long-lasting complications, especially from dehydration."

Alex called Willie to let him know the vet had finished his testing and treatment. Half an hour later, he arrived and paid the bill for the medical support from the IEG Security Department's funds. Twenty minutes passed and we arrived at our hotel room. Once inside, we settled the dogs in their baskets, and Willie hugged each of us. "Tell your Dad I'm proud of the work you've done. Now that we've recovered your dogs, you're free to go visit your mom and German friends."

"You're kidding, right?" I shook my head. "Dimitri and Genevieve tried to kill us."

Alex crossed his arms on his chest. "The Games aren't over yet and we need to catch those two."

"Don't make this hard, mates." Willie patted Alex on his shoulder. "You're limping when you walk." He pointed at me. "You're not recovered from being buried in the snow and almost being frozen in a pond." He shook his head. "And your dogs need rest and recuperation."

Alex and I stared at him.

"Mates, I can't in good conscience take you back on the team." He glanced at the floor, rubbed his left temple, and gazed right at us. "Besides, I promised your dad that when we found the dogs, you'd be off the case. I can't break that commitment." He shook his head. "I've done what I could. Be good and stay safe. The mission's over for you."

Neither of us said anything.

Our Aussie friend went to the door, opened it, and stepped into the hall.

"Willie." I ran into his arms. "Thanks!"

Alex hobbled over and embraced Willie too.

Seconds later, Willie broke away. "We'll keep in touch." He turned and left.

I raised my eyebrows at Alex. He grinned.

Chapter 62 – Delay

Wild Boar Hotel, Albertville, France
Sunday, 19 January 1992, 6:00 p.m.

Dad waited for us at the hotel's dinner table. "Still feeling a little under the weather?" He folded a newspaper he'd been perusing.

Alex winced when he sat. "That noticeable?"

Our father chuckled while I took my seat. "No. Not at all." He grinned. "How are you doing with the pain meds?"

"I take the next one in two hours." Alex braced himself against the back of his chair. "We left the dogs in the room after feeding them. They're not moving much."

Snagging a menu, Dad glanced at us. "That's incredible that you found them. I'll stop by to see them later. Great job."

"With our top-notch detective skills—"

Dad raised a finger. "Gabe, I have to be at a meeting this evening at seven. Let's order first, and then you can pour out the story to your heart's content."

About two-thirds of the way through the meal, after we'd finished describing the adventure, our father changed the conversation to the subject Alex and I didn't want to discuss. "Your mother and I will talk tonight to coordinate your trip tomorrow to Germany." Dad drank some water.

"Do we have to go?" My fork clattered on my plate. "Mom's happy right now, but two criminals that tried to kill us aren't behind bars."

"Who knows how far their reach is?" Alex wiped his hands on a napkin. "We need to finish this with Willie."

Dad paused a moment. While rubbing his jaw, his lips formed a firm line.

The aromas of fine foods, desserts, and the hotel's air freshener lingered in the air, making me hungrier, although I polished off a piece of chocolate truffle cake seconds ago. "While you're thinking, can I get a second dessert?"

Smiling, Dad's hands parted. He set his forearms on the table. "Sure, but not the expensive ones."

I knew what I wanted. Crème Glacée. The waitress thought the dessert was a splendid idea.

"Following cake with ice cream?" Alex sighed. "You're going to gain weight."

"I can handle it."

Dad checked his watch. "I have five minutes to get ready for my meeting before leaving. You two must stay here at the hotel tonight. Understand?"

We nodded.

"I plan on sending you by train to Germany. Can you handle the changes at the different stations?"

"The questionable ones will be in France." Alex sipped from his water glass. "We know the German Bahnhof system and the language."

"I'll make sure it's the most direct route." Dad dropped his napkin on the table.

"Can we invite friends over?" I glanced at Alex. "He's not going to be much fun. And he'll fall asleep before bedtime tonight."

Dad stood. "To your room, but don't go anywhere." He put a hand on Alex's shoulder and ruffled my hair. "I want you in bed by nine this evening. You need rest." He patted me on the back and left.

"How do you plan to capture the Russian and French woman if you can't move?" Sofia sat next to Alex's bed in one of the two chairs in our room, legs curled under herself.

Alex lay propped on his bed with pillows. Thunder sat next to him on the floor with his muzzle close to Alex's hand. Alex stroked his neck. Franco occupied the other room chair, which he positioned at the end of my bed, facing Alex. Izabella and I sat on my bed, a contented Lightning parked between us. He'd lick one of our hands occasionally and we'd reciprocate by petting him.

"Dimitri is easy to spot." I folded a piece of hotel stationery into a paper airplane.

"What makes you think Dimitri or Genevieve will show themselves in public now?" Sofia adjusted her chair to be next to Alex's bed and laid her hand on his.

"They've still got the Elim Games to ruin." I unfolded the plane and redesigned it. "We'd have to catch them when it's dark."

"But where will we find them?" Franco clasped his hands in front of him. "We'd have too many venues to cover."

Izabella tickled Lightning's ear. "We'd have to get some intelligence on which venue they're using. Like how Sofia found out where to go."

She stiffened. "I'm not buying drugs again. They will know it's a trap."

"Wake up." I threw a throw pillow from my bed at Alex. When it hit, he jumped and Thunder growled.

"That's my bruised ribs." My brother groaned. "Do that again and ...."

"And what?"

Someone knocked on the door.

Bouncing off my bed, I raced to the door and looked through the peephole.

I opened the door. "Hey, Dad. You're not supposed to be back yet. It's seven-thirty."

He stepped inside. "Good to see you too, son."

Lightning wobbled over to see him, lying at his feet. He lifted the fuzzball, let him lick his chin, and set him on the floor. My bud wandered back to his basket.

Looking at our friends, Dad smiled. "Hi, kids. Seven-thirty is sooner than I'd planned, but I'm going to ask you to leave to allow Alex and Gabe and their dogs to get a good night's rest."

My jaw dropped. "But you said nine o'clock."

Dad stiffened. His smile turned into a stone face. "That wasn't a question. You need rest. No arguments."

"We'd better go." Franco stood.

Our friends carried their chairs to their proper places and weaved past our father to get their coats.

"Can we see Alex and Gabe tomorrow to say goodbye?" Sofia threw on her coat.

"Perhaps we could have breakfast?" Izabella wrapped a scarf around her neck.

Dad's stiff posture relaxed. "I suppose, but not earlier than eight o'clock. Understood?"

Izabella adjusted her coat. "Thanks, Mr. Z. We'll plan on that." She waved from the door. "See you tomorrow."

Franco opened the door and our friends slipped away. The door made a soft click when it closed.

Dad stared at me. "Gabriel Zanadu, that was rude."

"Yes, but—"

"No buts. When I make a change, you don't question me in front of your friends. You talk with me later. Understand?"

My shoulders slumped. "Yes, sir."

"I want you in bed in half an hour." He turned and walked to Alex's bedside. He knelt, ruffled Thunder's fur, and inspected my brother. His tone softened. "You look a little better. How do you feel?"

"This time, the pain pill worked well." Alex pushed a few pillows around and sat straighter. "A little ache overall. My temperature? Normal an hour ago. But I'm tired and sleepy."

"Good." Dad examined Alex's face. "You'll have a big shiner in a few days."

"I think he looks better that way." I sat on my bed. Lightning joined me. "What did Mom say when you two talked?"

Dad's stare cut me to the core.

"Your attitude needs some work." Dad settled into a chair.

I shrugged. "I meant it like a joke."

"That's not what it sounded like to me."

"My fault." I drew Lightning into my arms. "But how's Mom doing?"

"She's fine, enjoying a good time with Karl and Frieda Schultz. They're serving her great German food and taking her on short little trips. She told me how finding Thunder and Lightning made her ecstatic. But not that Dmitri and Genevieve are still on the loose."

I began in earnest. "Germany's nothing compared to the Games—"

"She's safe." Dad inserted a little steel in his voice. "I also want you two to be protected. However…" He sighed. "She's made plans with Freida and Karl to go to Austria for an overnight. She said the two of you could stay another full day and join her the day after tomorrow."

Alex smiled. "That'll work."

Dad stood, pulled out some train tickets, and put them in Alex's night table drawer. "These are for your trip to Germany. Don't lose them. You leave at eleven o'clock in the morning on Tuesday, January twenty-first."

"Thanks, Dad." Alex tapped on the nightstand. "We'll take care of them."

"Can we spend tomorrow with friends watching the Elim Games?" I put on my best pleading face.

Our father rubbed the side of his face. "If you're feeling well. The restrictions are that you stay with friends the entire time and don't leave the venues you attend." He glanced at Alex. "Remember your brother's still recovering."

"And the dogs?" I didn't want anything left to chance.

Dad checked them out. Lightning drooped over the edge of my arm. Thunder sprawled on the floor next to Alex's bed. "We'll see in the morning. They don't seem perky right now."

I grinned. "Got it."

"See you tomorrow." Dad left after hugging each of us.

I jumped off the bed and swung a fist through the air. "Cool. We've got tomorrow to finish this."

Alex grinned. "Yep. And I didn't have to use logic...."

Chapter 63 – Free Tickets

Wild Boar Hotel, Albertville, France
Monday, 20 January 1992, 7:45 a.m.

The hotel's dining area contained a series of booths on the back wall. Open dining tables filled the rest of the space. Along one short wall, next to the kitchen, a few stations for hot food filled the air with the smell of sausage, sizzling bacon, frying eggs, French Toast, cheese, and vegetables.

Alex and I sat opposite each other at a booth for eight. Izabella sat next to me, Lightning between us, and Franco filled the rest of the space on our side. Thunder lay at Alex's feet in the walkway and Sofia sat beside my brother. Dad arrived at eight. Alex and Sofia scooted over to accommodate him, then moved back to their original position when Dad departed at eight-thirty.

What's the plan for today?" Franco raised his shoulders. "We haven't settled on anything."

Sofia glanced at Alex and me. "We know that the brothers are leaving tomorrow. I think they should make the choices."

"I'm still a little slow today." Alex rubbed his side. "And a little groggy from pain pills. I'd like to see the cross-country skiing first and come back to rest in the afternoon, followed by the Mixed Dance Ice Skating in the evening. Gabe can pick the other events."

I shoveled my second helping of French toast into my mouth. Speaking around the food, I gave my opinion. "Cross-country at Les Saisies is okay to start. But the ski jumping at Courchevel is more important to me." I swallowed. "We need to arrive in Courchevel before the start of the Men's competition. We leave at three o'clock to be in Albertville for the 5,000-meter Women's Speed Skating because it's an Elim medal event."

A jovial well-dressed man appeared next to Alex. "Bonjourno. How is your food?"

Alex twisted to see who it was. "Mr. Dubois, good morning." He glanced around the table. "We've enjoyed a terrific breakfast. Gabe's on his second helping and may get thirds."

Mr. Dubois smiled. "I'm glad." He scanned the area for a moment, then focused on our group. "The food is on the house today. I'm sorry for the trouble my son, Bastien, caused you." He placed a hand on my brother's shoulder. "I don't know the details yet, but your father told me you're leaving tomorrow and have one day to celebrate the Games with your friends."

I set my fork on the plate. "That's right."

"In that case, allow me to provide block seating for you and your friends at any event you would like today. That way you can enjoy each other. I'll send the tickets to your room for the group." His smile widened.

Alex told him our schedule decisions.

"But we may change our minds in the evening and go to the U.S. hockey game in Méribel instead of the Mixed Pairs Skating event in Albertville." I ignored Alex's glare. "We haven't decided that yet. Some of us like hockey better than skating."

Mr. Dubois waved a hand in the air. "No problem. Let me know when you are ready with your final plans. A call will suffice. My seating is flexible and I can hold them until six o'clock this evening." He patted Alex's shoulder and walked away.

"What's with the hockey game change?" Alex straightened his back and focused on me. "You know Sofia is a skater."

The others agreed.

"Remember Alex is not a hundred percent yet and you have a long train trip tomorrow." Izabella elbowed me.

"Let's revisit this at the speed skating event at five this afternoon." Sofia pointed at my food. "You need to finish. We have a bus to catch."

Chapter 64 – Gilbert's Message

Shuttle Stop, Les Saisies, France
Monday, 20 January 1992, 9:48 a.m.

I stepped off the bus at Les Saisies and took a deep breath of the sharp mountain air. The smell was clean and fresh. Sunshine warmed my face though the temperature hung around twenty-five degrees Fahrenheit. With Lightning bundled in my arms, I surveyed the walk to the cross-country stands. The crowd's buzz got me excited.

Alex and Thunder, Sofia, Franco, and Izabella exited the bus.

"You three go ahead and scope out our seats." Alex shooed us ahead. "We'll take our time." Thunder and Sofia joined him while they plodded to the stands.

"Let's go." Mr. Dubois' tickets would give us a spectacular view of the race. I speed-walked past the rear of the stands to the entrance. A small concessions area containing bathrooms and various admin offices occupied the space behind the seating area.

"Excuse me, sir." A man wearing an IEG Security uniform darted out of one of the admin offices and ran after our group. "Please wait."

I stopped and faced the man. "Who are you?"

"Thank you for waiting." The overweight security man, shorter than me by a few inches, threw his shoulders back. "I'm Officer Louis Bisset." He took a deep breath. "Gilbert, who works at the main IEG Security Headquarters, asked me to find Gabe or Alex Zanadu and give them this." He showed us a white envelope.

"Let me have it," I said, reaching for it.

Bisset jerked the envelope back. "First, you must confirm you are Gabe or Alex Zanadu.

I rolled my eyes, drew a folded copy of my passport out of my pocket, and handed it to the officer.

After a quick review, he returned the paper. "And your brother's full name?"

"Alexander." My brother skirted around the security man, followed by Thunder and Sofia. "Do you want to see a copy of my passport?"

After the officer confirmed his identity and returned my brother's paperwork, he handed the envelope to Alex. With a quick tip of the hat, the man left.

Alex ripped open the envelope and found one sheet of paper.

"What's it say?" I crowded around him with the others, reading over my brother's shoulder.

Alex read the words out loud for everyone's benefit.

> I hate to bother you, but my boss ordered me to find and inform Gabe and Alex Zanadu if anything strange occurred to him. Detective Gretzke did not show for work this morning at 6:00 a.m. I have called and searched his apartment for him. The apartment shows signs of a struggle. We are investigating and will keep you informed.
>
> Gilbert.

Alex folded the paper and handed it to me. "Dimitri and Genevieve have to be put behind bars."

"Now they've kidnapped Willie." I shook my head.

"I hope they didn't dip him in a pond." Sofia shivered at her comment.

"Can we do anything now?" Franco motioned at our surroundings. "We're stuck here until the next bus in about forty-five minutes."

"Maybe Gilbert can get us a private car?" Izabella shrugged. "We can at least ask."

"She's right." Alex pointed at the Security Office. "Let's check it out."

We tromped through the snow, made our way inside, found Officer Bisset, and presented our dilemma.

"We have no transportation for you to use at this time." He pointed to a phone. "But you are welcome to talk with Gilbert."

"Thanks." I moved in front of Alex. "Can you get him on the phone for me?"

I spoke with Gilbert a minute later, holding the receiver to let Alex listen in.

"Gabe or Alex?"

"We're both here." I glanced at Alex. "What's happening with Willie?"

Gilbert's voice seemed hurried. "I don't have much time. We leave in a few minutes to check possible places they might have taken him. We think it's Dimitri Vasiliev and Genevieve Fornier who've—"

"We need a ride to get back to Albertville. Five of us and two dogs."

"That requires a van." Gilbert paused. Called out to someone on his end and a heated conversation ensued in the background. He came back on the line. "I have something, but it's not good."

My voice rose. "What is it?"

"The vehicle will be available and arrive at your location at twelve-thirty. Don't arrive early at the Headquarters. I will not be here to receive you and the desk sergeant is on a rampage. This is the best I can do."

"We could take the bus back and meet the driver at the Headquarters." I tapped the counter, waiting for a reply.

"No good," Gilbert said. "I've already contacted the man. He is coming from Courchevel. But you will have the van and driver for the rest of the day. His name is Paul."

"Can't you—"

"If you arrive here early, the desk sergeant will make your life miserable. She goes off-duty at 2:00 p.m. Got to run. We'll connect later in the day." Gilbert shouted something at another person and the phone went dead.

"We've got some time to kill." I shook my head.

"What happened?" Franco said.

I motioned the group outside. Alex and I gave a rapid rundown while we walked to our seats.

"We'll need to eat lunch soon." Izabella sat next to me.

"Yes." Alex nodded. "We eat at eleven-thirty, use the restrooms, and arrive at the Security Office a few minutes before they expect us."

Thunder and Lightning parked themselves next to us while we watched the skiers. Izabella gathered Lightning into her arms and passed him to Franco later. Thunder lay on a blanket we brought, alternating to a sitting position at irregular intervals.

"The Cooperative Team is doing well with cross-country skiing." Sofia laid a gloved hand on Alex's arm.

"Because Russia's one of the six nations on the team." I snorted.

"But the other countries—Ukraine, Kazakhstan, Belarus, Uzbekistan, and Armenia—have some great athletes." Izabella pointed at the first person through for the Cooperative team. "Maybe the wins are real, even though the first person happens to be a Russian."

We waited, wondering if the Cooperative Team would win the race.

"Did you see that?" I yelled at the group.

"What happened?" Franco craned his neck to see the stadium.

"The Cooperative Team's second racer, Mariya Makarova, stumbled before the changeover." I jumped to my feet.

The rest of the group rose and strained to see what happened.

"The Norwegian Team is in the lead." Sofia grinned at me.

"I guess it's a real race." The third set of racers reached the first hill's summit and disappeared into the trees.

People around us pointed, made gestures, and shouted at each other when teams passed the start and finish line for the third lap. The crowd's restless energy infused the stadium with tension. When the racers completing their third lap came into the stadium, the noise levels rose.

"The Cooperative Team's in the lead again." I glued my eyes to the front person.

"One lap to go." Alex shoved his camera in a coat pocket after taking a few shots.

Izabella fiddled with a program. "The Russian anchor on the fourth lap is Veronika Solovyova. She's already won four gold medals and one silver."

"What about the Norwegians?" Alex thumped Thunder's shoulders.

"Nothing in cross-country." Izabella paused. "But Angelina, the Italian racer, has won a silver and a gold in cross-country."

"How long will the race take?" Franco glanced at his watch.

"At this rate, it will be less than fifteen more minutes for the winner." Sofia cheered for the Italian Team, currently in third place, pointing to their final racer. "That's Angelina Bianchi. She and Michelina Colombo are friends of mine." She raised a fist in the air. "Go, Angelina. Win."

I scooped Lightning off the concrete floor where Franco deposited him moments ago. "You're a bit cold, buddy." I unzipped my jacket and stuffed him inside. His head popped out to keep an eye on the world around us.

The cheering started when the final lap racers appeared on the last hill. Thunder leapt to his feet, checking out the crowd. Lightning, who'd gotten comfortable in my jacket, yipped until I silenced him.

"The Cooperative Team's leading." I zipped my coat a little tighter and kept my eyes on the track.

"Look at the gap." I handed Lightning to Izabella. He seemed to like her a lot.

The Cooperative Team took gold by finishing with a time of 1:01.27. The close battle for the silver medal between the Norwegian and Italian teams brought everyone to their feet. With 1.02.12, Norway won over Italy's time of 1:02.25.

Bouncing with energy, Sofia cheered her team to the very end. "They've won a bronze medal." She hugged Alex.

He winced in pain.

Her eyes widened and she grabbed his hand, squeezing it. "Forgive me? I forgot."

Alex made the okay sign and smiled. After watching a few other teams come in, he checked his watch. "Eleven-ten. We need to head to a restaurant."

We hunted until we found the Alpine Paradise Restaurant, where we could go inside and sit. The wooden log exterior and wooden beam ceilings made me feel at home. An alpine ski-lodge theme seemed perfect for the mountains around us. We squeezed into a small space filled with customers waiting for seats. I held Lightning in my arms to keep him from getting stepped on. After giving the maître de our name and party size, our group stood in a corner.

Thunder jerked Alex away from the group, sniffing and puffing.

Lightning squirmed to get out of my arm. "Where are you going?" I stroked his head. "Tired of crowds?" I laughed.

About half a minute later, a white poodle appeared, leading a rotund lady, about Sofia's height. The full-size poodle showed the latest expensive trimming on its legs and a bow in its hair.

"Fifi." The woman gave me the sad-eyes treatment when the poodle pawed my arm to get to Lightning.

Lightning wiggled, trying to get free to meet this new friend.

I set him on the ground. He and Fifi sniffed each other.

Thunder joined the party, dragging Alex behind.

"That's Fifi." I pointed to the dog and her owner.

Alex stared at her and tilted his head. "It's you."

The woman put a finger over her lips. "Don't say it."

Chapter 65 – Old Woman

Alpine Paradise Restaurant, Les Saisies, France

Monday, 20 January 1992, 11:40 a.m.

Gabe and the others' faces glanced at me with questions in their eyes. When the woman put a finger to her lips, I knew her. Genevieve.

I moved closer.

"Alex, you'll break my cover." She bent to click a leash onto Fifi's collar.

I began to back away, but before I took even one whole step, she clutched the sleeves of my coat. "I need to talk with you alone. Outside."

Sofia tapped on my back. "Alex, what's going on?"

I swallowed. Either I trusted her or I didn't. But curiosity drove me on. "Yes, I can help direct you to the next major event." I turned to Sofia. "I'll be back in a sec. I need to help this lady with some directions."

Sofia narrowed her eyes at me. She wasn't buying it.

I shrugged. "Be right back."

Knowing that the group would be talking about me until I returned, I grabbed Thunder's leash and tugged him to the door. Genevieve and Fifi followed.

Outside, she directed me around a corner. "That alley." She waved a hand to go forward. "We can talk there."

I stopped. "No. We talk here." I planted my feet.

"Alex, someone will spot us."

"We'll have to chance it." I petted Fifi. "Act like we're old friends."

Her body, tense at first, relaxed. She stepped closer and held my hand.

Fifi and Thunder lay at our feet.

I furrowed my brows. "You stood by while Bastien and your killers prepared to dip us in the water."

"No." Her fierce voice fired back. "I didn't stand by. Who do you think gave Willie the information to get him there in time?"

I dropped her hand and cocked an eye. "You're kidding."

She shook her head. "No. I can't explain it all now, but Dimitri is looking for me. He has Willie."

"When did he take him?" I gazed into her eyes, searching for telltale signs she spoke the truth. "Where?"

She glanced left and right. "I have to go. Everything you want to know is in this paper." She grabbed my hand, opened it, and jammed the note into my palm. She hugged me and whispered next to my ear, "You need to rescue him today."

Releasing me, she tugged Fifi's leash and hurried off, back bent over like an older woman.

Dazed, I stared after her. *She saved our lives?*

Thunder rumbled, rose to his feet, and headed back to the restaurant.

I drifted after him, lost in thought.

Sofia, jaw tight and arms folded, stood in the doorway of the building, staring at me.

Chapter 66 – The Note

Alpine Paradise Restaurant, Les Saisies, France
Monday, 20 January 1992, 11:50 a.m.

Sofia disappeared inside the restaurant.

I sighed. She didn't wait for me. Probably mad I spent time with a woman she didn't know. Odds were she'd put on a huge fireworks display the next time we were alone. When I led Thunder into the waiting area, our friends were gone. Did they leave? I checked with the maître de. "Did you seat a group of two girls, two boys, and a small dog?"

He stared at me. "Does this group have a name?"

"The Zanadu group?" I waited while he searched his list. He shook his head.

I racked my brain. What could my brother have told him? "The Gabe Table?"

"Oui." The man strode to our table and waited. "Is everything satisfactory, Monsieur?"

"Yes."

The man continued to stay in place.

Did I do something wrong? I pondered this for a second until my mind clicked with an answer. I frowned, patted my pocket, and withdrew my wallet. "Here it is. Thanks for taking care of me." I slipped a ten-dollar bill out, replaced the wallet, and removed my coat. "Would you mind hanging this on the coat rack behind you?"

I passed the money to him when he grasped my coat. He hung it on the rack and left. When the man blended back into the crowd, I plucked the note from my left pocket and sat at the table.

Franco shifted the remaining open chair for me. He sat on my left with Gabe to my right. Sofia sat across the table from me, frosty eyes watching me. Thunder deserted me and sat with her. Izabella stroked Lightning on her lap.

The waitress interrupted the moment by taking our orders. When Sofia gave her drink order, she lengthened the words while eyeing me. "I-c-e water."

I got the point.

"Hey, bro." Gabe smirked a little. "Find another mountain princess to court?"

Playing with the note, I ignored the barb and read it to myself.

Franco shifted his chair and craned his neck to read the paper over my shoulder, but I bent the sides in to keep it shielded from his eyes.

"We've got a bit of work to do before tonight." I passed the paper to Izabella.

"Come on, Alex." A smile wider than Texas lit Gabe's face. "Who was the pretty girl?"

Izabella tensed. "When can we talk about this?" She passed the note to Gabe.

My brother read the message, shrugged, and kept throwing verbal darts. "I wonder how many times this woman will keep you under her spell?"

Sofia's reaction came across worse than I expected. "Not again."

Franco grabbed the note from her hand. "Thanks." He read the message, folded it, and sat back in his chair. He slid the paper back to me.

"The best time to discuss this will be in the car when we drive back to Albertville." I locked eyes with everyone at the table. "We can't talk about it here."

"Then let's talk about the Games." Gabe whipped out a schedule from his pocket. "I bet—"

"Gabe." Sofia narrowed her eyes at me. "Not now."

"I wanted to—"

"Gabe." She glared.

And Thunder rumbled.

Chapter 67 – Limited Resources

Security Office, Les Saisies, France

Monday, 20 January 1992, 12:30 p.m.

Paul arrived with our transportation at the Les Saisies Security office at fifteen minutes past noon. The temperature warmed to thirty-one degrees. I enjoyed the sun's brilliant light and heat, which made the cold weather somewhat comfortable. However, the chill between Alex and Sofia would require an iron-smelting furnace to heat their relationship back to normal.

Franco, Alex, and I crowded together in the back bench seat to talk about the note. The girls sat in the middle row with Thunder and Lightning to get in on the conversation, leaving Paul in front by himself.

"Let's plan the next steps." Alex and Sofia glanced away in stony silence. "Come on, guys." I slapped the back of the girl's seat. "Our friend's life is on the line. We'll have to gather some equipment for the operation this evening. What time would be good to do that?"

"Not now, Gabe." Sofia faced her window, shutting me out.

I tried a different line. "To do a rescue mission, we'll need to co-ordinate with Gilbert. Why don't we find him the minute we arrive at Albertville?"

"What rescue mission?" Paul's French accent lingered over each word. "Who needs rescuing?"

Alex elbowed me. "Let's just say we have a friend we'd like to help out. I think we should talk to Gilbert first before making any other plans."

"Okay." Paul gunned the engine to pass a Datsun sedan.

"Maybe we can—"

"Gabe, stop." Alex glared at me.

"But you said—"

"I know what I said, but I'm wrong." My brother looked to the front of the van at Sofia. "Not everything I do is right. I make mis-takes."

The laughter bubbled out of me before I could stop it. "That's a true statement if I ever heard one. I can name a thousand times—"

"Enough." Alex's dagger-eyes told me I teetered on the edge of getting punched.

That wouldn't bother me, but if he hit me, I'd have to hit him back, and his ribs still bothered him. "That's okay, bro. I bet you don't feel good yet." I changed the subject. "I think the Cooperative Team may be using drugs to their advantage."

"Lots of positives on many teams, but not the Cooperative Team." Paul skidded around a corner. "I work at the testing center in Albertville."

I furrowed my brow. "What's your work level? Are you on Detec-tive Gretzke's team?"

"Not him." Paul glanced back at us, swerved to miss an oncom-ing car, and threw a hand into the air. "Terrible drivers. We have the International Elimination Games, talk about safe driving every opportunity we get, and what happens? People drive on the wrong side of the road, don't pay attention, don't learn how to drive in the snow—"

Sofia's tone sharpened. "Paul." When he lifted his head to hear better, she softened a bit. "Thanks for the information, but maybe there's a better place to talk when we get off the mountain."

Paul looked into his mirror. "For you, Cheri, I would do anything."

Sofia smiled like the sun. "I'm glad *someone* will take care of me."

The Main Security Headquarters didn't feel the same when we walked in without Willie being present. The grouchy desk sergeant flicked a hand at us to sit while we waited for Gilbert to arrive. The dogs sniffed the entire waiting area before he appeared.

"This way." He waved us back to Willie's office.

We settled into chairs after getting a drink from the coffee bar. I opted for my usual—hot chocolate. Sofia sat at one end of two chairs with Izabella beside her and Thunder at her feet. The other grouping of three chairs held me, Franco in the middle, and Alex. I cradled Lightning on my lap.

Gilbert sat, shoulders drooped, in another chair in front of Willie's desk. "I hope everyone is comfortable." He gave us a weak smile. "Not much progress to report on finding my boss. But we are making progress on the false positive drug tests and the information about the drops."

"Congrats on the testing. I stroked Lightning's hair. "Alex got information on where your boss is located. We need to review that and a plan to rescue him tonight."

Gilbert straightened. "That's wonderful. Let me bring in another detective to head this operation."

Alex stood, stepped over to Gilbert, and handed Gilbert the piece of paper from Genevieve. "We can't do that. The note gives specific warnings against getting any other Elim Games Security personnel involved. The woman who gave me this note risked blowing her cover to deliver the information." He walked to the door, leaned against the wall, and crossed his arms.

"Cover?" Gilbert glanced at the note, his eyebrows knit together. "Does the International Elimination Games Committee have an agent undercover that Security doesn't know about?"

"According to her, she's not an IEGC agent." I rubbed the back of Lightning's head.

"We still don't know if we can trust her." Sofia glared at my brother. "She uses some questionable methods to accomplish her mission. She can't stay away from Alex. He's like putty in her hands."

"Not true." Alex stiffened.

"The point is," Franco said, "she's the single lead we have right now."

"I'll get a real detective on this now." Gilbert rose and stepped to the door.

My brother, who still stood near the door, waved him off. "Gilbert, this room is wired to provide complete protection from bugs. Willie hasn't shared all of his work with your Security office. You will compromise him and the entire mission against the drug dealers if we don't keep this under the covers."

"Willie might not make it if we make this note public." I sipped on my hot chocolate. "Why don't we brainstorm a rescue plan here and now. We can't execute until it's dark anyway."

"That's not good." Willie's assistant wagged his head back and forth.

"Why not?" Izabella raised an eyebrow.

"We're supposed to have blizzard conditions on some of the mountains tonight. Officials might postpone some events until tomorrow. A terrible time to try to rescue my boss."

"Or the perfect distraction to slip in and fulfill our mission." Izabella's eyes shone.

"Read the note." I shifted in my chair. "You'll see."

Gilbert read the note and returned it to Alex.

"Let's take this line by line." Alex stepped next to the whiteboard behind Willie's desk. "Line one – Willie's hidden in a cabin near the Elim Games Park in Méribel." Alex put a black dot on the board and handed the note to Izabella. "Read it to me line by line."

"Line two – Form a small team of no more than four people."

I eyed the group. "Who wants to stay behind?"

"I should go." Gilbert stood. "He's my boss."

Alex waved him to sit. "We're going to need you here to protect us and be ready with more resources if we call."

"I'll stay back." Izabella patted Thunder's head. "I can be the prayer warrior."

I smiled. "Perfect. Hadn't thought of that angle."

"Line three – Bring three fast two-person snowmobiles. Haul the dogs behind one of the sleds."

Franco motioned at Gilbert. "Can you make that happen? It needs to be done by six o'clock tonight."

Willie's assistant tapped the arm of his chair with his knuckles. "It will be done."

"Line four – From the Elim Games Park at Méribel, follow the Ruisseau de Bourbon stream in the direction of the mountain's peak, past a road intersection. Reduce speed for fifteen more minutes to five miles an hour. Park the snowmobiles and hike in."

Alex drew a box for the park, a squiggly line for the stream, and the road intersection.

"We're going to need maps of the area." Sofia scratched the side of Thunder's face. "And the equipment listed at the end of the note."

Gilbert nodded.

"Line five – No police, no IEG Security, no officials of any sort. This must be done without notice to anyone. Below is a list of equipment you'll need. Don't come until it's dark."

"That means no one can see your people staging the snowmobiles or anywhere in the Méribel area." I gulped some hot chocolate. "When we leave here, we must have all the equipment."

Chapter 68 – Méribel Cabin

Mountain Cabin, Méribel, France

Monday, 20 January 1992, 1:50 p.m.

Genevieve threw off her oversized coat, tugging pillows and padding from the large-person net she wore earlier in the day in one of the single-floor cabin's two back bedrooms that shared a bathroom. She hated hiding the figure she'd worked so hard to maintain over the years. But deception required a high price of her for success.

She walked through the living room into the dining room and finished dropping the net and extra disguise pieces on the floor. She considered the layout. If she decided to build a headquarters, she would keep the open concept for the house's living, dining, and kitchen areas. Clear fields of fire throughout if someone attacked her. And the convenience of a large woodshed steps away from the kitchen door for fresh firewood also gave maintenance men and guards an outdoor space for their work.

"We'll never see the kids approach in these conditions." She considered the dense forest which covered the land outside about twenty feet from the cabin. "The snowfall's already thick." The previous owner cleared enough trees to allow for a gravel driveway and road to the house. A carport stood beyond the residence at the end of the road. "We're supposed to get snowed in later this evening."

"I've got plans for that." Dimitri smoked a Cuban cigar. He let out a couple of rings of smoke. "Did they buy your disguise and the note? I'll be glad to get rid of those insects."

She grabbed the pile of clothing and headed to the bedroom. "No question. They'll be here tonight." She passed Willie, sitting in the middle of the room, tied to a wooden chair nailed to the floor.

"You're crazy." Willie shook his head at her. "You're underestimating those boys and their friends. They'll turn you until your head's spinning."

Genevieve continued into the bedroom, threw the clothes in a closet, shut the door, and returned to the living room. Dimitri stood near the IEG Detective.

"You're not long for this world." Dimitri strolled behind Willie. "Tell me, who in my organization told you about the location of our house on the mountain."

"If I was going to tell you that, I'd have squealed earlier when your goons beat me up this morning. Besides, a detective never reveals his sources."

Dimitri slammed a fist into the back of Willie's head. "Tell me and I'll scare the kids off, and you'll be the only one who burns."

The Australian detective winced. "Those boys won't stop hunting you until you're in prison. The lot of you." He eyed Genevieve with a swollen right eye.

"Darling, for the benefit of the children, you should provide him the information." She ran a finger across his chin. "We can burn the cabin to the ground before they arrive and you'll be long dead."

The door of the cabin rattled with a gust of wind.

"Besides, I'd like to leave this rat-trap before the full blizzard hits tonight at nine o'clock." She smiled. "Driving in the snow has never been my best skill. And when I get nervous, the tension builds. When the tension builds, I get angry. And when I get angry, I lash out at anything or anyone." She slapped his face hard enough to leave a handprint. "Think about that, detective."

"She's not kidding." Dimitri checked the clock on the wall. "That gives her about five hours for the tension to build. She's never pretty when she's angry." He laughed and sauntered over to the dining room table.

"Let's talk about how we finish off this pesky investigation." Dimitri sat at the table, his vodka shot waiting for him.

"Boss, when do we get ready?" A Russian man peered out the kitchen door window.

Dimitri pondered for a moment. "Set the traps after dark. Seven o'clock."

Genevieve bristled that the Russian left her out of the loop for this particular piece of the operation. "What traps?"

He smiled. "I'll have the approaches wired to let me know when the boys and their friends are here. I'm sure you told them to walk in."

"You'd better have an army to take them out." Willie swallowed hard. "They'll knock out every defense you've got."

Dimitri chuckled. "Your confidence in two underage junior detectives is amazing." He shuffled some papers on the table and caught Genevieve's eye. "Have you framed him yet?"

"Why ask me? Am I here to do the dirty work?" She scowled.

"Your personal relationship skills are well above my men's capabilities."

She gritted her teeth. "Yes. Lieutenant Colonel Zanadu will take the fall. I planted the evidence myself today." She sniffed. "I even sweet-talked his Colonel supervisor into keeping him at work late tonight."

"You serve me well."

Genevieve slammed a fist on the table. "I don't serve you." Her nostrils flared. "We are a team. I do it for the good of my business."

Dimitri grabbed her left wrist and tightened his grip. "You work for me."

With a lightning-quick movement, she whipped a .22 caliber tiny pistol from the small of her back, cocked it, and aimed between Dimitri's eyes. "Let go."

Dimitri relaxed his hand. "You're not going to count to three?"

Genevieve detected movement out of her peripheral vision in the kitchen. She shifted around the table, keeping Willie in view and using Dimitri for a shield from the bodyguard's gun. "Tell your hitman to drop his weapon now."

"Stanislav, let it go."

A clatter came from the kitchen area.

"Nice team, mates." Willie laughed, but it turned into a coughing fit. "Fantastic working relationship you have."

"Stanislav, silence him." Dimitri eased back into his chair.

The bodyguard grabbed a gag from the table and completed the task.

"Now that we've taken care of the important matters let's plan the final stages of our International Elimination Games triumph." Dimitri puffed on his cigar and chuckled.

Chapter 69 – Sparks Fly

IEG Main Security Headquarters, Albertville, France
Monday, 20 January 1992, 2:15 p.m.

The meeting with Gilbert ended with the agreement that he would meet with me, Sofia, Gabe, Franco, and Izabella at four o'clock. Outside the Security Headquarters, Gabe and his two friends decided to head to our hotel to talk. Sofia slipped away from us without a word.

"Sofia, can I walk you to your hotel?" I jogged a few steps to match her speed, holding my left side.

She focused her eyes straight ahead. "Maybe. Depends on what we'll talk about."

"Us." I couldn't maintain her pace. I slowed to a turtle's pace.

She strolled a few steps in the direction of her hotel, paused, and turned back to me. "Coming?"

I grimaced and lurched ahead. "Sure."

When we'd walked half a block, Sofia stopped and pinned me to the wall with her look. "I can't believe you let that woman twist you around her finger." One hand on her hip, she threw the other into the air. "Am I too young for you? Or do you like relationships with older women?"

She fired off the accusation with a fierceness I had never noticed in her before. Was she worried about our relationship? I studied her. Dark-brown eyes narrowed. Nostrils flared. Jaw tight. And her black hair framed her face in beautiful waves.

"You look gorgeous when you're mad."

"Oo-oo-h." She swiveled and strode in the direction of her hotel.

I ignored the pain and hurried to catch her. "I mean…"

She pivoted and faced me. "What I mean is that you let your brain wander when a pretty woman is involved." She crossed her arms.

"What are you talking about?" I spread my arms." That's not true. And why do you care?"

"You are so dense." She spun to her right and stomped away.

"Wait." I loped a few steps until she faced me again. "Genevieve's undercover. She knew how to make our discussion seem like an innocent meeting between friends."

"She's turning you in circles with her emotional games."

"Not really. I acted out the ruse to protect her."

Sofia whipped around and left me behind again.

I rushed to walk by her side. She almost ran. We didn't talk for three blocks. Bad news for me. *What's it going to take to keep her with me?* I didn't want to make her angrier than her current state.

"Sofia." We kept moving, but she slowed a bit. "It's my fault."

"I'm listening."

She didn't face me but cut her speed to an average pace.

"Genevieve wanted me to go in an alley with her." I drifted closer to her to avoid another pedestrian. "I couldn't do that. Who knows what could have happened? I kept us beside the building where everyone could see and only got close for her to whisper and pretend to be close friends."

"You seemed *very* close to me."

I shut my eyes for an instant and rubbed my forehead. "I didn't know who might be listening. Speaking to each other while I hugged her meant we could keep the volume low."

"And I bet the heat went up in your bodies."

"We were in our snow coats. And she wore a fat-body disguise." I shook my head. "I acted out my part."

She sniffed. "An act I think you enjoyed."

"Sofia." I touched her arm and guided her to the side, by the outside of a building. "I'm sorry. First, she gave me the note. Next, she hugged me like a friend, whispered a warning in my ear, and left."

She glanced at the street and into my eyes. "What am I supposed to think? You still hugged her."

I rubbed my aching side. "I'm telling you the truth. She may have done it to protect herself. According to her, she saved us by telling Willie where we were at the pond. I wish our meeting could have been different. Trust me. You're far more important to me than her."

Sofia's eyes brightened at the end. "I'm glad to hear that." A church-tower clock chimed the time of two-thirty. "We don't have much time until our four-o'clock meeting." She slid her arm around mine. "We're almost at my hotel. You need to get back to your room and rest."

Chapter 70 – Go Time

Darkness surrounded Alex, Sofia, Franco, me, and our dogs. Six o'clock seemed like midnight. Wind-driven snow pelted us and our parked snowmobiles.

Gilbert delivered two machines, making us short one. He failed to get the necessary equipment we requested. His answer sounded like an excuse. *I am not Willie, whom people listen to without question. I must, how do you say, beg, borrow, and steal, to get what I want.*

I suppose he got that right. Willie could move mountains by telling people to make it happen.

But essential items dropped off the list. Two flashlights instead of four. No handcuffs, police web-belts, guns, gag material, riot batons, or bullet-proof vests. And instead of three flashbangs, tear gas, and smoke grenades, we got one of each. At least Gilbert acquired rope, some sacks for hoods, gas masks to strap on our legs, holsters for our belts, hundred-mile-an-hour tape, and some zip-ties. We would adapt and overcome.

Franco's voice came through the walkie-talkie. "Radio check. How do you read me?"

I couldn't see Sofia, but her voice came in strong. "Clear to me."

"Franco, plug in your earbuds and adjust the squelch and volume controls." I double-checked my equipment. "I can hear your walkie-talkie without my earbuds." Franco filled the trail member position for the group. Invisible to me.

"Done." His voice sounded clear through my equipment.

"Get ready to roll out." The howl of the wind almost blew my words away.

Alex, noticeable when he moved to within a few feet of me, nodded.

Bundled in our dark snow gear, each of us wore gators around our necks, pulled over our noses and ears, and skiing goggles to protect our eyes. We carried compact backpacks and wore different colored knit hats to distinguish between each other: Alex – black, Sofia – camouflage green, Franco – gun-metal grey, and me – dark navy blue.

I strapped on trick skis, which Gilbert supplied for the team. We could thread through trees better, and if we needed to switch from skis to boots, we would carry them and the collapsible poles clipped to our packs to keep our options open. At least Gilbert got that right.

Lightning kept my chest warm, occupying the front of my jacket in a baby front carrier. Thunder stood beside Alex, sniffing the air. The snow wasn't too deep yet.

"Gabe." Alex's voice filled my ears." "Take the lead. Avoid major trails—"

"I know what to do." We'd covered this in the planning meeting at four o'clock. "Stay tight." I glanced at my watch. "Six-thirty. Time to move."

I led Alex and Thunder, Sofia, and Franco, in that order. The blizzard arrived almost an hour before the predicted time. We started our operation about five o'clock at the Elim Games Security Headquarters in Albertville. Paul drove us in a civilian van to Méribel through a heavy snowfall, dropped us off at the snowmobiles, and ensured we got away without a hitch.

Hand and arm signals didn't work in the limited visibility. We bunched together when I stopped unless I used our commo gear. "Rest halt." I slid a few feet forward, catching my breath.

"When will we arrive?" Franco's voice came in short breaths from the climb and navigating through the trees.

Alex answered. "Ten minutes is the ETA."

"Seen any traps?" Franco's breathing became more regular.

"None." I scanned to my front. "They may have tripwires near the cabin. Since we don't know what it looks like, we'll have to play it by ear when we get there."

"Let's go." Alex's voice sounded strong and loud. "We need to be quick."

In less than five minutes, I called another stop. "Lights ahead."

Though difficult to make out, a dim glow filtered through the snow falling in front of me. I observed for a minute, but the light didn't go away.

I keyed my walkie again. "Time to stow our gear." I dropped my pack on the ground, released my skis, collapsed my poles, and strapped them onto my bag.

A noise startled me.

"Quiet." I crept forward, carrying my pack in one hand.

"Talk to us." Alex's voice rose in pitch.

"I see movement at the cabin, but it's hard to make out what's happening." Whispering, I dropped to my stomach. "Hide." I shouldered my pack and low-crawled next to a thick pine, observing the door in front of me. The glow by the door got brighter.

"Gabe, what's happening." Sofia's nervousness made her voice a bit shaky.

"A man—no, make that six men, came around the cabin's corner and are spreading out around the house in pairs. They have flashlights and knapsacks."

"They might lay traps for us on the trails to the house," Franco said. "I'm moving forward."

The men disappeared on the three separate tourist paths we'd seen on the map earlier.

Someone tapped my shoulder. I whirled; fist cocked. Ready to strike.

"Easy, bro." Alex raised a hand.

I dropped my arm and returned to watching the cabin while Alex and Sofia huddled next to my tree. Thunder stood alert next to my brother. Franco arrived seconds later. I pointed to the men spreading out.

"If they're setting traps for us, they'll probably be busy for at least five to ten minutes." Franco motioned with his head at the house. "We should attack now."

"Bad plan." Alex eyed the house. "We can't all go in at once. Remember, we don't know what the inside is like."

Thunder rumbled.

"Silent mode." Alex tapped his nose.

"One of us should look in the window." Sofia tapped herself. "I'll go."

"No." Alex and I said in unison and glanced at each other.

I spoke first. "We have experience in scouting different places. I'm going."

Alex's eyes widened, but he let it go. "Good choice since I'm still a little achy. We'll cover your back."

I hooked my walkie on my coat's collar near my mouth. "Warn me when they're returning."

Alex gave me a thumbs up.

Staying in a low crouch, I left my backpack and weaved through the underbrush to the door where the men exited the cabin. I zipped through the thick snowfall across an open space that's width was about the length of a full-sized car. It surrounded the building. The ground under my feet made crunching sounds, like gravel. I hugged the wall, ducked under a large window facing the trees where the group hid, and loped past the light pooling on the ground where the men first appeared at the edge of the building.

"All clear." Alex's voice assured me he watched the patch of ground.

I pressed my talk button, pushing the walkie close to my mouth. "Checking doorway now." I darted around the corner and edged onto the three steps to the door.

The top half of the door contained a pane of glass cut in quarters, a duplicate of the house we stormed to rescue the girls. Across from the entrance, beyond the cleared land surrounding the house, sat an open-sided shed with tools, lawn chairs, a mower, some other maintenance equipment, and wood. Inside the cabin, I heard shouting. I peeked in the window.

Genevieve strode across an expansive living room, cattycorner from the kitchen area near the door. She waved her hands, pointing at Willie, whose head swiveled back and forth between her and Dimitri. The Russian smoked a cigar, jabbing it at her to emphasize his points. She reached the dining room table, grabbed several papers, and stuffed them in a briefcase. Dimitri yelled, "Nyet." and flung the cigar at her.

"Inbound," Alex warned me. "Pair number One."

With the racket going on inside, I figured I could talk. "Argument going on inside between our targets. Willie tied and gagged at the living room's center. I'm going to the woodshed opposite the door and observe." I ran to the woodshed's backside away from the cabin but peered around the edge to keep observing.

"Negative, scout." Alex increased his volume. "Return to base. We need to eliminate the extra manpower."

Two men appeared at the corner of the cabin, cutting off any retreat. When they heard the shouting, one of them shook his head and pointed at my hiding place. I snuck behind the woodshed, where a small extension, with a door for a room, jutted from the middle of the building. I discovered an old ratty tarp covering a stack of wood. I loosened the cords holding it in place and crawled underneath it. Moments later, I smelled smoke. The men began talking.

I crept out from under my concealed position and investigated. Using extreme caution, I rounded the corner to the backside of the shed and peered around the corner to the front.

"Blue cap." Alex raised his voice to the drill sergeant level. "I said, return to base."

I spun my earbud's volume to zero, praying the people in front of me failed to hear Alex's loud voice.

The two men sat out of the blizzard on wooden fold-up chairs under a metal awning, with a cut piece of log about knee-height that they'd positioned like an end table. One wore gray snow gear and the other wore green camo. Both faced the kitchen door, waiting for the shouting to stop. They laughed at each other, oblivious to my presence. The one in gray smoked a fat cigar.

I backtracked to a spot behind the shed and raised my volume to level four. "Pinned down by Pair One. I'm stuck. Your team needs to eliminate pairs Two and Three."

I contemplated my options. Taking these guys out wouldn't be easy.

Chapter 71 – Hogtied

Trails near Mountain Cabin, Méribel, France
Monday, 20 January 1992, 6:37 p.m.

Pair One trapped Gabe." I beckoned Sofia and Franco closer. "We need to take out the other two teams fast."

"But Alex, that's impossible." Franco made a sweeping motion with his arm. "We don't know where they went or when they'll return."

I tightened my jaw. "Gabe's life is on the line now, along with Willie's." I stabbed my finger at the trail. "I'm not going to let men like that win. Got it?"

Sofia touched my arm. "What do you need?"

I laid out a plan in the snow.

"You're still hurt, Alex." Sofia pointed at my side. "You won't be able to do everything you described."

"Not to worry." I patted my backpack. "I took a couple of pain pills before we started and brought some with me. Plus, my Karate instructor taught me how to ignore pain when necessary. Did both of you understand the plan?"

When they both signaled yes, I grabbed my pack and Gabe's. Sofia and Franco shouldered their gear and we hurried away. I led the group through the trees to the smaller of the two trails with Thunder trailing behind.

The gap between the trees was wide enough for three burly men to walk side by side. Hustling about twenty feet further on the trail, I found two trees we could use. I strung a cord across the path, burying it below the surface of the snow. Franco and I used other cord pieces we cut moments ago to make lassos wide enough to fit around each man with ease.

After making his lasso, my Italian buddy brushed a loose pine bough back and forth on the trail to hide our work. He sprinkled the ground with snow from the woods to match the blizzard's effect.

"Grey hat, take the left side." Franco faded into some brush about three paces from the line lying across the path. He'd be behind the pair when we attacked. I took the same position opposite him on the right side.

"Green hat, are you set?" I checked her work to ensure the cord wound around the trunk was about calf-high on the tree. I inspected the path of the cord around another smaller tree. The extra tree would help Sofia keep the line tight when the men struggled. She'd followed my instructions and tied the end to a broken tree branch she'd trimmed to make a handle she could put her weight behind with two hands. "Excellent."

"Black hat," Franco whispered on the walkie. "Pair Two approaching."

"Roger." I patted Sofia's shoulder and moved into position.

I focused on the men and realized their position presented a problem. The bigger of the two men trailed a step behind the smaller guy, shuffling along. The short guy seemed skinny but wiry. He moved with a lithe step. The tall guy's barrel chest told me I needed to use extreme caution in taking him. But he wandered onto my side of the path. That would help.

Two steps until contact. I keyed my walkie to whisper the command.

One step.

"Now."

When Sofia yanked the cord taut, she grunted. A good distraction. Franco and I glided behind the two men, still unaware of our presence.

The short man tripped on the line and stumbled to the ground, falling on a knee. His head swung to Sofia.

Franco threw his lasso over the man's head, draping it over his arms near the elbows, and tugged the cord tight. The man tumbled to the ground. Sofia burst out of the trees to help Franco.

I tossed a lasso over the head of my guy, kicking his right knee in the process. The man yelled, falling on his uninjured knee while I jerked the cord tight around his arms. He rolled at me and kicked with his good leg. I jumped over him, rapping the injured knee hard as I went.

He bellowed.

I sucked in a deep breath to reduce the pain in my side. I rammed an elbow in the man's kidney. Rolled him on his stomach. Securing the loop on the man's back, I wrapped the cord around his good leg and tightened the rope, pulling toward the middle of his back. Almost like tying a hog or calf.

With two injured body areas, the guy's struggle to escape weakened. He twisted and turned, tearing at the rope with his hands. He kept fighting until I wrenched the leg with the injured knee.

Sofia and Franco secured their guy's legs and arms with zip-ties. They completed the takedown by gagging their man.

"Help." I motioned them over to my captive and they followed the same procedures. Standing next to them, I guided their actions while holding my side. "Pull the zip-ties tighter. Check the other man too."

"Sacks." I grunted, sank to one knee, and tugged a sack on the big man's head, securing it. My teammates wrestled with their man, but their work paid off when a bag covered his head.

"With these blizzard conditions, our captives will seem like fallen logs in no time." Franco waved at the wind-blown snow.

"Better for us." I paused to listen through the howling wind. "I'm sure someone heard those yells. Prepare for company." Searching both men, I found their guns and took them. "Either of you comfortable with a gun?" I held one out to them. Sofia shook her head.

Franco, however, stepped forward. "I've fired a rifle before."

I showed him the gun's safety, clicked it on, how to load the first round in the chamber, and talked him through a few pointers. "Guns aren't that accurate unless you've trained with them. Use it to scare someone or signal for help. Remember, bullets can ricochet on metal."

He hefted the gun and aimed at the big guy.

"Careful." I pushed his arm away from any people targets. "Use it only as a last resort."

He nodded and tucked the pistol in the holster on his belt, and I did the same.

I started to lead my friends through the trees to our next hidden location, five minutes closer to the cabin.

But Sofia grabbed my arm. "Alex, we're short on equipment, even with these guns." Her eyes widened. "Now we're fighting four guards instead of two. How can we win?"

Chapter 72 – Solo Solution

She Behind Mountain Cabin, Méribel, France
Monday, 20 January 1992, 6:57 p.m.

P air Two secured." Alex's comment spurred me forward.

I went back to a few of the traps I'd been setting in the last ten minutes. Lightning squirmed in the front-pack. I loosened his temporary home, took him out, and set him in the snow. Tapping his nose, I put a finger to my lips.

I executed a delicate approach to the two men smoking in front of me. With the noises in the cabin still raging with shouting, screaming, and crashing objects, I knew my best time was now. While Alex handled Pair Two, I kept myself moving.

Either the guards enjoyed the show, with an occasional glance in the window to see if they should intervene, or they didn't want to interfere with their boss and his business associate.

I constructed a simple first trap: a branch loaded with snow pulled back like a spring with one of my cords. A buried ladder and a few logs from the woodpile became the second trap. With a few other distractions, the grand finale would be the best.

I hefted the old ax handle and swung it like a baseball bat in the air. Poked it in front of me like a cattle prod. It would do the trick. I inventoried the stuff in my pockets: a can of pepper spray, zip ties, an empty ammo magazine, and a pad and pen. I showed Lightning what I wanted him to do, using hand signals. Taking a deep breath, I rubbed his cheek against mine. "Follow my lead, little buddy. We'll make it."

Chapter 73 – Spotter

Trails near Mountain Cabin, Méribel, France
Monday, 20 January 1992, 7:05 p.m.

Sofia tugged on my coat. "Alex, where is Pair Three?"

I shook my head. "Not sure. But they should arrive any second."

Franco pointed to the cabin. On the path, one man's silhouette approached through the driven snow. "They've divided their team."

"Either one of them is coming behind the first man or he went back to the house." I clenched my jaw. "Gabe might have unexpected company."

"We need to eliminate this guy," Sofia whispered.

"Be careful," Franco said. "The other guy might be laying a trap to eliminate us."

I tapped Franco's arm. "We split apart. You're going to be a spotter, in case we have the second man from this pair come to surprise us from behind." I handed Gabe's pack to him. "If we get attacked, you find Gabe. He'll tell you what to do next."

"What if they've captured Gabe?" He tilted his head in a question.

"Depends." I paused before my comment, wording it with care. "If we're not successful and the crooks capture both Gabe and us, then go to the police."

"Got it." Like a silent shadow, Franco slipped away.

Chapter 74 – Old Fashioned Remedies

Shed Behind Mountain Cabin, Méribel, France
Monday, 20 January 1992, 7:09 p.m.

I peeked around the corner of the shed. Partially obscured by falling snow, the two guys sat relaxed, smoking and joking. The loud arguments from the cabin got quiet, but Dimitri changed that with a shout. A dish flew into the cabin window and cracked the glass. The two men chuckled.

I rubbed Lightning's head, set him on the ground, and pushed him forward. He looked back at me and cocked his head. I sighed. Drama queen. I flicked my hands at him to direct him to the men. Satisfied I noticed him, he turned and trotted as I'd said. I ducked back around the corner and prepared to spring the traps.

Lightning's yapping wasn't that loud. Based on the increased noise in the cabin, I felt pretty sure they didn't hear him.

I lay on the snow around the back of the shed, behind a pine tree.

A taut cord to my right stretched from an anchor point behind me to my pine limb trap.

Lightning tore around the corner, making a beeline for the shed extension's open door. The first man in a grey jacket peeked around the corner, rifle at the ready. He aimed at Lightning right when he disappeared into the extension part of the building. Using my knife, I slashed at the first cord.

A pine branch loaded with snow released and slapped the man in the throat, throwing snow over his face and head. The second man, dressed in camo, peered from behind him, brushing snow from his coat.

The first guy held his rifle in one hand, coughing and clutching his throat with the other. He didn't sound happy.

"Take that, big man." I smiled. *No one hurts my dog and gets away with it.*

The man in camo clothes patted the other guy's back. Motioned him to move on.

Rubbing his throat, the grey-jacketed man scanned the area. He didn't see me huddled behind a tree.

Lightning reappeared in the storage room's doorway, barked, and disappeared back inside.

I jumped to my feet, threw a snowball at the first man, and sprinted to the small room where Lightning stood.

The two men shouted in Russian. They sprinted to the open door. Both men stumbled over small logs I hid earlier in the snow. The guy in camo helped his partner stand and inspected the ground in front of them.

"Chicken." I fired another snowball at the man in the grey jacket, smacking him in the head.

The guard roared and flew straight at me. He tripped, tumbling over the hidden ladder under the snow. I snickered. The second man, right behind him, stumbled on top of him. A crack sounded.

The first man, in grey, rolled on the ground, grabbing his right arm. The guy in camo rolled, grabbed his rifle, and abandoned his comrade howling in pain. The blizzard made it hard to see anything clearly, but his rifle swung sideways, aiming at my chest. I darted to my left inside the storage space. I whipped the connecting inner door to the other side of the shed open, squeezed through it, closed, and locked it. Lightning remained inside, barking at the man in camo.

I hightailed it at top speed through the open side of the shed, grabbing the ax handle. Rushing, I circled the opposite side of the shed, coming most of the way around the building toward the small room. I waited. Chest heaving. Listening.

The Russian in camo spoke to Lightning, who continued to bark.

I peeked around the edge of the building to check on both men.

The man who wore camo thrust a flashlight inside. He crouched sideways to the opening, back to me, rifle in his right hand. The man in grey still lay by the ladder where he'd fallen, holding the cracked arm to his chest, staring into the sky.

I stepped around the corner. Deciding against the baseball swing approach, I slammed the ax handle with maximum force into the guard's left kidney.

He swayed for a split second. Stumbled forward into the storage room. His flashlight fell on the ground and the rifle clunked onto the dirt floor.

I jumped inside, pulled the rifle out, and swung the door shut. I flipped the key in its lock.

I raced back to the opposite side of the shed's extra room, out of the other guard's sight. Lightning wiggled out through a small rabbit hole in the wall. He ran into my arms. "Nice work, buddy." I ruffled his fur. "Now we have to finish the job."

We sprinted to the front of the shed. I slung the rifle onto my back, grabbed a hoe and a rake, and finished the circle, checking around the corner for the Russian with the fractured right arm. He wobbled to his feet, holding his rifle in his left hand. He hunched over to balance the injured arm, walking to the storage room door.

While he trudged forward, he spoke to the man inside. I crept behind him with Lightning beside me. Before I could get in range with the hoe, he turned and saw me. He raised his rifle and leaned against the shed.

Lightning flew at him, leaping onto his chest. The rifle banged against the shed wall.

I dashed close, slamming the hoe into the weapon, hooking it, before the guard pulled the trigger. I jerked with the hoe and the rifle fell to the ground.

Lightning jumped and clamped his jaws on the man's right hand.

The man reacted with a barrage of Russian words and shook Lightning off.

I sprang forward, pulling the pepper spray from my pocket, and unleashed it in his face. He choked, coughed, and tried to breathe. I let him have it again and he went to his knees. I retrieved the tarp's extra cords from my other pocket and tied his hands and legs. I stuffed greasy rags in his mouth, securing them with a bandana, and covered him with the rotted canvas.

That's when Franco arrived.

Chapter 75 – War

What are you doing here?" I narrowed my eyes at Franco.

He held a finger to his lips and tapped his ear. "Two crooks are chasing Alex and Sofia—Pair Three. They're running away from the cabin and will circle back if they can capture them. If not, we have to grab Willie."

"How far away are they?" I took my pack from him.

He motioned us away from the Russians. We walked around the side of the shed. "At least seven minutes." He pointed at the cabin. "Seems pretty quiet."

I frowned. "They fought for a while." I tapped his arm. "Stay here. I'll do a little recon." I left Lightning with Franco and glued myself to the cabin wall. I snuck up the stairs and glanced inside.

Dimitri stood holding a smoking cigar in one hand and a drink in the other. He laughed. In front of him, Willie and Genevieve sat, tied to chairs in the middle of the room. I waved Franco over to me. Motioned for him to scope out the room.

"What's the plan?" Franco lowered his head and stared at me. "How do we get two people out?"

"Distraction works best." I pointed to the far side of the building. "I think that's a bedroom. I saw a doorway on that side. Go around. When I give you the word, shoot your gun in the air. Afterward, run into the woods, put your skis on, and come back to this side."

We descended the stairs together. "We don't have much time. Dimitri's men near Alex and Sofia will arrive soon or the guards I tied might free themselves." I dropped my pack and pulled out a flashbang. "If I lose control in the room, use this."

Franco nodded.

I keyed my mic. "Black hat – do you read?" Silence.

"Okay, we're on our own." I patted his shoulder. "Go. I'll give you two minutes to get in position."

Franco sped into the darkness.

"It's you and me, ole buddy." I cradled Lightning in my arms. "We've got this."

"In position." Franco's voice came in loud and clear.

I crept over the steps and glanced inside. Smiling, Dimitri dumped fuel from a gas can around the walls of the cabin.

"Go." After Franco fired his gun, I pulled out my earbuds and popped in earplugs.

Dimitri's head whipped around. His smile turned into a scowl. He set the can on the floor and rushed into the bedroom.

I opened the door, waved at Willie, closed the door, and slipped into the kitchen with Lightning. I dug into my pack, pulled out canisters of tear gas and smoke, and donned my gas mask from the pouch strapped on my leg.

Dimitri came around the kitchen's corner; his weapon pointed in my direction. "Nyet." He waved me away from my pack, directing me to Willie and Genevieve.

"Glad you could join us, my little friend. Where's your doggie?"

I looked around. "Not sure."

Dimitri shook his head. "Doesn't matter. Lay on the floor, face-down."

I did what he said. He tied my hands behind my back and my feet together. "Time to go."

Dimitri tossed his cigar onto a trail of gasoline. The gas caught fire, which traveled around the room and cabin. He turned in my direction. "You've interfered for the final time. At least you will have company—"

A metal canister crashed through a window and fell to the floor. I hid my face on the carpet and closed my eyes. The contents exploded.

Even with earplugs, the sound deafened me. Faint sounds of yelling filtered through my earplugs. I rolled right.

Alex and Sofia ran into the room.

Flames began to lick at the drapes in the windows of the cabin. Smoke billowed upward to the ceiling.

Dimitri crawled on all fours, searching for something solid to grasp. Alex shoved him to the ground and zip-tied his hands and legs. Both coughed several times.

Lightning tickled my neck with his tongue while Sofia rolled me over.

"My Swiss knife is in my right pants pocket." I tilted my head to direct her, but she didn't respond. Maybe the gas mask distorted the words. I repeated myself louder.

She nodded, eyes darting around at the flames. She dug out the knife. Opened it and cut the ropes off my hands. She slapped the knife in my hand and rushed to Willie and Genevieve.

I sawed through the ropes on my legs, patted Lightning, who hung right next to me. I bolted to my feet, ripped the mask off my face, and inhaled a lungful of smoke. I bent lower, coughing out the fumes.

Sofia ran to Alex and grabbed his arm. "We need to leave. Now." A coughing fit took her to a knee.

"Get low to the ground." Alex slit Willie's zip-ties, freeing him. "More oxygen there. Take Willie outside."

Sofia clutched Willie's hand, crouched, and yanked him to the door. "Hurry, hurry."

Willie sprawled to his side. He gathered himself to a sitting position, hacking and gasping for air. "Be a good Sheila and go for the door."

Sofia wrung her hands, frantic to leave. "Sorry." She hunched over and fled out of the cabin.

Willie rose, crouched low, and limped to the door.

Thunder guarded Dimitri while flames clawed at the ceiling. Lightning dashed beside me. Smoke filled the air, shrouding the room in a veil of black and grey.

Zip-ties held Genevieve's hands and feet together. She coughed like an engine trying to turn over. I slashed both her restraints in two and caught her arm to help her.

She shook me off, cupped a hand over her mouth, and stumbled to the bedroom.

"The other way is out." I pointed at the door.

The ceiling crackled. Fire blazed over the wooden rafters. "We're out of time." I coughed, bent lower, and motioned to the others. "Get out."

I hacked like a chain smoker with diseased lungs. Alex cut the cords around Dimitri's ankles and dragged him to his feet. I shoved the Russian from behind to get him moving with Lightning cradled in one arm.

Through the haze, Sofia reappeared, walking backward. Willie, who'd just reached the door, reversed course.

Sofia pleaded, "No. Don't make me go back in."

Pair Three entered the room, pistols drawn. They shoved Sofia and Willie farther back into the room.

"Let the boss go." The biggest of the two kicked Alex's side. He dropped to the floor.

"Burn them all." Dimitri sneered at us.

The two men waved their weapons at us while they backed away.

The snap of a gun came from outside, behind the men. Their heads jerked. Another crack sounded. Dimitri slumped to the floor. His men's pistols roamed from one of us to the other.

A thunderous bark roared over the fire. A black shape sprang into the room, growled, and slammed into Dimitri's guards.

While Thunder wreaked havoc, I kicked the ear of one guard. He crumpled to the floor. I jabbed the other man's rifle arm with my knife. Back on his feet, Alex used a Karate chop to relieve the gunman of his weapon, and knocked him off his feet.

At the far end of the room knelt Genevieve, weapon leveled at the group of us. "What are you waiting for?" She waved her pistol. "Get out. And take him with you." Her weapon dropped to Dimitri.

Lungs burning, I collected one rifle and handed the other to Alex. Spitting, coughing, and wheezing, we directed the two goons and Dimitri, shoving them toward the door. Genevieve came out last; her weapon still pointed at the Russian crime boss.

The cabin collapsed on itself. We made the entire group move back in the melting snow.

A siren sounded in the distance.

Alex and I stood on either side of the criminals, several feet apart, guns trained on the Russians. Opposite us, like the third point of a triangle, Genevieve kept her weapon pointed at Dimitri. Several yards away, out of the line of fire, Willie and Sofia bent over, gasping for a good breath. Franco stood beside them, checking on their breathing. Thunder stood by his Alex. Lightning pranced next to me, yipping and wagging his tail.

My brother and I exchanged glances, a question on both our minds.

I shrugged and smiled at Genevieve. "Are you with us or against us?"

"That's a long story." She smirked.

Chapter 76 – Wrapping Up

IEG Main Security Headquarters, Albertville, France
Tuesday, 21 January 1992, 9:00 a.m.

I walked into Willie's office and headed straight for the hot chocolate and donuts on the coffee table in the corner. Lightning trailed behind me. I glanced at Willie sitting behind his desk, a patch over his left eye and a sling on his left arm. "You're looking peachy."

"Thanks, mate." Willie smiled, which looked a little lopsided with his swollen lips.

"Gabe." Dad's eyes smoldered. "Have a little more compassion."

"I was going to chuck a sickie but decided we needed to tie things together before you left." Our Aussie friend leaned back in his chair.

"What?" Izabella laughed.

I snickered. "Call in sick." I bit into my donut. "He does look a little worse than normal."

Our gang positioned themselves around the room. Franco sat next to the door with Izabella beside him. Sofia and Alex filled the next two chairs, Thunder sitting at my brother's feet. The coffee table occupied the corner. I sat beside it for quick food access with Lightning on my lap. Dad sat on my left, near Willie's desk.

"Calling in sick would be an understatement." Dad shifted his coffee cup in his hand. "You look exhausted."

"A bit knackered, yes." Willie brought his chair forward. "But I've gone through worse. The Albertville Hospital cleared me to rest at home. But you're too important to me to not come to work."

"Did we do it?" Izabella straightened her back. "I mean, stop the drug ring?"

I grinned. "Did we ever. With fireworks and smoke."

Izabella cocked her head. "That's wild."

Alex, Sofia, Franco, and I informed Dad and Izabella about last night's operation.

Willie smiled. "Quite the dog's breakfast."

Thunder and Lightning both looked at Willie.

He laughed at the dogs' reactions. Glancing at the group, he smiled. "But I knew you'd figure it out."

Alex shrugged. "Even though it didn't go the way we'd planned, we still got the major criminals. Dimitri will be behind bars for a long time."

I gulped some hot chocolate to follow the second donut I'd snitched. "But Willie, we didn't hear your side of the story. What about Dimitri and Genevieve?"

"The Russian is in serious condition at the hospital." Willie glanced at a report on his desk. "He has a guard on him, but Genevieve winged him good. He has a deflated lung and some internal injuries that will heal. He'll spend a great deal of time in a maximum-security prison." The Aussie settled back in his chair.

"But what about the woman?" Sofia sipped from a coffee cup. "Shouldn't she be put behind bars?"

Alex rubbed his jaw. "She did a lot of crazy things that were bad but gave us good information, like tell us where Dimitri hid."

"But she tried to kill us, remember?" Sofia's eyes flashed with anger.

Willie drew closer to his desk, captured a pen, and twirled it in his hand. His right eye twinkled while he watched our debate.

"From what I saw, she controlled the entire drug operation." Franco wiped some frosting off his lips. "She should also be behind bars."

Izabella twisted a little to see the rest of us. "She did help Gabe—"

"Not everything we see reveals all that is happening." Willie tapped his pen on the desk to get our attention.

Dad raised an eyebrow. "Exactly."

"What does that mean?" I grabbed my third donut. For some reason, they kept drawing me to eat them. "She's not what she seems?"

"Mates, I can't reveal all the details." Willie shook his head. "But I've shared secrets with you in the past. I trust each of you to keep this to yourselves. Can you do that?"

We all nodded.

"I reckon Genevieve misled many people in her life. Her history as a young girl and woman was terrible. She suffered a lot at the hands of the Russians. When she grew old enough, she went into espionage work. She started in France, then went to England. Due to her help, which you may not have understood at the time, she galvanized us into action to capture Vasiliev while at the same time attempting to appear like a criminal."

Alex tilted his head. "But she told her subordinates to kill us at the pond." He licked his lips. "They were going to make us human popsicles."

Willie's lips curved in a grin. "She recruited Bastien to help in their operation and told him to notify us when the Russian's crew captured you. But she couldn't let Dimitri see that side of her. A discovery like that meant she would die. He originated from the KGB, remember? They're ruthless."

Izabella put a hand on her mouth. "You mean Bastien was a plant? He notified you of our location after going to the pond?

Willie shook his head. "He carried a tracer on him. When he took off on a snowmobile to 'notify Security,' he called us by radio. Next, he returned to continue his act in finishing you off."

"That's why he wouldn't let the guard throw us in the water right away," Alex said.

I positioned my hot chocolate on the end table. "And why he used one dose of that drug on us instead of two. He made sure we would wake up."

"Wheels within wheels." Willie winced when he rested his arms on the desk in front of him. The left-arm sling kept him from putting any weight on the arm. "He's back in normal life now. You may want to see him before you leave for Germany."

Izabella glanced at Sofia. "Speaking of insiders, what happened to Natalie?"

"Not sure." She shrugged her shoulders. "When the drop got difficult, she fled the scene. No word of her after that."

"We don't know where she went, but my staff informed me she left the country." Our Australian friend adjusted himself in his chair."

Dad drained his coffee and set the cup on a side table. "We need to let you get home to recuperate."

"You may be right." Willie smiled. "A little kip at home would help."

"You're going to take a nap and come back?" I snuck another donut.

He sighed. "Lots of paperwork to do, mates. Even though you saved the International Elimination Games Committee from a tarnished reputation, kept the record straight on those who competed under enhanced conditions, and helped crack the case, I still have to write the report."

Dad smiled and stood. "We'll let you get that nap." He reached out a hand to shake Willie's good one. "I appreciate everything. Including the extra effort to take care of my boys and the whole gang."

"They did most of the heavy detective work." Willie beamed. "Which left me with a mere smidgen of rough going at the end. I wasn't babysitting ankle biters but working with junior team members."

"What about the drug users?" Sophia said.

"Great question." Willie cocked his head to the side. "Each case is separate and all offenders will be prosecuted to the fullest. But I can tell you that several cases caused medals to go to the wrong individuals, such as the Russians beating the Norwegians and Italians in the Women's 5,000 Meter Cross Country Race. In the end, the Italian

Angelina Bianchi led her team to a Elimination Games Gold Medal after we discovered four different athletes from the Norwegian and Cooperative Teams had taken drugs."

"Awesome." Sophia jumped out of her seat and clapped her hands.

Alex stood and hugged her. "Congratulations."

The rest of us stood, grabbed our coats, and put them on.

I licked the glaze off my fingers, wiped them off on my pants, and grabbed one final donut. I wrapped it in double napkins and stuffed it in my pocket. When Alex glared at me, I grinned. "My morning snack before lunch."

After Dad stepped away from Willie, each of the rest of us walked over and said our goodbyes.

"Gonna miss you." I hugged him hard.

He slapped me on the back and patted Lightning's head, who yipped at him. "I enjoyed seeing you again too."

After Alex hugged Willie, Thunder rubbed against his legs. He knelt and patted Thunder's head. "Take care of this man until I see you again."

Alex raised his eyebrows. "Planning on seeing us again?"

Willie laughed. "The way our lives have been going, I'd almost bet on it."

Meet Aaron Zook

Aaron M. Zook, Jr. is a multiple award-winning author and speaker. He's thrilled thousands through his YA mystery/adventure Thunder and Lightning series about two inquisitive brothers and their dogs who solve one crisis after another around the world. Danger, intrigue, and excitement—all part of each book. Find out more about Aaron at Zookbooks.org. Aaron is a retired U.S. Army Colonel and lives with his wife, Joyce, in Holly Lake Ranch, TX. They have two married sons and four incredible grandchildren.

THE THUNDER AND LIGHTNING SERIES

The Secrets of the Castle—On a family getaway to the famous Neuschwanstein Castle in Germany, Gabe and Alex Zanadu and their dogs, Thunder and Lightning, find disaster at almost every turn. Their normal life is turned upside down when they're kidnapped near the castle and held for ransom. How will they survive?

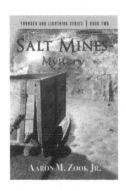

The Salt Mines Mystery—Visiting the Salt Mines in Berchtesgaden, Germany seems like a fun activity until one of Gabe and Alex Zanadu's friends lead them, their dogs, and other companions down a wrong trail. Lost, trapped by a dangerous human trafficking ring, the boys struggle to free themselves and find difficult life-and-death choices awaiting them as they navigate the mines and face-off with their captors.

The Phantom of the Fortress—A misguided man, who thinks he's Mozart, though Mozart's long been dead, carries a venomous hatred toward the townspeople of Salzburg, Austria for their mistreatment of him as a child. His diabolical scheme includes capturing the Fortress overlooking Salzburg and killing innocent citizens. Can Gabe and Alex Zanadu, their dogs Thunder and Lightning, and close friends save the town, capture the madman, and escape unharmed?

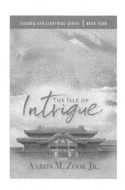

The Isle of Intrigue—

On a foggy Okinawan night, a stranger disrupts the Zanadu family's first island-unique dinner at a seafood restaurant. His violent search for a flying microbot leaves the family devastated, with Gabe and Alex Zanadu's mother unconscious on the floor. An Okinawan government official's son, Mike, whose father was also assaulted, leads the boys in a search for the fleeing thugs. Can they face the mafia and save their friends and siblings before its too late?

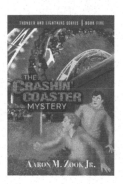

The Crashin' Coaster—

Gabe and Alex aren't having a fun summer experience at a Texas theme park. A mysterious man wearing a black hoodie releases the safety bars of the stalled coaster cars. Passengers scream in terror and one boy falls three stories to the ground. The saboteur races to a mainenance shed. The villain frames Alex. The FBI gets involved. Can the boys clear their names and capture the man in the hood?